Neil Broadfoot worked as a journalist for fifteen years at both national and local newspapers, including the *Scotsman*, *Scotland on Sunday* and the *Evening News*, covering some of the biggest stories of the day. A poacher turned gamekeeper, he has since moved into communications: providing media relations advice for a variety of organisations, from emergency services to government and private clients in the City.

Neil is married to Fiona and a father to two girls, meaning he's completely outnumbered in his own home. He lives in Dunfermline, the setting for his first job as a local reporter.

Also by Neil Broadfoot

No Man's Land

Neil
Broadfoot

No Place
To Die

CONSTABLE

CONSTABLE

First published in hardback in Great Britain in 2019 by Constable

This paperback edition published in Great Britain in 2020 by Constable

Copyright © Neil Broadfoot, 2019

1 3 5 7 9 10 8 6 4 2

The moral right of the author has been asserted.

A CIP catalogue record for this book
is available from the British Library.

ISBN: 978-1-47212-762-4

Typeset in Minion Pro by Initial Typesetting Services, Edinburgh
Printed and bound in Great Britain by Clays Ltd, Elcograf S.p.A.

Papers used by Constable are from well-managed forests and
other responsible sources.

Constable
An imprint of
Little, Brown Book Group
Carmelite House
50 Victoria Embankment
London EC4Y 0DZ

An Hachette UK Company
www.hachette.co.uk

www.littlebrown.co.uk

For Alex and Madeleine – don't worry, I promise Dad will get around to writing the Heroic Red Giant story soon . . .

CHAPTER 1

Her expression was hard. The sex was harder.

There was no passion. No tenderness. No intimacy. This was sex as desperation, both of them using the other to reach a moment, a heartbeat, where all the problems and pain and terror would be swept away, the car crash their lives had become temporarily forgotten.

Three sentences. That was all it had taken. Three sentences and here they were, hate-fucking, trying to use each other to hide from the storm.

He studied her face again – pulled tight into a frown that hinted at disapproval, eyes screwed shut, concentrating on her internal rhythm, reducing him to an afterthought. Felt a stab of something hot and shameful in his gut. He had done this. Taken everything they were and twisted it, perverted it, leaving them with only this – a drunken, frantic fuck in the gloom of their darkened bedroom. And for what? Despite himself, he swallowed the sudden urge to laugh.

What else?

He forced the thoughts from his mind, focused on her as he thrust his hips harder, faster. She moaned, ground down on him and he hissed with pain, the angle all wrong. He reached up for her, fingers tracing soft, sweat-slicked skin for an instant before he stretched out for the bedside table, fumbled around for what was there and pulled it close, the sound of it clinking off the forgotten wine glass like a backing track to her groaning.

He hauled her down. The kiss was as frantic as their fucking, teeth clashing together in their frenzy to make some kind of connection, however fleeting. She pulled away, eyes opening, blue-green gaze sweeping his face like a searchlight then tracing down to what he now held in his hand. She smiled, nodded understanding. Reached out and caressed the blade, finally showing the tenderness he had always loved. The tenderness three little sentences had destroyed.

He felt wine-soured breath tickle his face as she spoke. Just one word. But it was the only word he ever needed to hear.

'Now.'

CHAPTER 2

Connor Fraser heard the laughter just as he felt his chest catch fire. It was the sound of the playground – illicit, humourless, cruel. He blocked it out, focused on the agony in his chest as the weight bore down on him. Closing his eyes he exhaled as hard as he could, pushing the weight back up, arms shaking, the heavy clang of the bar finally hitting the rack the sweetest music.

But then he heard the laughter again.

He sat up, world swimming slightly in a moment of light-headedness from his exertion, then looked around the gym. It didn't take him long to spot the source of the laughter or its cause. If he was being honest, he felt a chuckle tickle in his own chest.

The kid was in the free-weights area at the far end of the room, looking like he was going to have a heart attack at any moment. His cheeks were angry scarlet, sweat-soaked T-shirt plastered to a sagging chest and a pendulous gut that hung halfway over the waistline of his shorts. The effort of lifting the dumbbells rippled through his chins like waves as he grunted and panted at the floor-to-ceiling mirrors in front of him. Finally, as he curled them up to shoulder height, his eyes gave a nervous twitch to the left, and the source of the laughter.

Standing around a bench, surrounded by an assortment of weights, were three young men. In their mid-twenties, Connor guessed. They might have stepped from the pages of a fitness magazine, designer workout gear clinging to every gym-sculpted muscle. Obviously no strangers to the salon attached to the gym, their hair was perfectly styled and their tans unnaturally healthy, even with the good weather Stirling had been enjoying recently. They were in a loose semi-circle, weights abandoned as they laughed and sneered at the fat kid.

Wankers.

Connor sighed, turned back to his workout. He was just racking another twenty pounds onto either side of the barbell when he heard the clatter of weights and an explosion of laughter from across the gym.

The fat kid was sitting on a bench, weights abandoned at his feet where he'd dropped them, head between his knees, taking deep, hitching breaths, knuckles white on the edge of the bench, gripping it as though it were a raft in a typhoon. With an irritated roll of his shoulders, Connor stood up and headed for the drinks fountain in the right corner of the gym. He took a paper cup from the dispenser and half filled it with water, then headed for the kid, feeling the eyes of the chortling meatheads following him.

'Leave him, man. Fatso's taken a whitey. He'll spew all over ye . . .' one called.

Connor ignored him, touched the kid's shoulder gently. 'Here,' he said, offering the water, 'drink this. Slow sips. It'll make you feel better.'

The kid looked up, pale green eyes watery with tears. His face was a mess of hectic colour, two scarlet plumes on his cheeks. Couldn't be much more than nineteen or twenty. Despite himself, Connor felt a vague snarl of contempt. How the hell did anyone let themselves get this out of shape so young?

'Th-thanks,' the boy said. 'Just went at it too hard, you know.'

Connor nodded briefly. He wasn't looking for a conversation, just didn't want to have to deal with the kid if he keeled over. 'Take it a bit easier,' he said. 'Get your breathing sorted. Inhale when you're relaxing, exhale when you're moving the dumbbells, okay? And drop the weight you're lifting a little, take it slow.'

The kid's head bobbed up and down eagerly, a nervous smile tugging at the corners of his mouth.

4

Connor watched the kid breathe for a moment, the gasping breaths becoming more even, the hammering vein in his neck calming. Satisfied, he turned and walked back to his own barbell. Started his set, got about halfway through when he heard the laughter again, followed by the same voice as before.

'Aw, fuck's sake, man, now *I'm* gonna puke. Lookadit jiggle!'

Connor finished his set, sat up. Saw the kid had moved to a running machine, gut and chest bouncing in time to his awkward half-jog. His eyes were locked on his own reflection, face set in loathing and bitter defiance. Despite himself, Connor felt a surge of admiration for the kid.

Decision made. He got off the bench, ignoring the small voice in his head that urged him not to get involved. Walked across to the trio of meatheads. The shortest of the three, who made up for his lack of height with width, turned as he approached and took a half-step forward. Connor watched as the other two fell in loosely behind. They might as well have painted a target on their friend's forehead.

'Problem, pal?' the meathead asked. No menace, just a cold smugness born of the knowledge that he was king of this castle and could handle anything that came his way. Connor studied him: the oily skin, the over-pumped muscles, the dilated veins that snaked up his arms like a roadmap. Wondered if the perfectly sculpted little shit in front of him had any idea how deep the waters he had just waded into really were.

'No problem,' he said, his voice low, even. 'Just keep it down, okay? Kid's doing his best, doesn't need you reminding him how far he's got to go.'

The meathead broke into a smile as fake as the rest of him. 'Fuck off.' He chuckled. 'Seriously, man? Who the fuck you think you are anyway?'

'I'm nobody,' Connor said. 'I just want to work out in peace. And I don't need to hear your shit when I'm doing it.'

The first meathead tried to take another step forward, but Connor was already moving. He stepped to the side, got an arm around his shoulders in a we're-all-friends embrace. Dug his fingers into the hard mound of neck muscle, heard a sharp intake of breath as he found the nerve cluster and squeezed. Leaned in close enough to smell sour sweat, eyes strafing the other two weightlifters, watching for them to make a move.

'Like I said, I'm no one,' Connor whispered, voice now as hard as the dumbbells. 'So let's keep it that way. You don't know me, I don't know you. Don't want to. But leave the kid alone. Otherwise . . .' He dug his fingers in deeper as he let the sentence trail off, pain delivering the rest of the message for him.

The meathead stepped back, his two friends crowding in on him. Connor stood, breathing slow and easy, eyes on the three of them. He saw the argument rage in the poisoned dwarf's eyes, the battle between humiliation and pain being waged.

'Ah, fuck ye,' he said at last, turning away as he rubbed at his neck. 'Nae fuckin' worth it.' He stormed off, friends trailing behind him. Connor watched them, just to be sure, then headed for the bikes. He saw the fat kid nod to him in the mirror, returned the gesture. He didn't want a friend, definitely didn't want a lost puppy following him everywhere. That only led to trouble.

He set himself up on a static cycle, was just getting into a rhythm when his phone buzzed in his pocket. Fished it out, irritated. Should have left the damn thing in his locker. But that wasn't an option any more, was it? As an employee, he could go off grid for a while, let Sentinel Securities run itself. But with Lachlan Jameson out of the picture, thanks to his part in three murders and an attempt on Connor's own life, Connor wasn't just an employee any more. The board – a strange blend of investment bankers and ex-service personnel – had asked him to stay on with Sentinel, and even elevated him to senior partner. It was, they said, good business. After all, the Jameson case had shown Connor could handle a crisis.

Connor had smiled at the compliment, but knew better. The former chairman of the board and founder of the company had been exposed as a cold-blooded contract killer with a taste for beheading his victims. The affair had very nearly brought down a government. Connor had managed to stay mostly out of the coverage. But, as always, there were rumours. And one of those rumours was that Connor Fraser was not a man to take lightly. So, along with a leg wound that still ached when the nights were cold, he had come through the Jameson affair with a reputation, and a job offer.

More money. More responsibility. More headaches. And a phone he could never switch off.

He opened the text message, read it. Let his legs come to a slow halt.

Time to go to work.

CHAPTER 3

Sitting on a hill that overlooked the three acres of carefully mani-cured grounds surrounding it, Robbie Lindsay was forced to admit that the Alloa House Hotel and Spa was an imposing sight. It ticked all the right boxes for a luxurious mansion turned country retreat – the secluded location, the sandstone-and-glass façade that screamed wealth in the uniquely restrained way Scots had perfected, the car-park at the side of the property just visible enough to show the high-end saloons and sports coupés of the guests to anyone arriving. This was a place that wore its exclusivity casually, like a four-figure handbag on the elbow or an understated watch that cost as much as six months' mortgage payments for a normal mortal.

Looking up at it again, Robbie was forced to conclude that the Alloa House was something else too.

It was a total pain in the arse.

He ground his toe into the perfectly raked slate-grey gravel that made up the driveway, looked out again at the view. A long, sweeping expanse of lawn led down to a thin copse of trees. He knew from studying maps of the place that there was a small stream beyond those trees, then about two square miles of dense woodland that backed onto a narrow, winding B-road that led, eventually, back to the main road to Stirling. No fences, no CCTV cameras, no security patrols. Normally, that wouldn't present a problem. The main house was covered by security cameras, the alarm system had a hot trip line wired directly to Police Scotland's area command centre in Stirling, and the main entrance to the hotel was manned by a rotating team of security staff twenty-four hours a day.

Problem was, this was anything but a normal weekend.

Robbie sighed, took another expectant look up the driveway. He hadn't wanted to call in Connor on this – he still felt the need to prove himself: he had almost let a client get away from him after a court appearance in Edinburgh. But after what he had been told when he arrived an hour ago, after what he had seen, what choice had he had?

None. Not when Blair Charlston was your client.

CHAPTER 4

The dull, echoing thuds of the punches ricocheted off the walls of the room, cut through by the almost-musical jangle of the chain anchoring the heavy bag to the ceiling as it danced and jerked. He glanced up at the clock mounted above the mirrors that dominated the far wall. Made a quick calculation. One minute more. Sixty seconds.

Plenty of time.

He darted forward again, chasing the bag, shock juddering up his arms as he dug into it with a combination of jabs, uppercuts and crosses. Saw faces in the bag, taunting, mocking him, heard voices in the shimmer of the chain. Those three sentences. The sentences that had transformed his life. And then there was her. That night. That room.

Now.

He blinked, forcing the thoughts away as he drove forward even harder, the thunder of his punches unable to drown out his thoughts. Felt his legs begin to shake with the effort, the air growing hot as he tried to take in ragged breaths, lungs not big enough to meet the growing scream in his muscles as his body clamoured for air.

He blinked away the sweat that stung his eyes, glanced at the clock. Fifteen seconds to go. Just fifteen . . .

'Mr Charlston?'

The voice startled him, made him stumble mid-lunge towards the bag. He whirled, anger churning with terror in his gut like acid, even as he felt instinct contort his face into a mask of practised calm.

A mask he had crafted after that night – the night that had changed everything.

Now.

In front of him, a tall man had the grace to look embarrassed at the intrusion. Blair placed his hands on his knees and leaned forward, using the moment it took to calm his hitching breath to try to remember the man's name.

'Yes, ah, Robbie?' he said, stars dancing across his vision in crampy waves as he straightened. He was aware of the heavy bag behind him, still swinging slightly, the chain's earlier jangling replaced by a dull, whispering squeak.

Now.

'Sorry to interrupt,' Robbie said, his eyes focused over Blair's shoulder on the heavy bag. The man hated making eye contact. It was something Blair was used to. People who knew about him had two reactions – disgust or indifference. He guessed Robbie Lindsay was veering towards disgust, but was forced to keep it indifferent because Blair was paying his wages for the next three days.

Too bad for him.

He waved a hand that had almost stopped shaking. 'No problem,' he said, giving Robbie a smile as practised as his expression. 'I'm done anyway. What's up?'

'Mr Fraser just arrived,' Robbie said, his eyes sliding to meet Blair's at last. Interesting.

Blair considered. 'Okay. Give me a couple of minutes to clean up. Tell Mr Fraser I'll see him in the suite in, say . . .' he made a show of looking at the clock on the wall '. . . twenty minutes?'

If keeping the boss waiting for twenty minutes annoyed Robbie, he hid it well. 'Whatever you say, Mr Charlston,' he said, as he gave a butler-like nod and backed out of the room.

Blair watched him go, the silence rushing in on him. He turned back to the heavy bag, which was now almost still.

Now.

Drove forward with a jab that sent the bag swinging again, then turned and left, leaving it to pirouette and twist, like his own thoughts.

CHAPTER 5

Connor stood outside the Alloa House, feeling a vague discomfort that had nothing to do with the sun beating down on him from a cloudless August sky. He took a deep breath, admonishing himself. He lived in a garden flat on one of the most exclusive streets in Stirling, had more than a few quid stored away thanks to an old-money inheritance from his mother, and had arrived in an Audi that cost more than some people could earn in a year. And yet, for all that, he couldn't shake the nagging feeling that he didn't fit in here as one of the wealthy. It was a feeling that had been magnified by his university days in Belfast, when he had studied during the week, then headed down to see his grandfather in Newtownards at the weekends. He and Jimmy O'Brien would spend their time either in the pub or in the home-made gym Jimmy had constructed in a shed at the back of the garage he ran, slowly building Connor into the man he was today. A man who preferred a gym to a 'health spa'. Or a Guinness to a gin and tonic.

He shook himself from his thoughts as he saw Robbie jog down the granite staircase that led up to the hotel's main entrance. Knew from the knotted shoulders and sheepish smile what he was about to say.

'So,' Connor asked as Robbie came to a halt in front of him, 'how long is Mr Charlston going to keep us waiting?'

'Ah, twenty minutes or so, boss,' Robbie said, a hectic red running around the line of his shirt collar. 'He was going hell for leather at a punch bag when you arrived.'

Connor arched an eyebrow. A punch bag? Interesting. Not exactly in line with the public image Blair Charlston was projecting these days and definitely not on message with what he was selling this weekend, but entirely consistent with what Connor had found out about the man.

The initial contact had come from Aaron Douglas, an investment banker who sat on Sentinel Securities' board of directors as a non-exec. Connor knew he had put money into the firm when Lachlan Jameson had set it up seven years previously. It had been Douglas who had approached Connor and asked him to join the board when Jameson had been charged with the Stirling murders – the case that had culminated in Connor beating Jameson half to death in the ground of the Holy Rude Church at the top of the town and nursing a knife wound to the leg. It was exactly the type of coverage that a firm specialising in close protection didn't need: operative moonlights as contract killer and political assassin. Rates competitive. Satisfaction guaranteed.

For three months after the Jameson affair, Connor had wondered if his elevation to the boardroom would be the shortest-lived promotion in history as the company hurtled towards ruin. But then Douglas had stepped in with this contract, and the work had started to flow.

Blair Charlston was a familiar name to anyone who had switched on the TV news or opened Twitter over the last five years. He had made his name as an investment banker in London, branded himself as the man who could raise the funds when a company needed them. He'd invested in everything from coffee shops to insurance companies, football clubs to high-street chains, stepping in and helping the companies to avoid bankruptcy through capital and aggressive growth plans. He'd been good at it, too, hauling firms back from the brink and into the black while pocketing a sizeable chunk of the profits.

But then came Perigee Designs. And Blair Charlston's life had fallen apart.

At first glance, it looked like just another deal. Perigee Designs was a bespoke kitchen design and manufacturing company, based in Kinross to the east of Stirling. It had grown popular in the 1990s and early 2000s when a Premier League footballer had agreed to a glossy magazine shoot of his mansion. The writer had become enamoured with the man's kitchen and expressed his feelings in the purplest of prose across two spreads. Connor wondered how much the owners of Perigee had paid for that affection, but it had done the trick – Perigee became *the* name in interior design for every fashionista and wannabe in the country. But, like fashions and political parties, Perigee had eventually dropped out of favour, overtaken by the Next Big Thing. Orders slumped and the company began to cut costs – with its workforce. Then the threat of Brexit delivered the killer blow by sky-rocketing the price of shipping its products, and Perigee found itself dancing around the business pages like a prizefighter about to collapse. Connor remembered the headlines that had been part of his briefing pack for this job: 'Kitchen Fitter Set for Last Supper', 'Perigee Set to Fall with Loss of 50 Jobs', 'Local MP Calls for Crisis Talks to Save "Heart of Kinross" Perigee'.

And then, just as Perigee had hit the canvas and the referee got to eight in his count, Blair Charlston had stepped in. A deal was agreed to buy the company and its assets, with Blair installed as finance chief and his fellow investors taking up other boardroom positions. At first he was hailed a hero, the visionary who had ridden to the rescue from the City to save a family firm and the community that depended on it.

Unfortunately, the goodwill didn't last long. Reports of asset stripping soon became rife, of Charlston and his team awarding themselves staggering bonuses, exorbitant salaries and expense-fuelled 'business trips' at the same time as they streamlined the business and set about cutting the workforce. But, like an abused partner clinging to the lie that 'they only hit me because they love me', the Perigee staff and the wider town had stood by Charlston and his team.

Until Graham Bell. And what Charlston had done after that.

Connor was roused from his thoughts by the soft crunch of gravel beside him. He turned to see Robbie standing in front of him, his face expectant, like a waiter about to take his order. Connor smiled. 'Sorry, Robbie, caught in my thoughts. Let's go inside, get a coffee and you can bring me up to speed. Shouldn't take more than, say, twenty-five minutes.'

Connor saw the calculation run behind Robbie's eyes even as his mouth dropped open. 'But, boss, that'll mean . . .'

Connor waited for Robbie to catch him up, a small smile tugging at the kid's face. He had potential, but he was still a little slow at reading the situation. Connor made a mental note to work on that with him.

He acknowledged the smile with one of his own – felt as though he was throwing a puppy a treat. 'Come on,' he said. 'Coffee. And you can tell me what's going on, and why Charlston needs to see me.'

CHAPTER 6

It was, Donald Peters realised, the quiet that was the problem.

He was sitting at his kitchen table, laptop in front of him, Donna Blake's familiar smile frozen on the screen. She was thinner than he remembered, and her make-up and wardrobe had definitely had an upgrade since her time at the *Western Chronicle* thanks to her new job as a reporter for Sky, but her eyes hadn't changed. Still that same glacial blue, made all the more piercing by Donna's habit of staring straight at you. She'd been labelled intense, even intimidating, by those she interviewed and those she worked with. It was one of the things Donald had liked about her. He hoped she still had that intensity, that it wasn't just an act for the cameras.

She was going to need it.

Lost in thought, his eyes wandered to the patio doors facing him and the garden beyond. He gazed out at it until the central heating gave a soft click and he heard the boiler switching on. And that was when it hit him. The near-perfect silence. The peace and quiet. He was used to the constant buzz and chatter of a newsroom as he worked, of calls being made, keyboards clattering, conversations shouted from one end of the room to the other. Even getting home had been no respite: Janet had been a noisy child, charging around the house, always making sure the TV was turned up too loudly, always eager to sit with her dad and listen to his stories. And then there was Carrie, his wife. A music teacher, she supplemented her income by giving private tuition, filling the house with music on the rare weekends that Donald had managed to get away from the *Westie*.

But that was a lifetime ago. Janet was half a world away now, enjoying a new life with her husband, Stuart, who had been lured Down Under by the promise of a high-paid job and a better life away from the UK. Donald saw the appeal, supported Janet when she told him of their plan, helped in every way he could. But he knew the truth, saw it in Janet's eyes every time they spoke. She wasn't emigrating. She was running away. From this house, from memories of her mother, who had been taken by a cataclysmic brain aneurysm one day when she was halfway down the stairs. Donald had found her when he got home that night after another too-long day at the office, could still remember the chill of her skin on his fingers. The doctors told him that Carrie would have felt only a momentary flash of pain before she knew nothing more. Donald took comfort in that, but what haunted him was the time: the time she had lain alone at the bottom of the stairs, the silence crowding in on her as her body stiffened and cooled. It was estimated she had died sometime in the morning, meaning she had lain undiscovered for at least ten hours before Donald got home.

All that time alone. In a silence like this.

He forced his attention back to Donna. It was a tight shot of her standing in front of an ornate entrance gate, the name 'Alloa House Hotel and Spa' carved into a sandstone wall in oh-so-tasteful lettering. He had paused the playback just as the wind picked up, teasing a stray strand of hair across her pale forehead.

Smiling slightly, he hit play, letting Donna reach up and brush the strand away as she spoke.

'. . . and it's here, five miles from Stirling, that Blair Charlston will host his ITOI weekend for more than three hundred guests. These three-day events, which Mr Charlston describes as an "immersive experience in personal power and liberation", have proven hugely popular since Charlston re-emerged as a lifestyle coach and business strategist following the Perigee scandal and the death of his partner, Kimberley George. While ITOI Consulting has refused to comment on attendees this weekend, I understand several A-list stars are expected to arrive over the course of the next few hours, undeterred by the ongoing controversy that surrounds Mr Charlston, or the threat of protests from those connected with Perigee . . .'

He tuned Donna out as she started to recount the details of Perigee. He knew them all too well. About how the cuts at Perigee had driven one of the workers there, a man named Graham Bell, to take his own life at the factory. This had set off a chain reaction which culminated in the company falling into administration for a second time and the death of Charlston's long-time girlfriend, Kimberley George. It had only been a month from Bell's body being found slumped in a toilet in the Perigee factory, arms opened from wrist to elbow, to the discovery of George's body in a London hotel room, Charlston slumped beside her, their blood mingling in a widening pool on the bed they lay on, but during that insane month five years ago, Donald felt he had lived a lifetime.

Seized by an urge to move, he got up from the table and busied himself making yet another cup of coffee.

He focused on the growing rumble from the kettle as it started to boil, using the sound to block out the maddening stillness in the room and the doubts that tugged at his mind. As he did, he tried to rehearse the conversation he would have with Donna when he gave in to the inevitable and called her. Found, again, he had no idea how he was going to tell her what he knew – and whether his courage would hold long enough for him to say it.

CHAPTER 7

If the hotel was luxurious, Blair Charlston's suite was nothing short of opulent. It was a study in understated good taste rendered in antique furniture, plush rugs and oversized soft furnishings. The suite was situated in the centre of the hotel's top floor, the grandeur of the living room's ornate marble fireplace offset by floor-to-ceiling windows that led out to a small balcony overlooking the grounds. To Connor, it looked as though the landscape had been designed to be best appreciated from this view: there was a symmetry to the hedge-rows, paths, flower beds and ponds that you just couldn't appreciate from ground level.

Aye, but tea is tea in a china cup or a tin mug, he heard his gran whisper in his mind, forcing him to suppress a smile. Ida Fraser, who now spent her days in a care home similar to this hotel – another grand house redesigned for residential use – had never been an easy woman to impress. And Connor doubted whether these shows of wealth would do the trick, nice views or not.

They were greeted at the door by a tall, thin woman who intro-duced herself as 'Anne James, Mr Charlston's personal assistant.' Her hand was a fragile thing in Connor's large paw, warm when he shook it. She had thin lips that she had attempted to plump up with fresh lipstick, and wore a blouse that looked as if it had been ironed onto her, its precision somehow at odds with the hectic colour in her cheeks and the glistening of sweat on her top lip. But despite this, it was her hair that Connor's eyes kept drifting to. It was a rich auburn, sleek at the front, but tousled around her long ponytail, almost as if—

'Mr Fraser, Robbie, sorry I kept you waiting.'

Connor turned away from Anne, his train of thought lost as Blair Charlston swept into the living area of the suite, eyes flicking between Robbie and himself. He was shorter than the TV footage, pop-up banners and posters dotted around the hotel suggested, with dark hair carefully teased into shape to give the impression of a thick fringe and full locks. Connor took a step forward, offered his hand, dimly aware of Anne retreating like an afterthought. 'No problem, Mr Charlston. I lost track of time while Robbie was getting me up to speed anyway.'

Charlston's handshake was like his smile – smooth, warm and undoubtedly practised. Connor watched as the man's eyes roamed across his face, as though looking for something. And there was another detail the posters hid well: the small squint in Charlston's left eye. There was also a slight over-exaggeration of his irises, which were a light hazel flecked with shards of green. Connor added the information to the small fading welts on the bridge of Charlston's nose, came back with two words – contact lenses. Not surprising – a visionary was always more convincing if he could see where he was going without glasses. And there, on his left shoulder, something that made sense of Connor's fascination with Anne's hair. He bit back a smile as he added the observation to the sheen on Anne's skin, almost as if she had been involved in some kind of frantic activity before she had opened the door to him.

Connor pushed aside the thought. So Charlston might be getting a little personal attention from his personal assistant. So what? Not his affair, pardon the pun.

Charlston broke the handshake, waved towards two leather sofas that bracketed a coffee-table so polished it glittered in the afternoon sun. 'Please,' he said, 'sit. Can I get you anything? Tea? Coffee?'

Connor declined, the coffee he'd had with Robbie still jangling in his veins. Strong stuff. But at the prices the Alloa House was charging, it had to be.

'So,' Charlston said as he settled into the sofa opposite Connor and

Robbie, the leather creaking softly, 'I believe Robbie called you in to go over some of the details for this weekend.'

Connor nodded, felt Robbie shift in his seat beside him. He really needed to work on his poker face. 'Yes, Mr Charlston, you see I—'

'Please, call me Blair. Ah . . . Connor, isn't it?'

Connor murmured agreement. 'Okay, Blair. Yes, Robbie called me in due to some justifiable concerns he's identified about the opening ceremony this weekend. Specifically, your plan to finish the first evening with an outdoor event.'

Charlston leaned forward, something catching in his eyes. It was as if a spotlight had suddenly been switched on.

Showtime.

'Ah, yes, the Destiny Bonfire and fireworks. But I don't see the issue. Mr Fra— Connor. We've carried out all the appropriate health and safety checks, have the necessary permissions from the hotel.'

Connor already knew that – he'd checked as soon as Robbie had called him, looking for a loophole. 'That's true, Blair, but the issue isn't so much one of health but of safety. Specifically, yours. Not to put too fine a point on it, not everyone is happy that you're holding the event this weekend. You know there have already been protests and, with the hotel grounds open, easy access to public roads through the woods, you being out in the open and exposed is a risk that I'd prefer we didn't have to take.'

Blair's face darkened, his expression becoming serious. But his eyes didn't dull, and Connor had the feeling that this conversation was unfolding exactly as he had expected and rehearsed. When he spoke, his voice was as muted as the cream walls of the suite. 'Look, Connor, I know I'm a divisive figure. Okay? And, let's be honest, I deserve to be. I . . .' He looked away to the windows overlooking the gardens, jaw clenching as though the words were bitter. 'What I did at Perigee was a disgrace, and it cost two people their lives. But I can't change that now, though I wish I could. What I can do is use that tragedy to help people. That's what this weekend is all about. And the Destiny Bonfire is a vital component of that work.'

Connor kept his expression and tone neutral. 'How so?'

'You know what I do here, right?' Blair asked, his face regaining

21

some of its previous animation. 'What the ITOI movement is all about? The whole weekend is about teaching people what I know – that the whole notion of God or a higher power is garbage, a prop we've created to comfort ourselves in the dark. So we have to become our own gods, master our own destinies. That's what ITOI means – In Thine Own Image. Over three days we immerse those who come here in that principle, make them take control of their lives, become the gods of their own existence. And to set them on that path, we use the bonfire. We write down everything that we were, every limiting belief, every problem and excuse that has held us back, then torch the lists on the Destiny Bonfire and celebrate our rebirth with the fireworks.'

Connor pushed back the vague snarl of unease he felt in his gut at Charlston's pitch. His grandparents were from a place where religion and belief could be a matter of life and death, and he had little time for the offer of salvation by soundbite. He'd read the background, knew that Blair had come up with his theory after being found with Kimberley George. As he told it, they had learned that Perigee was about to collapse in the wake of Graham Bell's death and, driven mad by a mixture of guilt, alcohol and cocaine, had decided to take their lives together. Connor remembered watching the interview Charlston had posted on his website, the tear-streaked remembrance of 'my sweet, sweet Kimberley and the promise we made'. They had gone to bed to 'make love one last time, then leave together'.

And they would have, if only they'd paused to hang a 'do not disturb' sign outside their hotel room. As it was, they were found by a maid, and the paramedics who had screamed to the scene had managed to resuscitate Charlston.

'I was gone for eight minutes,' he'd said, in the interview. 'And in that time, I saw nothing. Nothing but blackness. No lights, no Heaven. No God. And if this is all there is, then it's my duty to help people dominate their own existence and live life on their terms by becoming their own gods. It's what Kimberley would have wanted.'

Charlston's delivery was sombre, downbeat, with just the right amount of steel to honour his lost love glinting in his eyes. And yet, to Connor, there was something hollow in the vow – not least because he knew it was based on a lie. Brain damage from oxygen starvation tended to kick in at six minutes, so Charlston's claim to have been gone for eight was, at best, an exaggeration. But if he was willing to lie about that for his own ends, what else, Connor wondered, was he saying because it made a good soundbite?

Connor snapped his focus back to the present. 'I understand that, but surely you see the problem, Blair. There have already been protests at you hosting this event so close to Kinross and the Perigee plant, and there are rumours that some of the old workers are going to head this way over the weekend, which is part of the reason you called Sentinel in. And then, of course, there's the note you received last week.'

Connor saw the tension snap into Charlston's jaw, his eyes cooling. He became very still, staring at Connor, unblinking. 'Ah, yes, that,' he whispered.

'Yes,' Connor agreed. That. It had been a nondescript letter, delivered to Charlston's business address in London. Boring white envelope. Stirling postmark. Sent the day before. So far, so average. Unfortunately, the note it contained was anything but average. Connor remembered it, felt a wisp of disgust. One sheet of paper, obviously wiped in something vile after it had been written, the edges smeared with drying excrement. Two sentences slashed into the paper in angry red letters, like a kid being let loose with lipstick instead of a colouring pen.

Graham died because of you. And for that, you'll pay SCUM.

Connor had advised Blair to call the police, report it, partly because it was procedure, partly because it would take the whole mess off his plate. But Blair had refused and, despite himself, Connor could see his point. The moment the police were informed that a threat had been made against him, they'd either tell Blair to cancel the whole weekend or insist on sending officers in.

'And how would that look?' Blair had asked Connor at the time. 'I've got hundreds of people trying to design their lives, better themselves, all under the watchful eye of the police? Not likely.'

Reluctantly, Connor had agreed. He had no idea how credible the threat was, but it was just that. A threat. And it raised the stakes. He leaned forward in his seat, meeting Blair's gaze. 'Look. We can cover you and your guests in a controlled environment, but we've simply not got the manpower to seal off an open perimeter, which puts you at risk. I agree with Robbie on this one. If there's a way we can change or cancel this bonfire event, then we should.'

Charlston gave Connor a look that was almost sad, as though he was trying to teach a child how to spell and they just weren't getting it. 'I'm sorry, Connor, but that's just not possible,' he said. 'The Destiny Bonfire is the climax of the first night and kicks off the rest of the weekend – it's critical for launching my clients into the next stage of their development. If you feel you can't cover it, then I respect your decision and thank you for your time.'

Connor stayed very still, acutely aware of Robbie's gaze on him as a riot of calculations tumbled through his mind. The risk had been identified. The chances of a protester trying to enter the hotel grounds and disrupt the event or even get to Charlston himself were clear. But, then, if he walked away from this, what would that mean for Sentinel? Charlston might have been selling self-help bullshit, but it was popular bullshit. Hollywood stars, big names from the City and even a few politicians had come forward to endorse his work and, by proxy, Sentinel. If he pulled the plug on the operation, what would that mean for the company?

Connor sighed, let the tension out of his shoulders. 'Okay,' he said finally, the word feeling misshapen in his mouth. 'If you say it has to go ahead, fine. But we minimise your time outside, I stay by your side, and if there's even a whiff of trouble, you're gone. Agreed?'

Charlston held Connor's gaze for a moment, coldness bleeding into his eyes. Then he broke into a smile, offered his hand. 'Excellent!' he said, almost bouncing in his seat. 'Thank you, Connor. I really don't think there's any cause for concern, but I'm sure nothing will happen to me with you by my side.'

You'd better hope it doesn't, Connor thought. *For both our sakes.*

CHAPTER 8

The coverage was as he'd expected it would be – a few page leads in several papers, all with pictures of Charlston at various points of his career, from the fresh-faced financier to the born-again 'life architect and strategist' he now claimed to be. They detailed the upcoming weekend, the copy laced with the promise of controversy thanks to Charlston's involvement with Perigee and the death of Kimberley George, a dash of celebrity stardust cutting through with the mention of big names flocking to Stirling for Charlston's ITOI weekend.

It disgusted him. All of it. Didn't they know they were just playing into his hands, giving Charlston what he wanted – no, *needed* – more than anything else?

Publicity.

He turned from the kitchen table where he had spread out the clippings, feeling a stab of pain in his back as he straightened and headed for the log burner at the other side of the room. It was a warm day, the sky cloudless, the sun streaming in through the patio doors. But still he kept the fire stoked and burning, its orange glow and the soft crackling of the logs doing nothing to thaw the cold he felt at his core.

He flicked the door open, teased the logs inside with the poker he kept beside the burner. It was, he was forced to admit, a beautiful thing – almost like a work of art crafted in aluminium and stone. He stared into the flames, lost in thought. In a time before Blair

Charlston, in a time when he had been happy. When his back had not hurt and the house was warmed with people rather than fire.

When she was still alive.

He swiped at his cheek, anger and resignation churning somewhere deep inside him, like an echo of the flames, as he felt the all-too-familiar dampness. He reached to the mantelpiece over the fire and the picture that lay there. A perfect frozen moment, thawed by his tears.

The picture began to tremble in his hand and he placed it back on the mantel, suddenly seized by the fear he would drop it. Such a small, fragile thing, and his last memory of her. He could not, would not, lose that as well.

He forced himself to straighten again, blinked away the tears. Turned from the fire and walked back to the kitchen table. Besides the pile of newspaper clippings there was a brochure, along with printouts culled from Charlston's own website. Swallowing the bile that was rising in his guts, he began to read the words he already knew by heart after weeks and months of study.

The Destiny Bonfire is the culmination of the first day of the ITOI weekend, and attendees' first chance to truly commit themselves to becoming the gods of their own existence. In a ceremony led by Blair, attendees are invited to burn away their past to reveal their future in an event that is at once joyous and uplifting. At the conclusion, selected guests will have the opportunity to meet Blair face to face and enjoy the celebratory fireworks that mark the end of the first day of ITOI.

Despite himself, he smiled. 'Selected guests'. A look at the pricing structure tucked away at the back of the brochure revealed that those 'selected guests' had paid an extra three thousand pounds for the privilege of enjoying Blair's company.

No matter. Some things had a value beyond mere pounds and pence. This was one of them. He reached for the folder at the corner of the table, opened it to check, again, the contents. The registration documents, map to the Alloa House and, of course, the platinum ticket that guaranteed he would be one of the 'selected guests' to enjoy some one-on-one time with Blair Charlston. And he *would* enjoy it. Every single moment. For himself. For her. For everything Charlston had taken from them. The Destiny Bonfire could not have been more aptly named. What Charlston didn't know, yet, was that it would change his own destiny for ever.

CHAPTER 9

Sometimes answers to problems just came to you, the subconscious mind offering up the solution long after the conscious mind had abandoned the issue as impossible.

And sometimes, as Donna Blake had just discovered, those answers were delivered in a high-end Audi.

She had been sitting in Sky's outside-broadcast van with her cameraman, a lanky, greasy smear called Keith, who had a taste for *Star Trek* T-shirts and a high-sugar diet, if his complexion was anything to go by. She had been trying to work out her next step on the Charlston story when the answer had come to her. It had been a fairly typical problem – she'd covered the main story, but what else was there to do? Charlston wasn't accepting interview bids, and the staff on the hotel's main gates, who were giving her unhappy glances from their booth across the road, were hardly likely to let her drive up to the main foyer and doorstep him. There was one option, of course: sit it out. Make camp and wait to see what, if any, big names arrived for the weekend. But there were two problems with that – one being Donna's need to get home and see Andrew at some point, be a mother to her son, and the other was Keith. The thought of spending an extended period with the cameraman turned her stomach.

And then she had heard it – the snarl of a V8 engine. She glanced right, out of the van's window, just in time to catch sight of the low, sleek Audi as it powered away from the gate, the driver's bulk looming over the steering wheel like an advancing eclipse. She knew that figure, the huge shoulders and arms, could imagine the jade-green eyes twinkling from beneath a heavy brow, strobing across the road ahead. And even as she watched the car accelerate away, back end hunkering down onto the road like a sprinter on the blocks, Donna felt a small smile spread across her face.

Connor Fraser. Who else?

She had met Fraser six months ago, when she was working on the story that had, ultimately, landed her this job. A decapitated body dumped in front of the Holy Rude in the historic heart of Stirling was big news, and Donna, who was freelancing for the local radio station at the time, was determined to make the most of the story. She shivered, something cold scuttling up her spine. That story had got a little too close to home, especially when the body of one of her co-workers at the radio station was dumped on her car.

Panic seized her; hot, clammy fingers around her throat, making it difficult to breathe. She braced herself against the dashboard, forced herself to fill her lungs, push back the images of . . .

. . . of . . .

'You okay?'

She started, whirled round in the seat, heart hammering in her chest, mouth flooding with a sour cocktail of bile and adrenalin. 'Jesus Christ, Keith!' she barked, voice ricocheting around the van, harsh and discordant. 'You nearly gave me a fucking heart attack!'

Keith held up small white palms in a placatory gesture even as he shrank away into the back of the van. 'Sorry, sorry,' he said, voice as anaemic as his skin. 'You just looked a bit, ah, spaced out there for a second. Wanted to make sure you were all right.'

Donna blinked away the image of Matt Evans's decapitated head and wiped angrily at the tear she felt threatening to fall from her eye. *Get a hold of yourself, Donna*, she heard her mother warning in her mind. *Now's not the time.*

She looked away from Keith, back up the road, using the moment to compose herself and consider her next move. Then she turned back to the cameraman and gave him what she hoped was a conciliatory smile but which felt like nothing more than the tensing of muscles in her face. 'Sorry,' she said. 'Think I might have a lead on the Charlston story after all, one that won't mean we're stuck in this sodding van all night.'

Something that might almost have been disappointment flitted across Keith's face. 'Okay, then,' he said, the sullen edge to his voice confirming Donna's worst fears. 'What's the plan?'

Donna reached for her phone, started scrolling through the contacts. 'The plan is, Keith, I phone a friend and call in a favour. And while I'm doing that you head back for town. I think the Exchange might still be serving food, and I've no doubt Mr Fraser will be hungry after his shift with Mr Charlston this morning.'

CHAPTER 10

Unfortunately for Donna, by the time she found Connor's number he was already taking a call. And, unlike Robbie's earlier, it was one he had been looking forward to.

'What's this I hear about you terrifying our customers?' Jen MacKenzie asked, her voice slightly robbed of its vaguely west-coast lilt by the car's hands-free speaker system.

Connor smiled. 'Ack, they were just some dumb gym rats picking on a kid trying to get into shape. All I did was show them the error of their ways.'

Jen snorted a laugh. 'Connor, I've seen the CCTV footage. Darren looks about ready to shit a brick when you put that Vulcan neck pinch on him, and his pals aren't much happier.'

'Darren.' Connor called up an image of the kid he had encountered earlier in the day, the overdeveloped muscles and arrogant sneer, and added the name to his memory. Might come in handy if he ever met the little shit again.

'So, what you doing?' Connor asked as he hit a straight section of road and coaxed the car up to 90 m.p.h. He shouldn't enjoy the speed, should be more discreet, especially in his line of work, but still . . .

'You mean other than hearing about the legend of Connor Fraser, keeper of the bench press and defender of the flabby? Not much. Taking a Zumba class at four, then got a PT session. Should be finished

31

by eight . . .' She let the sentence tail off, an open door Connor could choose to walk through if he wanted.

They'd met about a year ago, when Connor had started to use the twenty-four-hour gym where Jen worked. They'd become friendly, engaged in some cautious low-level flirting, Connor being careful not to turn his workouts into an exhibition or sideshow for her. But they'd only really become close since the murders six months ago. And, no matter which way he looked at it, Connor couldn't escape the conclusion that he had used Jen at the time, made her just another chess piece in the deadly game he had been playing. And the thought of that gnawed at him.

'Still there?'

'Oh, sorry, Jen,' Connor said, staring out at the empty road in front of him, 'busy road, got distracted. You say you were finished at eight?'

She gave an overdramatic sigh. 'That's what I like about you, Connor. You always make me feel like you're really listening to me when we talk.'

Connor smiled. 'I'm sorry, long day. If you're free, how about we get something to eat? Or I could cook. I still haven't got round to making you my teriyaki salmon.'

'Defender of the flabby and a cook? Why, Mr Fraser, where do your talents end?'

Connor felt himself redden, the temperature in the car suddenly kicking up a notch. 'Wait until you taste it before you sing my praises,' he said.

She chuckled again, a warm, throaty laugh that made Connor glance at the heater to make sure he hadn't turned it up to full by accident. 'Okay,' she said. 'Want me to come to yours when I've finished work? I'll need to go home and change first, but it won't take long.'

Connor ran a quick calculation, plotting the path from Jen's flat in the Woodlands area of Stirling to his flat in Park Terrace. It was less than a mile and the traffic would be light at that time. But, still, Jen lived in the south of the city, in a suburban area that was popular with parents, for the schools on hand, and commuters, for its easy access to the road to Bannockburn and its access to the A91, which eventually led to the arterial route of the M9. But for Connor,

Bannockburn held a more personal connection: his gran was in the care home . . .

'Tell you what, how about I do the driving? I can head out to see my gran, make sure she's okay, then pick you up on the way back. Just give me ten minutes' notice and I can get you.'

'Okay, deal,' she said. There was a moment's pause, and when she spoke again, her voice was flatter, more serious. 'How's she doing anyway?'

Connor sighed, felt the all-too-familiar mix of frustration and res- ignation well up. Ida Fraser was slowly slipping into the quicksand of her mind, yesterday blending with today, the rising waters of her jumbled memory slowly erasing her identity, as though it had been written in sand at low tide. Some days she was perfectly lucid, talking to him about his work, his childhood and his late mother, Claire, who had cared for Ida until cancer had claimed her. Connor knew that had been a tipping point for his grandmother – his mum had acted as an anchor for Ida, tethering her to the world. When she died, the cancer eating away at her from the inside out, the loss had cut Ida adrift.

'You know how it is,' he said, feeling his grip tighten on the steer- ing wheel. Too many memories. None of them good. 'You never know what you're going to get from one day to the next. But they say she's comfortable enough, and that's all I can really ask for.'

'That's good,' Jen said, her tone indicating she wasn't sure what to say next. By asking about his gran, she'd led them into a conver- sational cul-de-sac. One that Connor now had to back them out of.

He forced a brightness he didn't feel into his voice. 'Aye, wait until I tell her I'm cooking tonight – and for a woman as well. I'll get every lecture on manners and respect there is, and be told to make sure I buy you flowers on the way back to town.'

Jen laughed again, the tension broken. 'Tell her the pollen would just get up my nose. And, besides, she should know that a girl's best friend is pinot grigio. Especially with fish for dinner.'

'Message received,' Connor said, making a mental note to pick up wine as well as dinner ingredients.

'See you tonight,' she said. 'Oh, and, Connor?'

'Yeah?'

'Next time you decide to go all Superman in the gym, at least wear the tights, will you? I know some of the women in here would pay a lot of money to see that.'

She cut the call before he could reply, the sound of her laughter echoing around the car. It soon faded, but the question in Connor's mind refused to.

Would she be one of the women willing to pay to see that?

Connor gave a self-admonishing laugh, then turned his attention back to the road. He had left Robbie in charge of arrangements at the Alloa House, but he had work of his own to do before he could visit his gran and make dinner for Jen. He glanced at the clock on the dashboard – almost 4 p.m. already. Pressed down on the accelerator, the car edging up towards 100 m.p.h. Hardly discreet, but necessary with time being so short. And even as he told himself that lie, his phone gave another chirp, telling him a message was waiting for him.

He darted his eyes from the road to the dashboard phone display, read the name that was there. Smiled. He should have known. The call had been inevitable from the moment he had taken the Charlston contract.

Connor thumbed a control on the steering wheel. 'Redial,' he said.

CHAPTER 11

Donna watched as Keith crammed another mouthful of burger into his face. Even as he chewed, his hand strayed across the table for the pint of Coke he had ordered with the meal. Donna's stomach gave a queasy clench as she noticed the tidemark of saliva and crumbs dotted around the lip of the glass.

This was not the afternoon she'd had in mind.

Connor had returned her call quickly. He'd confirmed that he was handling security at the Alloa House for Charlston, but politely declined the offer of meeting up in town for a late lunch and a catch-up. 'Sorry, Donna, I've got too much to do this afternoon,' he had told her, his tone indicating that wasn't the whole truth. Instead, he'd offered to meet her for coffee the following morning, and promised to see what he could do about getting her access to Charlston.

Which was, Donna thought, watching as Keith turned his attention to the fries he had drowned in tomato sauce, the least Connor could do for her. Deep down, though, she knew that was only part of it. The simple, irrational truth was that she felt snubbed by him – and jealous that he had priorities other than her.

She snorted, suddenly angry with herself. After Mark and all his empty promises of a life together and a bright, shining future, she had sworn she would never be hurt by a man again. And yet here she was, acting like a rebuffed teenager at the school dance, left with the other class misfits while all the cool kids hit the floor.

Keith looked up at her, gave her a smile that showed off the blotch of ketchup on his cheek. 'What's up?' he said, brandishing a fork towards the salad in front of her. 'You not hungry?'

She shrugged, tried to keep her voice even. It wasn't Keith's fault. No point in taking it out on him. 'Nah, not really,' she said, keeping her eyes off his mouth as much as possible. 'Just thinking about the Charlston story.'

Keith nodded excitedly, put his burger down and wiped his hands with a tattered napkin. 'Yeah, I was just wondering about that as well. What if we took the camera an—'

Donna's phone chirped, cutting him off. She gave him an apologetic smile, hoping it didn't betray any of the relief she felt, and dug around in her bag for the phone. Pulled it out, felt a tickle of curiosity and disappointment when she read the unfamiliar number on the display. Probably a junk call. But still.

'Hello, Donna Blake,' she said.

From the other end of the line, a ghost spoke to her and, for an instant, Donna was back in the *Westie*'s newsroom, being bellowed at to 'File your fucking copy now!'

'Hello, Donna, it's me, Donald. I saw you on TV earlier. You look great. Wonder if you've got time to visit an old man? If you're working on the Charlston story, there are some things I think you need to know.'

CHAPTER 12

Pulling up in front of the care home, Connor was again struck by its similarities with the Alloa House. Like the hotel, it was a former family home that had fallen into disrepair when the old money sustaining it had run out. It had lain empty for years, little more than an overly grand hangout for local kids to get away from prying eyes and do what kids driven by hormones and booze did, until it was bought by Carson Residential, a private health company that specialised in caring for the elderly.

The company had gutted the building and refurbished it, retaining the imposing Victorian façade and augmenting it with what looked like a block of flats to the side of the main building: residential units that were connected to the main house by an umbilical-like glass corridor that seemed to rise out of the perfectly manicured grounds. It was in this unit that Connor had secured a suite for his gran – effectively a small flat that featured all the comforts of home, along with added panic alarms, grab rails and twenty-four-hour care from the nurses who staffed the place. The cost was astronomical, so much so that Connor had been forced to sell his grandmother's home in town – a grand, limestone-hewn townhouse on Clarendon Place, almost in the shadow of the Albert Halls – and place the money in a trust that now paid the bills for the care home and made sure his gran was comfortable for . . . well . . .

He killed that line of thought along with the Audi's engine, and sat in the silence, steeling himself. He hated these visits – there was no way of hiding from that simple fact. Connor knew that Ida Fraser had not had the easiest of lives, her husband, Campbell, walking out on her and Connor's father, Jack, back in the sixties, when such an act of abandonment was still somehow seen as the woman's fault. Connor wasn't sure of the details. His only clue as to what had happened were his father's infrequent, drink-fuelled warnings about 'the Fraser temper'. On those rare nights, Jack Fraser would describe his father as some kind of Jekyll and Hyde character – charming in public but a monster in private – who railed against his lot and blamed his wife and son for shackling him to a lifetime of mediocrity.

'You've got the Fraser temper, son,' his father would tell him. 'Keep it in check, like I have.'

Connor sometimes wondered if that was his father's way of trying to explain why he had been largely absent from his life. When Connor was growing up, Jack Fraser had been both emotionally and physically absent, ploughing his energies and attention into his medical career rather than his wife and son. It was his absence that had driven Connor across the Irish Sea to Belfast when he left school. He had destroyed any chance of a relationship with his father when he had crushed Jack's lifelong belief that his son would follow him into the life of a doctor by opting instead to study psychology at Queen's University. Three years later he had thrown a grenade into the smouldering shell of their relationship with the announcement that he was joining the Police Service of Northern Ireland.

But, unlike his father, Ida Fraser had never judged Connor on his choices. She had refused to let whatever injuries Campbell Fraser had inflicted on her become a callus on her soul, and offered Connor all the love and support Jack either would not or could not give. And now Connor felt a duty to return that love, to make sure his gran was comfortable as her mind turned traitor and dementia robbed her of her present, filling it instead with garbled memories of her past, as jumbled and chaotic as the boxes that now littered Connor's home: packed-up belongings and mementoes from the house he had just sold. He had crammed most of them into the flat's spare room, promising himself he would get around to sorting through them, find anything that he could bring here to use to remind his gran of who she was for just a little longer.

Sighing, he got out of the car, unable to put it off any longer. This was what he hated more than anything – the long, uncertain walk up to the main entrance, mind racing with possibilities. Would she remember him today? Confuse him with his dad? Or would she be the Ida Fraser he had grown up with – a strange mixture of tenderness and pragmatism, with a dry wit and a keen eye that seemed never to leave him, as though she was expecting something from him at any moment.

He hoped that was the Ida Fraser who was waiting for him today. The ITOI weekend was a headache, and there was something about the philosophies and life-plan ideas Charlston was spouting that troubled Connor. Not that he was a particularly religious man – his maternal grandparents, sickened by the sectarianism that had blighted Northern Ireland for most of their lives, had largely shunned religion – but, still, there was something about the 'be your own god' schtick that stirred an echo of unease in Connor. Or was it the man rather than the message that Connor disliked? He had read all the interviews and explanations Charlston had given, his regret at the deaths of Kimberley George and Graham Bell, and the collapse of Perigee. And while his remorse seemed genuine and the testimonials from his rapidly growing client base were glowing, something indefinable disturbed Connor. He thought suddenly of the welts on Charlston's nose and the over-blinking eyes that were unused to contact lenses. He was a master of image, trying to sell the message and the version of himself he wanted others to see.

But what was behind that image? And how many problems would that create for Connor and Sentinel over the next three days?

He paused on the steps of the care home, pulling out his phone and tapping out a quick message to Robbie, which he would follow up later.

Then, knowing he could put it off no longer, Connor forced himself to relax, pulled a neutral, relaxed smile into place, then jogged up the last few steps.

Whichever Ida Fraser was waiting for him, the first thing she would see was her grandson's smile.

CHAPTER 13

The invitation had come as a surprise – and not a totally welcome one.

Donna made her apologies to Keith, grateful for the excuse to leave him and the ruins of his burger to themselves. She hopped into a taxi and headed for home, a new-build flat in an area that the estate agents had got away with calling 'central Stirling' thanks to some creative copy-writing and sideways glancing at the postcode. But that didn't bother Donna. After Mark had walked out on her, the flat had become the cornerstone of the new life she was determined to create. It was somewhat cramped and characterless, the walls and skirtings all smothering magnolia and high-gloss white, but the place was theirs. Home.

Her mother had made the usual complaints when Donna had asked her to stay with Andrew for another hour while she drove out to see Donald Peters, then agreed. It was a balancing act, and not always an easy one. She had found a great nursery for Andrew in the centre of town, not far from Connor's flat in the King's Park area. Despite her increased salary with the move to Sky, the cost of childcare remained astronomical, so Andrew was there three days a week. A combination of her mum and dad and Sam, one of the carers from Andrew's nursery who freelanced in the evenings and the weekend to supplement her wages, covered the others. But still, in the world of twenty-four-hour news and every resource being thrown at breaking the big stories first, there were times when Donna couldn't rely on the nursery or Sam at short notice. And that meant turning to her parents.

But, no matter how grudgingly she helped or disapproving she was of her daughter's choice of career and lifestyle, Donna knew Irene Blake loved spending time with her grandson. He was eighteen months old now, increasingly mobile and slowly taking over the flat, his toys, books and nappies strewn around the place like rubble. And one look at him with Irene told Donna that he was the centre of her universe, just as he was for her.

Not for the first time, the fierceness of her love surprised her. Children had never been part of the plan for Donna. She had committed herself to a job with long, unpredictable hours and little time for socialising. Even when she and Mark had got together, she had never seen them having children, rather existing as a family of two.

But then had come the pregnancy test. And Mark walking out on her.

She'd considered abortion, gone as far as making the appointment. But the night before something had shifted, the enormity of carrying a life inside her finally hardening from an abstraction to a cold, hard fact. And in that moment she had decided she would have the child, no matter the personal cost.

Preparing herself to leave him again, when all she wanted to do was scoop him into her arms and play with him, take in his smell as she held his warmth close to her, she wondered, not for the first time, who was really paying the price for that decision.

She got to her car and punched the address Donald had given her into the satnav. It was south of Stirling, in Larbert, just outside Falkirk. Like many of the towns and villages of the Forth Valley, it was a popular commuter town, those working in Glasgow or Edinburgh opting for a house with a garden and properly sized bedrooms rather than the nosebleed-inducing prices and cramped conditions city-centre living had to offer. She turned the radio on, tuning to Valley FM, recognising the voice seeping through the speakers. It soon became background noise to her, her mind drifting back to the last time she had seen Donald Peters.

He had been a legend of the *Western Chronicle* newsroom, an old-school journalist who gave stories only the space they were worth and refused to cut and paste a comment from a press release when the opportunity arose. He mostly worked the crime beat, straying into politics when the two areas almost inevitably collided. When the Perigee story had broken, and politicians scrambled to be seen trying to save the ailing firm, Donald was on the front line of the story. Donna remembered the splashes he wrote, the days he swapped reporting for working on the newsdesk, arguing with the editor of the day about which stories should run to ensure the *Westie* was at the front of the Perigee story instead of reheating what had been said on the evening news bulletins the night before. He had dug deep, covered the story all the way up to the deaths of Graham Bell and Kimberley George, then disappeared abruptly. Rumours of a substantial pay-off and a sun-soaked lifestyle still swirled around the newsroom but, like most big stories, Peters soon faded from memory as fresher office gossip jostled for attention.

And now he wanted to see her. Because there was something she needed to know about Blair Charlston.

Despite herself, Donna felt a shiver of excitement. She had resigned herself to the fact that Connor wasn't going to be much help, but now here was Donald Peters, the man who had effectively crawled inside the Perigee story and worked his way back out, with some juicy snippet of information for her. But what could it be? She knew Donald had worked the story as hard as he could, writing not just the hard-news pieces on the buy-out and the subsequent asset stripping, but also the feature articles and long reads that gave context to the story and showed the human impact the folding of a business could have.

But that was five years ago now, a lifetime. What could he possibly have to tell her that would give her the edge?

The chiming of the satnav shook her from her thoughts, forcing her attention back to the present. She glanced down at the screen, then followed the arrow as it guided her to take a left at the upcoming roundabout, past a large, open field that a sign told her was home to Stenhousemuir Cricket Club. She drove on, into Larbert, then turned onto Rae Street, where Donald lived.

She slowed to a crawl, counting out the house numbers on the street, which was lined with semis on one side, bungalows and villas on the other, pulling into the kerb beside the one she mentally calculated would be Donald's. She peered up the driveway to the door, and the large number 7 bolted to the brickwork. Yes, this was the place. She got out of the car, walked up the driveway, its appearance surprising her. The grass was neatly trimmed and edged, immaculately pruned shrubs dotted along the borders in rich, dark earth that looked and smelled as if it had been freshly tended. Donald had never struck her as much of a gardener, and this level of neatness was definitely beyond him in his days at the *Westie*. Even in a so-called paperless office, Donald's desk was always awash with drifts of paper, his computer spattered with Post-it notes, like a teen with acne. She knew his wife had died years before, wondered briefly who had brought this love of the garden to his life.

She shook off the thought as she reached the door. It looked like real wood, dark and heavily polished, the whorls and patterns of the tree it had been hewn from like God's own thumbprint.

A musical chime sounded as she pressed the bell. She took a step back, listening to the soft soundtrack of suburbia as she waited – the low throb of cars passing along the roads surrounding her, the shout of a child from a nearby garden, a flutter of wings as two pigeons squabbled over a perch on a tree in the next-door garden.

She took out her phone as she waited, flicked through work emails and social media. The usual crap – camera assignments for the following day, an email from Keith telling her that today's footage was good, an update on the staff pension plan. But there, near the top of the inbox, was something interesting. She'd signed up to Charlston's mailing list a month ago, the number of messages she'd received from his company increasing as the ITOI weekend grew closer. Today's message was a simple one, which could be boiled down to the subject title.

'One day to go! Are you ready to shape your own destiny with Blair?'

She clicked into it, skimmed the content – all short paragraphs and jagged, upbeat prose about the ITOI weekend starting tomorrow, and how it would help attendees 'become gods of their own existence'. And, of course, under the beaming picture of Charlston and the signature that was as enthusiastic as his smile, there was a small click-through box reminding readers there was 'Still time to grasp the moment and join Blair'.

Donna snorted. Yeah. Join Blair. And all it would cost was four figures to do it.

43

She pocketed the phone, considered the front door. Pressed the bell again, stood closer as she listened to the chimes echo through the house. She heard nothing else, no sound of footsteps, no shouted apology. Swallowed a prickle of annoyance. Donald had asked her here. Surely he wouldn't go out unless . . .

She looked back up the path. At the shrubs. Felt like slapping her forehead with a 'D'oh!' It was a warm, pleasant day. He'd been working on the front garden, then headed round to the back. That was it.

She cast her gaze along the side of the house, past a large bay window and a garage door painted a listless russet colour. Spotted a fence and a gate, headed for it. Saw that it was off the latch, swinging gently with the breeze.

'Hello?' she called as she stepped through the gate onto a small slabbed pathway between the garage and the fence. 'Hello, Donald? It's Donna, Donna Blake. You back here?'

The pathway led out to a garden bigger than she would have imagined from the front of the house. It looked like something from a garden show, the lawn lush, verdant and impeccably flat, the plants that bordered it tall and proud, as though standing to attention. In the back corner, just before a thick hedge so perfectly edged it looked like it had been pushed out of a mould, there was a small shed, its door open, a smattering of tools arrayed at the front of it, like toys discarded after a hard day's play.

'Donald?' she called again, glancing back at the house. The patio door was cracked open, a mug sitting on a garden table in front of it. She looked back, trying to decide between the house and the shed. The tools. The door left open. She saw it in her mind: Donald sitting at his table, enjoying a drink, surveying his work after a long day in his kingdom. Spotting something that bothered him, heading for the . . .

Donna stepped towards the shed. 'Donald, it's Donna Blake. You in there?'

She took another couple of steps forward, hoping Donald wouldn't mind too much as her heels punctured the lawn. Then again, he *had* called her here, made her come and find him so if there was . . .

The lawn.

She stopped dead, the sudden quiet of the day rushing in on her, taking on weight. Felt her heart begin to race in her chest as her mind processed what she had seen.

At the front of the shed, just below the door, there was a dark patch in the otherwise perfect grass. Glistening in the afternoon sun, it could have been anything. Oil, maybe – probably, given how dark it was – as if a shadow had taken physical form. But something told Donna it wasn't. A memory of another time, of sightless eyes glaring at her like accusing marbles glinting in the dark, told her it wasn't, sent panic screaming through her veins.

Oh, Christ, not again. Please. This can't be happening again.

Despite herself, she took a half-step closer, her focus zeroing down on the dark patch in front of her. And now she could smell it. Cutting through the sweet aroma of grass cuttings and flowers, dark and rich and metallic . . .

'Donald?' she called, her voice sounding like a stranger's to her ears. 'Donald, come on, this isn't funny. Stop playing about, okay?'

Her legs twitched as her instincts and her mind wrestled for control. Felt the urge to turn and run needle her legs, whisper at the back of her neck like a lover. Knew that if she ran now, she would never stop.

She peered into the darkness of the shed, every sense straining to pierce shadows that suddenly seemed too dark and deep for such a bright day. Reaching out, hand shaking, Donna swatted at the shed door as though it were diseased. Noticed the slick of red on the door frame, a thin tendril that connected the stain on the grass to its source.

It was like someone reached inside her and turned the contrast levels in her mind all the way up to 100. The world suddenly became a place of hard edges and lurid colours that crowded in on her senses. She heard her breath whistle through her nose, felt a scream tickle the back of her throat.

Donald lay on the floor of the shed, his head twisted to the right, as though he were trying to touch his shoulder with his chin.

Donna lurched away on numb legs, doubled over and vomited, her jaw aching as her body tried to expel the contents of her stomach and the memory of what she had just seen. She put her hands on her knees to steady herself, heart thundering in her ears, forced herself to breathe. Closed her eyes, felt hot tears, knew they wouldn't be the last today.

Her breath smelled of vomit and fear as she inhaled, but she filled her lungs greedily. Steeling herself, she turned back around, as if to verify that the horror she had just seen was real.

It was like looking at a flayed steak, a mass of dark red-black matter glistening in the harsh sunlight, contrasting with the horribly grey-blue flesh that surrounded it. From jaw to nose was little more than a blood-streaked mess of churned meat. Teeth poked out from the uneven undulations of flesh, small white gravestones amid the hills of minced gore. Donna felt bile rise again as her mind put together what she was seeing and she realised she was looking at a detached section of Donald's lower lip, which trailed along his pallid cheek.

Whatever was holding Donna in place snapped and she ran. Footsteps like gunshots up the garden path, barely slowing as she hit the gate and kept going. Back up the path, into the street . . .

The sudden blare of a horn and scream of tyres. Then the world was filled with shouts, as angry and hard as her own thoughts.

'Jesus, fuck! I just about hit you, you stupid bitch! What the fuck were you—'

Donna whirled to the car in front of her, chest heaving. 'Police!' she bellowed, her voice coarse with revulsion and fear. 'Call the police now!' She waved back to Donald's house. 'In there. He's – he's . . .'

The driver was out of the car now, casting wary glances between Donna and the house as he approached. 'You okay there?' he said, anger forgotten. 'Look, I'm sorry it's just that . . .'

Donna took a deep breath, wrestled her hysteria into submission. Gave him a glare so cold and hard it froze him to the spot. 'Call the police. Now,' she hissed. 'There's a man dead back there. I just found him.'

The man's eyes grew wide and he took a step back. 'Dead?' he whispered. 'Y-you sure?'

The image of Donald's ruined face flashed across Donna's eyes and she forced down fresh tears. 'Yes,' she said, her voice as cold as her gaze. 'Pretty fucking sure. Make the call. Now.'

CHAPTER 14

'So, just what happened here?'

Connor glanced over Jen's shoulder into the living room of his flat, the clutter and jumble that was there. It was a large room, the far wall dominated by floor-to-ceiling patio doors that led out onto the Chinese-style garden that had been installed by the previous owners to disguise the hunk of granite that made up the wall leading back up to street level. Connor loved the space, and the light the windows let into his flat, but today all it did was accentuate the mess. Normally the place was almost monastically minimalist and tidy.

'Ah, that, yeah, sorry,' he said, stepping past her to start scooping the drift of papers from the coffee-table and back into the cardboard box beside it. 'Been going through some stuff from my gran's place. I was planning to tidy it a bit before I picked you up, but then, well, you know . . .'

The truth was that, after visiting his gran, he'd collected the shopping and got back to the flat in plenty of time. After preparing the salmon and making sure the wine Jen had mentioned was chilling, he turned his attention to clearing up the box he had dragged from the spare room and making the place presentable for Jen.

But then Robbie had called back with the information he had requested, and the afternoon had taken a left turn.

'I've been through the databases and media reports from the time,' Robbie had said, his tone telling Connor he had enjoyed the task about as much as a trip to the dentist. 'No sign of any member of Graham Bell's family being arrested or charged with anything after he took his own life. Definitely no indication that any of them made any official contact with Charlston or his team, other than what you'd expect during the investigation of Bell's death.'

Connor had half expected this. Since speaking to Charlston, the origins of the threatening note he had received had been nagging at him. At the mention of Graham Bell, his family and those he had been involved with had seemed to be the logical prime suspects. They might still be, Robbie's checks showing only that no one in Bell's family had acted until now. Which gave Connor another problem. If someone who had known Bell had sent the note to Charlston, they had bided their time and waited for what they thought was the right moment. Which indicated someone who was organised and patient. Someone with a plan.

Someone who could be a problem.

He'd thanked Robbie for making the checks, told him to ensure all the correspondence Charlston received was being filtered as rigorously as possible. It wasn't easy: Charlston had pleaded client confidentiality as though he was some sort of therapist or doctor rather than a life coach, but Connor had given him a simple choice. Anything that rang even the vaguest of alarm bells, he was to inform himself and the team immediately. If he chose not to and something happened, the terms of Sentinel's contract stipulated that all liability would fall back on Charlston. And despite his rebirth as a self-development guru, enough of the City financier lingered in Charlston to tell him that this was a very bad idea.

Robbie agreed to get on to it, promising to give Connor an update as soon as possible. Which had left him free to clear up for Jen's arrival. But even as he turned to the task, the thought of the note, and Charlston's reaction to it, nagged at him. It felt as if something was missing, something in the blunt simplicity of the threat that Connor wasn't seeing.

Graham died because of you. And for that, you'll pay SCUM.

Before he knew what he was doing, Connor had abandoned the clearing up, pulled out his laptop and lost himself in the Sentinel file on Charlston and the ITOI weekend, rereading the reports and background, looking for something he had missed, something that would tell him if this threat was real or the analogue equivalent of a keyboard warrior letting off steam.

An hour later he emerged from the files with nothing to show for it – except a still-messy living room. He was about to start clearing up when his phone chirped, Jen giving him his ten-minute warning that she was ready to be picked up.

Which left him where he was now, desperately trying to clear the table, the thought of his gran's disapproval ringing in his ears. Not just for the mess, but for the fact that he'd left the history of her life strewn around his living room for anyone to see.

He heard Jen approach, felt her hand on his shoulder. 'Connor, it's fine, honest. I'm just not used to seeing this place so, ah . . . lived in.'

He turned, smiled at her. 'Yeah, sorry. Just that there was so much stuff from my gran's house, and I've not had . . .'

She flashed that perfect smile, which had been one of the first things Connor had noticed about her. Her teeth were like something straight out of a Hollywood movie – perfectly straight, dazzlingly white and contained in a warm, infectious smile that always made Connor unsure of what to say next.

'Look, I said it's fine. Go cook. I'll clear this up and you can tell me how your gran was.'

Connor darted a glance between the papers and Jen, the thought of what his gran would say flitting across his mind. But Jen wasn't just anyone, was she? Which raised another question he had been asking himself of late.

Who was she to him? Since the events of six months ago, work had kept him busy, given him a convenient excuse not to take things further. But, still, he had found his thoughts drifting back to her, hoping she was at the gym whenever he attended. And now here they were – wherever that was.

'Okay,' he said, more to himself than her. 'Just stick it all back into the box. I'll go through it later.'

'Fair enough,' Jen said, flopping into the couch and leaning forward. She was close enough for Connor to smell the conditioner in her hair, which was still damp, a small tidemark of moisture running around the collar of her T-shirt.

He stood up, took a half-step back. 'Didn't expect to start the evening with you tidying the place for me,' he muttered.

She looked up at him, the smile widening even as something in her eyes told him not to push the point any further. 'It's fine. I don't mind. Really. But if you're consumed with guilt, you could get me a glass of wine. This looks like dry work.'

He headed for the kitchen and the chilling bottle of pinot grigio. Got halfway back with two glasses when his phone started buzzing in his pocket. He stood the glasses on a patch of the table Jen had cleared, offering an apologetic shrug as he backed off and pulled out the phone. Disregarded the unexpected flash of guilt he felt when he saw the caller ID and hit answer.

'Donna,' he said, glancing across to Jen as he said the name. 'What's up?'

'Connor.' Her voice was hard and flat, telling him this was Donna the reporter he was speaking to, not Donna the acquaintance. 'Sorry to interrupt your night. I know we're meeting tomorrow, but this can't wait. It's to do with Charlston.'

Connor's shoulders tensed, the memory of the note flashing across his mind. *Graham died because of you. And for that, you'll pay SCUM.*

'What is it?' he asked, something in his tone making Jen turn and throw him a quizzical glance.

There was a pause on the line, Donna obviously trying to construct the sentence she needed to say next. When she spoke, her shaky voice told Connor she had been crying.

'I was meant to meet an old friend today. Used to work with him in Glasgow. He retired a couple of years ago, lived out in Larbert.'

She took a breath, evidently steadying herself, giving Connor the fraction of a second he needed to process the one word that told him where this conversation was going.

Lived.

'Anyway,' Donna continued, 'I got there and, ah, well, I, ah—' She broke off, sudden silence on the line as she waged a battle with herself. When she spoke, her words were clipped, brittle, as though she was using efficiency as a shield against her emotions. 'Well, I found him. Turns out Donald – did I tell you that was his name, Donald Peters? Turns out Donald was in the shed. Head caved in. The thinking at the moment is that he had a heart attack or seizure and fell, cracked his head open on the vice in the shed. But we won't know until . . .'

Her voice trailed off as the memories overtook her. Connor could tell from her breathing that the tears she was fighting back were close now. 'Donna, I'm sorry for your loss,' he said, trying to keep his tone soothing, hating that he couldn't. And there was something else. About that name. Donald Peters. Almost as if . . .

'You said this has something to do with Charlston. I don't see . . .'

'Donald called me because he knew I was covering the Charlston story,' Donna interrupted, impatient anger lingering in her words. 'Said he wanted to talk to me about it, told me he had something important to tell me.'

Recognition hit Connor like a punch. Donald Peters. Of course he knew the name, had seen it as the byline on the reports surrounding Charlston, the collapse of Perigee and the death of Kimberley George. 'Okay,' he said. 'An old colleague wanted to talk to you about a story he was working on. But I still don't see . . .'

'Of course you don't,' Donna said. 'You wouldn't know. No one did. It was part of the deal. I don't know what Donald wanted to tell me, Connor, but whatever it was it must have been important for him to risk everything.'

'Risk everything?' Connor asked, not sure he wanted to hear what was coming next.

'Yeah. See, Donald didn't quite retire. He left. Took a package, signed a non-disclosure agreement and said goodbye to a thirty-year career in newspapers. And all because of Blair Charlston.'

Connor blinked, reached for the wine glass on the table, exchanged a glance with Jen. He knew what Donna was going to say, had put the pieces together as she spoke. It was all there. A reporter. A controversial story. A non-disclosure agreement and a pay-off. 'So you mean . . .'

'Exactly,' Donna said. 'I only know what I heard at the time.

Donald was working on a story about Charlston, approached him for a comment and within a week he's out of the door with a golden goodbye and a gagging clause. Then he calls me this afternoon, the day before Charlston holds his triumphant homecoming gig, and by the time I get there to speak to him, he's dead. That ringing any alarm bells for you, Connor? Because I sure as hell don't like it.'

Connor took a swig of his wine, found he had no taste for it. 'No,' he said slowly. 'I don't like it at all.'

CHAPTER 15

The purring ring of the phone in his ear was a slow torture. Mark Sneddon worried at his nail as he listened, praying the phone would be answered, half hoping it wouldn't.

Bad time to call anyway. They were probably busy. Always were. Stupid. He should just hang up now, try again some other—

'Hello?'

The voice was like a dagger of ice in Mark's ear. Should have expected it. He felt panic crawling up his throat, forced his breathing to calm.

'Hello, Mrs Blake, it's ah, Mark. Mark Sneddon. How are you today? Is Donna there?' He winced as he said it. Where the fuck else would she be? 'Would it be possible to—'

'No, Mr Sneddon, it would not,' Mrs Blake's voice came back. 'Donna isn't here.'

He glanced at the clock on the newsroom wall. Nine a.m. Early for Donna to be out. Unless, of course, she had a lead on the Peters case. Something that . . .

The soft wail of a baby from the other end of the phone dragged Mark from his musings. He smiled, felt something hot flash behind his eyes.

Andrew.

'Ah, well, of course,' he said, the panic wrapping its cold, skeletal fingers around his throat again and beginning to squeeze.

53

'If you could tell her I called, ask her to give me a buzz when it's convenient.'

The only reply was a scoffing grunt, then the harsh click as the line went dead. Mark shook his head. '"Hell hath no fury like a woman scorned",' he whispered. 'Or her mother.'

He looked around the newsroom, empty at this hour, the paper not yet roused into life. Not that there was much life in this place any more. After he had been cut from the *Chronicle* in the latest round of redundancies and 'cost savings', Mark had found himself freelancing around the country. He'd worked most of the papers, finally catching some shifts at the *Capital Tribune* in Edinburgh. It was dull, unsatisfying work, mostly rewriting agency copy and throwing it onto templated pages, but it paid the bills. Or some of them. But then had come last night, and the news – little more than a few lines from the wire agencies that media outlets used – that Donald Peters, former reporter at the *Western Chronicle*, had been found dead at his home in Larbert. Mark had known Donald from his time at the *Westie*, was aware that Donna knew him as well.

Which had given him an idea. And an opportunity.

He rocked back in the seat as the enormity of the thought hit him again. A son. *His* son. Andrew. Born eighteen months ago. Now home with his mother and her parents as he, *his father*, sat alone in a rented flat in another city, the marriage he had abandoned them for little more than a smouldering ruin. But what would he have done if he'd stayed? Divorced Emma? Moved in with Donna, made a family and lived happily ever after?

He grunted. Happy ever after? Him? Hardly. It was one of the reasons he had been attracted to journalism in the first place. He hated the mundane, the routine. Loved the unpredictability of the job and the places it could take him. His marriage to Emma had been as empty as his bank account, but it had been an anchor, binding him to the dead weight of life with a woman who was happy to let him work whatever hours he needed or wanted to, all in pursuit of the next headline, the next exclusive, the next splash. He might have hated it, but Mark acknowledged that even if he had ended things with Emma when Donna fell pregnant, the next Donna, the next target, would be just around the corner. Happiness and stability were not part of his character.

But if that was the case, why had he not been able to shrug off the memory of Donna after what had happened in Stirling? Of those few short hours in her flat, almost under house arrest, as that man-monster Fraser hunted down a killer who had threatened them both. Of the gurgling from the baby monitor, and the unshakeable image of Donna switching from hardened reporter to protective mother in the blink of an eye.

It was those lingering thoughts that had finally torpedoed whatever was left between him and Emma. She could tell his mind was elsewhere, feasting on what-ifs and might-have-beens. But there had been no arguments, no confrontations. She hadn't argued when he'd moved out, had barely raised the interest to ask where he was staying. And now it was all in the hands of lawyers. Expensive lawyers. Which meant he had to keep working. Keep earning.

And if he was right, Donald Peters might just be his big pay cheque.

He'd heard the stories, of course, been party to the rumours that Donald had dug a little too deeply into Perigee and Blair Charlston than was comfortable. Whatever it was, it had been enough to make Charlston employ a team of six-figure QCs from London and set them on the *Westie*, which had barely enough money to defend its supplies of notepads, let alone a court action for libel. So a deal had been struck, and Peters offered a way out. All in return for his silence.

But what Mark knew, which he'd never shared during the whispered gossip sessions among the reporters, was a startling fact about the pay-out Peters had received. The information hadn't been difficult to come by. All it had taken was one night in Merchant City with one of the PAs to the *Westie*'s legal team when Donna had been home in Stirling visiting her parents. At the time he hadn't given it a second thought – it was another game, another chase, another story. But now he didn't know what disgusted him more: that it hadn't bothered him at the time or that he couldn't remember the girl's name.

He stood suddenly, as though the shame he felt had been spilled into his lap like scalding coffee. He leaned over his PC, tapped out a message to the news editor, Dennis, who had yet to make an appearance.

Stirling. Whatever was going on, the answers were in Stirling. He could compare notes with Donna, see if there was a way they could both get something out of this. From her mother's reaction to the call and the way she was blocking him he knew the reception wouldn't be warm. But it didn't matter. After all, he had something to offer her: the true cost of Peters's silence. And an all-access pass to Blair Charlston. After that, Mark would do what he always did.

He would play the game.

CHAPTER 16

Connor winced as he reached for his coffee, muttered softly when he saw the tremor in his hand. He focused on the mug in front of him, willing it to steady in his grip. Eventually it did and he took a swig, felt his eyes moisten as the coffee scalded his mouth.

Stupid, he thought. Stupid. After Donna's call, he had tried to return to his night with Jen, both of them knowing it was a sham. Oh, it was a pleasant enough evening – they'd laughed at each other's jokes, Jen had complimented Connor on his cooking – but it was as if there was a third person in the room, creeping into the pauses in the conversation, crowding in on the soft clatter and click of cutlery as they ate. When Connor had picked Jen up, she had greeted him with a hug, and something in that hug had told him what she expected the night to be. But then came the call from Donna, and their unspoken plan had been aborted. Connor had stopped drinking after one glass of wine and, when the conversation tapered out, he had driven Jen home. She had kissed his cheek when she left him, something sharper than disappointment in her eyes.

She had texted him before he was back on the main road – a simple message that burned his guts almost as badly as the coffee had his mouth. *Thanks for tonight. Hope you get work sorted out. Call me when you're ready x*

He had pondered the message all the way home, and why it felt like a goodbye. When he got in, he booted up the laptop and searched out the articles Donald Peters had written on Charlston and the collapse of Perigee Designs. There were plenty, but nothing to indicate what had led to the gagging order and his abrupt departure from the *Westie*. Frustrated, Connor had reached for his phone, scrolled through the contacts until he found the number for DCI Malcolm Ford. He had worked with Ford the previous year, when bodies had been dumped around Stirling as a calling card for him and, while he would hardly call them friends, he knew Ford was a man he could call on if needed – just as Ford could call on him. He was about to make the call when he saw the time on the phone – 00:17. He flipped to messages instead and thumbed in a text, telling Ford about Donald Peters's death and asking him if he'd heard anything, not really expecting an answer.

Before he knew what he was doing he was reading Jen's message again. *Call me when you're ready x*

Ready? For what? He knew he was stalling, keeping her at a distance. His last relationship had hardly ended well, and the thought of Karen, who was now living in Edinburgh, was like a sliver of glass in his guts if he gave it any attention. He knew their break-up had been his fault – he'd beaten the thug who'd used her as a way of threatening Connor half to death in Belfast, had shut down after that, too ashamed to tell her what he had done, too terrified that the violence he had unleashed could now never be fully contained. Then his mother had died, and Connor had retreated even further into himself, again becoming the insular, repressed boy of his youth. Karen had tried to reach him, but it was like trying to solve a jigsaw that you didn't have the picture for – the parts were all a jumble, nothing made sense, no combinations worked. They'd split three months later, Connor moving home from Belfast to Stirling, Karen to Edinburgh. He'd thought of reaching out to her, saying hello. But what would he say? More importantly, *why* would he be saying it? And what would that mean for him and Jen, and whatever might be between them?

When the thoughts had grown too much, he'd propelled himself off the couch, grabbed his keys and his kit bag and headed for the gym, knowing Jen wouldn't be there at that hour, hoping Darren and his steroid-enhanced pals were. Fortunately for everyone, the gym was nearly deserted, so Connor had to satisfy himself with the weights, stacking them heavier and heavier as though he could crush all thoughts of Jen, Donna and Donald Peters with enough plates. He had worked out for an hour, then driven home in a daze and fallen into a fitful sleep.

And now, here he sat, in the small café he liked on Bow Street, back to the wall, muscles aching from last night's exertions as he watched Stirling wake up and waited for Donna, wondering what she was about to tell him. Would it be something that would affect the ITOI weekend? Would he have to face down Charlston and force him to alter his plans for the bonfire that night? Or was it a horrible coincidence? After all, Peters had been an old man: he could have stumbled, smashed his head and torn his face open, bled to death in his shed. One of those horrible but prosaic accidents that underscore how random and cruel life can be.

Connor swallowed the thought with another slug of coffee. Yeah. Right.

The phone was back in his hand before he realised it, Jen's message seeming to sneer at him from the screen. He remembered the feel of her in that hug, her lithe body pressed against his, at once fragile and strong. The goodbye kiss, a ghost haunting its own dashed hopes.

Call me when you're ready x

He was about to hit dial when the door to the café clattered open, the soft sound of tyres on cobbles from the street outside wafting in with Donna. With a sigh, Connor pocketed his phone. From the look on her face, it was clear that he wasn't going to be calling Jen for some time.

CHAPTER 17

The sudden bark of laughter that echoed down the hallway felt to Ford like an insult to the chilled, antiseptic silence in Dr Walter Tennant's office. This was a place of cold steel, harsh lighting and icy air. The brash, enthusiastic sound of life had no place here.

Ford pushed away the thought, forcing himself to focus on Tennant, who was sitting across an obsessively tidy desk from himself and DS John Troughton. Everything about Walter Tennant spoke of strength, certainty. From the barrel chest to the thick white beard and the hands that dwarfed the reports strewn across the table in front of him, he looked more built for life as a doorman or a rugby player than a pathologist. Yet Ford knew the appearance for the lie it was: he had seen Tennant dissect a body with a skill and grace that was as fascinating to him as it was sickening. Luckily for him and Troughton, Tennant had finished the post-mortem examination before they arrived, and was reviewing his notes again before speaking to them.

Nodding to himself, as though finding the answer to a question that had been bothering him, he looked up, steepling his massive sausage fingers on the desk as he did so. He was wearing a short-sleeved shirt and, looking at the slab-like muscle of his arms, Ford was suddenly reminded of Connor Fraser. Another man whose certainty and strength seemed imprinted in his DNA.

And, like Tennant, another man who invariably brought Ford bad news.

The text had been waiting for him when he had switched on his phone that morning, after an all-too-rare evening when he had turned it off to spend a night with Mary. Nothing fancy. Just dinner, a bottle of wine and conversation. It was, Ford thought, a good night. She'd hinted at his retirement only twice, didn't push the issue when he dodged the topic. After all, what would he say? Yes, love, I hate the fucking job as much as you do, but if I quit now, who's left? Troughton?

The message had been as direct as its sender, just five sentences. All business. *Unexplained death in Larbert. Donald Peters. Not your patch, but can you have a look? Might be connected to Charlston and the event I'm covering this weekend. Will call later.*

The first time he'd met Fraser, Ford had been investigating a spate of murders around Stirling. He'd marked Connor Fraser as a former policeman the moment he'd met him: from the way he scanned a room to the questions he asked and the actions he took, everything about Connor Fraser screamed police. Ford had done a little checking, found he had been a promising officer in the Police Service of Northern Ireland. Until, of course, something had happened that drove him home. He blinked away the sudden image of a head mounted on a spike at the Holy Rude, squealing softly as it bobbed in the wind, calling to him.

'Well,' Tennant said, jolting Ford from his thoughts, 'I'll say this for you, Malcolm, you always bring in the interesting ones.'

Ford felt unease tickle the back of his neck. Fraser. Connor bloody Fraser. 'How do you mean, Walter?'

Tennant pulled back his lips to reveal a row of white teeth that seemed too small for a man of his size. 'Well, let's see,' he said. 'Male, seventy-three years old, approximately eighty-seven kilograms. Identified from items in his possession and medical records as Donald William Peters. Deceased had significant injuries to his face and temple, consistent with being struck with a heavy blunt object.'

Ford felt the fragile sliver of hope that this was merely a domestic accident tremble and finally snap, like a frosted spider's web.

Fraser. Connor bloody Fraser.

'So you're saying this wasn't an accident,' he asked, almost embarrassed at the question. 'SOCOs said there was a vice on the workbench in the shed, found blood and hair on it. No way he slipped and fell, cracked his head open on it?'

Tennant's dead smile widened, something approaching amusement flashing across his eyes. It was momentary, but long enough for Ford to see his old friend in a new light. He was enjoying this. He knew something, and he was making Ford work for it.

Why?

'No, Malcolm, I'm afraid not,' he said. 'There's too much damage, too much force for this to have come from an accidental blow to the head. He probably hit his head on the vice after the first blow, when he'd have been dazed and going into shock.' He slid a picture across the desk, smooth as a Vegas card dealer. Ford glanced down, heard Troughton take a sharp breath and shift in his seat behind him.

The picture was a tableau of horrors painted in angry crimson and pink, shot through with flecks of white where teeth and bone gleamed like jewels in the glare of the pathologist's camera. Ford could pick out enough landmarks – a glimpse of ear, a patch of stubbled cheek, a hairline – to make sense of what he was seeing, but the centre of the image was a riot of violence that seemed to mock any notion that this had once been a living, breathing person.

Ford forced himself to look away from the picture, focus on Tennant. 'So if it was intentional, what can you tell us about the assailant or the murder weapon? Nothing was found at the scene.'

Another flash of cold humour in Tennant's eyes, as though he couldn't wait to deliver the punchline to the world's best joke. 'Whoever the assailant is, they were strong.' He gestured to the picture. 'It would have taken considerable force to inflict wounds like this. Probably with something like a ball-peen hammer.'

Troughton looked up. 'Ball-peen?' he asked.

'Used in metalwork, son,' Ford said, voice harsher than he had intended. Tennant really had got to him. 'Your grandda' probably had one. About yay long.' He held his hands roughly ten inches apart. 'Had one flat head and one smaller round one.'

'Ah.' Troughton grunted, his pen scratching across his notepad.

Ford turned his attention back to Tennant. 'So, given the force involved, the attacker was probably male?'

'Conjecture, but given what I've seen, I'd say it's a good bet. From the pattern of the injuries he probably came at him face on, the first blow shattering his nose and front teeth. Most likely whoever did this was right-handed, the blow an uppercut slashing from right to left.'

Reflexively, Ford sucked his lips across his teeth as though to protect them. 'Jesus. So what was cause of death? Blood loss from the injuries, or did the attack do some other damage?'

Tennant sat forward, teeth glittering in the overhead strip lights. His smile was no longer amused: now it was sharper, cruel. Almost predatory. He broke his gaze from the policemen, went back to shuffling through his file. Found what he was looking for and slid it across the desk to Ford, who read the piece of paper, then looked up at the doctor, dumbfounded.

'That's right,' he said. 'As you can see, the unfortunate Mr Peters did not die from his facial injuries or blood loss.'

Troughton looked between Ford and the pathologist, head darting between the two in irritated confusion. 'What? Then how did he . . .'

Ford handed the sheet of paper to him, eyes not leaving Tennant. The pathologist nodded, the conversation passing between them unspoken in the glance.

'As I said, Malcolm, you do always bring me the interesting ones.'

CHAPTER 18

They ordered a couple of coffees to go and headed out of the café, Connor claiming he wanted to walk and stretch out the previous evening's workout. But there was another reason, something that echoed deeper than the burning ache in his legs: anger. It was irrational, he knew, but when he had seen Donna the first thing he had felt was a flash of anger. For the interruption to his night with Jen, for the memories it had stirred up and the thoughts he didn't want to have. The café had suddenly felt confining, claustrophobic, and the prospect of sitting across from Donna was a confrontation he didn't want to face.

So now they were walking down the steep slope of Bow Street, the blunt façades of the pink and beige sandstone of the houses seeming to glow in the morning sunshine. It was going to be a warm day, Connor thought, not a cloud in the sky. Good news for the tourists, who were already milling around this part of Stirling. Bad news for him and any hope he had of Charlston's plans for that night being rained off.

'. . . you think?'

Connor pulled himself from his thoughts, aware that Donna had stopped walking while he had carried on for half a step. Her face was a mask of weariness, shock and something that could almost be disappointment, the make-up she wore doing nothing to conceal another lost night's sleep. Connor winced, felt his anger redirected at himself. The woman had just found an old friend lying dead in his shed. A friend who had a link to a client Connor was trying to protect. Of course she would reach out to him. What she needed was support, help, not his misplaced anger and complacency.

Stupid, Connor. Stupid.

'Sorry, Donna, lost in my own head. What were you saying?'

She chewed her top lip for a moment, giving him a look as cold as it was resigned. Took a breath, seemed to come to a decision. 'I was asking what you thought of all this. Did you hear anything from Ford?'

'Not yet,' Connor said, remembering the text he had sent to Ford the night before. He should have followed it up instead of feeling sorry for himself. 'Did you find out anything about why Peters left the paper you worked for?'

Donna's expression told Connor she knew the question for the diversionary tactic it was. 'Not much,' she said. 'I asked an old colleague at the *Westie* to look into it, but it's all tied up pretty tight. All they could say is that Donald approached Charlston's team about a story he was working on, and all hell broke loose. Lawyers, injunctions, threats to sue the paper into bankruptcy. Then, suddenly, Donald takes a pay deal and fades into the background. Until yesterday.' She took a hasty sip of her coffee, as though she could swallow with it the memory of finding Peters.

'Bad?' Connor asked, the word feeling inadequate and hollow even as he said it.

Donna blinked, nodded, jaw tightening. 'Bad enough,' she said, her voice nothing more than a caffeine-strained whisper. 'It was like his head had been caved in, Connor. There was blood everywhere. And his face . . .'

She shook her head, trying to deny the memory. Connor stepped forward, put a hand on her shoulder, painfully aware of how slender and brittle she felt. 'I'm sorry, Donna, I really am. But you said yourself, he was old, liked a drink. Any chance at all that this was an accident, that he just stumbled in the shed, cracked his head open?'

Her head darted up and she stepped back, shaking off his hand. Connor tensed, the thought flashing across his mind that she was going to hit him.

'No,' she hissed, her voice as hard as the walls of the buildings that surrounded them. 'No way. It looked like a bomb had gone off in his head, Connor. Christ, his jaw was – was . . .' She fumbled for the words, realised she couldn't find them. 'No way this was an accident. And don't tell me you believe that shit for a second. Look at it. He gets in touch with me, tells me there's something I need to know about your little fucking saviour Charlston, and turns up dead later the same day. That sound plausible to you, Mr Protection Expert?'

Connor ignored the insult, knew it came from a need to inflict on others the pain she was feeling. He sympathised. And, in truth, he agreed. There was something about this picture that was very wrong, and the conversation he was going to have with Charlston as soon as he finished with Donna would be as blunt and direct as an uppercut. Charlston thought he was the god of his own destiny. Connor was going to disabuse him of that notion.

'No,' he said, finding her eyes and holding them. 'No, Donna, it doesn't. I'll speak to Charlston, find out what the hell is going on, what happened between him and Peters.'

'And Ford?' Donna asked, impatience creeping back into her voice. 'What about Ford? I could talk to him on the record, but we both know he's more likely to open up to you.'

Connor nodded. Given the way Donna had hauled Police Scotland and Ford over the coals when the bodies were piling up on the streets the year before, it was a fair bet she wasn't on any press officer's Christmas card list. Which left Connor in an awkward position. If Ford told him anything, how much could he – should he – tell Donna?

'I'll call him on my way to the venue, let you know,' he said, then, seeing the hopeful gleam in her eyes, added, 'No way, Donna, not today. I need to talk to Charlston, figure out what the hell is going on. No way I'm going to be able to do that if I've got a reporter in tow.'

The nod she gave him told Connor she understood, but didn't like it. 'Okay, but you'll call me as soon as you hear anything? I'm not asking as a reporter, Connor. I need to know. For Donald.'

'That mean you're not going to report any of this?' he asked.

She snorted a laugh, took another sip of her coffee to mask the smile creeping onto her face. If the question had insulted her, she gave no hint of it. 'What do you think? All I've got at the moment is that a former reporter died at his home in Larbert. Police are investigating the circumstances. I go on the record with any of the gossip about his history with Charlston, my arse will be in a sling before you can say the words "super injunction". But someone did this to Donald, Connor, and I want them for that. If I can splash their faces all over the TV in the process, all the better.'

Connor bit down a smile. He admired Donna's determination, the way she had forced life to give her what she wanted when her plans had been torpedoed by a selfish prick who thought he was such a catch that little things like responsibility, obligation and loyalty didn't apply to him. He had a sudden memory of the last time he had seen Mark Sneddon, bruised and cowering in the boot of a car, felt the smile grow wider. 'Okay, come on,' he said. 'I'll go and see Charlston, you keep digging on Peters, see if you can—'

He was interrupted by the chirping of Donna's phone. She dug it out of her pocket, took a step back, as if the phone had reached up and slapped her, when she read the caller ID.

'Donna, you okay?'

She looked up at him, face pale. Held up the phone so he could read the caller ID.

'Mark, mobile,' it read.

'As if this day couldn't get any worse,' Donna said. 'What the fuck do you think he wants?'

CHAPTER 19

The disgust he felt was like a living thing, a parasite churning in his guts. It had started the moment he had turned off the road and onto the driveway that swept up towards the Alloa House. Flags lined the driveway like sentries, the ITOI logo writhing like a snake as the wind twisted and turned through them. About fifty feet along, a makeshift checkpoint had been set up, drivers handing over their passes for the weekend and being directed to the appropriate car-park. From the set-up, it was clear that the more you paid, the closer you got to the hotel, and the event itself.

And he would get close. He had paid dearly for the privilege.

His pass checked and identity confirmed, he drove to the main car-park just behind the hotel. Felt hot, accusatory glances as he guided the Fiat into a rarefied land of Audis, Jags and Mercedes, as though he was leading a mule into a paddock full of thoroughbreds.

He parked, then retrieved his bag, the weight somehow reassuring as he hefted it from the boot. The place had an almost festive vibe, as though everyone there was attending a show or a gig, anticipation mounting as they waited for the big act to appear. He smiled at that. They'd get a show, all right.

Up the stairs to the hotel, into the main lobby, the excited thrum of the crowd milling around like discordant chatter in his mind. He checked in, kept his head down as he made for the lifts. Felt a flash of rage as he passed a cardboard cut-out of Charlston, his perfectly manicured smile beaming out at him as though he didn't have a care in the world. He paused in front of it, forcing himself to breathe, blinking away the sudden tears that tore at the back of his eyes, and denying the urge to tear the image of the bastard apart with his bare hands, as though it was an oversized voodoo doll.

No memory of how he got to his room, the thumping of the case onto the bed snapping him from whatever fugue he had been in. He stepped back, took in his surroundings. Just another hotel room in a conference venue, all restrained comfort, soft furnishings and gleaming porcelain in the bathroom. He crossed to the window and opened it, let the over-eager clamour of the world outside seep into him, feed his anger.

The room was at the front of the hotel – one of the perks of the platinum pass for the ITOI event that had effectively bankrupted him. The windows looked out onto the grounds as they swept down to the woodland that acted as a natural barrier to the outside world. To the left of the main lawn, in an area that had been fenced off and was being patrolled by more security staff wearing high-vis tunics, what looked like a forty-foot-high Jenga tower had been constructed from pallets, logs and other flammable materials. He sneered at the sight of it, the pretence and the arrogance. The Destiny Bonfire. The place where Charlston would 'help participants burn away their old lives and emerge into their new, like the phoenix'.

Bullshit. All bullshit.

He turned away from the window, the rage unfurling in him, blackening his thoughts and making targets of the mirror that hung on the wall and the chair in the corner. Felt his arms twitch at the thought of seizing the chair, hurling it through the windows, then shattering the mirror, finding a shard big enough to gouge and slash and—

He gasped as he drove his fist into his gut, the pain a sudden flare of white noise that blanked out his thoughts. Not long now, he told himself. Stick to the plan. Be patient. You've waited this long.

He walked back to the bed and opened the suitcase. Skimmed off the clothes at the top, like they were cream on milk, and set them aside, then reached in for the only three objects he had packed that mattered.

The first was her picture. He held it at eye level for a moment, then placed it gently on the small table beside the bed. The other two items he took back to the window. He looked at the bonfire, his earlier rage replaced by something purer, cleaner.

Excitement.

He bounced the bottle gently in his left hand, as though it was a piece of ripe fruit he was trying to weigh. Heard the liquid it held slosh gently against the cool plastic. Gripped by sudden panic, he looked down, making sure the seal was tight. He needn't have worried: he'd checked it half a dozen times after he'd filled it, eyes streaming, the scent scalding his nostrils.

Warily, he put it on the window ledge, watched as the sunlight played on the liquid, transformed into oily swirls of purple and red, as though a rainbow was trapped inside.

A rainbow in a bottle. He smiled. She would have liked that.

The thought was as sharp as the blade he held in his other hand. He took a deep breath and shut his eyes. Then he opened them and bent slightly, aligning the bottle until he could look through it to the bonfire beyond, as though it was some kind of prism.

He ran his hand across his stomach again, felt the pain from the punch run through him like an echo. Destiny, he told himself. Destiny was calling. Not long to wait now. For him or Blair Charlston.

CHAPTER 20

The hiss of driveway gravel seemed to echo the confused static of Connor's thoughts as he drove towards the Alloa House.

After leaving Donna hunched over her phone as she took the call from Mark, with the same stance as she would take a gut punch, Connor had headed back to the Albert Halls, where he had parked the Audi. Settling into the driver's seat, he noticed a message from Ford, a reply to his earlier text: *Call me.*

Firing the engine and switching the phone to hands-free, he had called Ford. Now, nodding to the security staff manning the checkpoint heading towards the hotel, Connor almost wished he hadn't.

Ford had answered the call even before the second ring had faded. 'Fraser, you took your time,' he said, the slight distortion of his voice from the hands-free doing nothing to mask the tension in his words.

'Sorry, sir,' Connor said, wincing at the title his time in the police forced him to give Ford. 'I was caught up with Donna Blake – you know, she found Peters's body. Didn't have much more to tell me. You find anything out?'

A harsh bark of laughter filled the car, seemed to darken the shadows for a moment. 'Find something? Christ, aye, you could say that.'

Connor twisted in his seat, a sudden discomfort that was nothing to do with his aching muscles. 'I take it this was no accident, then. He was murdered.'

Impatience in Ford's voice now. Connor knew he hated it when he wasn't the one asking the questions. Tough.

'Look, I'll get to that in a minute, but first, what is the connection between Blake and Peters? I'll be calling her the moment we're done, but anything you can give me would help.'

Swallowing his impatience, Connor filled Ford in on what Donna had told him about Peters's work on Charlston and the call he had made to her which had led to her finding the body.

'And why, in the name of Christ, did she not tell the interviewing officer when she called in the discovery of the body?' Ford asked, his voice sounding like the rumble of distant thunder.

Connor didn't answer, let the silence fill the car. After all, they both knew why. Whatever was going on, it linked Peters's death to Charlston and a weekend event that had already proved controversial. Aside from a personal tragedy, this was something else to Donna. This was an exclusive. A story that could put her at the top of the news cycle, leave her rivals in her wake and further her career.

And, as they both knew, Donna Blake would go to almost any lengths to get ahead of the pack. Keeping information from the police? Connor doubted that would rank as much more than an afterthought.

'Come on, then,' Connor said at last. 'It was murder. Donna said his face was a mess when she found him. So someone beat Peters to death.'

'Hardly,' Ford said, his voice telling Connor his face was twisted into an empty smile.

'Then what?' Connor asked, barely keeping the frustration out of his voice.

And then Ford spoke, and it was as if his voice was an icy fog drifting through the speakers, chilling Connor to the bone.

'He was poisoned, Connor. Pathologist says cause of death was organ failure brought on by a massive dose of . . .' the soft rustle of paper on the line as Ford consulted his notes '. . . ethylene glycol, more commonly known as antifreeze. Sweet-tasting, easy to add to the drink of someone who liked their tea hot and sugar-laden, and easily accessible at any DIY store or well-stocked garden shed.'

Connor felt as though he had just stuck his finger into the cigarette lighter. Thoughts sparked across his mind like lightning flashes. What the hell did it mean? Why would someone go to the trouble of poisoning Peters, then decide to cave his head in? There was something about that, like a shape felt in the dark you couldn't quite identify. The violence of the attack told Connor it had been personal, driven by hate. But the poisoning? That was something else entirely. Murder almost by remote.

And what had Peters been about to tell Donna? What he had discovered about Charlston that had earned him a golden gagging order and a slow slide into retirement? And here was another question, one with which Connor would have to confront Donna. If Peters had been killed because of what he was about to tell Donna, did the killer know the old reporter had been in touch with her? And, if that was the case, was she now a target as well?

'I'm heading for the Alloa House now, planning to speak to Charlston,' Connor said. He heard an intake of breath, Ford no doubt getting ready to object. Ignored it. 'I'll get off the line. Call Donna. I'll meet you at the hotel in half an hour and we can speak to Charlston together.'

'Fraser, this isn't a negotiation. What you've just told me makes Charlston a person of interest at the very least. I can't have you being present during a formal interview, which is what this will be.'

Connor grimaced, knowing where this conversation was headed. 'He's my client. I've been taken on to protect him during the ITOI weekend, and that's what I'm going to do. First job is to ascertain what he knows, what the potential risk is. Then I can make a decision on whether or not to pull the plug on the festivities tonight.'

'Potential risk?' Ford asked. 'I know there was talk of protests, but that sounds more definitive to me. Something I don't know?'

Connor ran the numbers in his head. Made a decision. Told Ford about the note that had been delivered to Charlston's London office, and his plans for the Destiny Bonfire that night.

'For fuck's sake, Fraser,' Ford grated. 'You should have told us the moment there was a credible threat to him. There'll be more than three hundred people there tonight, and if someone is going to take a pot-shot at Charlston, what are the odds that others will get hurt? Christ!'

'Not our call,' Connor said. 'I advised him to contact the police. He chose not to. Client confidentiality meant I couldn't do anything. But now that Peters is dead, and there's a potential live risk to Charlston, I have to tell you to protect him.'

'You work in a messed-up world, Fraser,' Ford said after a moment. 'You never should have left the polis.'

Connor shrugged. Hard not to agree. Even if he hadn't had much of a choice in the matter after what had happened in Belfast.

They agreed to meet at the hotel and Connor ended the call, urging the car forward. The message from Jen flashed across his mind again. *Call me when you're ready.*

Didn't look like that would be today. Not now.

He parked, cut his way through the growing crowd in the hotel's main lobby. It was like stepping into an experiment in group hypnosis – every face plastered with the same expectant smile, the eyes far away and dreamy, body language turned into a jerky, excited shorthand.

And why not? After all, this was the weekend Blair Charlston would change their lives. They all knew it. The brochures told them so.

Connor froze in the tide of people. He heard the shuffle of steps behind him and a startled squawk as someone moved quickly to avoid slamming into his back. Ignored it. Scanned the crowd for that face he had just seen . . . that . . .

There. About ten feet in front of him, head down, bustling along the hall. He turned briefly, a quizzical look on his face, as though Connor's glare had reached out and tapped him on the shoulder. Connor saw the kid's eyes narrow in momentary confusion, then widen with recognition. Connor lifted two fingers to his temple, offered a small salute, even as he felt something between sympathy and contempt fizz in his mouth. Made sense, though. The kid was chronically out of shape, an easy target for bullies at the gym until Connor had stepped in. No wonder he was looking for another way to change his life.

Connor watched him disappear into the crowd, then headed for the conference suite at the back of the ground floor that Sentinel had taken over as an operations centre. As arranged, Robbie was waiting for him, looking for all the world like a doctor about to deliver bad news to a patient waiting in his consulting room.

Connor ignored the look, decided to get straight to the headlines, then deal with the details. He told Robbie about his conversations with Donna and Ford, what he had learned, and that they would be interviewing Charlston as soon as Ford arrived. At the mention of this, Robbie's expression darkened, moving from apprehension to outright panic in the blink of an eye.

'What?' Connor asked.

'Well, there might be a problem seeing Charlston.'

'Oh, why? He too busy clearing his chakras to be disturbed or something?' Connor said. 'Well, tough. This takes priority, Robbie. He can play prophet some other time. We need to see him before this,' Connor gestured around, 'goes any further.'

Robbie held up his hands in a placatory gesture. 'Not arguing, boss,' he said. 'Problem is, no one's seen Charlston for the last hour.'

CHAPTER 21

'Oh, for fuck's sake, what the fuck is taking so long? *Christ!*'

Keith winced in the driver's seat, shot a nervous glance at Donna. She caught it out of the corner of her eye, turned to him, away from the tractor that was taking up the single-track road they were on, reducing the flow of traffic to a sludge-like crawl. Took a breath.

'Sorry, Keith,' she said, forcing the words out, her jaw refusing to unclench. 'Busy day. Lot going on.'

'Uh, yeah, okay,' Keith said, eyes fixed firmly on the road, hands clasped on the steering wheel, as though it was a lifebelt to cling to in the face of Storm Donna. The thought made her snort involuntarily. She felt laughter at the back of her throat, stubbing out matches behind her eyes.

Storm Donna? Shit storm more like.

The call had been textbook Mark. He had got past the façade of caring for Andrew or her quickly enough, dispensing with the issue after a few vapid questions about how they both were and how Andrew must be growing. She ignored the dig about calling the flat, and Mark's surprise at 'Andrew's gran being there and you being out so early'. Donna felt an answer tremble on her lips, asking what the fuck else she was meant to do when he had left them high and dry, the repeated promises of maintenance money and help as sincere and deliverable as a Tory manifesto pledge. The truth was, Mark was a distraction she didn't need today, especially with Connor about to speak to Ford in relation to what had happened to Donald. If this was going to turn into a murder investigation, and Donna had no doubt it would, it was only a matter of time until the link between Donald and Charlston would come to light. And if anyone was going to break that story, she was.

But then, in typical Mark fashion, he had twisted the knife, and Donna knew that her plans were about to go to shit.

'So, I saw Donald Peters died,' he said, static wash echoing down the phone, the blare of a horn an afterthought in the background. Was he driving? 'I take it you're working that line, Donna, especially with all the great stuff you've done on the Charlston story so far. That ITOI weekend of his kicks off tonight, doesn't it? Some kind of bon-fire event?'

She grumbled something noncommittal, struggled to rein in the panic that felt like an increasing weight on her chest. If Mark knew about Donald, and the Charlston link, he'd be working that line too. She had to get to Charlston or Ford first, get on air with the story before he could spike it with an online edition that—

The thought hit her then, stopping her dead. The horn. The blare of the horn.

'Why are you calling, Mark?' she asked. 'And where are you?'

She could almost hear the smile in his voice when he spoke. 'I'm calling because I've got some background on Peters and Charlston that you need,' he said. 'And I'm on my way to Stirling now to deliver it. Was thinking we could do an on-air interview as part of your package, bill me as an investigative journo looking into Charlston.'

Donna felt her grip tighten on the phone, resisted the urge to bounce the fucking thing off the pavement. Bastard. He was going to cut in on her story, use her to broadcast his CV to every publisher and TV station out there, and he was spinning it as a way to help her out. A sudden sourness clenched her stomach. What had she ever seen in the ruthless little shit? The answer came almost as soon as the question was asked: she had seen a ruthless little shit. A journalist who used charm, guile and contacts to get what he wanted. Donna included.

Her phone beeped, telling her a call was waiting. She pulled it from her ear, felt a blot of cold excitement race up her arm as she read the caller ID. 'Look, Mark, I've got a call coming in, have to go. Ring me when you get here – we'll meet up, okay?'

'Yeah, fine,' Mark said. 'But I'll save you some time. I'm heading straight for the Alloa House, so how about I just meet you there? Say an hour or so?'

The call-waiting beep was like a countdown clock to her thoughts. 'Right, fine, whatever. But do not try to talk to Charlston until we've spoken, okay?'

'Who me?' he said, and cut the call.

Cursing, she flipped over to the call waiting. 'DCI Ford, nice to hear from you. I was just about to contact you about Donald Peters.'

'Aye, I'm sure you were,' Ford said, his voice a blunt cudgel of vowels and syllables echoing down the line. 'Do you realise the level of shit you're in, Blake?'

'No, I don't think I do, Inspector. Why don't you tell me?'

So he did. About the penalties for withholding information relevant to an inquiry into an unexplained death. About how he could file charges against her, make sure the only thing she ever reported on again was how boring the life of a former TV reporter was, and how he was going to make sure she never spoke to anyone in the media team at Police Scotland ever again.

'So here's what's going to happen, Ms Blake,' Ford said when his tirade was over, the harsh words ringing in her ears, 'you are going to come to Randolphfield police station and we are going to have a nice little chat about everything you know about Donald Peters and Blair Charlston. And we are going to do it, as you say, on the record. Is that clear?'

'Totally, DCI Ford,' Donna replied, teeth grinding. 'But you made a couple of mistakes. You said Randolphfield when you meant to say the Alloa House. I'm on my way there now with my cameraman. And as for on the record, I'll make sure Keith gets you full frame for any statement you want to make. See you there. Bye!'

She hung up before he could reply, heart hammering. Met Keith at the van and bundled him in, telling him to head for the Alloa House. And now they were stuck on the A90, the ageing tractor in front of them, like a rusting blood clot on the road.

She glanced at her watch, felt a sting of panic. Was Mark already there? Trying to speak to Charlston? If so, what could she say, what could she . . .?

The phone was back in her hand before she knew it, number dialled. She smiled out at the tractor in front of her as the idea solidified in her mind, now half hoping there would be a sudden barking rasp of an exhaust followed by a belch of smoke from the tractor's engine bay. Anything to slow them down.

After all, she was about to reintroduce Mark to Connor Fraser. She knew what Connor thought of Mark, so it would be a meeting that Connor would want to linger over, for old times' sake.

CHAPTER 22

Sunlight played across the knife like molten gold dripping down the blade, sparking now and then as it turned the metal into a shaft of flame. He twisted it lazily, as though washing it in the light, hypnotised by its lustre.

Now, she whispered, and a chill shivered its way through him. *Now*. He remembered the urgency of that last kiss, the hard clash of their teeth as tongues strained to touch, connect, bridge the gap greed had driven between them. Felt a moment of revulsion at the sudden arousal the memory ignited within him.

Blair Charlston took a deep, steadying breath, forced himself to become still. He supposed it would reflect badly on Robbie, and Sentinel, that he had managed to get away from them. But that was the point, wasn't it? Years of planning, preparation and sacrifice. All leading to this one moment of escape, one night when he could erase the three fucking sentences that had destroyed his life and cost him the only woman he had ever loved. Three simple sentences.

Graham Bell took his own life. Can we be exposed? What now?

The knife seemed to take on extra weight at the thought of that last sentence.

What now?

And then he could see her, feel her. Her body entwined around his, the desperation in her lovemaking, the hot tickle of her breath on his ear. One word. The only word he ever needed to hear.

Now.

Charlston opened his eyes, took in his surroundings. Wheeled round suddenly and buried the blade in the window frame, the shock a blunt judder that crawled up his arm. Studied the blade for a moment, remembering the last time it had been used, the last flesh it had tasted.

It didn't take long to find the number he was looking for in the phone. It was the only one there, no name ascribed to it. He hit dial and lifted it to his ear, an old, ugly lump of plastic that was pocked and scarred with the passage of years. Listened to the buzz of the ring, seized by a sudden hope that it wouldn't be answered.

The voice oozed from the phone, cold and clinical. Charlston locked his eyes on the knife, used the sight to keep him tied to his rapidly evaporating calm.

'We're ready,' he said. 'You and the rest of your party can arrive at any time.'

'And what about security?'

The voice was cultured, soft. But, then, Charlston thought, monsters only ever really scream in the movies. 'In place,' he said. 'As promised.'

'Good.' The word was uttered as though it was an insult. 'We will arrive within the next two hours. This had better work, Charlston. Otherwise it's not just going to be your clients looking for their own god tonight. Understood?'

'Understood,' he said, lips and tongue numb.

The line died without another word. Charlston took the phone from his ear. Looked at it for a moment, a hateful, ugly thing, then dropped it to the floor and stamped on it, as though the act could somehow inflict pain on the owner of the voice that had just bled from it.

He stopped after a moment, chest hitching and rising. Composed himself. Then turned, grabbed the knife and yanked it free, the soft wood of the window frame squealing in protest.

'Now,' he whispered to himself, as he cleaned the blade. *'Now.'*

CHAPTER 23

Connor stood at the threshold of the gym in the hotel basement, the sour smell of old sweat biting at his nose, the latent heat of activity tickling his skin. It was like a call to him, delivered in a language only he could understand. Urging him to stride into the gym, pick up the weights, get to work. Add his sweat and effort to the atmosphere.

Instead he kept his eyes fixed on the punch bag that hung in the middle of the room, like some kind of sacrifice. Took a breath, forced himself to remain calm.

'One more time, Robbie,' he said.

He heard Robbie shuffle behind him, awkward and uncomfortable.

'Well, it's like I, ah, like I said, boss,' Robbie said, his voice as jagged and stuttering as his movements. 'Charlston's been coming down here regularly, getting his workouts in. Likes to go at it on the punch bag, like I told you. Anyway, he said he wanted to get a session in, asked me to wait outside. So I did, just like all the other times he's been here. Except, ah, except this time he, ah, well . . .'

Connor strode into the gym, leaving Robbie's excuses behind him. It felt like there was a steel band clamped around his head and Robbie was tightening it with every word. 'So, let me guess,' he said. 'It went quiet. You gave it, what, a few minutes, then decided to see what was going on?' As he spoke, he studied the floor-to-ceiling mirrors that made up the far side of the gym, his eyes falling to the heavy rubber matting that covered the floor to protect it from dropped weights and give those working out something more comfortable to lie on.

'Yeah, boss,' Robbie said, following Connor into the room. 'But when I stepped in, he was gone. Just vanished. I've tried his mobile, asked the staff. They've not seen him.'

Connor made a noncommittal grunt, stepped closer to the middle mirror. Leaned in. Smiled. 'And, of course, you swept this room?'

'Course,' Robbie said quickly. 'Couldn't find a thing. I mean, I turned away from the door once, to take a call from Callum, but I don't see how he managed to slip past me in that time. Connor, I'm . . .'

Connor held his hand up, resisted the urge to clench it into a fist and do what he really wanted to do. 'Tell me, Robbie,' he said, turning now, the flinch Robbie gave him revealing that his thoughts were written all over his face. 'What do you see on that mirror?'

Robbie rearranged his face into a mask of calm, then slowly, warily, stepped past Connor to the mirror. Studied it. 'I, ah, well, I . . .'

Connor felt frustration rasp at his throat like cheap whisky. 'For fuck's sake, Robbie,' he said. 'You let the primary get away from you, then you miss the basics at the locus. Did you check the plans for this room before you let Charlston access it?'

Robbie reddened, eyes darting everywhere but Connor's face. 'Well, I checked the room out, boss, made a sweep. But . . .'

'So that's a no,' Connor said. 'Course you didn't, because if you did, you'd know what those marks on the mirror and the floor mean.' Connor pointed to the mirror and three small smudges at roughly shoulder level.

'Fingermarks,' Robbie said, leaning in again.

'Yes, Robbie, fingermarks. And coupled with those,' Connor pointed down to small arced scores in the rubber matting, 'that should tell you what this mirror is for.' He stepped forward, pressed where the smudges were. Heard a click, the mirror at first pushing in then springing forward, a soft squeal as it caught on the flooring.

Robbie stared at Connor, face slack. 'A door,' he said as Connor swung the mirror fully open, revealing a small, harshly lit corridor beyond.

'A service door,' Connor said. 'Easy way to get equipment in and out of the gym without putting guests to the inconvenience of seeing the work being done. Also a handy and discreet way of getting a guest out quickly if they have a turn in the gym. Bad for business to see folk being carted through the main lobby having a heart attack.'

'Jesus, Connor, I'm sorry,' Robbie said, craning his head into the corridor. 'Even so, where is he now?'

Connor winced. Wondered again about his wisdom in giving Robbie so much responsibility so quickly. He had been recruited by Connor's predecessor, Lachlan Jameson, when the pressure of working for Police Scotland's call-handling centre at Bilston Glen in Midlothian had got too much. He was a technical and logistical genius, could play a keyboard like a concert pianist and, with his training, could multitask like a Swiss Army knife on steroids. But, as Connor had seen on previous cases, what Robbie lacked was field experience. He had thought he could train him in that, which was part of the reason he had given him such a prominent role in the Charlston operation. But now, he was forced to wonder, had he pushed Robbie too far, given him too much to handle on this assignment? Seen some imagined potential in him that just wasn't there?

He pushed aside the thought. Got on the phone, called the ops room upstairs. 'Kyle? Connor. Do me a favour. Pull up the rooms of every ITOI staffer staying at the hotel this weekend. Should be about twenty of them. Then have a look at the door codings, tell me if any have been swiped in the last ninety minutes, will you?'

He waited, the sound of Kyle's fingers flying across a keyboard filling the line.

'Okay. Names?' Connor listened as Kyle read out the four names and room numbers. Smiled when he heard the one he wanted.

'Thanks, Kyle. Be up soon. Call me if that reporter I told you about turns up, okay?' He pocketed the phone. He could deal with Mark Sneddon later.

He turned to Robbie. 'He's in room three ten,' he said.

Robbie's eyes widened. 'How did you . . .?'

Connor bit back another snarl of frustration, tempered it with the knowledge that Robbie was going to spend the rest of the weekend in Sentinel's ops room with Kyle. Let him play to his strengths for a while. He could worry about his field training later. 'Think about it,' he said. 'The ITOI event starts in less than three hours. Charlston's staff will be running around like good little drones getting everything ready. They'll hardly be going back to their rooms for a siesta unless they need to change clothes or get something they forgot.'

'But you said there were four rooms accessed in the window Charlston disappeared. How do you know which one he's in?'

'Room three ten. Anne James,' Connor said. 'You know, his assistant – the one who let us into his suite yesterday? The one whose hair was slightly rumpled, even though her lipstick was perfect and her blouse freshly adjusted. She lost one of those hairs on Charlston's shoulder, in case you missed that. Not conclusive proof that there's something going on with her and Charlston, but suggestive. And, if that's the case, who would she give a spare room key to, just in case?'

'Charlston,' Robbie said.

'Exactly,' Connor said. 'So, come on, let's go and see them. I've got some questions for Mr Charlston, and I want to talk to him before the police get here.'

Robbie opened his mouth as if to say something. Closed it. Then headed for the door.

Connor followed him, pausing at the punch bag. Snapped out a right jab before he had realised he was going to, pivoting at the hip, driving all his strength into it. The bag bucked as if it had been electrified and jangled on its chain, swinging up to almost 90 degrees and brushing the balsawood board that protected the ceiling.

Robbie looked at Connor as though seeing him for the first time. 'Fuck,' he whispered.

'Not on the first date, Robbie,' Connor said, voice flat and empty. 'Now, let's go find out what the hell he's playing at.'

CHAPTER 24

Connor hammered on the door, an old-school wrath-of-God frame-trembler he'd learned from his old partner Simon McCartney during his time in the Police Service of Northern Ireland. The sound rolled down the hall like thunder, Robbie casting glances behind them, as though worried someone would stick their head out of a room and complain.

That would be bad. Very bad. For them.

'Charlston!' Connor called again, his voice more intimidating than the hammering on the door. 'Come on, we know you're in there. Open the door – now. We need to talk.'

The sound of shuffling, the *thunk* of the bolt being unlocked. Metallic click of the latch. Connor followed the door as it swung open, forcing Charlston to stumble back.

'Connor,' he said as he turned and walked into the room, trying and failing to look as if it had been his choice all along. 'That's some racket to make. What's going on?'

Connor held up one finger, cast his gaze left, into the bathroom, then strode past Charlston, taking in the rest of the room with a cold, clinical sweep of the eyes. Nothing out of the ordinary. And no Anne. Just the bed, still made, a desk on which some notes were strewn like autumn leaves, a free-standing wardrobe in the corner, to the left of the window.

The window . . .

Connor took a step towards it, pushed the net curtain aside. Looked out onto the main stretch of the driveway, took in the hustle and bustle of the ITOI crew setting things up and his security staff herding guests to where they needed to be. At the checkpoint, he noticed a car pulled to the side to let others through. A dark-haired man in suit trousers and shirtsleeves was standing beside the car, gesturing between the hotel and the security staff. Despite himself, Connor smiled. Mark Sneddon had arrived. And, unlike Robbie, Kyle had done his job.

He stepped back, made his face implacable again. Eyes caught on the window frame for a second, a small mark grabbing his attention. What was—

His phone buzzed in his pocket and he pulled it out.

'Connor, look,' Charlston said. 'I'm sorry I gave Robbie the slip. I just needed some time alone to collect my thoughts before the opening address.' He gestured to the table. 'I was working on my presentation, that's all. Needed to get away, have some time alone. Robbie,' he turned slightly, 'I'm sorry. Hope you understand.'

Robbie gave a grunt of acceptance that buzzed in Connor's ears, like a tune played in the wrong key. He thumbed in a reply to the text he had just received, then turned his focus back to Charlston. 'Look, Mr Charlston,' he said, his eyes not leaving the man, who looked like he wasn't enjoying being the sole focus of Connor's attention, 'what you did was irresponsible but, ultimately, Robbie should have secured the room you were in and I'll deal with that failing later. I apologise that your security was compromised by his negligence.'

Charlston moved to say something, but Connor got in first, barging his words aside. 'However, that's not why I'm here. We need to talk, Mr Charlston. There was a death in Larbert yesterday, a person I believe you knew. The deceased's identity and the manner of the death raise significant questions for you, and about the wisdom of me allowing tonight's event to go ahead.'

Beneath his fake tan, the colour bleached from Charlston's cheeks. His mouth fell open and he blinked rapidly, as though Connor had just thrown dirt into his eyes.

'Now, just a minute,' he said, straightening his back and thrusting his chest out in what Connor knew Charlston described as his 'power pose to help dominate any situation'. 'We've been through this, Connor. I told you, the bonfire has to go ahead tonight. It's integral to the whole weekend. And what's this about someone I know dying? I haven't been back in Scotland in years. Anyone I know is either down south or attending the event tonight. And I've not heard—'

'Donald Peters,' Connor said.

It was as if he had stepped forward and slapped Charlston across the face. He flinched backwards, eyes widening, power pose collapsing like so much soft sand.

'Wh-what?' he stuttered. 'Peters? Donald Peters? The reporter? I haven't heard from him in years. What happened? And how can that possibly have any bearing on this weekend?'

Connor turned to Robbie. 'Robbie, get Mr Charlston a drink from the mini bar, will you? It looks like he needs it. He's got just enough time to finish it before DCI Ford arrives.'

He saw the confusion twitch across Charlston's face, punching through the shock. 'Oh, sorry, Blair,' he said. 'That's who texted me a moment ago. Detective Chief Inspector Malcolm Ford. He's here to talk to you about Donald Peters. And, after he has, you and I are going to decide what we're going to do about this weekend.'

CHAPTER 25

Jen swore under her breath as the phone began to buzz on the coffee-table, interrupting her as she bustled around the flat, trying to get ready for a shift at the gym. She reached for it, unsure what angered her more – the interruption, or the pathetic schoolgirl flash of hope that Connor was phoning her.

The hope was short-lived, killed by the name on the screen, making her sound sharp when she answered. 'Hiya, Dad. Whassup?'

A pause on the line. Duncan MacKenzie considering her voice.

'Jen. Jennifer, you okay, sweetheart?'

She exhaled, realising she had been holding her breath. 'Sorry, Dad, just in a rush to get out of the door to work. Whassup?'

'Does something have to be up for me to call my wee girl?' he asked, his voice as forced and strained as hers a moment ago.

Jen felt unease snake up her spine. She knew this tone from her father. Knew what it meant. 'No, I suppose not. But I really am in a rush, Dad, so if there's nothing specific, can I call you back later on?'

'Well, there was one thing,' Duncan said, and Jen had to force herself not to hold her breath again. 'Jen, have you any plans to see Connor this weekend?'

What? Confusion strobed through Jen's mind. 'Connor? What? Why would—'

'He's working up at the Alloa House, isn't he? On the weekend that character Charlston's running. Some bullshit about helping people get in touch with their best selves?'

Jen found herself nodding along, the earlier irritation returning like an old toothache. After the call from Donna Blake last night, she had managed to wheedle out of Connor a few details on what was happening at the Alloa House. But everything he had said was vague, couched in generalities. They had gone through the motions, but from the moment he had put the phone done, she had known she was on her own for the night, that his focus was on the hotel, Charlston, and whatever Blake had called to tell him. Jen knew she should understand – after all it was Connor's job to worry about worst-case scenarios and anticipate problems – but it didn't stop her feeling a certain jealous resentment at the intrusion. Especially given the way she had planned on the night ending. Was that why she had sent him that text? Part supportive, part passive-aggressive dig. *Call me when you're ready x*

She hauled her thoughts back to the present. 'Yeah, that's it. He's running security there. Why? You want me to ask if he can get Paulie a ticket?'

Laughter trickled down the line, warm, clean and deep, like a summer stream, and Jen found herself laughing. The thought of Paulie, her father's so-called executive assistant, whose taste for designer suits and luxury cars did nothing to disguise a man who traded in others' pain, attending some kind of self-awareness seminar was ridiculous to both of them.

'No, nothing like that,' her dad said, the warmth fading from his voice as he spoke, 'but I've heard there are a few people coming in this weekend, might keep Connor busy. So it may be an idea to give him his space, let the boy get on with his work.'

A hot flash of resentment clenched Jen's hand on the phone. Who the hell did her dad think he was talking to? Was she twelve again, being told to keep away from boys? Or fourteen, and being told to keep away from boys and booze? She stopped suddenly. No, of course not. He thought she was twenty-two again, and in some kind of trouble. She loved her father, knew that love would not endure some of the hard questions she would have to ask if she let herself contemplate the too-tight hugs and the anguished blend of terror and relief with which her mother had looked at her the night she had come home from the hospital after a hit-and-run. But, still . . .

'Dad,' she said slowly, 'what's going on? Is there something Connor should know?'

'No, no,' Duncan replied, his chuckle now as false as their laughter had been genuine a moment ago. 'Nothing like that, sweetheart. Just I heard a few of my clients are coming in for the event, Christ knows why. But it'll be busy, and I don't want Connor being distracted when he's working.'

Jen smiled at that. Her dad, worried about Connor? Hardly. Their first meeting had been like a stand-off of two alpha males warily circling each other, all pained smiles, hard handshakes and warm words as they sized each other up. Jen knew her father respected Connor, especially after he'd put Paulie on his arse so easily, but worry about him? Hardly. Which meant . . .

'Are you saying I shouldn't be near the Alloa this weekend, Dad?' she asked, her voice suddenly becoming her mother's.

'I'm not saying that, Jen,' her dad replied, his own voice flat, as though he were in a contract negotiation rather than a conversation with his daughter. 'I'm just saying that Connor is going to have a busy weekend so it might be better if you caught up with him after it. We can do something, if you want. Head across to Edinburgh, get dinner and a show?'

'Thanks, Dad, but no. I'm working all weekend. If Connor calls, I'll tell him you were asking for him, though.'

'I'd prefer it if you didn't, Jen,' her father said.

She sighed. 'Okay, Dad. Look, I really have to get ready for work. I don't think I'll see much of Connor this weekend, but if I do, I'll suggest we meet away from the Alloa, okay? Might ask him round here.' She regretted the last comment almost as soon as she had said it, the sudden need to lash out at her dad for treating her like a child overtaking her tongue.

'Whatever you think best, sweetheart. I just worry about you, want to keep you safe. And we both know Connor can attract trouble when he wants to.'

Jen nodded despite herself. Hard to argue with that. 'Okay, Dad. Look, I really have to go. I'll call you tonight. Love you.'

'Love you, too, sweetheart,' her dad mumbled, then killed the call.

She dropped the phone onto the couch, ran the call through her head. She knew her dad was into more than just the haulage company that bore his name, but had never probed just what he was involved in. She knew it wasn't all legal, had never felt the need to open that particular Pandora's Box. But now here he was, telling her people he knew were attending an event Connor was supervising that weekend and she should stay away. A sudden memory hit her: her father coming home late one night, clothes dishevelled, hair slicked with sweat. She had sat on the stairs, watching him, entranced by the angry red of his knuckles and the red-brown smear that had soaked through his shirt-sleeve like a tattoo.

Her eyes drifted to the window as she remembered her dad's parting comment: *I just worry about you, want to keep you safe.*

She stepped over to the window, gently pushed the blinds aside. Looked down on the car-park below, eyes searching for . . .

There. Tucked into the corner, nose just peeking out from beneath the canopy of a tree. A black bonnet, gleaming in the afternoon light. She didn't need to see the front grille to know it was a high-end Mercedes. Didn't need to see through the driver's side window to know that a large, squat man with a bullet-shaved head was sitting there, kneading the steering wheel between his massive hands, as though it was a stress toy.

Paulie. Her dad had sent him to keep an eye on her. Which told Jen two things. He was worried about something that might happen at the Alloa House that weekend.

And, whatever that was, Connor would be at the centre of it.

CHAPTER 26

Ford took his time settling into the couch across from Charlston, some sallow-faced officer he had introduced as Troughton beside him, earnestly checking his notebook and pen.

Connor had met Ford in the corridor outside Charlston's suite a few moments before, and he didn't need to look at the policeman's hunched shoulders, set jaw or unblinking glare to know how angry and frustrated he was.

'I should just arrest the bastard, put this all on the record,' he had snarled to Connor in the corridor.

Connor understood the impulse. If he was still a copper, he would do the same himself. But he wasn't. Much as he didn't like it, he had to speak for his client.

'You said Peters was poisoned before or at the time he was attacked. That means yesterday afternoon, before Donna found him at approximately three forty-five p.m. We've got Charlston on CCTV here for the entire day yesterday, either moving around the hotel or in the main conference suite practising his spiel for tonight. As alibis go, it's fairly compelling. And what would you be arresting him for, anyway? Because he had a previous relationship with the deceased? Okay, he's a person of interest to the inquiry. But a suspect? Don't think so, sir.'

Ford had shot him a glance, cold and accusatory. 'Still, this is hardly ideal, is it, Fraser? We're turning a police inquiry into a three-ring circus, and it's my balls that are in a sling if the chief finds out.'

93

'Finds out what?' Connor asked. 'That you're interviewing someone with a link to the accused? A person who has been in the media spotlight over the last couple of weeks and is holding a high-profile event this weekend? Seems to me the chief should be thanking you for keeping this quiet at the moment. Last thing you need are the headlines this could generate. No, this is better. You know you can trust me in there and I promise, if he says anything that gives you or me one moment of doubt as to his safety or that of those attending this weekend, I will shut this whole thing down.'

Connor held Ford's sceptical glance, making sure the policeman was in no doubt about his sincerity. Yes, Charlston was a client, and he was paying Sentinel handsomely in cash and referrals to make sure this weekend went ahead. But money only bought so much leverage. If Connor got wind of something that was a threat to Charlston or anyone attending the ITOI weekend, he would end it, consequences be damned.

So now he stood, arms folded, back to the ornate fireplace that dominated one wall of the suite, looming over Charlston and Ford who were sitting opposite each other as if the coffee-table was a barricade.

'Mr Charlston,' Ford began. 'First, thank you for agreeing to meet us at such short notice. I believe Mr Fraser has already filled you in on the details, and why we wanted to speak to you.'

Charlston flashed something that could almost be called a smile. 'Of course I know about the death of Donald Peters. It's tragic, Chief Inspector, but I'm not sure what it has to do with me or what bearing it has on the ITOI weekend which, I must add, I really should be preparing for.'

Ford tilted his head in an apology, his scalp winking in the light beneath his thinning hair. 'I know, Mr Charlston. We'll be as brief as possible. However, it's my understanding that you had, ah, a history with Mr Peters, during his time at the *Western Chronicle* and your time at Perigee Designs. I wonder if you could tell us about that.'

Charlston eased back from the table, the leather of the sofa murmuring a soft soundtrack as he moved. He took a second, chest expanding, back straightening as he inhaled. And in that moment,

Connor knew he was about to deliver a performance he had rehearsed a thousand times.

'Let me begin by saying that, for legal reasons, there are matters I cannot discuss with you unless my legal representative is present.' He held up a hand, as though warding off the objection Connor could see Ford wanted to make. 'However, as you know, I was interviewed by Mr Peters on several occasions during my, ah, association with Perigee. I had no personal relationship with him, if that's what you're implying.'

Ford chewed his lip, sizing Charlston up. He was too experienced an interviewer to show his disdain for the man, but Connor could feel it pulsing off him in waves.

'These matters you can't discuss without a lawyer, Mr Charlston, would they have anything to do with Mr Peters's sudden departure from the *Chronicle* due to a story he was working on about you and Perigee?'

Charlston blinked once, slowly, regaining his composure as he rearranged his hands on his lap. 'As I said, I can't—'

'See, the problem I have,' Ford said, leaning forward now, elbows on knees, 'is that we've got some unanswered questions here. We know about the threat that has been made against you. Now we find that a reporter who led coverage of the collapse of Perigee was killed the day before you are about to hold a large seminar less than ten miles from where he died. Now I find out that there's a story he was working on that cost him his job, and is covered by some kind of gagging clause. In case you forgot, Mr Charlston, I'm a police officer. I can have those records unsealed. So why don't you save us all a bit of time, tell us what the problem with you and Peters was.'

Charlston held his position as if he'd become a statue. He glanced up at Connor, accusation in his eyes.

Connor had told Ford about the threatening note, true, but the information about the gagging order could have come from anywhere, not just Donna. He returned the gaze, felt anger prickle the back of his neck. He'd been uncomfortable with Charlston and his be-your-own-god shite since the moment he'd first heard of it, but his current games had intensified that discomfort into active disgust.

Charlston's life had been threatened. A man was dead. And he was throwing lawyers at them?

Charlston exhaled, as though he had been holding his breath on behalf of everyone in the room. Made a sound that was halfway between a grunt and a chuckle, then extended his arms and relaxed his back as he smiled. 'We're all friends here,' the pose said.

Connor didn't buy it.

'Chief Inspector Ford, please,' Charlston said, his tone now warm, jocular, 'I'm trying to help as best I can, even agreed to talk to you without a lawyer present. As I told you, I knew Mr Peters for his work on the Perigee story. Yes, he approached me with an accusation that forced me to involve lawyers. It was an ugly process but, as you say, an agreement was reached that meant I received an apology from the publishers of the *Chronicle*. The details of Peters's deal with them are for them to describe, not me. What I can say is that, due to the terms of the deal that was made, I cannot discuss the allegations he made at the time in any further detail without legal representation.'

'Why?' Ford snapped, his voice as hard as the stone of the fireplace Connor was leaning against.

'Because to do so would be to violate the terms of the agreement, and leave me open to legal action. I'm sorry, Chief Inspector, I want to help, but my hands are tied. I've probably said too much already.'

Ford's expression suggested the thought of tying Charlston's hands wasn't a bad one. 'Fine,' he said. 'We'll do it your way. Now, about the threat you received at your London office. Can you think of anyone who might want to—'

There was a knock on the door of the suite. Anne James glided into the room before the sound had faded. 'Sorry to interrupt,' she said, eyes darting around everyone in the room, head moving in a jerking, birdlike motion. 'Blair, Donna Blake from Sky has arrived. She's setting up in the main conference room now.'

Connor swapped a glance with Ford. Donna? They had arranged to meet. But her interviewing Charlston had never been part of the plan. What the hell was she playing at?

'Gentlemen,' Charlston said as he made a show of checking his watch, 'I'm sorry, but I really have to press on. I've told you as much as

96

I can, and Anne will put you in touch with my solicitors if you need to know more. Regarding the note we received, I'm sure it's just a crank, but Connor and his team can fill you in.' He stood, extended his hand to Ford. 'Now, if you'll excuse me, I have an interview to give and a seminar to prepare for. It's going to be quite a night. Of course, you're welcome to stay.'

'Of course,' Ford echoed as he took Charlston's hand, eyes flicking over the man's shoulder to find Connor. 'Thank you, Mr Charlston. You've been a lot of help.'

Charlston smiled, headed for the door, Anne behind him. When they were gone, Ford looked to Troughton. 'Get the details of the legal team and find out what the hell was in that agreement.' He turned to Connor. 'And you. Mind telling me what your pal is playing at? Thought she was going to talk to us first.'

'So did I,' Connor said. 'So did I.'

CHAPTER 27

'Ah, for FUCK'S SAKE!'

Mark pulled the phone from his ear, sneered at it as though it had offended him. Stabbed the 'end call' button on the screen then drew his arm back, ready to throw the damn thing into the dashboard. Instead, he tossed it onto the passenger seat and hammered the palms of his hands against the steering wheel, the car rocking with the impact as pain juddered up his arms.

Cunts. Fucking cunts. Who did those jumped-up Nazi bastards think they were anyway, with their suits, earpieces and calm assertion that he couldn't get to the hotel because it was 'hosting a private event and you're not accredited as press or as a guest'?

He had argued, harassed, threatened. They wouldn't budge, or let him past. That overgrown fuckwit Connor Fraser had obviously trained his little troop of monkeys well. So Mark had eventually turned his car around, gravel spitting up from the tyres and pinging off the wheel arches in tinny explosions as he over-accelerated back up the driveway.

Childish, he thought now. And stupid.

He parked across from the main gates, then phoned Donna. He'd agreed to meet her here, had seen the Sky News van nestled in beside the hotel when he was arguing with the security staff. What the hell was she playing at? She knew he had information that would help her with the story, and ensure she had some very awkward questions to ask Charlston. But her phone was going straight to voicemail, and it didn't take a genius to work out why. He chewed his lip as he thought it out, fought to contain the cold, impotent rage he felt.

She had the cameraman, the broad brush of the story and, most importantly, the access. She didn't need to know what he had done to make life uncomfortable for Charlston – that was one of the joys of TV journalism. Print journalism, *real* journalism, was a binary equation, black and white. You wrote down your facts for the world to see, sourced everything. But broadcast was, literally, a more colourful palette. You could tell your story in hues of grey, casting shadows with innuendo and open-ended questions that left the interviewee gasping in front of the camera like a fish on the hook. Who needed a no-comment statement or flat-out denial when you could do even more damage with a glistening top lip or a nervous flick of the eyes?

No, Donna was going to hang him out to dry, take the story for herself.

Again, he cursed his stupidity, even as he appreciated the irony of the situation. After all, wasn't that exactly what he'd done when he'd found out she was pregnant? Left her high and dry, frozen out? And now she was returning the favour.

Or so she thought.

He forced himself to think. Retrieved the phone and called up his email, finding the message he needed with the attachments he absolutely should not have. Scrolled through them again, smiled.

Donna might think she knew what she was doing. Fine, let her. She had an arrow to throw at Charlston. But Mark had a fucking Exocet missile.

He glanced across at the hotel gates. All he had to do was get inside. Keep his head down, away from Fraser and his army of thugs, find Charlston or one of his people. A few carefully chosen words and he'd be sitting down with him, asking all the questions Donna didn't know to ask. He could still scoop her, sell the story to one of the nationals or, maybe, stick the finger up to the bitch and approach a few old friends at the Beeb or STV.

Smiling at the thought, Mark flicked over to Google Maps. The road he was on seemed to run about a quarter of a mile, then hook right, following a snaking path around a patch of green that ran up to the hotel. He hit satellite view, confirmed what he thought. Yes. It was a patch of woods that ran from the road into the grounds. He looked away from the phone, up the road, calculated. The security operation at the front gates was impressive, but would they have the manpower to close the whole perimeter? He doubted it. More likely they would throw a tight ring around the immediate vicinity, covering the bonfire he had spotted and the grounds just in front of the hotel. Okay, there might be fences in the woods, but Mark wasn't averse to a little climbing. And, besides, what other choice did he have? Let Donna use that fuckhead Fraser to freeze him out of the story? *His* story?

No. Fuck that.

He thumbed in a text message, hit send, making sure he would get a warm welcome. Then he slotted the phone into its holder on the dashboard, fired the engine and followed the map on the screen. He would find a quiet spot on the road, dump the car and cut through the woods into the hotel.

And when he got the exclusive, he would make sure that the first person to know about it was Donna. And if, along the way, he got the chance to make Connor Fraser look stupid by poking a massive hole in his security operation, then so much the better.

CHAPTER 28

The room Charlston was using for the ITOI weekend was a typical multi-purpose function suite, large enough to be a ballroom, banqueting hall or wedding venue. Today, though, it had been transformed into something that, to Connor, looked half-altar, half-rock-gig venue. The front of the room was dominated by a stage with a catwalk that extended into the room like a finger. Huge TV screens hung above either side of the catwalk, the screens flickering with slogans and the ITOI logo as the technicians tested them. Spotlights strobed the room in a kaleidoscope of colours: red, purple, blue, gold, then searing white.

It was in one of these flashes that Connor glanced to the stage, watching as Donna interviewed Charlston. He felt anger as bright as the spotlight, banished it. He should have known, really. Donna had come to him after she'd found a friend murdered in his own back garden, with something that might link the murder to Charlston. And what had Connor done? He'd kept her at arm's length, tried to put a bit of distance between her, Charlston and the ITOI weekend. It didn't take a genius to see that whatever her prick of an ex had been after when he'd called, it related to this story, which had forced Donna to cut Connor out of the picture and go straight to Anne with an interview bid for Charlston. It was, potentially, a high-risk strategy for Charlston to accept, questions about Peters being almost inevitable, but Connor understood why he had decided to get in front of the camera and give the interview. After all, he was a visionary, the man with the answer to all your problems and the key to a better life. What would it look like if he started to duck the media just before he strode out on stage at the biggest event of his career? And, besides, as he had shown in his discussion with Ford and Connor earlier, if awkward questions about Peters came up, Charlston had an ace to play. 'I can't discuss that for legal reasons. I'm sure you understand.' It was a short-term fix, and it would generate yet more questions, but it would get him past the initial interview – and keep him in the headlines as well.

Win-win.

When they'd finished their interview with Charlston, Connor and Ford had held an impromptu council of war in the suite. A council with only one item on the agenda.

'Well, he's a slippery little fucker, isn't he?' Ford had hissed, the anger in his voice tempered by a weary resignation that was written all over his slumped shoulders and rounded back. 'Question is, what do we do now? Cancel tonight?'

Connor shifted his weight, flexed his arms, tried to use the post-workout ache there to concentrate. 'I don't think we can at this stage,' he said. 'Look at what we've got. He has a cast-iron alibi for the time Peters was killed and he's admitted to a tangential link to him, even if he's "bound by confidentiality" not to go into detail about what the exact nature of the link is. As for the threat made on him, I'm not sure that's grounds to cancel an event that people are paying up to four figures to attend. We've had one vague, threatening note that was more cliché than chilling, and no follow-up. Christ, do you know how many threats like that the PM gets in a week?'

Ford grimaced, face twitching into something that could almost have been mistaken for a smile. Almost. 'Depends on how much time I get to write them,' he muttered. He sighed, straightening as he massaged his eyes. 'You're right,' he said. 'It's one crank threat, not enough to cancel the event. Police advice, not that it's been sought,' he flashed an accusatory look at Connor, 'would be to proceed with caution. He's a public figure, divisive, only natural that he'd get some negative reaction, and a poison-pen letter with no follow-up is hardly cause to call in the blues and twos. Especially with budgets the way they are at the moment.' He looked up at Connor, a thought occurring to him. 'I take it you've got everything else in place for tonight?'

'Sentinel's here to provide security for Charlston himself,' Connor said, 'but I checked with his people and, yes, everything is in place. Fire Service is sending a pump for the bonfire tonight, ambulance staff will be on site for the duration, there are trained first-aiders in the conference hall and,' he smiled, 'Police Scotland have been informed, are fully briefed and will be monitoring the traffic situation in and around the venue for the duration in case it causes congestion.'

'Right,' Ford said, voice more exhausted than ever. 'Well, there's nothing more that we can do at this stage, then.' He placed his hands on his knees. 'We'll check into the deal between Charlston and Peters, see what it throws up. In the meantime, keep me up to date with what's going on, will you? I know he's not a realistic suspect in Peters's murder, but still . . .'

Connor took Ford's outstretched hand, surprised by how cold it was. Shook it. 'Will do, sir, and don't worry, I won't let him make a true believer out of me tonight.'

Ford laughed. 'God forbid,' he said. 'But watch him, Fraser. There's something, I don't know, off about him. A little too practised, a little too perfect.'

Connor had agreed, accompanied Ford and Troughton back to their car. Then he had stalked into the conference room to watch Donna at work.

She took another five minutes, then turned to her cameraman and nodded. Job done: they had what they needed. Connor was too far away to hear what was being said but he could read the body language. Large, open-arm gestures, Charlston on the balls of his feet, showing Donna his kingdom. Enthusiastic nods, smiles, then Charlston bounded off, back ramrod straight, chest out. Exuding confidence and certainty.

He swept past Connor, heading for the exit. Connor took a half-step in front of him, forcing Charlston to stop short. 'Ten minutes, your suite,' he said. 'Want to go over the last preparations for tonight.'

'No problem,' Charlston said, wariness in his eyes. 'Look, Connor, I just wanted to say thank you. I know DCI Ford could have come down on me a lot harder, and that I've got you to thank for him agree-ing to talk to me here.'

'No problem,' Connor said. 'All part of the service.'

Charlston clapped him on the shoulder. 'It's appreciated. Right, ten minutes?'

'Ten minutes,' Connor confirmed.

Charlston walked off, the enthusiastic bounce still in his stride. Connor headed for Donna.

She raised her hand as she saw his approach, the cameraman doing a double-take as he saw Connor emerge from the gloom of the room.

'Before you say it, I didn't have a choice,' she said.

'Bullshit,' Connor said. 'Donna, you agreed to meet here, called to warn me that Sneddon was sniffing about. I said it wasn't a good time to try to talk to Charlston but you cut me off at the knees. What were you thinking?'

'I was thinking,' Donna said slowly as she removed a lapel mic from her jacket, 'that there's a story here, and another reporter was moving in on it. I was thinking of finding Donald Peters and his pulped face. I was thinking that maybe, if I got to Charlston first, I could find out what Mark was trying to string me along with.'

Connor ignored his irritation. No time for it now. 'And did he give you anything?'

Donna pursed her lips. 'Nothing bloody useful,' she said. 'Con-dolences to Donald's family, of course he knew him for the stories he did on Perigee, the usual bullshit.'

'Nothing to indicate what Peters had been getting too close for comfort to, that got him fired?'

Donna shook her head, hair tumbling over her fringe. She swiped it back. 'Not a word. Kept it very general, steered everything back to tonight and the weekend. He's slippery, Connor, and good. Knows how to take an interview where he wants to.'

Slippery. Connor was reminded of Ford's words. 'Yes, he is,' he agreed. 'So what now?'

'Out to the van, get some establishing shots, edit this and get it to Sky. Then find Mark, see if he can shed any light.' Donna's expression told Connor she was looking forward to that discussion as much as she would to root-canal treatment.

'You all right, Donna?' he said, the question out before he knew he was going to ask it. 'He's not giving you any hassle about Andrew, is he?'

Donna's face reddened, her gaze darting to the cameraman standing behind them. *Not for discussion in front of an audience*, her eyes told Connor.

'Yeah, I'm fine,' she said, voice telling him the opposite was true. 'But I've got to get this package together. We okay to catch up later, Connor?'

'You sticking around for the opening?'

She chewed her lip. She should really get home, back to Andrew. But Mark was still out there with something he thought was important, some snippet of information that might give her the edge on the story . . . even if he thought it would give him the edge on her. 'Maybe,' she said. 'Depends on what the newsdesk wants. Check in with you later?'

'No problem,' Connor said. He turned to leave, letting them pack up the last of their equipment, his mind already on the next problem.

CHAPTER 29

Excitement arcs through the air like static after a lightning bolt, amplified by the hammering of bass from music so loud it echoes in his chest. He feels as if he's walking like an eighty-year-old, shuffling as the crowd snakes its way forward, into the auditorium. The discordant sound of chatter, smiles caught and frozen in flashes from the spotlight, mixes with the pounding bass and snarl in his head and he has to bite back the urge to scream, to lash out and wrap his hands around the neck of the nearest brainwashed moron, wipe the idiotic smile off their face, as he yells, 'Can't you see? Can't you see what he is?'

A moment of panic, pure and clean, cauterising like fire, as he makes it to the front of the queue and shows that oh-so-valuable platinum pass. The usher flashes the same simpering smile he's seen too many times, nods and gestures for him to go into the auditorium.

'Follow the gold line, sir. It'll take you straight to the VIP area. Enjoy the night – you're about to have the time of your life. It'll *make* your life.'

He smiles, hoping the urge to lunge forward and sink his teeth into the soft flesh of the man's neck, rending and tearing, hot blood splashing onto his face, isn't written in his eyes. If it is, the stupid bastard is too wrapped up in Charlston's lie to see it: he simply widens his empty smile, gestures gently to the gold lines taped to the floor.

So he does.

It takes a couple more minutes of shuffling but finally he's in what looks like a pen with all the other sheep. He smiles at that, the feeling at once familiar and alien. Just one of the flock. Yes. Just another brain-dead sheep ready to be dipped in Charlston's bullshit and shorn of all my cash.

Shorn the Sheep. She would have liked that: she always liked puns.

He reaches down into his cargo pants – baggy, loose clothing, as recommended by the ITOI brochure – and taps the bottle there. He knows it's impossible but, for an instant, he could swear he feels it warm to the touch, a hint of the heat to come. But then, that makes perfect sense, doesn't it? He needs reassurance, comfort, support. Especially now.

He looks up at the stage, at the vantage point his life savings have bought him. It's close, admittedly, and not too high, only about a foot above those Charlston is here to proselytise with his bullshit pseudo religion. He's studied the videos on YouTube, knows what Charlston will do as well as he knows his own pain. It's a tired script, as worn and faded and familiar to him now as her picture. First, there will be the music. More high-energy, bass-heavy crap to whip up the audience. Then the slogans will start on the monitors above. 'You are your own god'; 'Master your destiny today'; 'Seize your existence: be the life you want to be'. All meaningless crap, packaged as deep and insightful. Then the voiceover, smooth and friendly, as though read out by a favourite uncle.

'Ladies and gentlemen, welcome to ITOI. Over the course of this weekend, you are going to destroy the person you were and become the person you were meant to be. You will be the god of your own life, your own existence. And nothing is out of your reach. And now, to guide you on that journey, Blair Charlston.'

Cue an explosion of adoring cheers and applause from the audience as Charlston makes his appearance, arms held aloft in arrogant triumph as he welcomes the adulation. If he follows his normal form, he'll bound around the stage, encourage the audience to scream more, smile, clap. Cheer. Then he'll run out on the catwalk, deep into the crowd, deep into his people.

A moment of panic. Will he be recognised? Could Charlston spot him among the crowd? He feels a thrill of terrified excitement at the prospect of Charlston feeling his hatred, his loathing, Just enough to throw the man off his stride as he looks down and sees him and, in that instant, understands. But, he reminds himself, it doesn't matter if Charlston doesn't see him, if he remains oblivious until it's too late. The result will be the same. This was destined to happen, an event made inevitable the moment she died. It was only a matter of time. Patience, he tells himself. Preparation. Since the day his life fell apart, through all his work, he has been sustained by the thought that this day would come. That he would finally, irrevocably, deprive Charlston of the one thing that meant more to him than anything else.

After all, it was destiny. For both of them.

CHAPTER 30

Charlston paced around the suite, ducking and weaving like a fighter in the ring. He had changed into a tight white T-shirt that accentuated his chest and biceps. He looked, Connor was forced to admit, trim, lean, and the way he was moving made sense of the hours he had spent on the punch bag in the gym.

It was a good show, but Connor knew that was all it was. Show. His physique was sculpted in the gym, his muscles swollen and developed for aesthetic reasons rather than function. It was his wrists that told Connor this. His biceps and forearms were corded with muscle, but his wrists remained thin and reedy. He'd never put the time into wrist raises with weight plates, pinching the weights between fingers as he rotated the wrist, building the muscles. It developed grip strength, helped protect the wrists from the impact of landing punches. But Charlston didn't know these things. He knew six-packs and building biceps. Everything that made him an attractive package and nothing that made him effective in a fight.

'So, one last time, tell me,' Connor said.

Charlston looked up at him, vague annoyance on his face. 'Okay, okay,' he said. 'I take the stage as normal, you'll be in the wings. I see anything, I say, "Special guest," and head for you. But really, Connor, don't you think this is a little . . .?'

Connor held up his hand. He was done having this conversation. 'And heading out to the bonfire?' he asked.

Charlston gave a bored sigh. 'I exit the stage, meet you in the wings. You walk me outside with another member of your team, stay close at all times. I don't stop to talk to people when I lead them out of the hall, stay with you outside.'

'And?'

Another sigh. 'When we get outside I take the podium only when you indicate you're happy for me to do so. I address the crowd, start the Destiny Bonfire, then step beside you when they start filing up to throw their destiny cards on the fire.' He paused, saw Connor looking at him expectantly, held up his hands in surrender. 'And when the crowd's done, I make the closing statement, get them to follow my team inside while you and your guy escort me back to the VIP zone. Okay?'

Good enough. It wasn't perfect, but it would have to do. If he insisted on the bonfire going ahead, there was always going to be an element of exposure. Risk. But, then, risk of what? His team had reported anyone trying to get into the grounds of the hotel looking to protest Charlston's presence and, other than the initial letter, whoever had threatened him had faded into the background. But still, something niggled at Connor. Something about Charlston's use of a legal shield to avoid talking about Peters, and the way Mark Sneddon was trying to shoulder his way into the coverage with something he claimed he knew. Connor pulled out his phone, thumbed in a quick message to Donna. *Heard anything from MS? You sticking around?* Hit send. Was about to pocket the phone when he scrolled back to Jen's message.

Call me when you're ready x

Considered. Typed in *Hiya. Sorry, work's keeping me busy. Missing you. Hope we can finish our night soon.* Paused. Added *x*, then hit send before he could change his mind and stuffed the phone into his pocket. Looked up to see Charlston studying him.

'You okay there, Connor?' he asked. 'Bad news? Just you looked a little . . .'

'I'm fine,' Connor said, hating the sudden rush of heat he felt in his cheeks. He glanced at his watch. 'You ready to go?'

Charlston smiled, pulling on the mask of the performer. 'Whenever you are,' he said.

Connor tugged his earpiece from his collar, wedged it into place. 'Alpha Tango One this is Team Leader. We are go. Primary is moving to position one now.'

'Copy,' Kyle said, into Connor's ear. 'We're ready when you are, boss.'

'Copy,' Connor replied. 'Showtime,' he said to Charlston, motioning for the door. 'Let's not keep them waiting.'

CHAPTER 31

Donna paced around the outside of the hotel, phone clamped to her ear as she cast glances towards the bonfire at the end of the lawn. Wondered if she concentrated hard enough she could channel her anger and ignite it.

'Yes, Mum, I know. I'm sorry. But it's late, and Sam can't cover. You think I'm happy about it?' She winced, voice harsher than she had intended.

'No, Donna,' her mum said, 'I don't imagine you are. We love having Andrew, you know that, but all these long shifts . . .'

Donna took a deep breath, swallowed the vile cocktail of anger and guilt that burned the back of her throat like acid. Her mother was right. She couldn't keep dumping Andrew so she could chase the latest story. She should be at home, with her son. But . . .

She glanced at her watch. 'Look, Mum, I'm sorry, really, but it's the job. I've one more line to follow up, then I'm done. An hour, no longer. I promise.'

Donna's mother gave a grunting snort down the phone, a sound Donna had become all too familiar with over the years. It articulated her mother's doubts, disappointments and sorrow over her daughter's foolish choices more elegantly than words ever could.

'Fine, Donna, it's not as though your father and I have a choice now, is it? But, please, for Andrew, try to make it back.' A pause, just long enough to underline the importance of what she was about to say next. 'I'll make us all dinner.'

Donna ended the call with an assurance that she would be as quick as she could. Then she let the irritation she had been holding back flood in. No messages while she had been on the call with her mum, no missed calls. No emails.

Where the hell was he?

She felt the guilt stab at her again, let it fan her annoyance into hatred. Typical fucking Mark. Dangle a titbit in front of her, something exclusive about the story, then pull a disappearing act. It was his fault she had lied to her mum, his fault that she was still standing in front of this fucking hotel instead of heading home to Andrew.

But what choice did she have? Mark knew something, was using it to play an angle and buy himself a bit of cachet and free marketing. How could she leave without knowing what he knew, without making sure he didn't steal this story, like he had already stolen so much from her?

She flipped into her contacts. Found his name. Hit dial. Swiped the angry heat from her eyes as she listened to the ringtone. And, for an instant, it was almost three years ago and she was in her flat in Glasgow, pregnancy test in one hand, phone in the other. She remembered sitting on her couch, the ringing of the phone like an echo of the emptiness she felt in her chest. She had known that night what she knew now. He wasn't going to answer.

Then she had known where he was – at home with his wife, trying to ignore the consequences of his actions. Fine. That was then. This was now. And, unlike that night, now Donna had only two questions.

What did Mark know?

And where the hell was he?

CHAPTER 32

Connor had to give him one thing: Blair Charlston could command a room.

He had bounced onto the stage just as the music had hit a pulsing crescendo, the 327 people in the room erupting into a rapturous roar so loud it hit Connor like the wall of sound created by a concussion grenade. He watched as Charlston prowled the stage, toying with the audience, clapping along with them, building a rapport. And then, slowly, he started to bring it down, the music fading just as his voice rose.

'Why are you here?' he asked the crowd as the music died away, and the question was mirrored on the huge screens above the stage. 'Take a minute, and really, really think about it. Look at where you are, what you gave to get to this point. What brought you here tonight? Desperation? Curiosity? The need to start again, heal your life?' He stood like a preacher in front of a grave now, hands clasped together in front of him, head bowed, voice low. 'Think about that. Contemplate it. Feel it. Because whatever it is, whatever brought you here, it's brought you to the most important moment of your life. Because tonight . . .' He trailed off, a rapt, expectant silence falling over the crowd. Connor felt the first pulses of bass rumble through his shoulders, the music being faded up slowly '. . . tonight we begin a journey.' The music rose again, the crowd beginning to shuffle and sway with excitement. 'Tonight we dare to reclaim our lives and be the gods of our own existence!'

Charlston punched the air and the crowd erupted again. He stepped forward for a second and Connor felt himself move before he was aware of it. He had warned him. With the threat still ongoing, however vague, he should stay away from the catwalk that stretched into the crowd. It added an extra degree of risk, brought Charlston one step closer to a potential threat. But if he went for it, what would Connor do? Charge onto the stage and yank him back? Or let the staff he had placed in the crowd around the catwalk do their jobs?

He didn't have to find out, Charlston diverting from the catwalk at the last minute and whirling on his heels with an overly dramatic flourish. He then launched into the spiel Connor had read in his book – about how, over the course of the weekend, they would all DARE to change their lives. They would *decide* what they wanted and how they would get it. *Act* on this desire. *Review* their progress and *evolve* their plan accordingly. To Connor, it wasn't anything you couldn't read in any self-help book that extolled the wonders of neurolinguistic programming. But Charlston wrapped it in enough showbiz glitz and personal pathos – 'You all know me, the mistakes I made to make me DARE to change my own life' – to ensure the crowd gobbled it up.

Connor tuned out as Charlston continued his sales pitch, clicked on his ear mic and asked for a call in from all agents in the room and on the perimeter. One by one they acknowledged the transmission and reported situation nominal. Connor nodded, satisfied. Yet still something niggled at him. Something that kept replaying the moment he had spotted the fat kid from the gym. The awkward nod of acknowledgement, the retreat into the crowd. Something . . .

He forced his concentration back to Charlston. The show was on, the planning done. Whatever happened next, Connor would just have to react to it.

He feels the excitement pulse through him as he steps towards the catwalk, pricking his skin with a thousand needles.

Close now, so close.

He strains forward, trying to give himself as much space as possible among the tightly packed throng of sheep. Feels eyes fall on him, sees a blank-faced man swivel his head to look straight at him. Knows in that instant who this man is, what he is. After all, he was warned. He's not a concern. All he needs is a few seconds, a sliver of time, and for Charlston to step onto the catwalk, walk forward . . .

He bites down on a scream as Charlston wheels away, turning back to the main stage. *No. NO!* he thinks. *He can't. Not now. Not when he's so close!*

But he does, and he has to force himself to be calm. To breathe. To think.

No, this is better. If Charlston's movements have changed, it must be part of the plan. He closes his eyes, blocks out the clamour and chaos of the crowd around him. Feels her hand on his cheek, her breath hot as she whispers into his ear.

Patience. Patience.

Charlston talks for what seems to be an eternity, throwing out platitude after platitude as the sheep roar their stupefied approval. How can anyone believe this crap? Can't they see what he is, what he's done? *Not that it matters,* he thinks. *They will soon. So very soon.*

And then, finally, Charlston stops. Gives the crowd their first instruction of the night.

'We're going to take a break now,' Charlston says in a voice that is like shards of glass in his ears. 'And you're going to take thirty minutes to write down what we've spoken about. Everything that drove you here, all the lies you've told yourself, the disappointments, the regrets. Then, when that's done, we're going to head outside and literally burn the past away. The Destiny Bonfire is about to be lit, and it's a beacon to your future!'

The crowd explodes as though at a revival meeting and the preacher has started chanting in tongues. The lights come up and ushers step through the crowd, gently cajoling and moving them on.

He's moved outside, given paper and a pen, like a child being told to draw a picture. And as he begins to write, he feels it call to him, drawing his eyes to it even as he hears Charlston's words.

'We're going to burn the past away. The Destiny Bonfire is about to be lit.'

He smiles. He knows what to write. After all, this is destiny.

And even as he does, even as he commits to paper the words that

116

have sustained him all these years, he hears another voice. Her voice. Whispering that one word, the only word he ever needed to hear her say.

Dad.

CHAPTER 33

Connor called for another check-in from his staff, all chiming off one at a time, reporting situation nominal. Satisfied, he passed one last sweeping gaze over the assembled crowd in front of him. They were packed into a roped-off area of the main lawn outside the hotel, the bonfire behind waist-high metal barricades. To the left, on a raised stage, a podium was emblazoned with the ITOI logo. About twenty feet away, tucked under the canopy of a massive oak tree, Connor could see a fire engine parked, doors open, crew milling around outside it looking bored. It was a requirement of the permit to hold the event – with a large fire, the service had to be on site to dampen it down and step in if anything went wrong.

Again, Connor felt a niggle – the fat kid in the hotel lobby, the awkward glance of recognition. Something . . .

A light flared into life by the side of the stage and Connor spotted Donna taking her position in front of her cameraman, a spotlight from the camera trained on her. He wasn't surprised she had stayed, wondered if she'd found out what that prick Sneddon wanted to tell her yet. There was an impatient hiss from behind the stage, something between a cough and a sneer. Connor looked over, saw Charlston waiting expectantly. Gave a nod. No point in putting this off any longer.

Charlston bounded onto the stage, the crowd erupting in yet more enthusiastic cheering. They waved pieces of paper over their heads, as though it was a rock concert and this was their version of holding their phones aloft. Despite himself, Connor smiled at the thought.

He felt his phone vibrate in his pocket, ignored it. No time to get distracted. Not now. Pushed away the memory of the text he had sent Jen. Later.

'. . . and now,' Charlston went on as Connor tuned back into what he was saying, 'it's the moment you've all been waiting for. Now is our time. Now is the time to burn away the past and rise from the ashes. Now is the time to set alight our futures. Now is the time to embrace our destiny!'

An aide scuttled onto the stage, handing Charlston what looked like a large baton. Connor knew that its tip was soaked with accelerant. The aide produced a blowtorch, its blue flame licking Charlston's baton. It caught, the flame quickly turning a rich, deep orange as it devoured the lighter fuel, and Charlston waved it above his head to the screaming approval of the crowd.

'And now,' he said, 'the bonfire is ready. You'll be guided forward, and when it's your turn, throw your past into the flames and begin the work of creating your future!'

He walked across the stage to the barricade that surrounded the bonfire, then hurled the torch at it. It arced through the night like a shooting star, flames guttering and sparking, and Connor had the briefest thought that Charlston had missed. But the torch landed about halfway up the pyre and the pile of wood erupted into flame. The crowd roared, Connor smiling. They didn't know about the technician behind the stage, watching, waiting for Charlston's torch to hit. Didn't know the bonfire was rigged with accelerant and charges that were detonated the moment a button was pressed.

It was, Connor thought, just like Charlston. All show. Flashy, superficial. Giving you just what you wanted when you wanted it.

Charlston wheeled back to the crowd, arms aloft again, beckoning them. At this, stewards in high-vis vests started shepherding them forward into a fenced run that led them down a path that led on past the bonfire. Charlston was as good to his word, stepping back to the side of the stage and to Connor, just close enough to reach out to the crowd, shake a hand, pat a shoulder. Congratulate those who had thrown something onto the fire. Connor wondered if any of them realised it was their money they were burning.

As if sensing Connor's thoughts, Charlston looked up at him, eyes reflecting the flames.

'What do you think?' he whispered, one hand curled around the mic that snaked from around his ear and across his cheek. 'Not a bad way to start the weekend, is it? Can't believe you thought we could cancel this. Imagine!'

Connor said nothing, gave Charlston a neutral stare even as his phone buzzed in his pocket again. Needing something, anything, to get him away from Charlston's arrogant, feverish gaze, Connor gave the crowd another glance, then took his phone from his pocket. As he suspected, a text from Jen: *Need to speak to you, it's important. Can you call? Doesn't matter the time.*

Connor frowned. Thought back to the message he had sent her. *Hiya. Sorry, work's keeping me busy. Missing you. Hope we can finish our night soon. x*

Would that be enough to make her want to talk to him regardless of the hour? He didn't think so, but then, what did he know? Confused, feeling the pressure to get back to the job bearing down on him, he tapped in *OK. ASAP*, hit send, then pocketed his phone and looked up.

And felt his world freeze.

A chaotic avalanche of thoughts tumbled through Connor's mind as he processed what he had seen. It was only the briefest of glances but, when he saw it, he understood what had been bothering him about the sight of the kid from the gym. And why he had been wrong.

It wasn't the kid and his shy, embarrassed acknowledgement that had been niggling at Connor.

No. It was the man he had seen behind the kid.

He remembered now. The shy nod, the aborted wave of acknowledgement. The kid sloping away, body swerving a man on his left, who was standing like a rock in the flowing river of people milling around the hotel lobby.

The man looking up at the poster of Blair Charlston with something akin to revulsion on his face.

The man who was approaching the bonfire now, his face bathed in the flames. Excited. Waiting.

Ready.

Connor grabbed Charlston by the elbow, yanked him back. Ignored the strangled cry of 'What the—' as he spun him away from the bonfire and plipped open the channel on his ear mic.

'Team leader to all personnel. Code Blue. Repeat Code Blue. I'm bundling Primary, passing off to Foxtrot now.' He looked up, saw Kyle striding from the wings towards him. 'All other assets, move in on the man approaching the bonfire now. He's second back from the front. Late fifties, sandy hair, I think, lean. Wearing a white shirt and cargo pants and—'

And then the screaming started. Alerted by Connor's snatching up of Charlston, the man surged forward, barging the woman in front of him out of the way. People scattered, setting up a ripple effect that bucked through the crowd like an aftershock. People jostled and tried to keep their footing, a panicked stampede as those behind him in the queue tried to back up and get away, only to run straight into those behind them, like waves crashing into a sea wall.

Connor saw his people try to muscle their way through the crowd, get to the man. They were still moving as he held up a bottle that winked like burnished copper in the light from the fire . . .

. . . the fire . . .

He smiled, tipped the bottle over himself. Connor surged forward, vaulted off the stage, felt something sting his eyes and burn its way up his nose. The ancient part of his mind, the part that had caved in the skulls of its enemies with rocks, reacted to the smell, knew what it meant.

Oh, Jesus, no.

'Charlston! I know what you did! This is for her. It's all for her!' the man screamed. And then he jumped. Connor dived forward, reaching, stretching, willing himself to catch the man. He felt a shoe whistle past his face, that same smell burning his nose, knew he was too late. Heard the man hitting the bonfire even as he landed and tucked into a shoulder roll, his grunt as the breath was forced from his lungs doing nothing to drown out the dull *whump* as the fire devoured this new offering.

An offering doused in petrol.

Connor turned, the man's screams in his ear. He saw feet kicking and bucking wildly, as though the bonfire was trying to eat the man.

Felt his stomach lurch as he caught the sickly sweet smell of burning hair and melting flesh.

From far away, too far, he heard the wail of the fire engine as the crew scrambled into action. Knew it was too late. In front of him, the man had managed to scramble to his feet and was standing stooped over, thrashing in the flames. Connor watched, unable to turn away, as the man's flesh erupted into huge boils, turned scarlet, blackened. He hauled off his jacket, took a step forward, desperate to do something. Anything.

And then the man did something that stopped Connor dead, something that would haunt his dreams for the rest of his life.

He smiled.

A huge, leering grin, the skin at the corners of his mouth cracking and splitting open into a horrific rictus of joy. He locked eyes with Connor for a second, something more intense and consuming than the flames that were devouring him dancing in there.

For Connor, an eternity passed in a millisecond as he was held in the grotesque intimacy of the man's gaze as it bored into him. Then, suddenly, whatever was in his eyes guttered and left them and he toppled forward to the ground, steam rising up as the cold grass doused some of the flames on his chest. Connor covered the distance in an adrenalin-fuelled charge, threw his jacket over the smouldering body, ignored the agony in his hands as the heat from the flames bit into his palms and he felt skin slough off in a sickeningly liquid rending beneath the jacket as he hauled the man from the fire.

Then, rough hands on his shoulders, trying to pull him away. Connor whirled round, caught his assailant by the throat. Squeezed as he drew his fist back. Felt other bodies fall on him.

'Christ, Fraser! Fire Service! Fire Service! Let him go. We've got this. Stand down. Stand the fuck down!'

Connor blinked. Forced the rage back down and willed his grip on the firefighter's throat to ease. He dropped the man and staggered back, terror and fury roiling in his eyes and across his face.

'Fucking nutjob,' the firefighter whispered.

Connor was pushed back, away from the smouldering corpse as the remaining firefighters crowded in. 'Back, get back, we've got this,' he heard a voice say.

Connor backed off, keeping his eyes on the fire crews. Saw paramedics sprinting towards them now, his own staff and the ITOI crews doing their best to keep the crowds away.

As though he was being operated by remote, Connor found his hand by his ear, clicking open his comms. 'Team leader to all units. Secure Primary and crash venue. Repeat. Crash venue. Assist ITOI staff with the civilians. Make sure there are no injuries.'

A sudden scream of static as the water jets from the fire engine were trained on the bonfire and it hissed its defiance at them as thick, acrid smoke roiled into the night sky.

He glanced back to the knot of firefighters and medics at the foot of the blaze, tending the man who had just thrown himself into the fire. Knew they were too late. Connor had seen it in the man's eyes. Something had happened to him to drive him to this. He was already dead. This was just tidying up unfinished business. What was it he had said?

Charlston! I know what you did. This is for her. It's all for her!

He clicked open his comms channel again. 'Team leader to Ops. Robbie, you there?'

'Yuh. Yeah, Chief,' Robbie said. 'You okay? Jesus, I . . .'

Connor ignored the concern in Robbie's voice. 'Pull the CCTV footage of everyone filing out of the main hall to the garden. Find me someone who matches the description of this poor fucker. Late fifties. White shirt. Cargo pants. Sandy brown hair, I think. About five ten, thin build, slight paunch.' A flash of the man holding the bottle above his head. 'Probably right-handed. Might help if you can get him writing down those fucking letters they were meant to throw into the fire.'

'Okay,' Robbie said, tone clipped and hard. The professional at work. 'Anything else, boss?'

Connor sighed. Felt weariness bite into his shoulders and back as the high tide of adrenalin started to ebb. Reached into himself and crushed the feeling. 'Yeah,' he said. 'Call DCI Malcolm Ford, tell him what happened. I assume police have already been called, but Ford deserves to know from us.' A cold feeling in his guts. 'Though if he's anywhere near a TV or a Twitter feed, he'll know already.'

CHAPTER 34

Ford didn't need Twitter or a TV to tell him what was happening at the Alloa House Hotel. He had a much more trustworthy source of information in the grandly titled Fire Scotland head of service delivery, Gary Strachan. They knew each other the way many police and firefighters did: too many years of being on the wrong side of the cordon, picking their way through the aftermath of a fire or a fatality, trying to sift through the devastation to try to piece together what had happened.

They were of similar ages, their careers on parallel paths as the promotions mounted. Until, that was, last year. Strachan had already been named an Assistant Chief Officer for the unified Scottish Fire and Rescue Service and given the title Head of Service Delivery for Central Scotland, a fancy way of saying he was the chief fireman for Stirling and the surrounding area. Ford had been expected to step into the shoes left by his boss, Chief Superintendent Robert Doyle, but then had come the case that introduced Ford to Connor Fraser. A political blowback had made him the last person anyone would promote, especially a chief constable battling to save his job from a vengeful First Minister who had seen her party taken to the brink of civil war by what Ford and Connor had uncovered. So he had stayed a DCI and listened to Mary's slowly increasing hints to take the pension. And why not? He had done his time, done his bit. Any further progress up the career ladder was virtually impossible now. So why not leave, take the money and run?

The answer was nights like this. And calls from friends like Gary Strachan.

He had been at home, meal settling, whisky warming in the crystal glass he held. Saw Mary's irritation as the phone chirped in his pocket, ignored it. Felt a niggle of confused wariness as he read Gary's name on the screen.

'Gary. How you doing? I—'

'You want to get the fuck down here, Malcolm,' Gary had said, his voice a calm, toneless counterpoint to the cacophony of sirens and shouts Ford could hear in the background.

'What? Hold on.' Ford felt his dinner give an oily heave in his guts. Oh, fuck. Oh, no. Please. 'You're at the Alloa House event, are you? Gary, please don't tell me—'

'One fatality. Victim threw himself into that fucking bonfire they'd set up at the front of the hotel. Used an accelerant of some kind – he lit up like a petrol bomb. One of my men's got some minor injuries – he was grabbed by some fucking roid-monster who was protecting Blair Charlston.'

Ford pinched his nose between two fingers, screwed his eyes shut. Fraser. Had to be.

'You need to get down here, Malcolm, get your boys on the scene to help with crowd dispersal. Get an MIT operational. I'll liaise with you on the ground.'

Ford groaned. Made sense. Any event like this, especially with the press involved, the chief would want a heavy police presence. A major investigation team wasn't normal practice in a suicide, but it sounded like this was far from a normal case. And if he was in charge of the major investigation team, he could maybe bypass some of the bullshit and wrap this up quickly.

Yeah. Right.

'Okay, I'll call Control now, make assignments. Thanks for the heads-up, Gary. I owe you one.'

'Don't thank me,' Gary said, his voice colder now, harder. Ford knew the tone all too well: he'd heard it too many times when Gary had told him about sights no man should ever have to see. Bodies warped and cracked by flames, eyeballs popped by heat, fluid congealing like egg whites on ashen, blistered cheeks. Ford briefly wondered how Gary coped with it all, smiled when he remembered the glass in his hand.

The same way he did.

He had ended the call, stood. Considered, then downed the whisky as his mind turned to the calls he would have to make and who he would need that night. It was against protocol – an officer going on duty should never have a drink beforehand, and it was one of the few rules he had followed over his career. Drink was for after. Not before. But . . .

But. Why not? If what had happened at the Alloa House was as bad as Gary had just indicated, he was going to need it.

CHAPTER 35

Connor sat in the ops room clenching and relaxing his fists. He'd been lucky, the paramedics had told him, his bundled jacket had protected him from the worst of it, leaving only superficial burns. But still, it hurt, and he used the icy waves of pain radiating from his palms to drown out the urge to grab his phone from the table and smash the fucking thing on the wall. Donna had been calling him since the man had jumped into the fire, but she'd been way down Connor's list of priorities.

After ordering Robbie to call Ford and alert the police, Connor knew what he had to do next. He hadn't forgotten the police training: a crime scene was a crime scene and his first job was to secure the location and preserve any evidence. He'd approached the firefighters who were on the scene, singling out the white helmet that denoted the incident commander. He was a tall man, rangy, with a thick jaw that seemed too big to be contained by the strap that held his helmet in place. From the shadows cast by the peak of the helmet, harsh, beady eyes glared out at Connor with a fury and animosity every bit as intense as the fire they had just extinguished. Connor put on his best smile, forced his shoulders to relax, his spine to curve, make himself less imposing. After all, he was at fault.

'Fire Officer . . .' he glanced at the name badge on the man's right breast '. . . Johnston, I'm Connor Fraser, Sentinel Securities.' He extended his hand, paused. 'You'll forgive me if I don't shake your hand. I, ah, well . . .' He flipped his hand palm up, the skin an angry scarlet.

Johnston had raised himself to his full height. 'Aye, I saw what you did, Fraser. Saw you assault one of my men too. If I had my way I'd—'

Connor held up his hands. 'Mr Johnston, I apologise. It was a fraught situation, and I overreacted to being manhandled from behind by an assailant who failed to identify himself.' Connor winced as he said the words. He knew he was wrong: he had let his temper get the better of him and lashed out. But he needed a working defence. And for this guy to know it.

The expression on Johnston's face didn't change, but in the absence of 'Fuck off' Connor decided to press on. 'Anyway, Mr Johnston, I've asked my men to alert the police, but in the meantime we're going to have to preserve as much of the crime scene as we can. I was hoping we could liaise on that?'

Johnston's face twisted into a sneer. 'My boss is already contacting the cops,' he said, jutting his jaw back towards the hotel, indicating his location. 'And as for securing the scene, my boys know how to do that. They don't need an amateur like you fucking it up for them.'

Connor had felt his shoulders stiffen, his back straighten. His hands clenched, the white-hot explosion of pain seeming to galvanise him. He saw uncertainty flash across Johnston's eyes, saw it wrestle with the urge to stand his ground. Took a deep breath. Forced a smile onto his face that felt like a blade. 'No problem,' he said. 'If my people or I can assist, just let us know. I'll speak to the police when they arrive, tell them how helpful you've been. And, please, tell the officer I had the run-in with that I'm sorry.'

He had stalked off then, heading for the hotel, swatting aside the offer of assistance from a paramedic who zoned in on him, one word burning through him more intensely than the pain in his hands.

Amateur.

He had made his way back to the ops room, made sure everything was in hand. His staff had done exactly as they had been trained to – in the event of an emergency, they were to protect Charlston, then turn to crowd control, make sure no one else got hurt. There had been a few bumps and bruises, Kyle told him, but nothing serious.

It could have been worse. A lot worse. It should have been.

Amateur.

He glared down at the phone, the display telling him Donna was calling. Again. Clenched his hands and unleashed another wave of agony.

He deserved it.

What the fuck had he been thinking? Taking his eyes off the Primary during an active event to check his phone? Fuck amateur: that was just downright stupid. And why? Because he was worried how a girl would react to a text he had sent? What was he? Twelve?

He snorted in disgust. Later. Right now, he had work to do. Connor did the maths in his head. Robbie had called the police ten minutes ago. But Ford had been contacted by a firefighter before that, so that gave him, what, maybe twenty minutes before the police arrived?

Connor felt a shudder twist down his spine as a sudden flash of the man in the fire rose in his mind, gaze locked on Connor even as he burned, as though he was trying to tell him something. What was it he had said before he jumped?

Charlston! I know what you did. This is for her. It's all for her!

Connor stood, grabbed his phone, flinched as his burned fingers protested. Glanced at the clock on the display. Twenty minutes. More than enough time to have a little word with Blair Charlston and try to figure out what the fuck was going on.

CHAPTER 36

When Ford pulled up Troughton was already outside the hotel, deep in conversation with a uniformed officer. Behind them, three police vans sat, the back doors open, blue lights strobing across the imposing frontage of the Alloa House, tattooing it with colour before it fell back into the darkness of the night.

Ford grunted as he got out of the car, fought off the stab of pain he felt when he stood up straight. Mary was right. This was a young man's game. He had done his bit. And then some. But the problem was that the young were people like Troughton and Officer Baby Face. And Ford wasn't ready to turn the keys over to them.

Yet.

He watched as Troughton disentangled himself from the officer he was talking to and trotted over to him. Ford could see the DS arranging his thoughts as he approached, made a bet with himself as to which policing-manual cliché he would deploy first.

'Sir.' He didn't salute, but Ford saw the policeman's arm twitch, bit back a smile. 'Arrived on scene seven minutes ago. Officers have been deployed to secure the immediate locus and take witness statements as required.'

Ford nodded. So far, so by the book. He ignored the smell that hung in the air: burned tyres and sweet meat. Tried not to let his mind wander down that path. He would have to face the reality of it soon enough. Speaking of which . . .

'How long before Tennant arrives?' he asked.

Confusion flitted across Troughton's face, like the police lights playing on the façade of the hotel. 'Sir?'

'Tennant, DS Troughton. The pathologist?'

'Eh, SOCOs are on scene, sir. I assume they've called him.'

'Get a call in, make sure. Last thing we need is a fuck-up.' He looked over Troughton's shoulder, peered into the gloom, heard the vague static of wind rustling through the trees that surrounded the hotel. 'You said you secured the immediate locus. Did you order a wider search of the grounds as well?'

Troughton glanced over his shoulder, following Ford's gaze. 'Not yet, sir. First priority was securing the scene and helping account for those who were attending the event. We're just in the process of starting to take statements now, but with more than three hundred people here and the bods from the Health and Safety Exec clamouring to get an update . . .'

Ford nodded. Manpower. It was always a question of manpower. And Troughton had done the right thing. Preserve the scene, get as many statements as possible while the incident was fresh in witnesses' minds. Not that this was something any of them was likely to forget.

'Fair enough,' Ford said. 'But get a couple of uniforms to sweep the grounds anyway. Large, unsecured location like this, who knows what might be out there?'

Troughton nodded. 'Anything else, sir?'

Ford felt bile crawl into the back of his throat. He knew what was coming next. It wouldn't be pleasant. 'First, let's have a look at what we've got. Then let's go and see Mr Charlston, try to pick apart what the fuck happened here.'

Troughton nodded. 'This way, sir,' he said, gesturing towards a harshly lit puddle of activity about sixty feet away, white-suited SOCOs buzzing around in the light like anaemic flies. 'Charlston's back in his suite. I've sent an officer up to him, but I believe the man from the security firm running this event is there already, the one we spoke to with Charlston earlier.'

Ford nodded. Fraser. Connor fucking Fraser. Why was he not surprised?

CHAPTER 37

Donna's hand shook as she thumbed through her phone for the number she needed. She told herself it was a hangover from what she had seen and the live broadcast she had just made to report the bonfire incident for Sky. She couldn't remember a word of what she'd said, but Keith had assured her she'd 'knocked it out of the park'. God knew, she deserved to. The only major broadcaster here, she'd scooped everyone, made sure all the networks and newspapers were aware that Donna Blake was a reporter who got the story.

But, as ever, there was a price. And now she was going to have to pay it.

The call was answered, her mother speaking before Donna had a chance to form the first word.

'Donna? My God. Your father and I saw your report on the TV. That poor, poor man. What happened? Are you all right?'

Donna took a second, composed herself. Not the reaction she had been expecting. 'I'm fine, Mum, honestly. I just wanted to call and say sorry for being late, make sure you and Andrew were fine.'

'Yes, yes,' her mother replied, that same breathless, gossipy tone in her voice. 'Of course you missed dinner, but we've got Andrew down now and we're just waiting for you to get home. I take it you're on your way now you've – what do you call it? – filed the story?'

Ah, Donna thought, that was more like it. The passive-aggressive dig and then the follow-up. Typical mother. Maximise the guilt.

'Well, Mum, I've got one more lead to follow up, then I'll be on my way, I promise. I'm sorry it's been a long day, but this is the job. I'm getting time off in lieu for this.' She winced at the lie, hoped her mother didn't hear it in her voice.

A sigh down the phone. One perfected through long years of disappointment in her daughter. 'Okay, darling, but please, don't leave it too long.'

Donna kept her tone neutral. 'I'll be back as soon as I can, Mum. And sorry again about dinner.'

'It's you who missed out, dear. It was stovies. Your favourite.'

Donna smiled, even as her stomach rebelled at the thought. Lucky escape. Just a pity her dad would have had to endure it with a hearty smile and warm words for his wife.

She said goodbye and ended the call. Toyed with the idea of calling Connor again, discarded it. He had his hands full. And it wasn't as if there was much more he could or would tell her than Keith already had on camera. No. Best to go back to the source. She scrolled through her contacts, found the name she was looking for. Anne. Charlston's PA. Was about to hit call when another thought struck her. Her mother was right. Mark really should be taking some responsibility. After all, it was his fault she was still here, no matter how well that had worked out for her. And all because he had something to tell her.

She dismissed the call to Anne, found Mark's number instead. He wasn't answering her calls earlier, and she was damned if she was going to listen to yet another answerphone recording. She thumbed out a message: *Tried calling. What did you want to talk about? All kicking off here. You probably saw me on the news. Going to be here for another half-hour. Call me back.*

She paused. Then added: *Don't be a dick. The silent treatment has me worried.* Hit send before she could talk herself out of it, then flicked back to Anne's number.

Time for Charlston to give her the second exclusive of the night.

CHAPTER 38

It hadn't taken Connor much to get past the police officer at the door to Charlston's suite – he knew his mood was written all over his face, emphasised by the flat, dead tone he used to tell the uniform that he was 'stepping in to see Mr Charlston, who I understand is merely a witness to the events of this evening'.

Charlston was hunched forward on the sofa, elbows on knees. A crystal tumbler of something amber and peaty-smelling sat in front of him. Charlston made no move to reach for the glass, just stared at it as if it had hypnotised him.

'Mr Charlston,' Connor tried again. 'Blair. Look, I know you've had a shock, but there are some details about tonight I need to go over with you. Now.'

Charlston blinked, looked up at Connor, smile flickering on and off like a faulty light as he tried to get back into character as the man who knew how to forge a great destiny. But Connor knew better. The projector was broken, the façade destroyed. Charlston had been reduced from messiah to man the moment someone had chosen to burn themselves alive in front of him. What damage that would do to Charlston and his brand as a life guru Connor didn't know or care. All he wanted was answers.

'Sorry, Connor, bit distracted, you know?' He looked over Connor's shoulder as Anne drifted in front of the picture window, phone clamped to her ear.

'I know this has been traumatic, but I have some questions. The man who jumped into the fire, he said something about knowing what you did. That it was for her. Any idea what that means? Who he might have been?'

Charlston cleared his throat, blinked again. 'I'm sorry, Connor, really, it all happened so fast. I've no idea what he might have meant, but the man was obviously troubled. I mean, to do that . . .' He trailed off, shaking his head.

Connor felt sharp pain in his palms as he clenched his fists. He knew bullshit when he heard it. Didn't need Charlston's averted gaze, sharp, shallow breaths or the fluttering of muscles in his jaw to confirm it. The man was lying through his perfectly bleached teeth.

'Look, Blair. The police are going to be here soon. They're going to ask you the same questions, and they're not going to be satisfied by your answers. So you can tell me what the hell this is all about, or you can tell them. It's up to you. This doesn't look good for Sentinel, but it looks fucking disastrous for you. If you tell me what you know, maybe I can help us both.'

Charlston looked up, something Connor couldn't read twisting his smile into a nervous leer before leaving his face slack and sallow. In that instant, Connor saw the man Charlston was when he was alone and the mask had been stripped away. Small, insecure. Scared.

'Look, Connor, I would tell you if I could, really. But I—'

A sharp knock that didn't fade before the suite door was opened. Connor whirled, curses on his lips ready for whoever had barged in just at the moment Charlston might have said something useful. The words died when he saw Ford stride into the room flanked by his DS and the uniformed officer from outside.

'I hear you played the hero tonight,' Ford said, heading straight for Connor, glancing at Charlston as though he was an afterthought.

'Just did what I could, sir,' Connor replied. 'Not that it meant much. Poor bastard was dead the moment he hit the flames.'

Ford let the silence stretch out. Connor held his gaze, the thought of the victim's eyes flashing before his mind's eye. The intensity. As though he was trying to tell Connor something, share with him something that mere words couldn't articulate.

135

'You have any luck identifying him?' Ford asked.

Connor smiled, glad they weren't wasting time with pretence. They both knew that, as a private contractor, Connor had no right or jurisdiction to investigate this. They also knew that he would. No matter what.

'Nothing yet, sir,' he replied, 'but I've got my people combing the security camera footage to see if we can tie the face with a room here. Of course we'll share whatever we find with you.'

Anger flashed in Ford's eyes, stiffening his back and cooling his tone. 'Bloody right you will. And you'll turn all the footage you mentioned over to us, let my people study it.'

Connor felt the pain flare in his hands. Grabbed it. Forced himself to be calm. 'As I said, we've already started looking at it. To stop now and give it all over to you would waste time. I don't want that. You don't want that. I'm happy to have an officer supervise my people as they work but, please, let us keep going.'

Connor saw the equation run in Ford's eyes. After a moment, he shrugged. 'Fine,' he said. 'But full cooperation, Fraser, or else I'll . . .'

Connor held up a hand. 'Understood,' he said. 'They're working in the ops room in the ground-floor conference suite now. You can send one of your people there, tell them I sent them.'

Ford turned to the uniformed officer standing beside Troughton. 'Weatherstone, isn't it? Go. Make sure they're not fucking with the footage. Get me a name.'

Weatherstone gave Ford a quizzical look. 'Sir?' he asked. 'Isn't that contrary to standard MI procedure? Shouldn't we secure all evidence to ensure its integrity?'

Ford looked as though he was chewing on something bitter. 'Christ, and there was me thinking I was a DCI in charge of the investigation. Very good, sir. You want to double the hours and the manpower we spend on this, fine. Or you could let me run the show and see if we can actually get some bloody answers as to who he was and why he decided to dive into a bonfire after a petrol shower.'

The air in the room became dense, heavy, as Ford glared at the uniformed officer, who was now the focal point of everyone's attention.

Connor willed the man not to speak. Luckily he didn't, just turned on his heels and scurried out of the room.

Ford turned to his DS. 'Troughton, go with him, make sure everything is logged properly.'

'Sir,' Troughton said, then left.

Ford exchanged a glance with Connor. 'What a fucking mess,' he whispered.

Connor was about to agree when Charlston found his voice, the run-in with Weatherstone giving him enough time to pull himself together. 'DCI Ford, thanks for coming,' he said. 'I'm afraid this has been a trying night for everyone but, as I was just telling Connor, there's not much light I can shed on the situation. I don't know the poor man who fell into the fire – I'd never seen him before tonight.'

Connor raised an eyebrow. Interesting. Only minutes ago Charlston had said he hadn't got a look at the man. Now, with the police here, he was denying he ever knew him. Defensiveness in front of the police, or something more?

He felt Ford's gaze on him, accusatorial. 'Yes, I asked Mr Charlston about what happened tonight. Specifically, if he knew the victim.'

Ford's eyes became sharp, predatory. 'And was there any specific reason you thought Mr Charlston here might know the victim?'

I know what you did. This is for her. It's all for her!

Connor shot a glance at Charlston. Saw nothing there but weary defiance. Made a choice. 'Might be nothing,' he said. 'But I was just asking Mr Charlston about what the victim said just before he jumped into the flames.'

Ford turned his gaze to Charlston, who almost flinched. 'Have a seat, sir,' he said. 'You'll excuse me for a moment while I speak to Mr Fraser. But get comfortable. Sounds like we've a lot to talk about.'

CHAPTER 39

Duncan MacKenzie shook his head, drained the whisky from his glass, eyes not leaving the TV and the images from the Alloa House. A man standing on a stage, all teeth and tan, gesticulating wildly as he preached some bullshit about 'setting alight our futures and embracing destinies'. The crowd lapping it up, as if it was a rock concert instead of a con. Then chaos, confusion, the camera jerkily tracking and zooming in on one man who was screaming, pouring something over himself as others shrieked and fled in confused panic. Then he lunged forward, intent clear, before the footage cut to a young woman, haunted eyes staring into the camera with something like defiance as she reported what happened next.

'While the images are too distressing to broadcast, the man then threw himself into the bonfire. Emergency services on the scene were unable to reach him in time, and it's my understanding that he succumbed to his injuries a short while later.'

Another cutaway shot now, this time showing a scrum of firefighters and paramedics huddled over a body. And, standing like a referee at the periphery, a large man in a suit, all shoulders and attitude, glaring at the firefighters as though he was trying to pick targets, decide who to attack first.

MacKenzie shook his head again.

Connor Fraser.

He raised the glass to his lips, tutted when he found it empty. It was a mistake calling Jen. He'd known that the moment he had put down the phone. But what choice did he have? She was close to Fraser, and everything MacKenzie had learned about the man told him that wasn't the worst thing in the world for his daughter.

Paulie had vouched for him, told Duncan that Fraser could 'handle himself', which for Paulie was close to gushing. But with what Duncan knew about the Alloa House – and who was visiting that weekend – the last place he had wanted Jen was anywhere near that hotel or Fraser. But calling her? Stupid. He might as well have told her to put Fraser on speed dial.

He moved across the room, legs feeling weary and slightly disconnected from the rest of him due to the whisky, heading for the drinks cabinet that sat beneath the portrait of Hannah. Stopped, as he always did, to study it, to see if he could spot in her eyes the shadow of the cancer that was eating her brain, that would kill her just months after the picture had been taken. He felt the old resigned anger tug at him as he searched it, the injustice burning more than the whisky he was pouring. Why her? Why Hannah, whose only crime had been to fall in love with a thug like him? He would have swapped with her in a heartbeat if he could, taken the poison into him, left her and Jen untouched.

But, then, that was the problem, wasn't it? Hannah had been afflicted with disease the moment they had met. What he hadn't realised until it was too late was that the disease she had contracted wasn't cancer. It was him.

He shook the thoughts away, whisky sloshing out of the glass and onto the polished surface of the cabinet. Wiped it away with his hand, felt Hannah's disapproving gaze on him.

'What was I meant to do?' he asked, keeping his eyes down. 'She's got a soft spot for him, Han, and you know what Jen is like when she gets an idea in her head. She's like you. She'll want to look after him, be there for him. And with all the bastards in the Alloa House Hotel this weekend, that's the last place Jen needs to be. So I called her, okay? Tried to warn her off.'

Nothing. No response.

Duncan took a swig of the whisky, felt it rush to his head. Walked back to the centre of the room, flopped down on the couch as though a lead weight had been placed on his shoulders. Forced himself to think. Jen would doubtless have seen the TV coverage by now, had probably made contact with Fraser already. Fine. Calling her might have been stupid, but he hadn't told her anything that Fraser could use. And if he had, and Fraser contacted him, he could laugh it off as the overprotective dad trying to keep his daughter safe.

He slid the whisky glass across the table, out of reach, removing both the temptation to have any more or to shatter it. Then he reached for the phone on the table, letting the weight of what he was about to do settle on him like a shroud.

Two calls. That was all it would take. Two calls and a promise. And maybe, maybe, he could keep Jen safe from the nightmare Connor Fraser had just stumbled into.

CHAPTER 40

Connor stood in the hotel corridor, facing Ford. He wanted to lean back against the wall, take the weight off his aching legs, but with Ford there that wasn't an option. He'd been too well trained by the Police Service of Northern Ireland to show a superior officer such disrespect.

'"I know what you did. This is for her. It's all for her"?' Ford said, quoting back what Connor told him the man who had jumped into the bonfire had screamed. 'What the hell does that mean? Who is the "she" he's talking about?'

Connor gave a noncommittal shrug. Dousing yourself in petrol and leaping into a bonfire were hardly the acts of a sane and rational mind. But there was something about the man, something in his eyes even as he burned, that stopped Connor agreeing with Ford. They might have been ravings. But Connor somehow knew that they meant something very specific to the victim. Something that wasn't based on madness but . . .

'You think this is connected to the threat made against Charlston?' Ford asked, interrupting Connor's train of thought.

'I considered that,' Connor said, 'but I'm not sure. The threat delivered to Charlston's London office made specific reference to Graham Bell and what happened to him. Whoever jumped into the fire was very specific in referring to a woman. There may be a link, but we won't know until we talk to Laughing Boy and get some answers, or we can get an ID for the victim.'

Ford blinked slowly, eyes holding Connor's as an unspoken conversation passed between them. Connor had very deliberately said 'we' when talking about interviewing Charlston, his way of telling Ford he wanted in on the investigation. Now it was up to the police officer to shoot him down or let him in.

'Fine,' Ford said, his shoulders sagging. 'Let's get this over with. But if he asks for a lawyer at all, you're out, okay? And I'll have to go through this again at the station with him, get him formally interviewed.'

'Fair enough,' Connor said. It was what he had expected. Ford was a police officer but, above all, he was a pragmatist. He had little time for the rules and regulations of police work, preferring results over red tape. Right now, Connor was a resource.

A thought struck Connor then, the instincts of the police officer he had been elbowing aside the man who had been hired to protect Blair Charlston. 'How do you want to play it?' he asked. 'Want me to hold back, play the pal and try to get him to talk when I can?'

Ford smiled despite himself. Once a copper, always a copper. 'Yeah, that works. I'll be Mr Stern, you be Mr Supportive. See if we can get him to tell us something useful. Christ, someone has to have a clue about what the fuck is going on around here, don't they?'

'Sir, we'll get this,' Connor said, surprising himself with the words. 'Charlston will open up. He has to. We'll get an ID for the victim tonight. He was at the event, so he paid for a room here – I saw him checking in. We'll find him on CCTV, get a room number and a name. Even if it's fake, we'll get a name. And that'll tell us something. Something we can use.'

'Never took you for an optimist, Fraser,' Ford said.

Connor smiled. 'What can I say? Charlston's changed me. I'm a better man for this weekend, after all.'

'Away tae fuck,' Ford said with a chuckle as he turned and headed back for the suite.

Two floors down, Donna nodded thanks as she took the cup of coffee Anne James was offering to her. They were in one of the smaller suites booked by ITOI as the venue for what was meant to be Charlston's triumphant meet-and-greet with VIP guests after the bonfire. Tables with canapés and snacks were dotted around the room, forgotten, beside glasses of pre-poured champagne that would now never be drunk. Behind a small bar that had been set up in the corner, a waiter in a bow-tie milled around, trying to find something to do.

'So,' Anne said, gesturing to two chairs that sat on either side of a coffee-table, 'what can I do for you, Ms Blake?'

Donna took a seat, sipped the coffee. Bitter. But it would do the job. 'Well, Anne, you'll have seen my report earlier. All the networks have it. They'll be sending reporters now and I'm guessing your press-office phone has already gone into meltdown?' Anne gave a nod of confirmation. 'So it's simple. I've already done a pre-record with Blair. We were forced to can that after . . . ah, after what happened outside. But we can still use it. If I can get an interview with Blair, we can cut that in with what we recorded earlier – him talking about his hopes and dreams for the event, and how he wanted to help so many people. It'll give you the chance to shape the story, show Blair as a compassionate, caring man who was only trying to help the kind of people driven to the desperate act we saw tonight.'

Donna could see the idea take root in Anne's mind as she considered the angles. It was, after all, an easy way to get a good PR spin on the situation after the disastrous images from earlier.

It was also total bullshit. Donna didn't care how this looked for Charlston, Anne or ITOI. Didn't care if they could spin Blair into a benevolent guru who had been touched by the cruel madness of the world and resolved to work harder to fight it. No. All she cared about was getting Blair Charlston in front of a camera and on the record before anyone else did. And in that interview Donald Peters's name would feature heavily, lawyers and Mark be damned.

'Well,' Anne said, 'it's an intriguing offer. And Blair did say your earlier work was very good, insightful. So . . .'

Donna gripped her notepad, pushing down the urge to punch the air. She had them. The interview was hers.

Anne pulled her phone from her bag, tapped in a message, then stood, looking down at Donna. 'I've given Blair a five-minute warning.

143

We should head up to the suite and meet him. He'll be wanting an interruption from the police anyway.'

Donna stood, felt excitement bubble and froth in her, like the forgotten champagne. The interview with Charlston was golden. The chance to barge in on the police – and DCI Ford – was priceless.

'After you,' she said, fishing out her phone and scrolling through the contacts for Keith's number. She wanted him to be ready.

Anne bowed slightly, then headed for the door. They walked along the corridor, took the lift up to the top floor. Had Charlston's suite door in sight when all hell broke loose.

CHAPTER 41

They came up behind the two women fast, exploding out of the lift before the doors had fully opened and barrelling along the corridor, footsteps like thunder in the enclosed space.

'Move, move, step aside!' the officer boomed, a shorter man in a bad suit trying to keep pace with him.

'Jesus Christ, what's the rush?' Donna shouted as she bounced off the wall and Anne James's shoulder barged into her as she lost her balance.

The officers didn't reply, just kept sprinting for Charlston's door. There was an oddly comic moment when they pinwheeled to a halt, arms flailing, before they hit the buzzer.

Anne exchanged a glance with Donna, panic digging deep grooves into her features and hollowing her eyes. 'What do you think?'

'Why don't we find out?' Donna said, quickening her pace. They reached the door just as it swung open, Donna exchanging the briefest of glances with Connor Fraser. He moved to close the door behind the police officers, but Anne pushed past Donna, held out a hand.

'It's Anne, Mr Fraser,' she said. 'I've got every right to be in that room with you.'

Connor's eyes darted to Donna, then back to Anne. 'She's with me,' Anne said.

Connor shrugged, stood aside. 'Off the record for now, okay?' he said to Donna.

She gave him a smile. 'No promises, Connor,' she said, hoping he heard the humour in her voice, worried he hadn't.

Connor closed the door behind them, rejoined Ford, who was now staring at the breathless police officers in front of him.

'What?' he said. 'Kitchen out of milk? You found Lord Lucan in the basement? What could possibly make you run through the hotel like a couple of teenagers on a dare? Why not just call me?'

The officers exchanged glances, eyes darting between Ford and Charlston, confusion and embarrassment making their facial expressions ripple in time with their breathing.

'Sorry, sir,' the detective sergeant said.

Troughton, Donna thought suddenly. His name is Troughton.

'But you left your radio in the car and I did try to call you on your mobile . . .'

Ford grunted. 'On silent while I was interviewing Mr Charlston,' he said, something a lesser person might mistake for regret tingeing his words.

'Quite, sir,' Troughton said. 'But we couldn't contact you. And we thought you'd want to know straight away.'

'Know what?' Ford asked, impatience raising his voice now. 'What the hell is going on?'

This time, it was the uniform who spoke. His jaw was tight, face pale, and Ford was sure he could see flecks of vomit drying on his tunic. 'We searched the grounds as ordered, sir. And we found something. SOCOs are securing the locus now, and Dr Tennant is en route to make initial examinations.'

Ford's eyes darted to Fraser even as his jaw tightened. 'Wait. Tennant. Dr Tennant. The pathologist. You mean . . .'

'Yes, sir,' Troughton said, his voice suddenly very loud in the silence of the room. 'We found a body, sir, in the woods. Hanging from a tree.'

'Hanging? Christ, not another suicide? What the fuck is going on here tonight?'

'No, sir, you don't understand,' Troughton said, his voice so remote and detached that Donna flinched. 'Whatever this is, it definitely isn't a suicide. You see . . .'

He handed his mobile to Ford. The DCI looked down, the light from the screen playing across his features and turning his face into a gruesome jack o'lantern. Donna saw him blink rapidly then swallow, the clicking of his throat like a gunshot. He stood like that for a moment, frozen, then looked up at Troughton, disgust contorting his face into a death mask. 'Jesus,' he whispered, as he passed the phone to Connor.

He took it clumsily in his burned hands, saw what was there, jaw working as his shoulders stiffened. He passed the phone back to Ford, then looked across at Donna, something almost apologetic in his gaze.

And in that moment, even as panic clamped a cadaver's hand around her throat, as the world seemed to tip on its axis and tears began to claw at the back of her eyes, she knew who was in that picture.

Knew her son would never see his father again.

CHAPTER 42

Connor sat on the sofa beside Donna, close enough to feel the heat from her body and the shuddering catch of her breath as she forced her lungs to keep functioning. He cursed himself for his stupidity in letting her read on his face whose body had been found in the grounds of the hotel. But at least she hadn't seen the image.

And if Connor had anything to do with it, she never would. Mark Sneddon might have been a self-centred little prick, but he was still Donna's ex, and the father of her son. Better to remember him as that rather than the butchered, mangled knot of bloodied flesh Connor had been shown.

He blinked away the thought, focused his attention back on Donna. When she realised it was Mark who was dead, she had buckled, rocked back as though Connor's glance had become a punch to the stomach. He moved towards her, barging Troughton out of the way, and she'd held up her hands, backing off as her eyes became wide, glittering jewels framed with tears.

'No,' she whispered, 'no, no, no . . .'

He got to her, put his arms around her. Felt her stiffen then fall into his embrace, chest hitching, stifling her tears against his chest.

Connor made soothing sounds, rocked her gently. Looked up, glanced at Ford, then Charlston. 'Can we have the room, please?' he said, his tone telling them both it wasn't a request.

Charlston looked at Connor as though he had just spoken in

tongues. 'What the . . .' He blinked, as though the words were written in front of him but he was having trouble making them out. 'What's going on? What? How?'

Anne walked over to him, took his arm, glanced across to Connor. 'I'm sorry, Mr Fraser, but, as you can imagine, this is a lot for us to take in, especially after what happened earlier. We'll give you both some privacy.'

She placed a gentle hand on Charlston's back, shepherded him to the door of the suite, pausing at Ford, seeming to read a question in his eyes.

'I'll take him to my room,' she said. 'Three ten. We've been using it as an office and green room. Is that all right, Inspector? You can send an officer with us, if you want.'

Ford gave Anne a look that was somewhere between professional courtesy and respect. No denying it, she knew how to assess a situation and cover the angles. 'We'll need a statement from him,' he said, eyes sliding to Connor for the briefest of moments. 'But as long as you stay in the room, that'll be fine. If you need anything, just let us know.' He reached into his jacket and handed her his card.

Anne pocketed it, then got moving again. Ford watched them go, started to mobilise his own men. Stopped when he was passing Connor. 'I'll send a liaison officer up,' he said. 'But I'll need a statement from her as well, Fraser. And there's the little matter of formal identification to be dealt with.'

Connor heard the barb in Ford's tone. Yes, he'd made a mistake. Looking straight at Donna was a reflex. Stupid and amateurish. But it was done. And it didn't change the fact that Mark Sneddon was hanging dead from a tree, stomach ripped open, intestines glistening in the light of the flash like gore-streaked ropes. In that instant, Donna held close to him, Connor had a sudden memory of collecting raw sausages from the butcher with his grandfather, the cold firmness leaking through the waxed paper they were wrapped in. He felt his stomach lurch, bit back the flood of sickness at the back of his throat. Not now. He could deal with it later. Right now his friend needed him.

He waited till the room was empty, moved Donna gently to the couch and sat her down. Busied himself at the drinks cabinet as she wiped angrily at her cheeks, battling to get herself under control. He placed a glass of whisky in front of her and sat, abandoning an awkward attempt to put an arm around her when he saw her shoulders tense.

'Is it me?' Donna said, after a moment, her words as hard and cold as the glass in front of her.

'Sorry, Donna, what? I don't—'

'Is it me?' she repeated, anger giving her voice heat now. 'First there was Matt Evans and all that insanity last year. Then I find Donald with his head caved in, and now you're telling me Mark's dead. So is it me?' She turned to face Connor, anger and pleading in her eyes. 'Am I cursed or something? Three people, Connor . . . three.' Fresh tears streaked down her cheeks.

Connor reached forward, took her hands in his. Squeezed. He'd seen this before. Survivor's guilt, the living trying to make sense of death. But, as he knew, there was no sense to any of it. Life was cruel and unfair. Bad things happened to good people. Donna was just the latest person to be trapped in the crosshairs.

'No,' he said, giving her hands another squeeze. He could feel her knuckles clenched tight, wondered if her nails were digging into her palms. 'Donna, this is not your fault at all. None of it. You know that. Matt was killed as a message, and we don't know if what happened to Donald and Mark are connected.'

She turned to him, eyes defiant. 'That's shit and you know it, Connor,' she said. 'Donald wanted to see me, tell me something about Charlston. Then Mark called with the same bloody line, telling me there was something about this story I had to know, and now he ends up dead in the woods.' She jerked her hands up suddenly, shrugging off his grip as she stood. 'Three people dead because of something that fucker Charlston,' she jabbed a finger at the door, 'knows or did? No way. I'm going to find out what's going on here. And Charlston is going to tell me.'

She stood up, whirled round when Connor put a hand on her shoulder.

'What?' Her voice was as cold as her eyes. 'You're really going to stop me? Protect your precious client? Fuck that, Connor. He knows something, and I'm not waiting for the press release from the police to find out what it is. Donald and Mark are . . . are . . .'

She trailed off, blinking back angry tears. Connor stared at her. He should wait for Ford, make sure Ford spoke to Charlston and Donna first. The last thing anyone needed was Donna getting something out of Charlston that could prejudice the investigation into what the hell had happened so far tonight.

But then. The memory of waxed paper in his hands, the chill of raw meat bleeding through. Sneddon hanging in the woods like the devil's own piñata, guts exposed to the world, a look almost like surprise on his face. And then there was that voice. That scream. *I know what you did! This is for her. It's all for her!* And those eyes. Trying to tell him something from the heart of the blaze.

He straightened. Took his hand from Donna's shoulder. 'Let's go.'

CHAPTER 43

Abattoir.

The word screamed across Ford's mind as he surveyed the scene in front of him. It was the only word that fit. He was standing about twenty feet from the tree where Mark Sneddon hung, white-suited SOCOs buzzing around like flies attracted to the carcass, while fire-fighters erected makeshift scaffolding to reach the body.

'Jesus,' Strachan said, beside Ford. 'Some fucking night, Malcolm. What the fuck . . .'

The sentence trailed off, questions rushing in to fill the silence between the two men. Just what the hell was going on here? First, an old reporter is found with his head caved in. Then a man takes a petrol shower and jumps into the centrepiece of Charlston's night, screaming about some woman and knowing what he did. And then, just to top it off, this.

The photograph Troughton had shown Ford barely did the scene justice. On the phone it had looked grotesque, unreal, but in reality it was like looking through a crack into the bowels of Hell.

Sneddon hung about ten feet off the ground, from a branch of an oak tree so gnarled and twisted that it looked almost prehistoric to Ford. His face was untouched, features slack and waxy as his head lolled back at an impossible angle, ear touching his shoulder. It was, Ford thought, almost as if he was trying to look away from what had been done to his torso. He was topless, the paling grey of his cooling flesh making the wound even more vivid. The slash ran across his entire lower stomach, like a leer framed in lipstick. From it, tendrils of slick, glistening intestines and viscera oozed like an octopus's tentacles. Ford's own guts gave another lurch, and he felt his throat constrict even as the urge for a cigarette wrapped itself around his mind. He had stopped smoking twenty years ago, mostly without too much thought. Until nights like this. Nights when the acrid tang of cigarette smoke in his nose was the only thing that would block out the smell of blood and fear.

And tonight there was plenty of both to go around.

Movement startled him from his thoughts, and he looked towards the tree to see Dr Tennant lumbering towards them, the white SOCO suit straining to contain his massive frame. He stopped in front of the two men, gave a curt nod, answered their question before it needed to be asked.

'We've got all we can with the body in situ,' he said, eyes locked on Strachan. 'You can tell your men to bring him down now, Gary. Just be careful, eh?'

He nodded, gestured over Tennant's shoulder. Ford watched as the firefighters scuttled up the scaffold to reach the body, felt another pang of nausea as Sneddon began to swing gently, the intestines oil-dark in the sharp floodlights and writhing like snakes. 'So, what can you tell me, Walter?' he said, relieved his voice didn't have the brittle edge of his thoughts.

Tennant sighed, gave Ford a you-know-better look. 'There's not much I can tell you at this stage other than the obvious, Malcolm. I won't commit until I can run further tests back at the lab, but most likely he's been dead for at least two hours. Cause of death seems fairly self-explanatory – rapid blood loss following a catastrophic injury to the abdominal cavity.'

'Hold on,' Ford said, mouth filling with sand as he spoke. '"Following"? You mean that,' he gestured to the body, 'was done to him before he was hauled up into the tree?'

Tennant's gaze hardened with disgust at the inevitability of the conclusion. 'Yes, Malcolm. He was slashed open, then hauled up into that tree. Blood spatter confirms it. The distance of traces from the body and the patterns could only have been made while the heart was still pumping blood. The dislocation of the internal organs is consistent too, as are the gouging marks of the rope in his neck. He would have been thrashing for life even as his guts slithered out of him.'

'Christ,' Strachan whispered, his eyes not leaving the body as his men brought it down. 'This is no place to die, Malcolm.'

Ford was forced to agree. Gutted and left hanging in a wood, the sounds of the ITOI event probably in your ears as you gagged and choked for life and felt the liquid sloughing of your internal organs slither from your body? No. This was no place to die.

'Can you put a rush on the full post-mortem?' he asked Tennant, his voice cold and distant now.

The pathologist nodded, weary acceptance making his features suddenly slack and old. 'Yes, Malcolm. I'll accompany the body, get the post-mortem done ASAP.' He paused, eyes locking with the DCI's. When he spoke, his voice was as dark as the blood pooling around Sneddon's shattered corpse. 'Whoever did this is a savage, Malcolm. You need to find them. Now.'

Ford nodded agreement, made a silent promise to his friend. He would find out what was going on here. Charlston was the key to it, he was sure of that. It had been a calculated risk, giving Fraser the room with Blake. But he knew Fraser, knew he was driven by the same compulsion to know as himself. He said goodbye to Strachan, turned and headed back to the hotel. If he was right, Fraser and Blake would be talking to Charlston now, warming him up.

By the time he got back to the hotel, Charlston would be ready to tell Ford everything he wanted to know.

CHAPTER 44

There was no surprise on Anne's face when she swung open the door to Connor and Donna, just an arch of the eyebrow in Connor's direction.

'We're here to see Blair,' he said, keeping his eyes locked with Anne's even as he felt unease prickle his back. Technically, he was Charlston's employee, hired to handle security for the ITOI event, which included keeping reporters with awkward questions away from the boss. But he was also a friend of Donna, and had just seen her former partner's body hanging from a tree.

Fuck it. Answers first. He could have the moral debate with himself about employee relations later.

Anne nodded, as though she had been expecting this, and stepped back. 'You're welcome to come in,' she said, 'but Blair's not here.'

Connor's jaw tightened. He knew the answer to the question before he asked it. 'Where is he?'

'He said he needed to unwind, clear his head. Went down to the gym for a go at that bloody punch bag.' Distaste pulled her mouth into a tight, bloodless line. 'Barbaric. But it means I can get on with some work.'

Connor was turning away when Donna spoke, breaking the stony silence she had maintained since they left the suite. 'What work?' she asked.

155

Anne blinked, processing the unpredicted question. 'Well, ah, we've had to cancel the event, of course, so there are people to inform, arrangements to make.'

Donna twisted her face into a smile that doubled as a sneer. 'Sorry, this must be so inconvenient for you,' she said, and walked away.

Connor caught up, showed her the way down to the gym. He half expected the room to be empty, for Charlston to have pulled another disappearing act. But, no: the thud of the heavy bag, the jangle of the chain and the presence of a PC outside the gym told him Charlston was here.

He nodded to the uniform, who returned the gesture. 'Here to see my client,' he said. The officer's tired eyes told him he would get no argument.

Charlston was dancing around the heavy bag, weaving and ducking, snapping out the occasional jab or roundhouse. Telegraphing every move, Connor noted. All about the presentation, no concern for the result. If he was throwing those punches for real, Connor doubted he would feel any of them if they connected. He was surprised when he realised he wanted to discover what a punch from Blair Charlston felt like.

'Mr Charlston,' Donna called. 'Blair. I need to speak to you, I've got a few—'

Another jab snapped out, sending the bag swinging. Charlston ducked around it, turning his back on Connor and Donna.

'Ignorant bastard,' Donna hissed, taking a step forward. Connor reached out, touched her shoulder, ignoring the flash of pain in his wounded hand.

'Ear buds,' he said, tapping his ears as he stepped past Donna towards Charlston. He waited until another punch was thrown, moved forward and grabbed the bag, absorbing the momentum with his chest. Charlston's head jerked up and he stumbled back, terror forcing his eyes wide.

'Jesus! Connor!' he shouted as he dug out the ear buds.

Connor heard a small voice bleed from the earphones as Charlston fumbled in his pocket for his phone and killed whatever he was listening to.

'Sorry,' Connor said as he released the bag. 'But we need to talk, Blair.'

Charlston's eyes darted towards Donna, who was crossing the gym towards them. 'I don't think this is the best time for an interview, Ms Blake.'

'Good,' Donna said. 'I'm not here for one. I just want answers, Mr Charlston. Now.'

Confusion flitted across Charlston's face as he looked at Connor for an explanation. 'The man who was found in the woods tonight was her ex,' he said, watching Donna's shoulders tense.

Charlston took a moment, his features rearranging themselves. To Connor, it was like watching an actor get into character. 'I'm sorry for your loss,' he said, his voice warm and deep now, body still, 'but I'm not sure what I can tell you. I don't even know—'

'Sneddon,' Donna said, voice as taut as her shoulders. 'His name was Mark Sneddon. He knew someone else you knew, Blair, who died recently. Donald Peters.'

A tight smile twitched across Charlston's face. 'Ah, Mr Peters. Another tragedy. But as I told the police, and Connor here, there's nothing I can really tell you about Mr Peters. I haven't seen the man in years, have no idea what he was doing prior to his death.'

'He was going to tell me something about you. That's what he was doing,' Donna said, anger chilling her voice now. 'Something about you and Perigee. And now he's dead. Just like Mark. Got anything to say about that, Mr Charlston?'

Charlston gave an apologetic smile as he repositioned his ear buds. 'I'm afraid I can't help you, Donna,' he said. 'I've never heard of, ah, Mark, was it, before you told me his name just now, and as I've told the police, I can't discuss my dealings with Peters or Perigee for legal reasons. If there's anything else I can do for you, let Anne know. But now I'd like to finish my workout.'

He threw a jab before Donna could object, began the pantomime again. Connor stood back, let the bag swing past him like a pendulum. Saw the fury swirl in Donna's eyes, felt it call to his own. Feed it. Held up his hand.

My turn, the gesture said.

He backed off, let Charlston take a few more digs at the bag, get into a rhythm. Caught the bag as it swung away after a sloppy round-house, put his hip into it, stopped it dead.

'Good idea, Blair,' he said. 'It's been a long night for everyone, be good to get a couple of digs in. You mind if I join you now that Ms Blake is done?' He waved at Donna, praying she would play along. She did, heading for the door of the gym.

'Great! Like I always say, movement creates the moment. Exercise exorcises,' Blair said, something in his smile making Connor queasy. 'But your hands?'

'Let me worry about them,' Connor said. 'Brace the bag for me, will you?'

Uncertainty rippled across Charlston's face. 'Eh, okay.'

'Thanks,' Connor said, tone casual. 'See, thing is, Blair, it's been a hard night. I've got two people dead, one of them gutted like an animal. That doesn't sit well with me. You see that, don't you?'

'Well, of course it's only—'

The bag punched the rest of the air out of Charlston's lungs, killing the sentence. Connor had flashed out an elbow strike, pivoting at the hip, hitting the bag at roughly the level of Charlston's head. 'Sorry, Blair, got a little carried away.' A flat forearm slash this time, the bag dancing and jerking on its chain. 'So now I've got two people dead, and another death that, from what Donna says, is probably connected. So you can see I'm frustrated.'

Connor whipped his knee up, drove it forward like a hammer, into the bag, then followed with a sweeping roundhouse kick that tore the bag from Charlston's grip and sent him sprawling across the floor, his pained yelp drowned out by the gunshot thunder of the heavy bag crashing into the wall.

Connor shouldered it aside, loomed over Charlston, offered a hand. Charlston hesitated for a moment, Connor's gaze telling him refusal would be a very bad idea.

Connor clamped his grip on Charlston's forearm, hauled him up and pulled him in close. 'Two dead tonight, Blair, three in total,' he said slowly, feeling his disgust crawl into his eyes and crystallise there as his gaze bored into Charlston's. 'And they all had one thing in common. You. So forget legal niceties, forget the fact you hired me for this weekend. None of that matters. What matters . . .' he tightened his grip, felt tendons in Charlston's arm jump in protest even as the pain forced his eyes wide and pinched his face '. . . is that you tell me what the fuck is going on. Right now. Otherwise, I won't stop with the heavy bag. Clear?'

He released Charlston and the smaller man staggered back, rubbing his arm and blinking at Connor as though seeing him for the first time. In a way, Connor realised, he was. This was a side of him he kept hidden most of the time. The Fraser temper. Over the years, Connor had mostly learned to control it, channel it, make it work for him. And there was no doubt it was working now. The fear in Charlston's eyes told him that even as the man nodded like an enthusiastic child being told an exciting story.

Connor heard Donna's heels click on the gym floor as Charlston took out his ear buds with a hand that wasn't quite steady. Something in the gesture stuck with Connor, chimed with another thought deep in his mind. Something about the way Charlston had looked when they'd first entered the gym . . .

. . . something . . .

'Let's start with Donald,' Donna said. 'What was the story with you, him and Perigee?'

Charlston looked between Donna and Connor, face collapsing into weary resignation, the long, nightmarish night having finally delivered the knockout blow.

'Okay,' he said, 'okay. I'll tell you what I know. But not here. Let's get a drink. I think we could all use one.'

CHAPTER 45

It was an hour later that Connor collapsed into his couch, physically and mentally drained. After hearing Charlston's story, he had checked in with Kyle, Robbie and the team, made sure they had eyes on the client at all times. There had been a discussion about how safe the hotel was after the discovery of Mark Sneddon, the conclusion being that it had been swept, staff and police were in position. Moving Charlston to an unexamined location would create a world of headaches for Connor and DCI Ford. And there was another factor in the equation, Connor had agreed with Ford. Whatever was going on, Charlston was connected to it. If he was moved, it might plant the seed in his mind that it was time to head back to London, away from Police Scotland's reach, with lawyers waiting to make sure he never again set foot north of the border. And Connor wanted him here. So it was agreed that his room would be watched in shifts when DCI Ford left. If, that was, the chief inspector didn't decide to haul him into the nearest police station and make the conversation as uncomfortable as possible.

Considering what he had just heard, Connor couldn't decide if that was what Charlston deserved. Either that or a medal.

Following their confrontation in the gym, Connor had effectively frog-marched Charlston back to his suite, Donna tagging on behind. He had a moment of indecision when they reached the suite, unsure whether he should ask Donna to stay out. One look at her told him that was a bad idea. The set of her jaw and the flaming scarlet rash that raged up her neck, angry against the paleness of the rest of her, told Connor she was running on adrenalin and rage. He didn't like to think of the crash she would endure later, when everything was done and she was sitting in the silence, grief and loss soaking into her, like an ache she couldn't touch. But that was for later. Once they had their answers from Charlston.

Charlston prepared drinks, pushing aside the whisky Connor had poured for Donna earlier, replacing it with a crystal tumbler so full it sloshed its contents onto the table. Connor saw that Charlston's hands trembled slightly as he did so, felt a sudden rush of guilty glee. There had been something in the man's smile in the gym, some sickening need to please and ingratiate, that had turned Connor's stomach and hardened his opinion of Blair Charlston into something cold and ugly. Beyond the desire to sell himself as a guru, to have others learn from his mistakes, there was something else. Some need to be accepted and respected, to fill some hole at the centre of himself with the adulation of others.

He was, Connor realised, selling salvation to salve his own conscience.

Charlston sat across from them, staring into his own glass, which he turned gently, the crystal whispering softly against the wood of the table. Then he rubbed his eyes and snapped his head up, defiance stretching his face tight.

'You wanted to know about Donald Peters, what he might have had to tell you about me,' he said, keeping his eyes on Donna, careful not to look in Connor's direction.

'That's right,' Donna said. 'He called me the day he died, said he had something to disclose about you and what happened at Perigee. Then he turns up dead and everything . . .' she reached for the glass, lifted it to her lips, paused '. . . everything went to shit here with the bonfire and then . . .' She drowned the end of the sentence with a slug of whisky so deep it burned Connor's throat just watching her.

Charlston nodded, mirrored Donna's action. 'Like I said, it's not what you think, and I can't see how it has a bearing on what . . . what happened tonight.'

'Tell us,' Connor said, surprised to hear his father's voice escape from his lips. Cold. Disconnected. Cynical.

Charlston dared a quick glance in his direction, twitched his face into a smile.

'You know what happened with Kimberley and me, don't you?' he said, now looking into the space between Connor and Donna, as though addressing a ghost. Or the elephant in the room.

'I've read your book, heard your speeches,' Connor said. 'You two made a lover's pact, slashed each other's wrists. Only you got lucky and she didn't. Can imagine your lawyers had to spend quite a lot of time trying to dance you out of a culpable homicide charge.'

Charlston's face hardened, hate leaping into his eyes. Connor returned the look, his body a statue. He was through playing with this man.

'I wanted to go with her,' Charlston said, wistful defiance making his voice a low whisper. 'But I didn't. But do you know why we decided to end things, what drove us to that?'

This time, it was Donna who answered. 'Your book says it was because you were overcome with grief at what happened to the guy who took his life at the Perigee factory. Gareth Bell.'

'Graham,' Charlston corrected, voice sharp with old pain. 'Graham Bell. He was part of it, of course, that and the fact we knew Perigee was going to collapse despite our best efforts. But what I didn't put in the book, what Donald Peters found out, was that Kimberley and Graham were, well, together before I arrived at Perigee.'

Connor added that to what he knew, frowned. Nope. Something missing. He could see it in Charlston's face, read it in his hunched shoulders and defensive body language. 'And?' he prompted. 'I can see that's a bad headline. Ex-boyfriend takes his own life after being dumped for the new boss, but bad enough to warrant a gagging order and a pay-off to the reporter? No way. So what else?'

Charlston finished his drink, stared into the glass, whatever he was seeing making his eyes glisten with tears. When he spoke, his voice was empty. 'No, I don't suppose it was enough. But it was for Kim. She couldn't get over it. Told me she felt like she'd killed him twice. And when we found out Perigee was going to fold despite everything we'd done . . .'

Connor felt irritation flutter in his chest. He was tired and sore,

162

burdened with memories from tonight that made the thought of sleep a cruel joke. He was in no mood for riddles. He sighed once, loudly, saw Charlston look up at him.

'When we met, she was pregnant,' he said, voice still empty. 'Briefly.'

Connor heard Donna hiss a breath out. 'Christ,' she said slowly. 'You're telling me you and Kim started something when she was pregnant with Graham's baby, and she got rid of that child to be with you?'

'No!' Charlston barked, an almost feral rage in his eyes. 'It wasn't like that. At all. I knew that was how it would be played in the press, knew that's how Peters would write it. But that's not what happened. We – we met when I arrived at Perigee. She was working in the IT department, helped show me the systems. She told me she was pregnant early on. Didn't matter to me, child or no, I wanted to be with her. So she left Graham. They hadn't told anyone at the factory they were a couple for obvious reasons as she was technically his boss, so that wasn't an issue. But something went wrong. See, she miscarried. I would have loved that child as much as I loved her, but it just wasn't . . .'

'Killed him twice,' Connor muttered, the comment making sense now. 'So this is what Peters approached you with, asked for comment?'

Charlston met his eyes for the first time since they'd left the gym. He looked deflated, defeated, the weight of the past crushing any resistance or instinct for self-preservation.

'It was just after . . . after Kim died,' he said. 'Peters had been digging, found out about Bell, the baby and me. See, I made a mistake. When it happened, when Kim lost the baby, I approached Bell, gave him a pay-off from Perigee. Straight into his wages. Very generous. Get him away from painful memories. He hit the roof, went for me. Told me it was blood money. Took his own life two days later. I don't know how Peters found out about it – maybe Bell went to him – but he got wind of it. Came to me with a query about the pay-off, and using company money to clean up my personal mess.'

Donna sat forward, eyes hardening. 'Misappropriation of company funds,' she said, 'and a nasty little love triangle. No wonder you wanted to keep it quiet. Doesn't do your reputation as a life coach much good to have a skeleton like that in the cupboard, does it?'

'It was nothing to do with that!' Charlston snapped. 'Peters could write what the hell he wanted about me after Kim died. I didn't care. But I did care about her memory. So I arranged for the gagging clause and the pay-off for Peters. It wasn't hard. His publisher was shitting bricks the moment I threw my lawyers at them.'

Connor leaned forward, a memory flashing across his mind, the sickly sweet smell of burning flesh tickling at his nose. '"I know what you did",' he muttered. 'That's what the man who jumped into the bonfire said. You told the police you didn't know him, but that's not true, is it, Blair? Who was he?'

'I'm honestly not sure,' Charlston said, his eyes telling Connor he no longer cared if he was believed or not. 'I only got the briefest glance of him. And I only met the man once, at the funeral, but it could have been . . . Well, it could have been Kim's father, Jonathan.'

'Jesus Christ,' Donna whispered. 'He blamed you for his daughter's death. But why do what he did? What the hell drove him to that?'

'I don't know. I don't even know for sure if it was him,' Charlston said. 'I only got a fleeting look at him. But it could . . .'

'What about Mark?' Donna asked, voice blunt. 'Mark Sneddon. The . . .' she cleared her throat '. . . ah, the man they found in the woods. What about him?'

'I've never heard of him before tonight,' Charlston said, the conciliatory tone in his voice grating on Connor's nerves. 'Donna, I'm sorry for your loss, but I have no idea why anyone would do that to him, why—'

The suite door opening stopped Charlston, and Connor turned as Ford and Troughton entered the room. He stood, crossed to the two police officers, cutting them off before they could get any closer to Donna. Gave Ford a questioning look.

'It's done,' the chief inspector replied, eyes darting to Donna, voice low. 'We found his ID on his body, can do the rest with dental records. If I can spare her seeing him, Fraser, I will.'

Connor nodded his thanks, then turned to Charlston, raising his voice to be heard. 'I'm glad you're here, Chief Inspector. Mr Charlston was just telling us a very interesting story, which might help identify whoever it was who jumped into the bonfire this evening.'

Ford's gaze became sharp. 'Really? Then we'll have to get that on the record, won't we, Troughton?'

'Yes, sir,' the younger policeman muttered.

'We'll leave you to it, then,' Connor said, glancing at Donna who, taking the hint, stood. Her gaze never left Charlston, an appraising look, as though she was studying an expensive piece of art that she neither understood nor liked.

'I'll be in touch to get all this on the record myself,' she said.

Connor had made arrangements to coordinate with Ford, checked in with his team. He said goodbye to Donna, giving her a hug that went on just a second too long to be comfortable, felt the desperation in her grip when she dug her fingers into his shoulders.

And now he was home, head throbbing in time with his scorched hands. What did it all mean? Charlston's situation with Kim, and Graham Bell, was a mess, there was no doubt about that. But had he acted purely to protect the reputation of the lover who had died beside him, or was there something more? And, if so, how did Mark Sneddon factor into it all?

He sighed in frustration, stood. Began pacing around the flat, poking disinterestedly at one of the boxes piled up in the corner. Mostly photographs, some documents. He pulled out a couple, found he couldn't concentrate on them. Went to the kitchen and poured himself a Bushmills. He wasn't much of a whiskey drinker, but when he did drink it, he always went for the brand his maternal grandfather had favoured. It reminded him of those long nights training in the makeshift gym in the back of the garage in Newtownards, Jimmy Fraser supervising, drink in hand, as Connor built himself into the man he was now, with endless reps of ever-heavier weights . . .

. . . weights . . .

An image of Charlston dancing around the heavy bag, ear buds wedged in. And suddenly Connor knew what had been annoying him when he had confronted Charlston in the gym. Something so obvious that he felt like kicking himself for not seeing it sooner.

If Charlston had, as Anne said, gone straight to the gym and hit the bags after leaving the suite, that had given him at least twenty minutes' start on himself and Donna. Plenty of time to get the bag swinging. But if that was the case, why wasn't he sweating or breathing hard when Connor had arrived? What had he been doing? And whose voice had Connor heard when Charlston had removed his ear buds?

Connor drained the glass, knowing it would do nothing to slow his thoughts. All he had were questions. What he needed was some answers.

Time to start finding them.

CHAPTER 46

Looking into the blank, obsidian screen of the laptop was, Murphy thought, like looking into the eye of someone you had just killed. Light still reflected off its surface, and you could still see yourself in there if you looked hard enough, but its purpose was gone. Eye or screen, the plug had been pulled and all that was left was something through which you could peer into the void.

He sensed rather than heard Boyle move across the room with fluid, unsettling grace. Thought briefly of him moving through the woods earlier this evening, a predator among sheep, stumbling upon prey that, while hardly worthy, would at least provide a few moments' entertainment.

Boyle stopped, turned. Dark eyes falling on him, forcing the temperature in the room to plummet. He had the type of face your eyes would simply slide off if you passed him in the street. Everything was average, from his jaw to his nose to his neat dark haircut. It was only if you looked at his eyes that you would notice Boyle was far from average. There was something in the cold gaze, something that reached past rational thought to the less evolved part of the brain where fight or flight ruled. Something that said this man was an imminent lethal danger. Someone whose attention you did not like to catch.

As Murphy just had.

'Problem?' Boyle asked in his calm, measured tone, a hint of the east coast clipping the vowels and elongating the consonants.

'No, no, nothing at all,' Murphy replied, glad to hear his voice was calmer than he felt. Boyle was an asset, of that there was no doubt. But he was like all lethal weapons – uncaring about whom he injured.

Boyle let the silence stretch out. Then, 'Any word from him?'

'Got a call about an hour and twenty ago,' Murphy replied. 'Understandably, he's busy with the police after Jonathan George's little head dive and your handiwork in the woods earlier on. But he'll be here soon enough.'

'Good,' Boyle replied, the room cooling further. 'Less time we spend here, the better.'

Murphy murmured agreement. As ever, Boyle was right. It was one of the reasons Murphy had hired him. He could assess any situation dispassionately, then come up with a calm, rational plan to extract them from it. It was why they had managed to extricate themselves from the Perigee mess a year ago, why they were sitting in a hotel suite rather than a prison cell. But, still, there was another side to Boyle, a cold savagery that Murphy found both hypnotic and horrifying. There had been no time for details on the brief call earlier, but it was clear that Boyle had gone medieval with the reporter in the woods, just as he had done with the old man the day before. Murphy was the first to admit he himself was no angel, his hands far from clean, but Boyle was on a different evolutionary level. What, he wondered, drove a man to such violence, and such utter calm in its aftermath?

He was startled from his thoughts by the impatient buzz of his phone on the table, felt a flash of cold surprise as he read the name on the display. Gave a small shake of the head to Boyle, who was looking at him expectantly.

Not who we're waiting for, the gesture said

He clicked answer, held the phone to his ear.

'Duncan MacKenzie,' he said. 'Well I never! I've not heard from you in an age. How are you? And how's that daughter of yours? Jen, isn't it?'

CHAPTER 47

As Murphy was listening to a voice from his past, Connor was study-ing a computer screen. But, unlike Murphy's, the screen in front of Connor was far from dead. And what was on it made for compelling viewing.

It was the matter of one phone call to Kyle at the Alloa House and accessing a secure Dropbox file for Connor to have what he wanted: video footage from the gym in the hotel basement. Under their orig-inal agreement, Charlston had stipulated that the CCTV in the gym be disconnected to allow him to 'work out and meditate in peace'. Initially, Connor had agreed. Secured room, on the hotel grounds, with access controlled by a member of the Sentinel team on the door. It was a low-risk environment, and Connor didn't have any pressing desire to see Charlston work himself into a puddle.

But then Charlston had pulled his disappearing act on Robbie, and Connor had reconsidered the agreement, ordered the cameras reacti-vated. It was a shame he had forgotten to mention it to Charlston but, hey, when people are busy details sometimes get overlooked.

So now he was watching footage from the gym, starting from about ten minutes after he had been there with Robbie to the cut-off point he had stipulated to Kyle, which was ten minutes before he had called. It was mostly dull stuff, the gym in darkness, only the strip lights glowing in the gloom, the emergency exit sign above the door a strangely comforting beacon.

And then the strip lights flared into life, the screen whitening as the contrast control on the camera readjusted. Charlston walking in, circling the bag, prodding it gingerly, building momentum until it swung on its own. A couple of half-hearted jabs, followed by a rummage in his pockets. Ear buds appeared but, instead of being stuck in place, were draped around his shoulders, like a necklace. Connor leaned forward, watching intently as Charlston gave the bag a few more half-hearted jabs. Found himself nodding, putting the pieces together. Typical Charlston. Ever the showman, he was setting the stage, picking the soundtrack. All he needed was the squeal of the chain and an occasional thump on the bag to convince the copper outside of what he was doing.

A furtive glance up at the door, then another object appeared in his hand. The camera angle gave Connor only a fleeting glance, but it was enough to tell him it was another mobile phone, older this time, more bricklike. He had a sudden memory of one of his first mobiles, an old Nokia with an LCD display. No camera, no internet access, no email. Just a phone doing what it was meant to do. Be mobile. And make calls.

On the screen, Charlston stared at the phone as he turned half away from the bag, as though protecting it from the phone. Then, with a sagging of the shoulders that Connor could almost feel through the screen, he juggled the phone in his hand and lifted it to his ear. There was no audio on the footage, but Connor didn't need it to know what the nature of the call was. Tense shoulders, wild gesticulations . . . he wondered how hard Charlston had had to work to hold back the scream of expletives he was telegraphing with every gesture. But even as he spoke, he kept digging at the bag, keeping the soundtrack going, the illusion real. Another thirty seconds, then he stepped away from the bag, nodding. Dropped the phone, looked into the middle distance. Did a slow half-turn around the gym, as though taking it in for the first time. As his head swept past the camera, Connor saw his mouth was pulled into a shape that was only made by a very specific word. A word Blair Charlston would never use in front of those he was exhorting to take control of their lives. Another glimpse of the man behind the façade. Connor found his grudging respect for Charlston and the efforts he had gone to in order to protect the memory of Kimberley George begin to recede, replaced by a more familiar impression of the man.

Disdain.

Charlston pocketed the phone, stared at the bag. Wedged in his ear buds and fumbled for his smartphone, stopping to make the call Connor presumed he had interrupted when he and Donna had arrived.

He watched himself and Donna walk into the room a few minutes later, struck again by the fury that seemed to pulse off Donna in waves. To Connor it was as if there was a spotlight on her, focusing all the attention in the room on her ramrod-straight back, squared shoulders and set expression. He made a mental note to call her when he had finished with the CCTV footage. She was obviously using anger to ward off whatever else she was feeling about Mark Sneddon's death. Connor was no stranger to such a strategy. But he also knew its cost.

And the last thing he wanted was Donna ending up like him.

As though illustrating the point, he watched as Charlston went flying when his first elbow strike hit the heavy bag. But there, too, was something he had missed at the time, something he could not possibly have seen until now. Donna. Leaning forward, a grim, cheerless leer of a smile twitching at her lips even as tears streaked her cheeks.

The knee strike came next, followed by the roundhouse. Despite himself, Connor smiled. Good form. Solid contact. And Charlston sprawled across the floor. Message delivered. But then his smile faded, pride curdling into something uglier as he heard another voice. A voice he had heard earlier that night when questioning Charlston. His father's. And that all-too-familiar warning.

You've got the Fraser temper, son. Just watch for it. Like I have.

Frustrated, he reached out, felt the cool of the laptop sting his burned fingers as he flipped the lid closed. Considered. So he had been right. Charlston's little trip to the gym had been an excuse to get away from everyone and make a phone call. No. Two phone calls. But to whom? And why was the first call made on what looked like an antique? A burner phone that could be used and disposed of without

171

fear of it being traced back to him. And if he was so concerned about his privacy, why did he use his own phone to make the second call? Why not keep everything confidential?

Connor sat back in the couch, stared up at the ceiling. Closed his eyes, tried to think it through, reorder what he knew into a chronological timeline of events, let any disruption in the chain show him what he could feel he was missing.

Okay. First, Donald Peters was found with his head caved in after getting in touch with Donna about Charlston. Then a man, possibly Kimberley George's father, doused himself in petrol and took a running jump into Charlston's Destiny Bonfire, sparking off a night of hell for Connor, Donna and DCI Ford. Then Sneddon was found in the grounds of the hotel, gutted and left to hang like a felled deer. And Charlston's reaction to all this? To the fact that three people, all connected with him in some way or another, had died violently in the space of forty-eight hours? He didn't fall apart. Didn't beg for protection or answers. No. He slipped away and made two phone calls, two calls that . . .

Connor sat bolt upright, fast enough to send a sharp dagger of pain lancing through his neck. He called up the screen again, scrambled around the laptop and through his notes for what he needed. Studied the frozen image of Blair Charlston sprawled on the floor, himself looming over him.

Connor felt anger rise, cold and scalding, in the back of his throat. Heard his father's words again, nodded silent agreement. Yes. This was the Fraser temper. Instead of ignoring it, he embraced it, let it become something hard and unyielding in the centre of his chest as he stared at the screen. And in that second, he willed his other self to move to grab Charlston again and haul him to his feet. But this time to clamp his hands around the little bastard's throat and squeeze. Squeeze until his wounded hands screamed and Charlston's eyes bulged as he gasped and clawed for breath.

Because if Connor was right, that was the least he deserved.

CHAPTER 48

After leaving Connor, and giving a formal statement to the police at the scene, with the promise of a visit to Randolphfield station in Stirling the next day, Donna finally made her way out of the hotel. She had called her parents, told them what had happened, talked her mum down from the hysteria and inevitable tears.

She was walking in a daze, no real concept of where she was going, compelled by nothing more than the urge to move and the desire to get away from this place. Her head was a riot of questions and memories, of Mark, of Donald.

But mostly of Andrew. She stepped out of the hotel, took a deep breath of night air. Felt her stomach churn as the acrid smell of smoke hit the back of her throat, made rich and sweet by the after-taste of something else that had burned that night, something she didn't want to think about. She looked down the manicured expanse of lawn to an area that was marked off with yellow police tape, two officers standing sentry. Bile surged up her throat even as her vision doubled and the woods somehow seemed to grow darker. That was where he had died. Mark. Her Mark. The Mark who had promised her a life, then snatched it all away, leaving her literally holding the baby. Andrew. Her son. *Their* son. The son who would never have the chance to know his father.

She turned away from the wood, started back along the gravel path of the hotel, heels digging in and making her wobble in her haste. Marching now. Almost running. Trying to get away, trying to . . .

'Donna?'

She bit back the scream that clawed its way up her throat at the voice, whirled round. Was confronted by Keith, his face pale, dark rings mascara-like under his eyes.

'Jesus, Keith,' she said, breathing deeply. 'You gave me a fright. Hold on, what are you doing here anyway? We filed the story about the bonfire hours ago. I told you to head back to the studio well before . . .'

'Yeah, I know,' Keith said, the gloom of the night doing nothing to mask the sudden darkening of his cheeks. 'But I wanted to stick around, get some establishing shots. And when I heard the rumours that someone else had been found on the grounds, that . . .'

Donna's head came up, Keith's words hitting her like ice water, focusing her thoughts. 'Hold on,' she said. 'Rumours? You mean the police haven't put out a statement?'

'Nope,' Keith said. 'No official statement and nothing on the wires. Anyone who picked up your story only goes as far as mentioning that there was a disturbance during the opening of the ITOI night and police were called in. Nothing more about a body being found, though all the reporters and crews had left to file before that. And I only heard about it from a fat kid in the lobby who was struggling to keep his dinner down and moaning about how much money he'd wasted trying to get here.'

Donna glanced back at the hotel, careful not to look at the woods. Dizzying calculations danced across her mind, searing away her exhaustion, thoughts of Donald and Andrew, leaving her with just one name to focus on, one problem to solve.

Mark.

He was her ex. The father of their son. The personal connection couldn't be more blatant. But he was also something else now. A story. No, an exclusive. A way to get ahead of the pack and show she could still break the news, no matter how it affected her. Christ, she might even find a book in all of this somewhere.

And yet . . .

Unease roiled in her gut, along with something uglier and purer. Guilt. The rest of the reporters drawn there by the promise of a gory death and a celebrity scandal had missed what came next: the police managing to keep the discovery of Mark's body quiet, either by design or, more likely, blind luck. But that meant there was a clock ticking. And a decision to be made. Leave the story, bank what she had learned about Charlston, Kimberley George and Graham Bell and work that angle, give the police time to identify Mark formally and inform his next of kin, let the story get out and keep herself away from it. Or did she double down? Get in first, report the line everyone else had missed, what she had been in the room to hear when the young detective sergeant had told Ford, and use that to put pressure on the police and Charlston, force them to talk to her and give her the answers she needed in ways she didn't fully understand?

Tick, tock. Tick, tock.

She chewed her bottom lip, ignoring the sharp pain, eyes darting between the hotel and the wood.

The wood . . .

A sudden flash of Connor looking up from the sergeant's phone to her, his eyes telling her everything she'd never wanted to know.

'Donna?' Keith, behind her. 'Come on, van's still in the car park. I'll give you a lift home. Looks like you could do with getting to bed for a—'

'Better idea,' she said. 'Let's get to the van. You call the newsroom, I'll send a line to the desk. Tell them they've got a story coming.'

Keith's face creased into a scowl. 'What? I don't . . . You mean you've got another line on this?'

'Yeah,' Donna said, a rancid taste flooding her mouth. 'Could say that. It's an exclusive. And, trust me, this one is going to make a name for both of us.'

CHAPTER 49

Duncan MacKenzie's office sat at the heart of an industrial yard on the outskirts east of Stirling, about halfway between the city and Bannockburn. It was out of the way, further than he would have liked from the main arterial routes of the A91 and the M9, but back when he was just starting out and he had bought the yard, cost had beaten location. Now, thirty years later and with one of the biggest haulage businesses on the east coast of Scotland, Duncan could have afforded to move anywhere he wanted. But he liked the yard, had a fondness for it as the birthplace of the empire he had built.

And, besides, some of the business he did benefited from having a place that was slightly off the beaten track.

He reflected on this as he listened to the coffee machine grind and hiss its way through its work. He would have been happy enough with a kettle and a jar of instant, but Jen had insisted that he needed 'real coffee, not that instant crap'. So he'd accepted the machine, an overly complicated thing hewn from chrome and sleek, shiny plastic, with a smile and a hug.

Anything to keep Jen happy.

After making the call last night, he had fallen into a fitful sleep on the sofa in his living room and woken, cold and disoriented, at just after six, breathing hard, jumbled images and undefined panic dancing on the edge of his thoughts. Unable to settle, he had showered and dressed, headed for the yard. So now he stood, looking out of a grimy window

176

as the rising sun turned the sky into a glowering bruise of purple and gold, waiting for the coffee which would hopefully slough away the bitter taste of last night's whisky and fortify him for another day.

And what a day it promised to be.

The call to Murphy had been brief, business-like and, as with most of Duncan's dealings with Murphy, unpleasant. He had first met the man when Perigee was putting itself back on its feet under Blair Charlston's leadership. He had bid for some of the contracts to ship their kitchens around the country, attracted by the company's sheen of popularity with A-list clientele and the promise of funding from a team of City financiers led by Charlston. MacKenzie Haulage hadn't won any of the official contracts but, as Duncan quickly found out, that didn't mean there wasn't enough work to go around. Providing you had the right people for the job. And a yard that was quiet and out of the way.

It was during this time that he had met Murphy. Duncan struggled to define what the man actually did and settled for facilitator. It was Murphy who had commissioned Duncan for several deliveries to and from Perigee, all through third-party drivers in vehicles that just happened not to have MacKenzie branding on them. It was quick and lucrative, and Duncan made no secret of enjoying the financial benefits of the deal, especially when he learned how far the tendrils of Perigee had spread into haulage and transport businesses around the Central Belt. So when the ITOI event at the Alloa House Hotel was announced, Duncan wasn't surprised to hear that a few of his former competitors and colleagues would be heading to the event. Of course, he was the black sheep of the family, the secret that dared not speak its name. But as for the rest of them, why wouldn't they enjoy Charlston's hospitality? They had done business with him and Perigee in the past, little wonder therefore that he would invite his former associates to his latest business venture as a life coach.

And Duncan was under no illusion that the ITOI weekend was any more than that for Charlston. A business. And a bloody one at that.

He turned from the window, busied himself with making coffee, tutting in time to the hisses and clicks of the coffee machine as he did so. Yes, he had a fair idea of what the ITOI event was really about, which was why he had called Jen and clumsily warned her off getting close to Connor Fraser over the course of the weekend. The last place he wanted her was anywhere near the Alloa House, people like Murphy or, worse, his diseased colleague Boyle.

Neither man had mentioned Boyle during their call, and at the time, Duncan couldn't have sworn the man was there. But then he had turned on the TV as he got dressed, seen Donna Blake's gaunt, haunted face staring into the camera, reporting on 'the discovery of a body in the grounds of the Alloa House', and he had known Boyle was there.

Just as he had known he had been in Kinross before.

So he had called Murphy, made arrangements, some of which involved Connor Fraser. Not that he gave a fuck what happened to the overdeveloped meathead. As far as he was concerned, any harm that befell him would be fair payback for the humiliation he had inflicted on Paulie the year before. But, as ever, there was a bigger picture to consider. A picture that had Jen at its forefront. For whatever reason, she cared for Fraser. The thought made Duncan uncomfortable, but he was forced to admit that the man was a step up from the feeble idiots she had been attracted to previously.

He finished the coffee in a gulp, forcing down the memories he didn't want to have with it. Retreated to his desk, checked emails. Nothing there that couldn't wait.

Satisfied, he typed a quick message to the site manager, Eric, about expected shipments for the day. Nothing untoward, just the usual ebb and flow of lorries and pallets in and out of the yard. The out-of-the-way yard. Where no one ever looked.

He felt the coffee kick in as he stood up, the caffeine lightening his chest and making his legs tingle. Maybe Jen was right after all. The real thing was better.

The real thing.

He grabbed his jacket, patted himself down, making sure everything was there, including the comforting weight that pulled at the lining of his lower pocket just a little too heavily to be hidden. Grabbing his keys, Duncan headed for the door, fumbling his mobile as he dialled Jen's number.

She was right. Real was better. And while Paulie was watching over her, would give his life for her if he had to, sometimes only the attention of her father would do.

Just to be sure.

CHAPTER 50

Connor was at the gym just off Craigs roundabout when he saw Donna's report. He was racking plates onto the leg press when he glanced up and Donna's gaunt face was staring down at him from the TV screens. Normally, they would be tuned to MTV or another high-energy music channel, but that was too much for even the most ardent gym bunny at 6 a.m. So instead the TVs were set to Sky News. It made sense to Connor – with the state of the world, the news induced more than enough frustration and rage to fuel the most strenuous workout.

He plugged his earphones into one of the static cycles in front of the TV screens, tuned it to the TV channel. Listened to Donna's report about the discovery of a body in the grounds of the Alloa House Hotel, 'which was last night the scene of a horrific incident as an attendee died in the bonfire that was meant to signify the start of the weekend retreat led by former financier turned life coach Blair Charlston'.

Connor felt the anger snarl again at the mention of Charlston's name, momentarily overwhelming the flash of concern he felt for Donna. The crash was still coming for her, grief and sorrow stalking her from the shadows of her mind, and she was using work to delay the inevitable. But the forced cheer in her voice and the febrile glitter in her eyes told Connor she was heading for the edge of a cliff.

He unplugged his earphones, jacked back into his phone, let the

180

sounds of Bach wash over him as he took deep, steadying breaths. After all, that was the reason he was here: to calm himself with a workout, blunt his rage with exhaustion, let his rational mind take over again before he spoke to Charlston about the CCTV footage he had watched the previous night. The CCTV footage that had told him Charlston was playing some kind of game for which Connor had yet to work the rules out.

That Charlston had made two phone calls in quick succession was troubling enough, but it was the timing of those calls that most concerned Connor. To steal away after one man had burned to death and another had been found eviscerated in the woods told Connor two stark, ugly facts about Blair Charlston.

The man was an even better showman than Connor had thought. And he had been expecting something to happen the night before.

Connor paused between sets, considered the fact, turned it over like a jewel in a spotlight. No matter which way he looked at it, the answer was the same. Charlston had been looking for an excuse to get away from the crowd and make his phone calls, which were, evidently, more important to him than his own safety and the deaths of two people at an event that was all about him. After last night, and Donna's report, Connor was in no doubt that Charlston's career as the 'Soundbite Saviour' was as dead as Mark Sneddon. Charlston would have known that the moment Kim George's father took a dive into the bonfire. So why wasn't that his pressing concern the night before? Why wasn't he trying frantically to implement some sort of damage control, to get in front of the story and become the god of his own destiny? Why instead was he intent on making two phone calls?

The conclusion, Connor realised, was simple. And as crushing as the weight he was now pushing against.

But why?

He was considering the thought when he felt the presence of someone in front of him. Looked up, Bach still drowning out the world, saw Jen in front of him, a mixture of concern and bemused humour playing across her face.

Connor popped his earphones, took a deep breath. 'Sorry, Jen,' he said, suddenly self-conscious. He could feel the anger coursing through his veins, pulsing like a bass beat in his soul, hoped Jen didn't see it in his eyes.

'No problem,' she said, cranking up the smile a little. 'Saw you come in, wanted to make sure you were okay after last night. I was wondering why you didn't reply to my text, then I saw what had happened. It must have been awful.'

Connor blinked away the memory of eyes glaring into his own as flames leaped and capered around blackening, bubbling flesh. 'Aye, not the best day at the office,' he said, raising his hands and inspecting them. They were still an angry pink, and they stung from the sweat now coating them, but he would survive. 'Anyway, how you doing? Sorry again for the other night, I just—'

She raised a hand, swatted away his words, something like uncertainty forcing her eyes from his. 'It's no problem. I know it was work,' she said. 'Speaking of which, are you going back there today?'

'You mean to the Alloa? Yeah,' Connor said. 'Got a few things to wrap up. Not sure how long I'll be. Why? Want to do something later on?'

The uncertainty deepened, became clouded by something Connor couldn't read. He watched as she chewed her bottom lip, perfect white teeth flashing briefly in the lights from the gym. 'Well, yeah, maybe, but no, it wasn't that, it was ... Well, it was just ...'

Despite himself, Connor felt a rush of irritation. He wasn't in the mood for games. He'd had enough of that with Charlston. Took a breath. Steadied himself. 'Jen, what is it? What's wrong?'

'What? Oh, nothing, nothing. It's just that, well . . .' Her voice trailed off and she glanced away, up at the TV screens and the image of Donna. When she spoke again, the words came out in a rush, tumbling over each other as though there was pressure behind them.

'It's just that Dad called last night, wanted me to keep away from you this weekend. Something about some of the people who were visiting the hotel, and how busy they would keep you. And then I saw what happened on the TV, and I was worried that ...'

Connor felt as though a shard of ice was lodged in his throat. Out of respect for Jen, he hadn't looked too hard into her father, Duncan. He knew that he ran a haulage business, that not all of his cargo was

182

legal, and that his right-hand man, Paulie, had two distinguishing features other than a nose that looked as though it had been crafted from putty: his protective feelings for Jen and his propensity for beating people up, then storing them in the boot of his car. Connor suppressed a shiver as he remembered a night a year ago when he had handed Paulie a gun, then turned and walked back to his own car.

It had been the longest walk of his life.

'Did your dad say anything about who was visiting?' Connor said, forcing his tone to remain casual.

'No, no,' Jen said, relief on her face now, as though telling Connor about her conversation with her father had unburdened her somehow. 'He just said you'd be busy and maybe we could do something instead. Dad's always been overprotective, especially after . . . But this, with what happened afterwards, just seemed odd. Maybe you shouldn't go back there today, Connor, stay away. We could do something, like you said.'

Connor didn't reply, both of them knowing what he would say. He had to go back, find out what Blair Charlston knew, what was really going on. But this was unexpected. Who was Duncan MacKenzie so worried about that he had warned Jen away from Connor for the weekend? From what little Connor knew of the man he was astute, shrewd. So why fire off the flares and paint such a huge warning sign about the Alloa House for Jen, one that he must surely have known would get back to Connor?

'Jen, look, if it's okay with you, I'm going to give your dad a call, have a word with him about all this. Two people died at the hotel last night, and if your dad knows something, he's better talking to me about it than the police.'

Jen nodded with a weak smile. 'I knew you'd say that,' she said, 'which is part of the reason I wanted to see you. Dad called about ten minutes ago. I finish at seven, he's going to pick me up and we're going for breakfast. So I was wondering . . .'

Another pause, a flash of perfect teeth.

'Do you want to join us?'

CHAPTER 51

Too much coffee and too little sleep, plus an ill-tempered exchange with Mary about how pale he was looking and the 'long hours taking their toll' had Ford in no mood for any crap by the time he got back to Randolphfield and the MIT room at just after 6.30 a.m.

Which was, he thought, precisely why the first call he received that morning was from Police Scotland's chief constable, Peter Guthrie. Ford had encountered Guthrie the previous year, when decapitated bodies had started to appear on the streets of Stirling, and had taken an instant dislike to the man. A political creature moulded by four years' studying politics and history at one of Scotland's most prestigious universities followed by fast-tracking up the ranks of Police Scotland, Guthrie was a bureaucrat rather than a copper. But he had one skill that his political masters valued above all others.

He knew how to make Police Scotland look good. And, more importantly, how to shift the blame when they looked bad. For proof, Ford had to look no further than his former mentor Detective Chief Superintendent Doyle. What had happened to him in the wake of the headless-bodies case was a textbook example of scapegoating. But to Ford, it was something else. Something more personal.

It was an injustice that cried out to be righted. And he would. Some day.

'Sir, how can I help you this morning?' Ford said, after Guthrie's PA had put him through.

'You can start by telling me what the hell is going on at the Alloa House,' Guthrie said, his voice as clipped and precise as the ridiculous moustache he had taken to wearing. No doubt some PR guru had told him it lent him an air of authority. To Ford, it made him look even more like a kid playing dress-up.

'I made sure your office was copied into my reports, sir,' Ford said, keeping his voice light and pleasant even as his mood darkened. 'We were called in after a suspected suicide at the ITOI event being run there last night. While on the scene, officers discovered another body, this time in the woodland that surrounds the hotel. We've made a formal identification, an MIT has been assembled and we're beginning enquiries.'

Guthrie grunted. 'Ah, yes, all well and good, Chief Inspector. I saw the reports you mentioned. I was struck, and temporarily impressed, by the fact that you hadn't issued a press statement on the body found in the woodland, that we had managed to contain that for the time being.'

Ford felt the beginnings of a headache, poked into life by a pang of unease at one word Guthrie had used.

Temporarily.

'Yes, sir,' he said cautiously. 'I thought it would be better, in light of the other activity and coverage that evening, to hold that back for the time being. We're—'

'Yes, yes. Very good, Chief Inspector. I quite agree. But if that's the case, can you tell me why I'm watching a full report on the matter on the TV right now?'

'Sir?' Ford said, a terrible certainty causing the headache to push its way to the forefront of his mind even as he fumbled for the remote for the wall-mounted TV in his office.

'Sky News, right now,' Guthrie said, impatience making his voice sound hostile. 'A woman called Blake. I believe she reported on the man who jumped into the bonfire. Seems remarkably well informed about the body found in the woods. Care to comment on that, Chief Inspector?'

Ford tightened his grip on the remote as the TV flared into life, Donna Blake's face filling the screen, the Alloa House behind her.

It was obviously prerecorded from the night before probably, Ford guessed, just after she had given her formal statement. He clamped his jaw shut, used the tension to offset the dull hammering of his headache.

'Sorry, sir,' he muttered. 'Ms Blake was at the event last night, was on scene when the first incident occurred. I'll get the press office to put lines out now, reassure the public. And I'll make sure someone talks to Ms Blake personally.'

'See that you do, DCI Ford. This has the potential for taking a nasty turn. The last thing we need is the public thinking there's another bloodbath in Stirling, especially after the fiasco last year. Am I clear?'

'Crystal, sir,' Ford said, the cliché bitter and ugly in his mouth.

'Get on to it, Inspector,' Guthrie said, his tone indicating he had lost interest in the conversation. 'I've a meeting with the justice secretary in an hour. I *want* to be able to tell him that this matter is in hand, that my best people are working on it. Can I tell him that?'

'Yes, sir. I'll deal with it.'

'See that you do. And keep me updated.'

The call ended before Ford could say anything else. He listened to the dead line for a moment, resisted the urge to slam the phone down and placed it gently back in its cradle. Then he aimed the remote at the TV and increased the sound, listening to Donna's report.

'The body, which has yet to be formally identified, was found in the grounds of the Alloa House Hotel after Blair Charlston's ITOI event was abandoned. A participant died in the bonfire that was meant to be the centrepiece of the weekend, which was billed as a "journey into mastering your own destiny", led by former financier Blair Charlston. Charlston, who hit the headlines last year when—'

Ford snapped the TV off, stared at the blank screen. Impressive, he was forced to admit. Blake had reported the discovery of Sneddon but kept herself, and her relationship to him, out of it. Made sense. She was hardly a suspect in the killing, but she was definitely a person of interest.

Ford sat back in his chair, considering this. Given what Connor Fraser had prised from Blair Charlston the previous evening about his past, it was obvious that the lifestyle guru was the common denominator between Donald Peters, Mark Sneddon and Kimberley George's father, Jonathan. The formal identification had yet to be made, but from what Charlston had said, it fitted that he was the man who had thrown himself into the bonfire. Ford had been so keen to look at Charlston, to get under that perfectly presented veneer and prove the man was no messiah, that he hadn't looked at the other possibility: that Jonathan George was just a grief-stricken father driven mad by his loss, and that nothing else was at play. After all, George had, albeit dramatically, taken his own life. But Sneddon and Donald Peters most definitely had not, one bludgeoned to death after being poisoned, the other gutted and strung up like an extra from *Game of Thrones*. And the common factor between them?

Donna Blake.

Ford reached up, ground his thumb into his temple and rubbed, used his free hand to grab the phone and call the press office. First he would get them to issue a statement in response to her report – they were probably already working on one anyway, that report making it open season for the press.

And then he would go and have a chat with Donna Blake, and find out a little more about her history with Mark Sneddon and Donald Peters, and why men she knew seemed to meet bloody, violent ends.

CHAPTER 52

It took only one glance for Connor to read exactly how breakfast was going to go. They walked out of the gym, the smile on MacKenzie's face collapsing like a house being hit with a wrecking ball as his eyes slid from his daughter to Connor. He closed the arms that had been thrown wide to embrace Jen as his steps became smaller, slower. Connor felt a rush of sympathy for the man, even as the image of Mark Sneddon reared in his head like the memory of a lost nightmare.

No matter what else MacKenzie was, he was still a father who had been looking forward to spending time with his daughter. A daughter who had failed to tell him she was bringing her . . . her what exactly? . . . along with her.

'Jen,' he said, pulling her into a hug, even as he pivoted her away from Connor. 'And Fraser. This is a surprise.' He reached out a hand and Connor took it, playing along as MacKenzie clamped his grip around his palm and squeezed. No point in getting into a pissing match with the man. Especially if he wanted answers.

'Mr MacKenzie,' Connor said, returning the cool gaze he received. 'Pleasure to see you, sir. Jen mentioned you were meeting for breakfast, suggested I tag along. I hope that's all right?'

A dart of eyes to his daughter. 'Why, yes, of course,' MacKenzie said, the warmth in his voice doing nothing to thaw the ice in his eyes. 'I thought we could go to Cisco's. It's only five minutes up the road.'

Connor heard Jen's approval, nodded his own. It was a small café on Port Street, heading back into the centre of town, maybe a ten- or fifteen-minute walk from Connor's flat. He'd been in a few times after an early-morning gym session, finding the coffee hot, the staff friendly and the food filling.

Not that he expected to have much of an appetite with the company he was keeping this morning.

'Good!' MacKenzie said, the same false note of cheer in his voice hitting Connor like an off-key note. 'Shall we walk? It's a fine morning after all.'

They set off, heading up the hill and into Stirling. Connor didn't need to look behind them to know that a sleek black Merc had grumbled into life the moment they started moving and would be tailing them all the way. If MacKenzie was worried enough to warn Jen about what was happening at the Alloa House, then it stood to reason he had put Paulie on guard duty. Connor wasn't sure if the thought should cheer or horrify him.

He kept a discreet distance as they walked, letting Jen and her father catch up. His own relationship with his father had been non-existent, but it was clear to Connor that Duncan and Jen were close. They walked together, steps in time as though marching, body language open and expressive, all wide smiles and eye contact. Connor felt guilt niggle at him. Yes, he was intruding but maybe, just maybe, Duncan MacKenzie knew something that would help him understand all this, get him one step closer to whoever had killed Mark Sneddon.

And that was a step Connor found he wanted to take. Very, very badly.

He was so engrossed in his thoughts that he missed MacKenzie's words, the older man's impatience needling him back to the present.

'Oh, sorry,' Connor said. 'Lost in my own head. You asked me something?'

'Yes,' MacKenzie said slowly. 'Jen was just telling me about the drama up at the Alloa House. Said you were hurt last night. Nothing serious, I hope?'

Connor couldn't help but smile at the contrast between MacKenzie's words of concern and his crocodile-dead stare as he spoke them. 'Nothing serious,' he agreed. 'Just got a little scorched. Though actually, now you mention it, Jen did say that you knew some people who were attending the event last night. Hopefully none of them got caught up in what happened?'

A warning flashed across MacKenzie's eyes even as his head jerked in the slightest not-now shake. 'A few of my former business associates were attending as guests of Charlston,' he said. 'Got an invite myself but decided not to bother. Glad I didn't, the way things turned out.'

Connor smiled, mind turning to the attendee list he had scanned for the ITOI event. Specifically, the corporate clients and VIPs. He remembered a few City-listed companies, recognised a few reality-TV stars, an odd Premier League footballer and then . . .

He snapped his fingers. 'Kinloss Construction and Robinson Haulage, right? Eh, Nicolas Davis, Mark McIntyre and Audrey Robinson.'

MacKenzie caught the admiration that flitted across his face, crushed it with a scowl dark enough to threaten rain. 'Very good, Fraser. I see you do your homework.'

'Part of the job,' Connor said. 'I thought I recognised some local companies, but with the way things happened, I never got the chance to meet any of their representatives. I assume they'll have gone now, if they've given the police their statements.'

'Yes, long gone,' MacKenzie said.

They got to the café, found a table and ordered, MacKenzie making a big show of ensuring the waitress put it on his tab. Connor wasn't sure if he was trying to impress Jen or him. Found he didn't care, his attention drawn to the car that had just pulled in across the road.

He turned back to the table in time to see Jen rise, chair scraping back, eyes fixed on Connor. 'I'll be back in a minute,' she said. 'You two play nice while I'm away.'

Connor gave a smile as fake as MacKenzie's, rose slightly as Jen stood and left. Watched her go, conscious not to let his eyes roam anywhere inappropriate in her father's company. Then he sat down again, let the mask slip from his face. 'So, Mr MacKenzie, I hear you told Jen that I would be quite busy this weekend, that she might be better off staying away from me. Tell me, any hints for the Lotto tonight?'

MacKenzie made a noise as close to a laugh as Connor had ever heard him emit as he reached forward and took the sugar bowl in the centre of the table into his palm. 'I told you, I knew some of the people who would be there, knew some would be high maintenance. Didn't want Jen getting in the way. Thought I was doing you a favour, is all.'

'Thanks,' Connor said, watching as MacKenzie spun the sugar bowl, knowing at least part of him was analysing how effective it would be as a weapon. 'Problem is, I'm not sure I buy it. Why warn her away from me when you knew it would get back to me? And why make sure Paulie,' he gestured towards the window, 'is back on duty shadowing Jen? Sounds to me like something has you worried, Mr MacKenzie. Care to tell me what that is?'

Colour flared around MacKenzie's bull neck, knuckles blanching as he bore down on the sugar bowl. 'Look, Fraser, just leave it. You've seen yourself there's a world of shit going on at the Alloa House this weekend, some heavy people involved.' A small flicker in his eyes, as though an unpleasant memory had stirred. 'People I don't want Jen anywhere near. And since, for reasons I can't understand, she seems to like you, I wanted to make sure she was away from it, okay? Nothing more.'

Connor felt a flush of anger as hot and black as the coffee in front of him. 'I appreciate that, Mr MacKenzie, I really do. You're just looking out for your daughter. But, in case it escaped your attention, two people died at the Alloa House last night. Both of them, like you, were fathers. One to a young boy who will never remember his dad.' Connor shifted his weight forward, the chair squealing. 'So let me be clear. I don't give a fuck about these "heavy people" you're so worried about. I want to know what's going on up there, and if it has anything to do with Mark Sneddon's murder. I swear to you I'll keep Jen safe. But you started this when you called her. So tell me, what or who are you so worried about? And believe me, if you don't tell me, I will shove a microscope so far up your arse it'll take Paulie a month to find it with a torch and tweezers.'

MacKenzie's eyes darkened. Connor felt a tingle in his temple as the sugar bowl scraped across the table. MacKenzie leaned forward, nose almost touching Connor's. When he spoke, his voice was a whisper rasped with hate. 'Now listen, you little shite, I'll tell you this and this only, I—'

'Dad? Connor? You both okay?'

MacKenzie whipped his head around so fast that Connor felt the breeze tickle his face. 'Yeah, fine, darling,' he said, voice calm and gentle again. 'Just telling Connor a joke that isn't really suitable for this time in the morning.'

Connor shrugged his shoulders, pulled his face into what he hoped was an embarrassed smile.

'Hmm,' Jen said, eyes telling them both she was unconvinced. 'Well, lighten up, the pair of you. I know you had some worries about Connor's work this weekend, Dad, but, as you can see, he's fine.'

MacKenzie turned to Connor, eyes cold and dead. 'Just fine,' he echoed. 'Hopefully it stays that way, especially now there's been a body found in the grounds of the hotel.'

Connor raised his coffee cup, tipped it slightly towards MacKenzie. 'Not to worry, Mr MacKenzie,' he said, 'I know the police. Know how they work. I'll be heading up there to coordinate my teams with their officers after this. But don't worry, I'll make sure to keep an eye out for your friends and say hello if I find them.'

MacKenzie nodded, a stiff, halting movement, as though he had glass shards in his neck. Connor smiled, glanced down at the sugar bowl the man still held. Sipped his coffee and wondered briefly how much pressure the thing would take before it shattered.

Heavy people, he thought again, running through the names he had recalled on the street. Nicolas Davis, Mark McIntyre and Audrey Robinson. Time to find out how heavy they really were.

CHAPTER 53

She sat with her back to the bathroom door, knees drawn up to her chin, hugging herself again, the shakes that racked her body coming in waves. From the living room she could hear the vague, discordant sounds of some kids' TV star belting out another overly cheery song, and her father cooing over Andrew. They had refused to leave when she arrived home, her mother stating in that cool, my-word-is-law way that she used in times of crisis, 'Now is no time to be alone.'

Donna tended to agree, but not for the reasons her mother might have expected.

She had held it together through the chat and the platitudes, her father's awkward hugs and her mother's insistence that she would look after Andrew while Donna took a break. There was no judgement in her mum's tone or gaze, none of the usual passive aggression that was the price Donna paid for them helping out with Andrew. And the realisation that her mother only truly became a real parent in times of crisis tipped Donna over the edge. She made her excuses and lurched for the bathroom, fumbling the door lock then sliding down, her legs suddenly liquid. She arched her neck, opened her mouth and screamed silently at the ceiling, willing the hammering of her blood in her ears and the stabbing pain from her jaw to drown out her thoughts.

They didn't.

What had she done? What had she become? At the time, it had

seemed so clear. So simple. She had an exclusive so she reported it. After all, what did she owe Mark, and what had he been to her anyway? The ex who had dumped her the moment she had become pregnant? The man who didn't have the courage to leave his wife and his comfortable lie of a life for her?

The father of her child. The man she had, at one time, built her life around. And how had she honoured his memory? She had turned him into another line, another soundbite. Made him the story instead of the man reporting it.

And why? For what? So everyone would know Donna Blake was the woman who could find the stories no one else would? So the big stations would beat a path to her door, begging her to front their 6 p.m. or 10 p.m. news bulletins? No, the clip she had recorded had already been dropped into the mincer of the news cycle, mashed, pulled apart and recycled into every other news station's rolling coverage.

She had done it out of revenge, pure and simple. The last laugh on Mark, using him to further the career that having Andrew had almost destroyed.

No wonder she was on her own. After all, who else would want to be with such a petty, vindictive cow if they didn't have to be?

She felt tears burn at the back of her eyes, ground the heels of her hands into them until angry white sparks danced across her vision. Took a deep, liquid breath, banished the tears and the self-pity. What was done was done. She could no more undo it now than she could go back and warn Mark and Donald about what was ahead of them.

The question was, what could she do next? What *should* she do?

As if in answer, her phone buzzed in her pocket. She didn't need to know what it was trying to tell her. She had diverted the call from DCI Ford straight to voicemail as soon as she had seen the caller ID flash up on screen. Of course he was going to want to talk to her: she had found one man dead, been intimately linked to another.

Linked.

The word stuck in her mind, like a piece of food she hadn't been able to swallow. Linked. Donald had got in touch, promising something on Charlston that would put her ahead of the game. A titbit, she now knew, that involved a messy love triangle, financial misdoings at a company that had gone belly up shortly after that, and a chain of events that ultimately led to two suicides, three if you counted Kimberley George's father.

But how much of that had Mark known when he'd got in touch? He'd seen the line about Donald's death and his first instinct had been to call her. What was it he had said? *I've got some background on Peters and Charlston that you need. Was thinking you could bill me as an investigative journo looking into Charlston.*

Was that why he had died? Because he had found something? It had to be. The alternative – that Mark had randomly fallen victim to a psycho while in the woods, to which Donna, indirectly, had sent him with her warning to Connor that he was in the grounds – was too horrifying to contemplate.

Whatever Mark had found, whatever he had teased Donna with in that phone call, it couldn't have been what Donald had wanted to tell her about Charlston and his past. Yes, it was embarrassing, potentially damaging for Charlston to be painted as a love rat who thought he could solve all his problems by throwing money at them, but worth killing for? No.

And there was another link, something else that bound Donald and Mark together. The manner of their deaths. Both incredibly violent, but something else, something more.

Both over the top. Overkill. One man with his head caved to a pulp, the other left to die with his guts dangling from his chest. Donna knew Connor had tried to protect her from that detail, and felt a strange mix of gratitude and resentment, but it had taken only one call to a source at the police's Bilston Glen call centre in Midlothian to discover the grisly truth.

Donna forced aside her disgust, tried to look at the facts objectively. Donald was an old man and Mark, while fit, no fighter. It was almost as if whoever had killed them viewed murder as a performance rather than as a means to an end.

But why? Why kill them at all? What was it they knew?

She took another deep breath and stood, sliding her back up the bathroom door, not totally trusting her legs, which still felt disconnected from the rest of her. She steadied herself, moved to the mirror

195

over the basin. Looked past the greyish hue of her skin, the puffy red bags under her eyes and the deep lines around her mouth that she couldn't remember being there yesterday. Instead, she forced herself to stare into her own eyes, see the person who lurked there, the real Donna Blake. The woman who wasn't motivated by selfishness or petty revenge or the need to be first.

She turned on the tap, splashed cold water in her face, slapped her cheeks lightly, bringing some colour to them. Looked herself in the eye again, nodded as she made a promise to herself.

She would find out why Mark and Donald had died so violently. Not because it was a story, not because it would put her on the TV. She had made a decision: no matter what happened, she would not report one more word of this story. Her penance for breaking the news of Mark's death.

No. There was only one story Donna was interested in now. Whatever had happened, it had robbed her son of his father. One day Andrew would ask why. And on that day, Donna would tell him. She owed him and Mark that much at least.

CHAPTER 54

Connor gunned the engine of the Audi, throwing the car into the corners on the twisting road that led from Stirling to the Alloa House. Houses and fields blurred past the car's windows, the landscape more agricultural the further away from the city he got. How long, he wondered, before the developers moved in, harvesting the land in their own particular way, raising crops of kit-form houses and cheek-to-jowl flats for would-be home-owners and commuters to snap up? Couples looking to start families and build a life. Couples who had never been forced to endure the horrors Connor had.

He pushed away the thought, focused on the road ahead. He always liked driving when he had to think – there was something about letting reflexes kick in and handle the mechanics of steering, clutch and accelerator that seemed to free his mind to attack a problem from a different angle.

And, right now, Connor had more than enough problems to attack.

After leaving Duncan MacKenzie and Jen, and receiving a cheerless nod of acknowledgement from Paulie as the Merc slid back into the traffic, Connor headed back to the flat. He jogged the whole way, kitbag bouncing on his back, part cardio work-out part anxiety to get home and start digging.

He ran the names MacKenzie had mentioned through the guest list for the ITOI weekend, found them all marked as complimentary VIPs with access to the after-party on the first night. It made sense on one level – invite your former partners, show them how well you were doing. But then, something about that bothered Connor. Construction and haulage were a world away from Charlston's new calling as a lifestyle guru, and it was hardly likely there would be many opportunities for Kinloss Construction or Robinson Haulage with ITOI. They delivered and built the bespoke kitchens Perigee had designed before it went bust. So why invite them along?

Thinking back to Charlston's performance with the punch bag, Connor knew the answer. Charlston wanted to torture his former partners with his new-found success.

Or was there something else?

He recalled the calls Charlston had made in the gym. Could they have been to someone at Kinloss Construction or Robinson Haulage? Possible, but – again the question persisted – why?

Frustrated, Connor had called Robbie, who was back at the Alloa House for the morning shift. Connor could hear restless tension in his voice, understood it. He had made a mistake in letting Charlston slip away from him but, if Connor was being honest, it was as much his mistake as Robbie's. He knew Robbie's strengths and his weaknesses. He had put him in a position where his weaknesses had been exploited. Time to play to his strengths.

He asked Robbie to do a background check on Kinloss Construction and Robinson Haulage, looking for links to Perigee or Charlston. Connor wasn't quite sure what he was looking for, but there had been something in MacKenzie's warning, something he couldn't quite articulate but could feel in his mind.

'Kinloss Construction, Robinson Haulage,' Robbie repeated, the sound of keys chattering in the background as he spoke. 'I'll see what I can dig up. Directors' names are on the guest list. I'll look at them as well.'

'Good,' Connor said. Then, on a whim: 'Add Duncan MacKenzie and MacKenzie Haulage into the search as well, see if there's anything. Biggest haulage firm in the Central Belt – if there were contracts going, he might have pitched for them.'

'Fair enough,' Robbie said, keys still rattling. 'When do you need this by, boss?'

'Soon as you can,' Connor replied. 'Thanks, Robbie.'

He'd killed the call, got up and made for the shower.

Now, heading for the Alloa House, he mused on how he was going to confront Charlston. With the weekend abandoned, Connor's only real job was a wash-up with Charlston, a check in with the police, then writing up the whole sorry affair for the Sentinel board. But something about the CCTV footage Connor had found of Charlston refused to let him go. His reaction to two deaths was to hide away to make two phone calls. Why? And to whom?

A memory of Mark Sneddon hanging from the tree flashed across Connor's mind, blurring with the eyes of the man who had leaped into the bonfire.

Two dead. On Connor's watch. And Charlston knew more than he was letting on. Connor was sure of that.

He pushed down on the accelerator, urging the car forward, eager to get to the hotel and whatever answers Charlston could give him.

CHAPTER 55

After failing to contact Donna Blake either at home, on her mobile or at work – where he was told by a brusque reporter with a voice almost as thick with Glaswegian as it was with contempt that she was off for the rest of the week – Ford had briefly toyed with the idea of sending Troughton and a uniform to her house. Had been distracted from the idea by the ringing of his phone. He snatched it up, felt his throat tighten as he prepared to give Blake a bollocking for not getting back to him sooner.

'Ford,' he barked.

'Malcolm? Malcolm, it's Walter. You okay?'

Ford sat back in his seat, let the tension drain from his shoulders and his voice as he hissed out a breath that was part disappointment, part relaxation. 'Walter, sorry. Been a bit of a morning already.'

'Yeah, I heard the chief constable was on the warpath,' the pathologist said, stretching out the syllables in 'constable', putting emphasis on the first. Walter Tennant's opinion of Police Scotland's bureaucrat in chief was an open secret, but the source of his rancour was not. Ford knew it was something to do with an incident at Tulliallan, the police training college in Fife, but the nature of the incident remained elusive to him. Whatever had happened, both men had gone to a lot of effort to keep it quiet. It was, Ford knew, something that curiosity would force him to ask his friend about one day, probably after too much to drink. But not today.

'You got something for me?' he asked, pulling his thoughts back into focus.

'Yes, actually,' Tennant said. 'You asked me to put a rush on the post-mortem of Mark Sneddon. Nothing hugely surprising. Cause of death was exsanguination and massive organ damage due to the wound in his abdomen. He had a significant injury on the back of his head, consistent with blunt-force trauma. Best guess, and this is off the record, Malcolm, is that he was clobbered from behind, then gutted before being strung up.'

Ford felt something cold scuttle between his shoulders, like ice-chilled spider legs. What would that feel like? Gasping for breath, kicking, fighting, feeling your internal organs slough out of you with every buck and twist?

'Jesus,' he muttered.

'Indeed,' Tennant agreed. 'Whoever did this was savage, Malcolm, utterly.'

Ford found himself nodding in agreement, memories from last night flooding back to him. 'Does the head wound give us anything to go on for the perpetrator?' he heard himself ask.

'Well, that's where it gets interesting,' Tennant said, something like humour warming his voice. 'I thought there was something familiar about the wound pattern, so I went back and had a look. And I was right. It was consistent with the wounds we discovered on a customer you brought in a few days ago.'

'Donald Peters,' Ford said, trying and failing to keep his irritation at Tennant's game from his voice. 'Oh, Christ.'

'Correct,' Tennant said, his voice quivering now, as though he was holding back a laugh. 'The injury I found on Peters, the one to the back of the head that probably stunned him, was the same as the one found on the back of Sneddon's head. Same pattern, similar location, too, which isn't surprising as both victims were roughly the same height. Probably caused by a ball-peen hammer.'

'Stand up in court?' Ford asked, almost absently, his mind racing.

'I'd say so,' Tennant replied, all humour gone from his voice. He had delivered the punchline to his own little joke. Now he was back to business.

'So whoever killed Donald Peters also killed Mark Sneddon? Fuck,' Ford said, a thought interrupting as he spoke. 'Don't suppose he went the extra mile and poisoned Sneddon as well?'

''Fraid not,' Tennant said. 'Of course, it was difficult to make a full inspection of stomach contents given that half of his stomach was spattered across the ground, but blood work doesn't show any trace of poison in his system.'

'And what was that again?' Ford asked, leaning forward and grabbing his pen. Just for an instant, a thought had scurried across his mind then vanished. Maybe the pen would help him remember it.

'Ethylene glycol,' Tennant replied. 'Or antifreeze, as it's more commonly known. Found almost two litres of it in his stomach.'

'Antifreeze,' Ford mulled, the thought tickling the back of his neck again. 'So somebody clobbers Peters then pins him down, forces a bottle of antifreeze down his throat, then smashes his face to a pulp. That sound wrong to you, Walter?'

'Not my side of the fence,' Tennant said simply. 'I just give you the facts and you interpret them. But it does seem like overkill to force him to down antifreeze then attack him anyway.'

Ford brought the pen to his lips. 'Yeah, it does. Thanks, Walter, you've been a real help.'

'No problem. Oh, and we're getting the dental records for Jonathan George sent over, should be able to formally identify him after that.'

Despite himself, Ford grunted a laugh. 'Christ, with everything else going on, I almost forgot about that. What type of a bloody week have we had that I almost forget a guy jumped into a bonfire? Anything else on that one?'

'Not really,' Tennant replied. 'Fairly standard. Suffered burns over eighty-five per cent of his body, but it looks like it was his heart that killed him. I think he suffered a cardiac arrest after he jumped.'

'No fucking wonder,' Ford said, trying not to imagine what it would feel like to have flames wash across your body like scalding water.

'There was one interesting thing, though,' Tennant said, as if he had just remembered it.

'Oh?'

'Yes, just what you said about him jumping into the bonfire. He had a prolapsed vertebra in his lower back, signs of surgery as well. Jumping like that would have caused him a considerable amount of pain.'

'Don't think that would have been on his mind,' Ford said, thinking of the single-mindedness it would take to douse yourself in petrol and leap into a fire.

The thought hit him like a punch, forcing him to sit upright and tighten his grip on the phone.

Single-mindedness.

'Donald Peters,' he said. 'Walter, can you tell if he was held down at all? Forced to drink the antifreeze? Or how long it had been in his system?'

The sound of papers being rustled over the phone. 'No signs of bruising to the chest, which would be consistent with someone pinning him down or sitting on him while they forced the antifreeze down his throat. Can't tell from the face, of course, as there wasn't enough left to see if there were any injuries consistent with being force-fed. Ingestion . . .' another flutter of papers '. . . looks like some of the glycol had been metabolised, but there was a lot in his stomach as I said. Why? What are you thinking, Malcolm?'

'That you were right,' Ford replied. 'That it is overkill. Poison a man, then beat him to death? Why? If you hate him enough to bludgeon him to death, why bother trying to kill him some other way?' He cradled the phone between ear and jaw as he spoke, calling up files on his computer. Found the case he needed, clicked open the file he wanted. The one that had been bothering him.

'It does seem unnecessary,' Tennant said. 'But who knows what goes on in the mind of a killer, Malcolm? Who knows why he did what he did?'

Ford didn't reply, instead staring at the screen in front of him. It was a crime-scene picture – the garden shed where Donald Peters had been found. Took a moment to understand what he was seeing, let the air whistle out between his teeth.

'Malcolm? You still there?'

'Yeah, yeah, sorry, Walter. Just lost in thought. Listen, thanks, I'll get back to you as soon as I can. And let me know when you get the formal ID for Jonathan George, will you?'

'Yes, of course. But what did you mean, Malcolm, that I was right about Donald Peters?'

Ford felt a smile play across his lips as he looked at the screen in front of him again. It was a wide shot of the shed, blood pooling on the floor, which was dotted with police evidence markers. In the corner of the room a bottle, neatly tagged, was sitting on a bench beside a stool. Ford didn't need to zoom in to see what it was.

Antifreeze.

'It was overkill,' he said. 'Poison, then physical assault? Doesn't make sense. But what if we got it wrong? What if whoever attacked Peters didn't force-feed him the antifreeze?'

'Hold on, you mean . . .'

'Yes,' Ford said, the idea hardening in his mind like setting concrete. 'What if whoever attacked him did so when he was already a quarter of a bottle of antifreeze down?'

'You mean he was trying to take his own life, and the killer just happened to interrupt? But why?'

'No idea,' Ford said. 'Not yet. But I know a woman who might. 'Scuse me, Walter, but I have to go. I've got an errand for Troughton to run, and a few questions to ask a woman who's been giving me the bum's rush for just a little too long.'

He ended the call, buzzed Troughton's extension and waited for the sergeant to get to his office. And, as he waited, he considered the facts. Peters had called Donna Blake, asked her to his home with the promise of information. Then, for some reason, he had decided to have an antifreeze happy hour in his shed. A happy hour that was interrupted by someone who didn't think poisoning was fast enough.

But why? Why call Donna then move to take his own life? And why had he been targeted by a killer anyway?

He was missing something. Some piece of the puzzle that would help the picture he was starting to see make sense. And, one way or another, Donna Blake was going to give him the answers he needed.

CHAPTER 56

Connor sat in the car, listening to the engine tick and cool as he stared up at the imposing frontage of the Alloa House Hotel. It seemed colder today, the stone walls and ornate sweeping staircase somehow harsher and more forbidding than he remembered. Not surprising, really, given everything that had happened over the last forty-eight hours. He doubted the place would be getting a big TripAdvisor rating any time soon.

He thought back to the call he had just received – Kyle telling him they had managed to track the bonfire jumper on CCTV, followed a trail that led them back to a second-floor room booked in the name of Geoffrey Kim. It didn't surprise Connor: if it had been Kimberley's father who had jumped into the fire, he would hardly have booked a room under his own name.

The room had been sealed by the police pending a forensics team getting in to examine it, and the thought irked Connor. He wanted to get into that room himself, see where Geoffrey or Jonathan or whoever he had been had spent his last hours before taking his great leap. Try to get into the mind of the man, see what lay behind those eyes that had bored into him even as he burned to death.

Questions. Too many questions.

He got out of the car, pulling his mobile from his pocket as he did so. Hesitated for a moment, then hit dial.

'Fraser, what do you want?'

Connor smiled despite himself. 'Sir. I just heard from my staff that they've identified the room most likely used by Jonathan George. I understand you've got teams going in to examine it shortly?'

Ford grunted. 'Aye. Should have formal identification on the body shortly as well. But why are you telling me what I already know?'

'Well, sir, I'm not asking you to compromise any part of the investigation, but if there's anything you can share about what your people find in the room, I'd be grateful. After all, I've got a vested interest in this case.'

Another grunt, deeper this time, as though Ford was trying to cough something up. 'Hmm. No promises, I'll see what I can do. But this isn't a one-way street, Fraser. I want something from you in return.'

Connor came to a stop, vague alarm bells ringing in the back of his head. 'You know I'll help you in any way I can, Chief Inspector.'

'Donna Blake. I need to talk to her but I can't find her anywhere. You got any idea where she might be?'

Connor winced. The truth was he knew exactly where Donna was. Glasgow. Chasing down a lead on Donald Peters. She had called him just before Kyle had, told him what she was doing, and that she needed to see him later that afternoon. He had agreed to meet her at the Settle Inn, a pub at the top of the town in Stirling, about five minutes from the castle. Not that Connor had had much choice about it: Donna's tone had left him in no doubt that they would be meeting, whether he liked it or not. All of which left him with a problem.

'Well, I spoke to her earlier,' Connor said, deciding to hedge his bets for now. 'I know she's still working on the story, following up a line about Donald Peters and Mark Sneddon, I think.'

Ford sighed. 'There's a fucking surprise,' he said dully. 'If you hear from her, tell her I'm looking for her, and that it would be in her best interests to stop fucking me about and get in touch ASAP.'

'Will do, sir,' Connor said, then ended the call. He looked down at the mobile. What was he doing? Protecting Donna? Hardly. She was close to the case, with ties to two of the three deceased, but she was hardly a suspect. So why not tell Ford she was in Glasgow? Why play coy?

The answer, Connor realised, was simple. And, he was forced to admit, a little childish. If Donna did find something in Glasgow, he wanted to hear it from her first. Before Ford and the rest of Police Scotland could take the information and pound it into whatever gap they could find in their investigation. After Donna's report that morning, Connor knew that Ford would be under pressure from the high heidyins to get a result on the murders, be seen to be enforcing justice and protecting the general public. Which meant corners might be cut. Not necessarily by Ford, but by someone else in the chain. And that was a risk Connor wasn't willing to take. He had watched a man burn to death, seen another swinging gutted from a tree. He wanted justice for those atrocities, but he wanted something else too.

The truth.

He thumbed a quick text to Donna, warning her that Ford wasn't going to stop looking for her, then headed up and into the hotel. He had called ahead, told Charlston's assistant, Anne, he was dropping in to 'go over the last of the wash-up with Blair and review next steps'. He could just have taken that meeting and walked away: with the damage done, the weekend cancelled and the police on site, there wasn't much need for Connor's services. But still, there was the matter of the note sent to Charlston's offices: *Graham died because of you. And for that you'll pay SCUM*. It made more sense in light of what Charlston had told him about his past relationship with Graham Bell and Kimberley George, but it was still a loose end that nagged at Connor like a mis-hung painting. And there was something about that note, something he could feel rather than see, that told him it was important.

He shook his head. Right now he wanted to talk to Charlston about two phone calls and a very ugly mobile phone.

Anne ushered Connor into the suite almost before he had stopped knocking on the door. He found Charlston had arranged himself in one of the deep leather couches in front of the fireplace. To Connor, he seemed to have shed his skin overnight. Gone was the open-necked shirt, expensive jeans and wristband, replaced with a sharp suit, crisp white shirt and a watch that looked big enough to choke on. The only

207

thing that spoiled the look was Charlston himself. His skin was pale and a sheen of sweat twinkled on his top lip, as though it had caught the same fever that was making his eyes glitter. Not that Connor could blame him. Overnight, the man had seen his brand and business effectively destroyed – for the second time. For Blair Charlston, his rebirth as a lifestyle guru had become a stillbirth – after all, who would take advice from a man who had had two people die around him in less than twenty-four hours?

'Connor, good to see you,' he said, standing and offering Connor his hand.

Connor took it, gave it a squeeze. Not enough to hurt, just enough to remind Charlston of the previous evening in the gym. 'Thanks for seeing me,' he said, waving aside Charlston's gesture towards the drinks cabinet as he settled into the couch opposite. 'How are things? You manage to get any rest?'

A thin smile stretched Charlston's face tight. 'Not really. As you can imagine, this has been a total nightmare. What with pulling the plug on the weekend, I've barely been off the phone with my clients, the legal team and everyone else who needs to make alternative arrangements.'

'Yeah, that makes sense,' Connor said. 'Tell me, is that what you were doing in the gym the other night before Donna Blake and I arrived? Calling clients?'

Charlston started, and Connor saw something flash across his eyes. Then it was gone, smothered like a candle flame engulfed by a rising tide of liquid wax.

'I'm not sure what you mean, Connor,' Charlston said, his tone aiming for confused amusement, his shoulders telling Connor he was feeling something else entirely.

'Before Donna and I found you in the gym, you made a couple of phone calls, Blair. One on an old mobile phone that looked like it came straight from Keanu Reeves in *The Matrix*, then another on your own phone. It got me thinking. Were they clients you were calling? And, if so, who was so important that, as soon as you heard a man had been found dead in the grounds of the hotel, you decided to slip away and call them? Because,' Connor shifted forward, propped his elbows on his knees, 'if they're that important, I should know who they are. For security purposes obviously.'

Connor could see from the minute twitching around Charlston's eyes and the flexing dome of muscle in his cheek that the man was working hard at his poker face. Problem was, he was holding a busted flush, and Connor had four aces.

'I'm not sure . . . I – I mean I . . .'

Connor held up a hand. 'Here's the way I see it,' he said. 'You hear about the murder of Mark Sneddon, then slip away as soon as you can. Grab a phone no one can trace and make a call. Then you use your own phone to make arrangements, probably with Anne here.' Connor turned and gave her a brief smile. 'So my questions, Blair, are simple ones. Why were you using a second phone to make a call straight after Sneddon's murder? And what did you arrange? See, something like that happening so close to a body being found hanging in the woods makes me uneasy. And there's still the small matter of the threatening note that brought you to Sentinel in the first place. Bottom line, I'm here to ensure your safety for as long as you're in Scotland. But I can't protect you if I don't know the whole story. So what's going on?'

Charlston exchanged a glance with Anne, found no answers there, realised he was on his own. 'Look, Connor, it's like I said. When we pulled the plug on the weekend, we had to let our clients know. Now, some people I work with are keen to be in the limelight and be seen with me. But there are others who think that trying to remould their destiny and admit they need help is a form of weakness. These clients pay a premium for discretion. I hope you understand that.'

Connor gave a noncommittal nod. He understood. It sounded plausible. But there was something . . . something about the way Charlston had set the scene in the gym, made sure the bag was swinging, given the soundtrack for the officer outside the door, that nagged at him, told him there was more to it.

'I take it, in that case, you wouldn't be willing to provide the names of who you called.'

Charlston gave him an indulgent smile. 'I'm sorry, Connor, I can't. You know that,' he said.

'No problem. Tell me, have you spoken to anyone from Kinross Construction or Robinson Haulage about what happened this weekend? Maybe Nicolas Davis, Mark McIntyre, Audrey Robinson?'

Charlston blinked, eyes filling with panic as his Adam's apple bobbed in his throat. 'No, ah . . . I mean, I know them, obviously, they were on the VIP guest list, but, no, I, ah—'

'So they weren't the people you called?'

'Connor, I . . .'

Connor let the silence stretch out, eyes never leaving Charlston's. Then, after a moment, he nodded, as though coming to a conclusion. 'Okay, Blair. I can't force you to tell me who you were calling, or why. I'll just have to take your word for it. I'm not sure if you'll be able to make it fly with the police, though.'

'Police? What do you mean?'

'Well, I'll have to tell them, of course,' Connor said. 'It's part of the timeline after the body was found. But if it was just clients you were calling, it won't be a problem. Though I guess they'll insist on knowing who you called, just to be sure.'

Charlston shot another glance at Anne, who seemed fascinated by something on the other side of the suite.

'Well, of course I'll give the police my full cooperation, Connor,' Charlston said with all the conviction of a doorstepping politician.

'Good,' Connor said, standing and offering his hand, which Charlston took. 'Well, I'll make sure one of the boys keeps an eye on you, and if we get anything else I'll let you know. Though I think you're fairly safe here now, what with all the police milling around.'

Another flash of panic in Charlston's eyes, brighter this time, almost feral. Then it vanished into a smile Connor guessed was almost causing Charlston to pull a muscle in his face.

'Of course. Thanks for everything, Connor,' he said.

'All part of the service,' Connor replied. He headed for the door, Anne materialising beside him to open it for him. She didn't say a word as he left, but the way she slammed it told him all he needed to know.

He stood in the hallway, thinking. What was it MacKenzie had said? 'Some heavy people'? Robbie hadn't turned anything up yet, but

Connor knew he would be doing a deep delve into the companies and, as much as that frustrated him, it took time.

But yet . . .

Heavy people.

He felt the urge to slap himself on the forehead. Stupid Connor, he thought. Stupid. There was more than one way to find out what he was dealing with here. If MacKenzie wouldn't tell him, Connor bet he knew someone else who would. Someone to whom he had once handed a gun. A man whose hand Connor had smashed the first time they met. A psycho who wore his suit like a costume, as though he was at a fancy-dress party and that was his idea of what normal people looked like.

Connor flicked through his contacts, found Paulie's number. All he had to do was frame the question in the right way and he was sure he would find out everything he needed to know.

And to do that, the question he was about to ask would have to involve Jen in some way.

CHAPTER 57

The thought was like a sewer rat. It slunk through the shadows of his mind, sleek and insidious, the chittering of its sharp little claws seeming to harmonise with Charlston's whining at the other end of the phone.

Murphy tuned the man out, making supportive grunts and uh-huhs at the appropriate times. Looked over to Boyle, who was standing next to the window, arms crossed, head turned to the light to show his unremarkable profile. To the casual observer he would look as if he was daydreaming or taking in the view. But Murphy knew better. He had seen this before. The stillness that would settle around the man like a shroud, the slack features and relaxed posture belying the mind that was running a hundred calculations and scenarios at once, like a lion watching its prey.

A sudden silence on the line drew Murphy's attention back to the call. Charlston had finished his rant, was now waiting to be told what to do next like a good little boy. Not for the first time, Murphy felt the sting of regret at agreeing to any of this in the first place. They had been lucky enough to get out of the Perigee clusterfuck unscathed, thanks to Charlston and his proclivities, so going back for round two was insane. He had known it at the time, his instincts, which had served him so well over the years, only dulled and placated by the promise of the potential rewards that lay at the end of this. Payment in full for the Perigee disaster. And a business opportunity that would make him one of the richest and most powerful men in Europe, Brexit or no.

But, still, that meant dealing with Charlston.

He took a deep breath, straightened in his chair, forced down a sudden shiver in his guts as Boyle turned from the window and regarded him with those cold, expressionless eyes.

'Look, Blair, it's fine. Meet us in an hour. We'll conclude the transaction then say our goodbyes . . . No, there won't be any problems . . . Yes, you did the right thing.'

He sighed, put the phone down harder than he'd intended, reaching for the crystal tumbler sitting beside it.

'Problem?' Boyle asked, taking a half-step back into the room.

'Charlston,' Murphy said, slugging back a knock of the vodka. 'Seems his security man just paid him a visit, somehow knows about the calls he made after the fun and games last night. Says he managed to fob him off with some crap about clients, but the spineless little shit is rattled.'

'How rattled?' Boyle asked, his tone indicating his preferred course of action depending on the answer.

'Enough,' Murphy said. 'Best we get this sorted out sooner rather than later. You were right. We don't want to be here any longer than we need to be. Especially now.'

Boyle glanced back to the window, as though he had heard something. 'So, this security guy. He's the boy toy of MacKenzie's daughter, right? I thought you had assurances.'

Murphy felt the vodka curdle in his stomach, viscous and dark. This was the last thing he needed. 'I had, and it's fine. He's poking around at the edges, has no idea what's really going on. By the time he figures anything out, if he figures anything out, we'll be long gone.'

Boyle turned back from the window, bland face slack and empty. But he couldn't hide the gleam in his eyes, a gleam that tightened his normally perfectly modulated voice. 'Two things.' He held up his hand, bunched it into a fist, then popped up a finger. 'One, we know Connor Fraser is a player. I looked into him when Charlston told us he was on board for this gig. He's an ex-copper. PSNI. Not a guy you readily fuck about with. If he gets his teeth into this, he won't let go, believe me. So we have to decide what we're going to do about that.'

Murphy felt his head nodding. Wanted to top up his glass – fuck, wanted to drain the entire bottle – but instead stayed where he was, pinned by Boyle's gaze. 'Okay. Second?'

Something that could almost have been mistaken for a smile twitched at the corners of Boyle's mouth. It stripped away the bland façade of his face, made his features taut and cruel, exposed the predator he really was.

'Second, we know MacKenzie can't be trusted. He gave you his word about this, and Fraser, yet here we are. Charlston is freaking out, we're sitting on top of a crime scene and the clock is ticking. Why? Because Duncan MacKenzie just wants to look out for his little girl.'

Murphy gulped the last of the vodka. After what had happened five years ago, he couldn't blame MacKenzie for being overprotective. Christ, if it had been his Gayle instead of MacKenzie's daughter, he would never let her out of his sight again. He suppressed a shudder at the thought that it had almost been Gayle. And if it had been, would he have done what MacKenzie had to ensure she was safe? He hoped so. Hoped also that he would never have to find out.

'So what do you suggest? You heard me. I'm meeting Charlston in an hour to finish this up. Then we can get the fuck out of here.'

Boyle nodded, a bored doctor listening to a patient list the symptoms of a common cold. 'One hour,' he said. 'Plenty of time. I suggest we keep close tabs on Mr Fraser, see what he does next. Won't be hard.' He jerked a thumb over his shoulder to the window. 'I saw him when he was leaving just now, clocked his number plate. So an hour gives us plenty of time to check up on him and deal with the other item at hand.'

'And what's that?' Murphy asked, the thought from his call with Charlston resurfacing.

'Charlston,' Boyle said, smile widening into a leer. 'I think we need to have a very serious conversation about Blair Charlston's next career move.'

CHAPTER 58

The café was on Royal Exchange Square in Glasgow, which sat behind Buchanan Street, one of the main shopping streets in the city. The square was dotted with a smattering of shops, restaurants and pubs and, of course, one of Glasgow's most idiosyncratic landmarks. The massive statue of the Duke of Wellington that sat outside the Gallery of Modern Art was just like any other, an imposing work mounted atop a stone plinth with the duke on horseback, staring resolutely ahead. Except, Glasgow being Glasgow, someone had decided that a little more colour was needed, and added a traffic cone to the statue's head. Efforts had been made to remove it at various times, but it had always reappeared, and when the council tried to raise the plinth to deter any more headwear, a protest campaign and a rally were held.

Donna sat at a table by the window, staring at the statue as she sipped coffee and braced herself for her encounter with Rimjob Ronnie.

Ronald Jeffries, a.k.a. Rimjob, was a legend in the increasingly shrinking village that was Scotland's print-media industry. Not for his prodigious talent or nose for news, but rather for his ability to survive and thrive. He had started his career as a general reporter at the *Westie*, worming his way onto the newsdesk and beyond by inserting his tongue firmly up the arse of the person just above him on the corporate ladder. He had earned a reputation for piling his failings on other reporters while playing favourites with those who could further his career or offer something else he wanted. Case in point, the six months he'd spent writing news schedules for a reporter on the newsdesk who barely knew how to type. It hadn't taken Donna long to find out that the reporter's skills had lain in her oral reporting rather than her longhand, and Rimjob was enjoying her career development a little too much.

It was never confirmed but the threat of newsroom scandal – and a sexual-harassment claim from an NUJ rep who was looking to make a name for themselves – had earned Ronnie a promotion out of the newsroom and into the wonderful world of Benedict Media's 'digital journalism' project. The plan, the brainchild of CEO Brenda Anderson, prioritised online news content over traditional news stories. Everything had to go online as soon as it was written, or sooner. The mad rush to get the story out first led to a slew of mistakes, both minor and major, and a *Westie* website that regularly crashed or spammed users with so many pop-up adverts that the story was rendered unreadable. Not that any of this mattered to Ronnie, who spun his best line of bullshit about the success of the project into a career leap to a national tabloid with the promise of 'revolutionising their content' as well.

All of this was irrelevant to Donna. She was in Glasgow to see Ronnie for one reason. He had been on the newsdesk at the *Westie* when Donald Peters was working the Charlston story. And, Ronnie being Ronnie, if there was legal action in the air, Donna was convinced of two things. He would have made sure he was in the clear. And he would know every single detail.

She looked up as he bustled into the coffee shop, threw him a wave and a smile which she hoped was at least halfway to genuine. He returned the wave, wove his way to her.

'Donna Blake! Well, this is a surprise,' he said, settling into the seat across from her. Still the same Ronnie, his skin unnaturally pale, bottle-dark thinning hair teased and gelled into some abstract shape that a mad professor would have been proud of.

Donna shrugged, ignored the way his eyes seemed incapable of meeting hers, drawn downwards by the seemingly irresistible gravitational pull of her chest. 'Well, I was in town, Ronnie, thought I'd look you up. Besides, I need your help with something.'

That pulled his gaze up to hers, and she saw keenness in his eyes. She'd piqued his interest, knew he would already be running the angles.

'Oh, what's that? I saw your work on the Charlston weekend, very nice. You working a line on that?'

'You could say so,' Donna said, looking down into her coffee for a second. 'I'm not sure if you've heard, but Donald Peters died a couple of days ago, and I wanted to talk to you about him and the Charlston story.'

'Donald? Really? I hadn't heard. I'm so sorry,' Ronnie said, his voice devoid of conviction. 'But we worked together years ago. I'm not sure how anything back then would help now.'

'Come on, Ronnie, you said it yourself. Charlston. You were on the desk when Donald was working on the Perigee story. He called me just before he died, told me he had something to tell me about Charlston. He never got to tell me, but I'm guessing you will.'

Confusion pulled Ronnie's face into a fleshy knot, then released it. 'I'm not sure I can help. Everything Donald did at the time is online – you can find it on the *Westie* site. I'm not sure what else I can add.'

Donna rearranged her cup on the saucer, framed the words in her head before she spoke them. 'You can tell me about the last story, Ronnie,' she said finally. 'You know, the one that never got published. The one that earned Donald a golden goodbye and a walk out of the door. What was it he wrote? I've heard the official line from Charlston, but now I want to go back to the source. So tell me.'

Ronnie's face paled, eyes growing dark and hard with anger. When he spoke, his voice was cold, clipped, as if he was reading a prepared statement. 'I can't help you, Donna. You should know that. It was all part of the settlement, which I had to sign as well, by the way. I can't discuss that with anyone, especially if there's a chance you'll report it.'

Donna shook her head. She'd been expecting that. 'I'm not going to report it, Ronnie, I promise. But I need to know. Charlston's already told me about Kimberley George, Graham Bell and the pay-off bid. But I think there's something else, something Donald was going to tell me before he died. So I need to see the story, and the details of the deal to keep it quiet.'

Ronnie put his hands on the table, pressed down. 'Donna, it was lovely to see you again,' he said, 'but I can't help you with this, really. I'm sorry but—'

'Milestone Marketing,' Donna said, eyes boring into Ronnie's. She felt her temper rise like heat in the back of her throat, but forced herself to keep calm.

'Sorry, what?' Ronnie said as he sat back down, skin paler than ever.

'Milestone Marketing,' Donna repeated. 'That's the company you sold the *Westie*'s spamming algorithm to, right? The firm that makes sure it's their clients who are always the clickbait on the website and social-media channels. Tell me, you going to do the same deal with your new employer as well, or are you going to try and sell restricted commercial information to an even bigger client this time?'

'I, uh, I – I don't know what you mean. I never . . .' He scrabbled for words, eyes growing wide and moist, angry patches of colour running around the collar of his shirt.

'Save it, Ronnie,' Donna said, feeling a pang of self-loathing as she realised she was enjoying watching the bastard squirm. 'I did some digging, found out all about your meetings with them the last time you were in London. You know, when you're going to sell out your newspaper, it's not always a good idea to expense the taxi fares to and from the offices of the people you're selling them out to. And using a gmail account instead of your work email? Who do you think you are? Ivanka Trump?'

He opened his mouth and closed it like a fish fighting for breath, his eyes darting around the room as though he was looking for an escape. 'What do you want?' he asked at last, his voice a defeated whisper.

'Exactly what I said,' Donna replied. 'The original story or stories Donald filed and a copy of the hush-hush agreement he signed. I'll take yours as well, come to think of it, just in case there's something I've missed.'

'That'll take me a little time to pull together.'

'Get busy, then,' Donna said. 'You've got till close of play today. I need this, Ronnie, badly.'

'And if I do it, you'll forget about Milestone?' he asked, the pleading in his voice as naked as the desperation in his eyes.

'Of course,' Donna said. 'After all, what are friends for? Now get going, Ronnie, and call me when you've got everything. I take it you've still got my number?'

Ronnie nodded, his eyes telling Donna he had her number in more ways than one. Then he left, staggering out of the coffee shop as though he had been drinking pints. Donna watched him go, urged him to move faster. Pulled her phone from her bag and scrolled through her contacts. Found Connor's number and hit dial. Ford and Police Scotland could wait till later.

CHAPTER 59

They agreed to meet at the gym, Connor guessing that Jen was at work and Paulie was standing guard outside. Which led to another question.

He spotted Paulie's Merc on the street, wasn't surprised when the car door opened and the chassis rocked as Paulie levered himself out of the driver's seat. He was a short, squat man, making up for his lack of height with girth. To the casual observer he would look fat, with a gut that strained at his waistband and slab-like arms that looked like the flanks of a calf. But Connor had seen behind the lie of Paulie's appearance, knew he was fat in the solid, squat way that small tanks were. Their first meeting had ended in a scuffle in which Connor had broken Paulie's fingers, but Connor knew that was mostly luck aided by the element of surprise. Which was why he found himself forcing his shoulders to stay loose and his hands not to bunch into fists as he approached.

'Paulie, thanks for meeting me,' he said.

Paulie looked up at him, cold grey eyes flicking across his face. 'You said this was about Jen,' he said, voice as dead as his gaze. 'So talk.'

Connor glanced over Paulie's shoulder to the gym. 'Here? Fine with me, but you know Jen won't like it if she sees you here.'

Paulie grunted, followed Connor's gaze back to the gym. For some reason, Duncan MacKenzie liked to have Paulie check in on his daughter from time to time. It was on one of those occasions that

Connor and Jen had gone for their first drink, Paulie trailing them to a nearby pub. Out of respect for Jen, Connor had never pushed for an explanation of why one of her dad's hired thugs acted as her shadow. He also didn't ask the bigger question, the one to which he really wanted an answer – why she put up with it.

Paulie waved his hand to the street, pointing with a blunt finger. 'Let's take a walk, then,' he said. 'There's a KFC over there, and Ah'm hungry.'

They set off, taking the underpass that led beneath Craigs Round-about to the KFC and petrol station beside it. As it was on one of the main arteries into and out of Stirling, the roundabout was always busy, and the background rumble of vehicles distracted from the carefully manicured lawns, shrubbery and trees sunk into its heart.

'So, what do you want?' Paulie asked, keeping his eyes trained straight ahead, as though he was locked on his destination and looking at Connor was an unnecessary diversion.

'I need some background,' Connor said. 'You know I met with Jen and her dad this morning. He said there were some "heavy people" milling around Charlston's ITOI event this weekend up at the Alloa. The names Kinloss Construction and Robinson Haulage came up. I'm not asking you to go behind your boss's back, but it's pretty obvious he's worried about Jen, and if there's something going on that she could get caught up in, I need to know, Paulie.'

Paulie stopped abruptly and turned to Connor, whose gut clenched. He had seen the look too many times before, the darting glances as targets were picked and punches calculated. Was this why Paulie had agreed to meet him? To get him down here and beat the shit out of him?

'Just what did Mr MacKenzie tell you?' Paulie said, his voice rumbling in harmony with a truck on the roundabout above.

'Not a lot,' Connor admitted. 'Just that he knew some people who were attending the event over the weekend, that he didn't want Jen being exposed to them. Fine as far as it goes, there are arseholes you want to protect your family from in every business, but this felt like something more. And it doesn't explain why you're on guard duty again, unless, of course, the people in question are heavier than MacKenzie hinted. You know what happened up there, Paulie. If

221

something's going on that could affect Jen I need to know, because neither you or MacKenzie are going to stop her seeing me.'

Anger flashed across Paulie's eyes, blackening the pupils, sharpening them with hate. 'Aye,' he grumbled. 'And she's normally such a smart wee lassie an' aw.'

As he spoke, Connor saw the hate in Paulie's eyes gutter and die, softened by something sadder and more wistful. 'Come on, Paulie,' he said. 'Help me out here. We both want to keep Jen safe. I promise, if there's some shit coming to my doorstep, I'll keep her at arm's length, but I need to know what I'm dealing with.'

Paulie sighed, shoulders rolling in the crumpled confines of his suit. Then he grimaced, coughed, twisted his head and spat a wad of phlegm onto the tarmac. He looked at it for a moment, then turned back to Connor. 'The boss warned me not to talk to you, right?' he said. 'Ah probably shouldn't. But he doesn't always see straight when it comes to Jen.' He looked away again, back towards the road. Then he sighed, shook his massive head, and pinned Connor with a cold, empty gaze. 'You tell him or anyone you got this from me and I swear to fuck I'll gut you, clear?'

'Clear,' Connor agreed, trying to keep the edge of excitement out of his voice.

Paulie held Connor's eyes for a moment longer, then started to speak. He told Connor about the past, about a night when the world had gone wrong for Duncan MacKenzie, his wife Hannah and their daughter Jen. About how MacKenzie had pulled every favour he had with Kinloss Construction and Robinson Haulage to put things right.

Connor was rooted to the spot, the sound of the road fading, leaving nothing but Paulie's voice. He understood now. Why Paulie shadowed Jen, and why she permitted it. No wonder MacKenzie had tried to keep Jen away from him and the Alloa House Hotel that weekend. Connor would have done the same thing.

What he didn't understand was how Paulie's story fitted with the murders of Mark Sneddon, Donald Peters and Jonathan George. Yes, the last had taken his own life but, listening to Paulie, Connor was convinced the man had been driven to that last desperate act by someone.

Which left Connor with two questions. Who? And why?

CHAPTER 60

Killing time while she waited for Ronnie to get back in touch with her, Donna found herself wandering the streets of Glasgow, haunting the landmarks of her old life. After meeting Rimjob and impressing on him how urgent it was for him to get her what she needed, she had fully intended to head back to Queen Street station and the train to Stirling, let Ronnie tell her what he found out via phone or email. But at the station she paused, surveying the work being undertaken there, blocky seventies offices being torn down to reveal the latticed glass and metal half-moon that made up the original Victorian frontage of the station. Without conscious thought she turned left and kept walking, skirting the edge of the Buchanan Galleries shopping centre then turning up towards Cowcaddens, stopping outside the building she had been kidding herself into believing she wouldn't visit on this trip.

The *Westie*'s home was that increasingly rare beast in the Scottish print press: an office that had been designed and built to serve as the headquarters of a newspaper. In Edinburgh, *The Scotsman*'s original home on North Bridge had long since been converted into a luxury hotel, the paper squeezed and boiled down until it fitted into two floors of offices in an uninspiring high-rise in the north of the city. Across the country, other papers were meeting the same fate, their homes sold off for flats or supermarkets or whatever else the publishers could get the most money for. But while the cuts had come, cuts that had cost Mark his job, the *Westie* had hung on to its home, a granite and glass reminder of a different time.

Donna looked up at the newspaper logo emblazoned along the front of the building in script so ornate it almost hurt the eyes to read it. She felt heat behind her eyes, blinked it away. She owed so much to this place. She had started her career here, met Mark here. The *Westie* had shaped her life and, despite everything, she missed the place and the life it had offered her, even if that life had ultimately proven to be a lie.

She turned away, angry with herself. What was she doing, wasting time on a trip down Memory Lane? She had a job to do. And a son waiting at home. True, thanks to a combination of day care, her parents and Sam picking up the slack with Andrew, she didn't have to get back to Stirling immediately, but still the thought nagged at her. And reminiscing about what-ifs and might-have-beens was depressing and pointless.

She turned away from the *Westie*, heading back into the centre of town, determined to catch the next train home. She would get Andrew out of nursery for the afternoon, maybe take him to the soft-play or the park, anything to spend some time with him and make him laugh. She was so caught up in making plans for the afternoon, her head filled with images of Andrew giggling in her arms or cooing with delight on a swing, that she almost didn't hear the phone ringing in her pocket.

'Hello?' she said, stopping in the shadow of Donald Dewar's statue at the top of Buchanan Street.

'Donna? Donna, it's Ronnie.' His voice was as thin as his hairline.

'Thanks for getting back to me,' Donna said. Diagonally across from her, a flash of red caught her eye: a young woman's dyed hair dancing in the wind as she ducked into a comic shop on the street.

'Aye. Look, I found what you wanted. Managed to get the unedited copy and the stories Donald did about Perigee that were spiked.'

'And the non-disclosure agreement? You managed to get that as well, didn't you, Ronnie?' Her voice was harder than she had intended, given an edge by impatience and the sudden nervousness that was gnawing at her. For an instant, she felt as though she was standing at the edge of a cliff, one step away from a sheer, never-ending drop into the unknown.

'Yes, yes, I got it,' Ronnie hissed. 'I'm going to send it over to you now, personal email, not work, okay?'

Donna felt herself smile. Typical Ronnie. Cover his own arse first. 'Understood, Ronnie. And thanks. But give me the headlines. Anything jump out at you?'

'I don't . . . Ah, well . . .'

'Come on, Ronnie, don't try that on . . . No way you didn't have a sneaky little look at everything before you called me. So anything catch your eye?'

A pause on the line, the sound of Ronnie's nasal breathing filling the static. When he spoke, his voice was a low, urgent whisper, and Donna had a sudden image of him pressed into a corner of his office with the phone clamped to his ear.

'Look, we're even now, Donna, okay?' he said, the desperation in his voice telling Donna he didn't believe that any more than she did.

'Fair enough,' she said, feeling her impatience rise again, flitting across her mind like the scarlet streamers of the comic-shop girl's hair. 'So come on, what am I looking for?'

'You can see for yourself in the stories,' Ronnie replied. 'Some more background on Kimberley George, Graham Bell and how far their relationship went.'

'And?' Donna coaxed, knowing there was more to tell.

'Well, that's not the best bit,' Ronnie said, unable to keep the edge of excitement out of his voice now. 'The big stuff is in the deal between the *Westie* and Charlston – you know, the stuff about Donald's golden goodbye.'

'Yeah, how much was that anyway?' she asked.

'Half a million,' Ronnie snapped back.

Donna felt the world sway for a second, her heartbeat pulsing heavily in her temples as electricity arced through her chest. 'What?' she whispered. 'That must be a mistake, Ronnie. No way the *Westie* had that type of money, even with someone like Charlston breathing down their necks. You must have got that wrong.'

'I thought that as well,' Ronnie replied, his voice regaining its usual smug, self-satisfied warmth. 'But I went back and checked. The figure is right. But even that's not the best part of it.'

'Go on,' Donna said, her lips now numb, mind racing. Suddenly she wasn't sure she wanted to know what Ronnie was about to say.

'The *Westie* didn't pay the money to Donald. Not one penny. The payment came from CCI Ltd.'

Donna frowned. She knew that name, had seen it in . . .

. . . in . . .

A sudden memory of Charlston sitting across from her in his hotel suite, fumbling through his explanation to Connor and her.

When it happened, when Kim lost the baby, I approached Bell, gave him a pay-off from Perigee . . .

The thought hit Donna like a slap. For an instant, it was as if someone had turned up the colour contrast on the world – everything was too bright and harsh, crowding in on her.

'Hold on. CCI Ltd? That's Charlston Capital Investments, isn't it? The financing company Charlston was running in London?'

'Yup,' Ronnie replied, chipper now. 'The *Westie* didn't give Donald a golden goodbye after all. Charlston did it and then dressed it up as from the paper. The files show you how. As to why . . .' His voice trailed off. Then he went on, 'Well, that's the five-hundred-thousand-pound question, isn't it, Donna?'

CHAPTER 61

It was just another hotel room – small, clean, functional. A tight corridor led from the door to the main area, which was filled with a double bed, an industrially upholstered armchair and a bureau on which a TV sat alongside a kettle and a phone. The far wall was taken up with a large window that looked out onto the front of the hotel and the charred ruin of the bonfire beyond.

The thought lingered with Ford as he watched the SOCOs buzzing around the room with almost regimented efficiency, photographing, measuring, documenting. What would it have been like to stand at that window, looking down at the pyre, knowing what you were going to do when you got there? What could drive a man to that?

The identification had come in not long after Fraser had called him, dental records confirming that the man who had thrown himself into the fire after a petrol shower was indeed Kim George's dad, Jonathan. Ford didn't like to admit it, but Fraser's people had done good work sifting through the CCTV footage from the evening and backtracking George to this room.

Ford spotted a familiar figure, raised a hand. 'Jim? Got a minute?' he called to the massive man in front of him. With his pendulous gut, massive frame and facemask pulled up across his scrabble of beard, Jim Dexter looked more like the blank outline of a clown from a child's colouring book than a forensics specialist. But Ford had worked with the man for years, knew that if there was something to find in this room, Jim and his team would find it.

'Ah, Malcolm, 'mon, we'll talk outside,' Jim said as he lumbered towards Ford, gesturing for the door. Ford nodded and turned, feeling Jim's bulk at his back as he walked up the short narrow corridor, seeing the soft flashes of camera and hearing rustles of paper SOCO suits from the bathroom to his right, like a backing track.

He found he was glad to be out of the room, felt the tightening fist of claustrophobia ease in his chest. Ford had never been good with large crowds or over-busy rooms, the people and the bustle filling his brain like static, making it difficult to think. It made managing case conferences and leading major investigation teams challenging and draining as he fought to drown out the background noise and focus on the job in hand. But focus he always did, and he took a certain grim pride in it. Another weakness overcome, another demon faced down. God knew he had enough of them.

'So, Jim, what you got?' he asked as they emerged into the hotel corridor.

Jim pulled his mask down around his neck, exposing a beard that was now more white than red. His cheeks were ruddy, sheened with a thin layer of sweat that glistened in the light. 'Not a lot so far,' he replied, the faint burr of the Highlands giving his voice a slight singsong quality. 'Nothing out of the ordinary, that's for sure. Usual medical supplies in the bathroom, prescription painkillers consistent with the back injury Walter mentioned.'

Ford grumbled agreement, remembering what the pathologist had told him: Jonathan George had damaged his back at some point and undergone spinal surgery to correct a prolapsed vertebra. The man would have been on painkillers following such an operation, and significant quantities of the drug had been found in his bloodstream. Which made sense to Ford. The man was about to throw himself into a bonfire. The last thing he would want was pain in his back slowing him down. But there was another explanation, one that, after reading the post-mortem report on George, Ford hoped was true. That, knowing what he was about to do, the man had downed a large dose of painkillers to numb himself to what was to come.

'. . . to show anything untoward.'

Ford blinked. 'What? Sorry, Jim. Been a hectic couple of days. You were saying?'

Jim Dexter's smile grew indulgent. 'No problem, I know how it is, Malcolm. I was just saying that there's nothing untoward about the room, nothing to show anyone else had been there or that George was planning anything bigger than his taking his own life.'

This, at least, was a relief. When it had been established that George had used an accelerant on himself, every officer had been forced to ask the same question. Had he planned something more? Brought more petrol than the amount he needed for his own personal use? In these days of weaponised vehicles, homemade bombs, the word 'terror' bandied around all too casually, it was only natural that the police would think worst-case scenarios. And while a sweep of the hotel and surrounding area had turned up nothing, the nagging worry had remained.

One less thing to worry about.

'You OK, Malcolm?' Jim asked, smile fading just a little. 'Don't take this the wrong way, but you've looked better.'

'Not the years,' he muttered, remembering a phrase from a film that his father had often repeated, 'but the mileage. I'm fine, Jim, thanks. Just a lot going on with this one and—'

He was cut off by his phone buzzing in his pocket. Flashing an apologetic smile to Jim, he turned away, felt a brittle amusement as he read the contact name on the screen. Christ, was the man psychic? He toyed with the idea of hitting cancel, diverting the call to voicemail. Instead, he thumbed the answer key and clamped it to his ear, turning away from Jim and another SOCO tech who had just joined him in the hallway.

'Fraser, funny you should call. You heard from Donna Blake yet?'

'Ah, no, sir, not yet,' Fraser said, the thin reverb on the line telling Ford he was driving as they spoke. 'Look, sir, I was just wondering if you'd heard anything about the search of Jonathan George's room yet.'

'Odd you should mention that, I'm standing outside it right now. Why the sudden urgency, Fraser? I told you I'd let you know what I could if and when I could.'

'Yes, sir, I appreciate that, but I've come into possession of some new information. While I can't divulge the source at the moment, I think I can predict some of what you're going to find in Mr George's room.'

Ford felt anger and frustration burn at the back of his throat like a cheap whisky. Who the hell did Fraser think he was? 'Look, Fraser, you know how this works. This is a police investigation. If you have information relevant to the case, you bloody well share it with me, along with the source it came from. Is that clear?'

'Totally, sir,' Fraser replied, his tone telling Ford that the message had been received, understood and ignored.

'So what's the big secret? What do you think we'll find?'

'Well, I, ah, I have reason to believe you're going to find pictures in that room, sir. I can't say for certain what, exactly, will be in them but I'm betting they'll feature George's daughter Kim quite prominently.'

'Pictures? What the hell do you mean pictures? Stands to reason a father would have pictures of his late daughter with him, especially if he planned to take his own life.'

'Yes, sir, I agree, but I think these pictures may be more, ah, intimate. They may show Kimberley George in, ah, well, compromising positions.'

'Compromising positions? What do you mean?' Ford's voice trailed off as he looked back towards Jim Dexter. The smile was gone now, replaced by a look that was halfway between shock and warning. In his hand, he held a small plastic evidence bag, through which Ford could see what looked like a splayed set of cards. He looked up at Jim, who nodded silent confirmation.

'Pictures,' he mouthed.

Ford felt his throat tighten. 'Get here, Fraser, now. Ask for Troughton when you arrive. He'll bring you to me.'

He cut the line before Fraser could reply, stepped towards Jim, who lifted the plastic bag for him and spread the pictures within as best he could.

The plastic meant the images were difficult to make out, for which Ford found himself grateful. There was enough to see, enough glimpses of exposed flesh and dark, seeping blood to tell him more than he wanted to know.

Two questions punched through Ford's revulsion. He seized on them, using them to block out the images in front of him. Why the hell would Jonathan George have these images? And, more importantly, how had Connor Fraser known about them in the first place?

CHAPTER 62

Murphy let out a sigh as they drove out of the Alloa House Hotel's gates, Boyle speeding up just as soon as they hooked a left and hit the main road. He felt tension he didn't know he had been holding on to ease in his shoulders, as though the imminent threat of a blow had finally been lifted.

It was done. Finally, after all these years, it was done. They were in the clear.

He should, he thought, have been elated. After the disaster at Perigee and the escalating nightmare that had been the last two days, it was done. After all the planning and plotting, all the long, sleepless nights waiting for a knock at the door or the flash of police blue to stab into the shadows of the room, it was over. The plan, the insane, improbable plan, had worked. He was set for life now. They all were. He would never have to work another day in his life. He could take Diane and Gayle and move wherever they wanted. Maybe to Skye, buy that cottage they'd always talked about. Put the past behind them. No more violence or pain or threats, no more scheming or plotting or running a half-step in front of the authorities. Instead, a quiet life filled with long days and relaxed nights.

Yes, he should feel elated. But all he felt was exhausted. Cored out. As though the last two days had robbed him of something vital, something he hadn't realised he would miss until it was gone.

He sighed, trying to rid himself of the thoughts. Melancholic crap, nothing more, brought on by the hangover from the adrenalin that had been pumping through his system for the last two days.

'You OK back there?' Boyle called from the driver's seat, cold eyes inspecting Murphy from the rear-view mirror. They gleamed like freshly polished stones under a jeweller's inspection light, and Murphy knew that Boyle was riding a hangover of his own. How long, he wondered, until the man in the driver's seat decided he needed a hair of the dog?

'Aye, aye, fine,' he said, not prepared to break eye contact with Boyle, willing him to look back to the road. 'Just tired after the last couple of days. Glad to get this shit behind us.'

'Agreed,' Boyle said, his eyes mercifully sliding back to the road. 'That Charlston really was a tiresome little toad. I don't know how you put up with him for so long.'

A memory flashed across Murphy's mind as a thick, coppery taste caught at the back of his throat. He pushed it down, wrestled the sudden gag reflex he felt tickling his chest. Not now. Not in front of Boyle. No weakness.

'He's good at what he did,' Murphy said, trying to keep his voice conversational as he writhed around in the seat, fishing in his pocket. 'A smug, sanctimonious bastard, maybe, but he knew his business, that's for sure.' He held up the item he had been looking for in his pocket, rolled it through his fingers. Amazing that such a small, innocuous item could hold such power. Could shape men's lives and destinies. Enriching some, ending others.

'Well, you don't have to deal with him any more,' Boyle said, a saccharine cheerfulness in his voice. 'I take it there are no remaining links with Mr Charlston that we have to worry about, that this was the final transaction?'

'Yeah, that's it, we're clear,' Murphy said. Yes, there were company records to, ah, manage and there would be paperwork, always paperwork, but the job was done. The item in his hand proved it.

He drifted back into his thoughts, fragments of his imagined life with Diane and Gayle. Walking around Portree, picking their way along the rocky beach down at the Sleat Peninsula, the mountains of the mainland jutting into the air like a monster's teeth across the water. Dinner at the Three . . .

'Hold on,' he said, noticing a street sign. 'Boyle, you missed our turn-off. The M90 was that way. Better turn around and—'

'No mistake,' Boyle said, his voice now as cold as the eyes that were back on Murphy. 'As I said, Mr Murphy, we've got a loose end to tidy up before we leave. Duncan MacKenzie put us at risk with his little chat to darling Jen, so we need to have a quick word with him about loyalty. Won't take long. Then we can be on our way. I also have to deal with Mr Fraser, but no need to trouble you with that. I promise I'll have you home in time for a nightcap with Diane.'

Murphy started, felt something in his gut shrivel and cower away at Boyle's mention of Diane's name. He opened his mouth to speak, protest, tell Boyle to forget it, just get going. Closed it, the words dying in his throat. It was useless. The look in Boyle's eyes, and the bloodied USB stick he now held, told him that.

CHAPTER 63

With its sturdy sandstone walls and gabled, slate-tiled roof, there was something vaguely school-like about Stirling railway station to Connor. He was in the car-park, leaning against the Audi, waiting for Donna's train to arrive from Glasgow. She had called him shortly after he had finished his meeting with Paulie, told him what she had found out. On top of what Paulie had told him, the new information on the deal between Charlston and Peters had slammed into Connor's mind like a caffeine overdose, making his thoughts run wild as his body itched with the need to move, act, rather than wait and plan.

It was, he told himself, this impatience that had forced him to call Ford. It had been a stupid, amateurish move to reveal his hand – and a potential bargaining chip – but it had proved productive, the inspector's blunt instruction to 'get here now' telling Connor all he needed to know.

But what did it all mean? He turned away from the car, looked beyond the station to the industrial estate at the other side of the tracks and the rolling expanse of the hills beyond as he tried to order his thoughts. So Blair Charlston had lied about the pay-off to Donald Peters. None of it had come from the *Westie*'s publishers after the threat of a defamation case, but from his own company's funds. But why? By Charlston's own admission, he wasn't above throwing money at a problem, as he had done with Graham Bell, but why do so for Donald Peters? Why throw half a million pounds at a reporter

235

who had written a few stories that didn't stand up to scrutiny or could be best described as tabloid titillation? 'City Slicker Takes Over Company and Gets Girl' wasn't a great headline for Charlston, but it wasn't a career-ender. So why pay Peters that sum of money? And was that linked to how Peters had died – bludgeoned to death in his garden shed? And then there was Mark Sneddon. What had happened to him in those woods? Who had he encountered when he was trying to sneak into the hotel? Connor had made sure his men had turned him away. And why had he had to die in such a brutal manner? If someone wanted him dead, it was the perfect location for a quick, silent kill. Why waste time mutilating and displaying the body the way the killer had? It was almost as if they were trying to attract attention, much like Jonathan George when he had jumped into the bonfire.

Connor felt a sliver of ice slide down his neck as he remembered the feel of George's flesh sloughing off his body like so much over-cooked meat as he dragged him from the fire. And then there were those eyes. Boring into him even as the fire consumed the petrol that had soaked into his body.

But what had Charlston done? And who had—

Connor's thoughts were interrupted by the buzz of his phone in his pocket. He half expected it to be Donna, glanced towards the station to see if a train was approaching. But, no, the caller ID told him it was someone else he had been waiting on.

'Robbie,' he said. 'What you got for me?'

'Did a background check on those names and companies you requested, boss,' Robbie replied, voice clipped and neutral. 'Nicolas Davis is listed as the chief exec of Kinross Construction, Audrey Robinson is chief exec of Robinson Haulage, while Mark McIntyre is company secretary. Both companies do pretty well, file their returns on time, so far so dull.'

Connor thought back to what Paulie had told him and the incident with Jen. A long shot, but still. 'Anything on criminal records?' he asked. 'Health and Safety fines, anything like that?'

'Nope, nothing, boss,' Robbie said, his tone telling Connor he had hoped he would be asked the tricky question. 'Both companies clean as a whistle, no haulage violations, no reports of drivers over-clocking hours or mileage, no accident reports. All above board.'

'I see,' Connor said, deflated. He had hoped for something more. He didn't know what, but he'd been sure there was something. Especially after what Paulie had told him.

'That's not the whole story, though,' Robbie said.

'Oh? Go on,' Connor said, cold needles prickling the back of his neck as he spoke.

'It's the company records, sir. You said to throw Duncan MacKenzie into the mix, see what came up. And what came up was interesting. We know Perigee did business with Kinross Construction and Robinson Haulage, but it seems it went a little further than that. There is a raft of companies that have been set up and subsequently folded that list Charlston, Davis, McIntyre and Robinson in various director roles. Probably to be expected if they're doing business together, better for tax purposes.'

'So what's the link to MacKenzie?' Connor asked, the vague outline of an answer forming in the back of his mind.

'Well, he's only listed in one, sir, Perigee Distribution Services, which was set up when Charlston took over at the firm. Thing is, he was struck off as a director just a month later.'

'Interesting,' Connor said, more to himself than Robbie. 'Thanks for that, Robbie. It's good work. Can you ping me over everything you've found and save it to the server? I'll have a look properly when I get to my laptop.'

'No problem, boss,' Robbie said. 'What do you need next?'

'Help Kyle with the wrap-up at the hotel,' Connor said, distracted. 'Check in on Charlston, make sure everything's in hand. Oh, and one more thing.'

'Boss?'

'Keep an eye on DCI Ford. I understand he's there now, for the search of Jonathan George's room.'

'No problem. Any message you want me to give him?'

'None at all,' Connor said. 'But I want you to call me the moment he leaves.'

'Okay,' Robbie said, voice heavy with wary curiosity.

'Great. Thanks, Robbie.' Connor said, then ended the call. A moment later, his phone pinged as the email from Robbie arrived – the information on the companies Charlston had set up, as requested. Connor was scrolling through the list when a text from Donna told him she was ten minutes out.

Ten minutes. Plenty of time to make one more phone call.

CHAPTER 64

How had he known?

The thought buzzed around Ford's mind as he surveyed the images splayed across his desk. How the hell had Fraser known about these?

They had been found in an envelope wedged under the mattress in George's room. It was A5-style, with George's address in Bridge of Allan printed neatly across it. Ford looked at the picture of the envelope, felt a dull shock shudder through his chest as he read the address: Fountain Road, just across from the library, all privet hedges and beige sandstone, barely ten minutes' walk from his own house. He looked up at the wall, at the photograph of Jonathan George he had culled from the internet and pinned there. An average man, tall, skinny, with a sharp, blade-like nose, intelligent eyes and a wide, heavily creased forehead topped with a mop of sandy hair. The face meant nothing to him but still, it haunted him. This man, this man who had turned himself into a Roman candle, had lived less than ten minutes from him. Had he passed him on the street, jostled him when he went for a pint at the Westerton? And, if so, had he been thinking of what he was about to do, planning the petrol and the leap and the painkillers, while the officer who would try to put together the pieces of the puzzle sat just feet from him, oblivious? The idea both repelled and fascinated him.

He tore his gaze from the photograph, forced himself to concentrate on the pictures on his table, the question again tugging at his mind.

There were about fifteen in total, all of Kim George. Some were of her smiling at the camera, a beach and a foreign sun providing the backdrop. But others were worse, pictures of moments no father should have to see. Of a woman lying on a bed naked, legs splayed wide, fingers playing. Of her from behind, the photo clearly taken by the man shoving into her. Ford let his eyes rove over the pictures, trying to push down the reaction they triggered with thoughts of Jonathan George. Ford and Margaret had no children due to some congenital problem that had left him with a cataclysmically low sperm count, but he could imagine how a father would feel at seeing pictures like these.

But they weren't the worst. Not by far.

At the bottom of the pack there were four pictures that turned Ford's saliva thick and poked at something dark in his guts with a blunt stick. Three pictures of Kim in another bedroom, again naked. In the first she was smiling at the camera, holding the point of a large, wicked-looking knife against a pale nipple. In the second she was lying back, exposed, the knife glinting on the bedside table.

Ford swallowed cold coffee and reached for the third image. It was a copy of the original, which was now with Forensics, but still Ford didn't want to touch it. He had seen worse in his career, from heads mounted on spikes to what had been done to Mark Sneddon, but there was something about this picture, about the grotesque intimacy of it, that filled Ford with a mournful fury that made him want to at once lash out, destroy something, and pick up the phone to Margaret. Tell her she was right, that he was done with all this. That he was on his way home, his warrant card left at the front desk along with a one-sentence letter of resignation.

Kim lay on the bed of the hotel, the cream sheets dyed almost black by the plume of blood that surrounded her like some kind of obscene halo. Her skin, golden and taut in the other pictures, was an ashen grey, her nipples now scarlet pinpricks on her exposed breasts. Her arms were stretched up above her, wrists pointing towards the camera, exposing the savage wounds that ran from her wrists to her elbows like bloody route maps. To her right, in the centre of the bed, lay the knife, the blade still glittering in the flash, this time not silver but black-red with blood.

The note was a photocopy of what was scrawled on the back of the last picture, of a hotel door, the number 617 on a brass plate above the peephole. Three sentences. Twenty-one words. Twenty-one words that would destroy any father, no matter how brave.

I know what Charlston did to your little girl. This was no place for her to die. I'll be in touch.

Ford tore his gaze from the note. The envelope had borne a Stirling postmark, showing it had been posted locally. Checks for DNA traces from the sender were ongoing, but Ford didn't hold out much hope. Whoever had sent this knew the effect it would have, what it could drive a grieving father to do. No, their best hope was that the search of George's home would turn something up, perhaps a follow-up note or a message from the sender. And then, of course, there was the other matter.

Connor Fraser. What was it he had said on the phone earlier?

I have reason to believe you're going to find pictures in that room, sir. These pictures may be more, ah, intimate. They may show Kimberley George in, ah, well, compromising positions.

Who had he been talking to? How the hell had he known? For an instant, the thought that Connor himself had sent the pictures flitted across Ford's mind. After all, it fitted. He knew what had happened to Kim George, wouldn't take much searching around Charlston's private files to find some intimate pictures of his former lover. Then it was only a quick call to some police contacts for access to crime-scene images and, hey presto, send them from a Stirling mailbox after you've removed the forensic traces you know the police will be looking for and you're set.

It was ridiculous, of course. Ford knew Fraser wasn't cruel. Angry, yes, but not cruel. There was no reason for him to torture Jonathan George with these pictures, to drive him, knowingly or not, to take the action he did. Ford remembered the report from the firefighters on the scene, of Connor pulling George from the fire, trying to help.

No, it wasn't Fraser who had sent these. But he had known about them. How?

Ford swept the pictures up, shuffled them into a rough pile, then slammed them into his desk drawer. Closed his eyes, willed away the after-images of Kim George. The he reached for the phone and dialled Fraser's number. One way or another, he would make him come clean about everything he knew.

CHAPTER 65

She handed him the bomb with a smile on her face.

Connor returned the smile nervously, feeling the warm weight settle into his arms and chest as the smile on the face of Donna's mother – Connor was finding it hard to remember her name – intensified.

'There you go, see,' she said, beaming now, eyes darting between Connor and Donna, who was standing beside him. 'He likes you. Thank you, Connor. Gives me a chance to say hello properly.'

'No problem,' Connor said, looking down at the child she had just placed in his arms. He had little experience with children, and what struck him was the almost staggering feeling of fragility. He was scared to hold him too tightly, even as Andrew squirmed and wriggled against his chest, burrowing in. And then there was the warmth the infant was radiating. It was like nothing Connor had ever felt before, a concentrated furnace. Connor felt his legs lock as his heart began to hammer in panic, sudden thoughts of dropping Andrew flashing across his mind even as the old stab wound in his leg began to ache. The injury had been inflicted six months ago, when Connor was fighting for his life in the grounds of Cowane's Hospital.

Thinking about it now, his current situation was almost worse.

After he had picked Donna up from the train, she had suggested heading back to her place, mentioning that her parents were looking after her son after collecting him from day care. Connor agreed.

He had taken a call from Robbie telling him Ford had left the hotel, which meant he could head back there if he needed to after Donna had told him what she had found.

Donna's mother had exploded into panicked activity when Connor had walked into the flat behind Donna, jerking up from the couch and offering her hand even as she exchanged questioning glances with her daughter. Connor had watched with embarrassed amusement as Donna reddened at her mother's questions, the girl bringing a boy home rather than the successful reporter and mother. It was, he realised, a side to her that he had largely forgotten existed. The last time he had seen it was on the same night he had fought for his life six months ago, when he had brought Mark Sneddon here, along with Jen, using her presence to rope in Paulie as a bodyguard for all of them.

Not his finest moment.

Introductions were made and Donna's mother – had she said her name was Irene? – had handed Connor the grandson-shaped bomb he now held in his arms.

'So, Mr Fraser, can I offer you a cup of tea?' Irene asked, eyes still darting over him. She had obviously passed on her looks to her daughter: the dark hair, high cheekbones and bow lips only slightly distorted by the passage of the years. Was this what Donna would look like in years to come?

'Ah, a coffee would be great if it's not too much trouble,' Connor said, trying to ignore the pain between his shoulder blades. With his size, he tended to hunch when he was introduced to new people, trying to make himself less intimidating.

'No problem at all,' Irene said. 'Donna?'

'Coffee would be great, Mum, thanks. But this isn't a social call. Connor is here to work.'

An expression Connor knew only too well from his own father flashed across Irene's face. Disappointment.

'Ah, of course,' she said. 'So you're a journalist as well, Mr Fraser?'

'Connor, please,' he said, ignoring the emphasis she put on the word 'journalist', making it sound like an expletive. 'And, no, I'm in security. I'm helping Donna with a story, and she's helping me.'

244

Confusion furrowed Irene's brow, as though the concept of someone helping a journalist voluntarily was alien to her. 'I'll get those coffees,' she said, as she headed for the living-room door.

Donna flashed Connor an apologetic smile as she stepped forward and took the baby from his arms. 'Sorry about that. Mum can be a bit, ah, funny about my job and looking after this one.' She raised the child in her arms with a casual half-shrug Connor would never have dared attempt. 'But she means well, I think.'

'No problem. I know how it is. My dad's not about to win any parent-of-the-year awards either.'

'Really?' Interest sparkled in Donna's eyes, brightening them. It made Connor uncomfortable, yet he was glad to see it. After what had happened with Donald Peters and Mark, it was good to see a little life back in Donna's eyes. Even if it was over something he would never tell her about.

'So, what did you get from your pal in Glasgow?' he asked, wincing internally at the clumsy attempt to change subject.

She held his gaze for a moment too long, making some kind of decision. Shrugged, then headed over to a desk in the corner of the room where a laptop sat.

'Like I told you on the phone, he got me access to the legal deal that was struck between the *Westie* and Perigee. It shows that the pay-off came from Charlston himself, not the paper, which is odd.'

Connor nodded agreement. If you were going to pay someone off to stop them writing a bad story, why dress it up as a gagging deal with the paper they worked for? Why not just do an under-the-table deal with the reporter directly and keep everyone else out of it?

'Anything else?' he asked, following her to the computer as she sat in the chair in front of it and settled Andrew on her lap.

'Well, there are the stories,' she said, using the trackpad and keyboard one-handed. 'I mean the ones that didn't see print . . . Can you take him while I find them?' She offered up Andrew like a sacrifice, and Connor took him, his leg aching anew.

'See, there were a load of stories that were subbed down or completely spiked. But I've got the originals here, or at least all the originals Rimjob managed to get his hands on.'

'Rimjob?' Connor asked, sure he had misheard her.

'Sorry, nickname for my contact,' Donna said distractedly as the light from the laptop screen danced across her face. 'Yeah, here they are.' She pointed a finger to the screen and Connor leaned in as far as he could. It was an attachment to an email – a zipfile, with what looked like a dozen stories and a handful of images attached.

'So you think there's something in here that explains all this?' Connor asked. 'Something that explains why Donald and Mark . . .' He trailed off, found himself unwilling to complete the sentence with a child in his arms.

'Maybe,' Donna said, face hardening. 'It's all I've got. And whatever is going on, it all started when Donald called me, so there has to be a link, don't you think?'

'Makes sense,' Connor said. 'But it's going to take time to go through all these, and I'm not sure time is something we've got a lot of. Charlston could leave as soon as the police tell him he's clear to go.'

Donna blew out a frustrated breath. 'No other way around it,' she said. 'We have no idea what we're looking for, so I can't run a search. Maybe the best thing to do would be to split up. You head for the Alloa House and I'll read up here, try to find something.'

Connor looked down at her for a moment. The plan made sense. After all, she had Andrew to consider, and working from home would solve a lot of her childcare problems. But was there something more to this? Was she trying to get him out of the way, keep whatever she found to herself? She had cut him out before, most notably when she had gone around him to get the interview with Charlston, so why wouldn't she do it again now? But if that was the case, why invite him into her home in the first place? Why call him from the train?

'Good plan,' Connor agreed. He moved to hand Andrew back to his mother, paused, a thought flashing through his mind.

Parents and children.

'Try searching for Kinross Construction and Robinson Haulage. Also the names Nicolas Davis, Mark McIntyre, Audrey Robinson and Duncan MacKenzie.'

'Hold on, MacKenzie. As in father of . . .?'

'Yeah,' Connor said, holding her gaze. He had called Jen before Donna had arrived, asked her if everything was okay. Had meant to ask her about the names he had just given Donna, found that, after what Paulie had told him, he didn't know how to.

'Right,' Donna said, as she typed, her grace and accuracy shaming him and his own clumsy picking at a keyboard when he had to type something up.

The computer made a small chime as it found hits, three stories among the files and two images. Donna swivelled the laptop slightly so Connor could see over her shoulder, then opened the first of the files.

A few minutes later, Irene came back and put coffees in front of them before taking Andrew 'for a feed before Sam arrives'. They mumbled their thanks and kept reading. After a few moments, Connor forgot about the coffee. Instead, his entire focus was on the screen in front of him. The screen that told him he had been handed another bomb, one which could go off at any moment.

CHAPTER 66

His thoughts were as splintered as the windscreen, random ideas and images radiating out from one moment of impact in an impossible jumble. He blinked, wiped a blood-streaked hand across his face, forced himself to breathe, to think. Let the world back in enough to hear the discordant howl of the car's engine, found that, for the first time since he had passed his test more than thirty years ago, he had to think through the sequence of events needed to change gear. Ease off accelerator. Press in clutch. Change up. Release clutch slowly. Foot back on gas. He went through the process slowly, mechanically, using the familiar mundanity to calm himself.

Checked the rear-view mirror, saw the road behind him was clear. Reluctantly, he eased off the accelerator, bringing the car back down to a more normal speed.

'Fuck!' The expletive was out before he was aware he was going to shout it, carried from him on a wave of anger and self-loathing.

Stupid. So fucking stupid. He had spent so long worrying about Jen, warning her to stay safe, putting measures in place to make sure she was, that he'd forgotten to worry about himself.

They had arrived at the yard without ceremony, pulling up in front of the main office in a large SUV that looked like it had just been driven out of a showroom. Duncan had recognised Boyle the moment he had slid out of the driver's seat, buttoning his forgettable

248

suit and moving round the back, opening the door for the passenger in the rear of the car like a chauffeur.

Despite himself, Duncan had grunted a laugh at the irony of that. One look at Boyle, at that gaunt face and small, hard eyes, told him that, while Murphy was calling the shots, it was Boyle who was in the driver's seat. In every sense.

He turned from the window and slid his jacket on, slipped his hand into the pocket and moved the dead weight that was there to his waistband. Then he turned and headed out of the office, meeting Murphy and Boyle in the small reception area. Didn't know whether it was good luck or bad that no one else was about, everyone either on the yard or out making deliveries.

'Ah, Duncan,' Murphy said, striding over and offering a hand. 'Good to see you again.'

'Ian,' Duncan said, taking Murphy's hand, noticing that Boyle slid to the corner of the room like a shadow. 'This is a surprise. What brings you here?'

'Well, you'll have heard about the, ah, unpleasantness up at the Alloa House surrounding Blair Charlston. I thought I'd take the chance to pop in on you while I was in the area. Could we perhaps talk in your office?'

'Ah, sorry,' Duncan said. 'I'm just heading out.' The last thing he wanted was to be trapped in a small room with either of these men.

A darting glance between Murphy and Boyle, the latter swinging around the room so he was behind Duncan. 'No problem,' Murphy said. 'This will only take a minute. We just wanted to check something with you.'

'Oh, what's that?' Duncan said as he moved towards the door slowly. He felt the weight of the gun press into his back, resisted the urge to draw it. Better to front it out if he could.

He managed to get outside, keys already in hand. Plipped the central locking on his car, which was only about thirty feet away in the director's space straight outside the office. Thirty feet. No distance at all, really.

Normally.

'Well, it's just that when I was talking to Blair earlier, he said that one of his security people had mentioned some mutual business associates of ours, Kinloss Construction and Robinson Haulage. Given the sensitivity of our dealings with them, we wanted to make sure you hadn't been bothered by this. After all, we know that Jen is, ah, close to the man leading the security operation for Blair.'

Duncan forced down the cold ripple of revulsion he felt at Murphy speaking Jen's name. 'No, no bother at all,' he said. 'And, yes, Jen does know the security chief up there, a man by the name of Connor Fraser. He uses the gym she works at. Wouldn't say they were close at all. But, no, he's not asked me about any of this. Not that it matters – you know I wouldn't say anything if he did.'

Boyle took a step forward, Duncan's breath catching in his throat as he reached into his jacket. He tensed, ready to reach for his own weapon, relaxed slightly when Boyle produced a phone and started to fiddle with it.

'Hmm, not close?' Boyle said in that average, forgettable voice of his. No anger, no real emotion at all. 'So none of this came up when you had an intimate little chat with Mr Fraser over breakfast the other morning?' He lifted the phone to eye level, showing Duncan the image that was there. Him and Connor, leaning conspiratorially close over the table at Cisco's.

'What the fuck?' Duncan whispered. 'You're having me followed? What gives you the fucking right to . . .?'

Murphy raised a hand. 'You know what gives us the right, Duncan. This weekend has been a long time coming. And while you didn't have the balls to see it through to the end, you know enough to drag us all into the shit if you want to. So when I see images like this of you cosying up to a former police officer, and then I hear from Blair that this same man is asking some awkward questions about former associates, I tend to get nervous. Surely you understand that.'

Duncan clenched his jaw, hissed his words through bared teeth. Outrage churned through him, mixed with something darker and more bitter. Guilt. Because they were right. He had spoken to Connor. Not about all of it. But enough.

'What I understand is that you can fuck off. Now. This guy,' he jabbed a finger at the phone, 'is seeing my daughter so of course I want to check him out. But you know me better than that. You think I told him anything about what's really going on? Why the fuck would I do that?'

'To protect your little girl,' Boyle said, his tone almost bored. 'We all know what happened a few years ago, that you'd do anything to make sure it doesn't happen again. And if we find out you've been telling Mr Fraser things you shouldn't, it will happen again, Mr MacKenzie. I promise you that.'

Duncan was moving before he realised it, lunging for Boyle, propelled forward by an explosion of rage and fear, his mind filled with thoughts of that night, years before. He grabbed Boyle by the lapels, drove him back into the roughcast wall of the office.

'Fucking cunt! I'll kill you!' he screamed, spittle peppering Boyle's insanely calm face. A smile flashed across Boyle's mouth, quick and sharp as a switchblade, then he grabbed Duncan's wrists. The grip was vice-like, irresistible, pinning him as Boyle twisted his body then swept Duncan's leg from beneath him and pushed him away. He fell to the ground, grunted as the hard earth punched the air from his lungs, and scrambled back.

Boyle advanced, smoothing his jacket down. He flashed a look towards Murphy, who sighed, then nodded agreement.

Duncan scrabbled back, trying to get his feet under himself, lurched into a crouch, flailed for the gun in his wristband. No time. Launched himself forward, aiming to rugby tackle Boyle, who pirouetted with impossible grace and dodged the blow.

Duncan screamed as he felt fire lance its way up his back, bounced off the wall, then drew himself up. The harled wall dug into him, dull needles of pain that seemed to intensify the growing warmth in his back. He reached behind himself, felt tacky, slick blood coat his hand even as Boyle raised the knife.

'Come on, then, you fuck,' Duncan hissed, voice thick now. He could feel his teeth beginning to chitter, knew he was going into shock. Tried to focus. All that mattered was that knife. Getting it from Boyle and shoving it into that dead, empty face of his as hard as he could. For Hannah. For Jen.

Boyle tilted his head then stepped forward, rotating the knife so the blade ran up the outside of his wrist. Duncan tensed, willed his legs to move. Felt frustrated tears prick his eyes as he fumbled for the gun in his waistband, blood-slicked hand sloughing off it.

Boyle smiled, a predator moving in on wounded prey. Was this what Mark Sneddon had seen in the moments before his death? The devil swathed in banality, only the eyes and teeth hinting at the savagery that lay behind the façade? Was this—

'Oi, boss, you okay?'

The shout pinned Boyle to the spot. Duncan blinked up, saw Eddie walking round the corner of the building from the main part of the yard that lay behind the office block. Felt a claustrophobic stab of panicked relief as his site manager approached, wary curiosity etched into his face.

Moving with practised precision, Boyle shifted to the side, shielding the knife from view, while Murphy stepped forward, hands up, placating, putting himself between Eddie, Boyle and Duncan. 'Nothing to worry about,' he said, voice velvet-soft. 'We're just having . . .'

'Eddie, fucking move!' Duncan bellowed, the effort causing a fresh column of fire to lance up his back. He twisted, finally managing to get a grip on the gun, levelling it at Boyle, whose smile shifted from artifice to genuine. He was enjoying this. The psycho was actually enjoying this.

'Jesus Christ!' Eddie's voice was a jagged squeak. He raised his hands in a what-the-fuck gesture. 'Boss, what the hell is going on? I—'

Duncan pushed himself off the wall, edged his way past Boyle, careful to stay out of arm's reach, gesturing for Murphy to step beside his partner, putting them up against the wall of the office and clearing a path to the car.

'Eddie, back off, slowly,' Duncan said, eyes not leaving Boyle. 'Get into my car. We're leaving.'

'Not happening,' Boyle whispered, his voice still bored and detached.

'Fuck you!' Duncan hissed, tasting blood in his mouth. He edged past them, got parallel with his car, eased the driver's door open.

'Come on, Eddie, get in, we really have to—'

The shot was an explosion in the charged silence of the yard, a thunderclap that drowned out the world. Duncan ducked down reflexively, saw Eddie bounce off the passenger's side of the car and fall to the ground in a plume of blood and brain matter. Looked up, saw Murphy standing there, gun in hand, training it on him now.

'Get away from the car, Duncan. There's nothing—'

Duncan lunged forward, landing roughly in the driver's seat. Stabbed at the start button on the console, heard the engine roar into life. Shifted into first, then buried the accelerator into the floor, the car lurching forward. The front end bucked violently upwards, and the cabin was filled with a wet, popping snap. Duncan felt his stomach lurch as he realised he had just run over Eddie's corpse.

He flailed for the wheel, got a grip of it. Felt the back end of the car kick out, then correct, aimed roughly for Murphy, who wasn't fast enough to get out of the way. A booming thud that Duncan felt reverberate through the car, and Murphy spun away, arms reaching for the sky, suit jacket pulled up and over his head. Duncan blinked, hard, trying to see past the crack Murphy's body had put into the windscreen with the impact. Looked in the rear-view, saw the bloodied smear of Eddie's body, Boyle rushing across the car park to his boss.

He drove out of the yard and turned left, heading for Stirling. Forced himself to slow down, ignore the panic that hammered in his chest and the agony in his back that urged him to drive, *just fucking drive!* as fast as he could.

He blinked, wiped a blood-streaked hand across his face, forced himself to breathe, to think.

They had been following him. The fuckers had actually been following him. And they knew about Jen, and her connection to Connor Fraser.

He reached for the screen in the centre of the dashboard, left bloodied fingerprints on it as he scrolled through menus and found the phone option. Hit dial on the contact he wanted, willed them to answer, Boyle's cold smile filling his thoughts as he waited. The memory of the man's words hurt more than Duncan's ruined back.

If we find out you've been telling Mr Fraser things you shouldn't, it will happen again, Mr MacKenzie. I promise you that.

He pushed down on the accelerator. No. No fucking way. Never again. He had promised Hannah. Nothing else mattered now. Not the business, not the secrets he had kept for so long, not the future. All that mattered was keeping Jen safe.

And if he had to kill again to do that, it was a price well worth paying.

CHAPTER 67

Connor could have sworn he heard the plastic casing of the phone creak as he tightened his grip on it. He saw Donna glance nervously at him, realised his voice must have been harsher on the phone than he'd thought.

He took a breath, forced himself to ease his grip. Spoke again.

'So you're telling me Charlston's getting ready to leave, Robbie, that right?'

'Yeah,' Robbie said, voice cold. 'Didn't think there'd be a problem, boss. I checked with the police, that DS Troughton we've been liaising with. He says they've completed their interviews with him for the moment, and they have his contact details for any follow-ups. The event here is done, and he and his assistant were keen to get away, so I didn't see a problem. Kyle's getting a car ready for him now, should be leaving for Edinburgh airport in about twenty minutes.'

Connor ground his thumbs into his eyes. Keen to get away, he thought. I bet he is. But to have one of Connor's own people drive him away from the hotel? Well, that was just taking the piss. He remembered his conversation with Ford, their agreement that, whatever happened, they wanted Charlston in the hotel where they could find him. If he headed back to London there was little chance he would come back to Scotland, which would complicate any investigation with the added layers of bureaucracy that cross-border policing always brought.

Neither Connor nor Ford had any time for that. For their own reasons, they both wanted answers – and both believed Charlston had them.

'Get on comms to Kyle. Tell him to delay that car. No, I don't care what he tells him, but I want Charlston to stay put. Tell him the location is secured, both by the police and us, so it's the safest place for him. I'll be back as soon as I can – tell him I'm running down some lines on the note he was sent and I'll drive him to the airport personally. Thanks, Robbie.'

He ended the call before Robbie could complain, cast a nervous glance at Donna. Saw nothing in her posture or eyes that told him his voice had given her another scare.

'I take it Charlston has tried to get the hell out of Dodge,' she said.

'Yeah,' Connor said, pocketing the phone.

Donna nodded. It made sense. After what they had just learned, the last thing Blair Charlston would want to do was stick around the Alloa House, or anywhere in Central Scotland for that matter.

From the files Donna's contact had managed to get, it was clear that Donald Peters had dug a lot deeper into Blair Charlston's dealings with Perigee than just his predilection for picking up pregnant women. It was all laid out in the stories and research notes he had compiled, dating all the way back to when Charlston had stepped in and bought Perigee Kitchens out of administration. It had been a standard deal: buy the company for a nominal fee with the understanding that the new owners take on the debt and the pension liabilities, which, in Perigee's case, totalled £8.5 million. But where it got interesting was the consortium Charlston had assembled to buy Perigee in the first place. Charlston Capital Investments, the City-based company he had used before his rebirth as a life-coach guru.

Where it got even more interesting were the other investors who, Peters had discovered, were listed as trusts based on Jersey. Company records for the time showed that the wages, accounts and assets of Perigee were handled by a White Cliffs Trust, which was based in Jersey's capital, St Helier. Charlston and his other business partners, including Nicolas Davis, Mark McIntyre and Audrey Robinson, were paid through this offshore company, with the majority of their payments being made in tax-free loans from the White Cliffs Trust. Connor was no finance whiz, but he recognised the set-up quickly enough: he had read about it a couple of years ago when some A-list pop stars, celebrities and comedians had been caught out using the arrangement to reduce their tax bills. It wasn't illegal but the morality was questionable – and it made for a hell of a headline, one of which Peters had suggested: 'Kitchen Firm Saviour Dines Out on Millions in Tax Dodge'.

Which was, Connor realised, a problem. Donna had told him that, from what she could see, the unpublished stories were solid. The facts were clear and undisputed, from the Companies House records to the timeline of Charlston setting up the companies and trusts and ultimately buying Perigee. It was strong stuff but, provided Charlston and the other parties involved were given a right to reply, the stories would stand up in court and be defendable by the *Westie* or any other newspaper. So why had they been pulled? And why had Charlston made such a massive payout to Peters?

Connor thought he knew the answer, could see in Donna's eyes that she had come to the same conclusion. But he kept quiet, not wanting to sully the memory of her former colleague, the friend she had found battered to death.

'So what do we do now?' Donna asked, startling Connor from his thoughts.

He shrugged. 'Keep digging,' he said. 'I've bought us some time with the promise to get Charlston out of town myself, and I think that, after what we've found in those files, it's worth looking at the other company records my people managed to dig up.'

Donna leaned back in her chair, groaned. Connor could tell from her eyes, reddened from reading through all of Peters's files, that the last thing she needed was more reading. But it was the logical thing to do.

She stood, straightened her back. 'Get yourself sorted out, then,' she said, nodding down to her laptop, 'and we'll take a look. You want more coffee?'

'Yeah, please,' Connor replied as he settled into the chair, which was still warm from Donna sitting in it. He pulled the laptop to him, flicked onto the internet. Called up the Sentinel site and, after disabling the remember-password setting on the Mac, logged into the server. As promised, Robbie had placed the files he had culled on Duncan MacKenzie, Kinross Construction and Robinson Haulage in a folder marked Charlston and Co. There was also a Word file in the folder, a short note from Robbie:

Boss, this is what we were talking about. Interesting stuff. Looks like Charlston was in bed with Davis, McIntyre and Robinson at various points. Makes sense. The one listing for Duncan MacKenzie is in Perigee Distribution Services. I've marked the file. Hope this helps . . . R

Connor smiled, closed the Word document and scrolled through the files Robbie had uploaded. He was, despite his failings over the previous days, a good operative, could handle the investigative work, wasn't afraid of doing a shift, as this showed.

Connor found the file Robbie had marked, clicked it open. Typical Companies House record of directors of the company, with MacKenzie listed as resigning one month after being appointed. But there, on a list alongside Nicolas Davis, Mark McIntyre and Audrey Robinson, was another director, with whom Connor wasn't familiar.

Ian Murphy.

He flicked off the server and onto the Companies House website, typed in the name and hit return. Was scrolling through the information he had found, eyes drawn to one line on the page, when his phone rang in his pocket. He fumbled for it absently, thinking it was Kyle calling to give him an ETA update.

'Hello, Kyle. What's the—'

'Fraser?' Voice as thick and hard as an old hammer, slurred with something veering on fury. 'Fraser, it's Paulie. We've got a situation. Can we meet at your place, say twenty minutes?'

Connor frowned. What the hell? What situation? And why would Paulie want to pay a house visit?

'Paulie, now's not a good time. I'm right in the middle of—'

'It's the boss,' Paulie interrupted, his tone darkening, commanding Connor's full attention. 'He's been hurt. Probably because he talked to you earlier in the day.'

'Wait – hurt?' Connor asked, the thought of Jen flashing across his mind. 'How bad? Shouldn't he be going to hospital? I can get Jen, meet you there in—'

'No,' Paulie hissed. 'No fucking hospital. And Jen stays out of it. We just need a place to lie low, figure out what the fuck to do next. Can't take the boss home, they know where he lives. But we can stash him and his car at yours. So twenty minutes, okay?'

'Okay,' Connor replied. What choice did he have? If this was something to do with what was going on, he had to see MacKenzie. And if he was hurt he had to help. For Jen's sake. Didn't he?

'Good,' Paulie grumbled. 'Oh, and Fraser, if you tell the boss one word of what we talked about earlier on today—'

Connor killed the call before Paulie could finish uttering the threat. He didn't need to hear it anyway. Turned back to the laptop, reading again the line that had caught his eye. Nothing special, just a listing of other companies Murphy was involved in. But there was something, something that . . .

'Right, coffee,' Donna said, walking back into the room and offering him a cup. Connor smiled and reached for it, already crafting his excuses to leave.

CHAPTER 68

He should leave.

Parked up a quiet lane about a mile from the MacKenzie Haulage yard, Boyle sat in the driver's seat and assessed his options. He focused on his breathing, used it to drown out the soft, pathetic sobs from the back seat where he had deposited Murphy. Grabbing him had been like trying to pick up a jumbled pile of twigs, which Boyle knew meant several broken ribs. From the pinprick pupils that searched his face for something to spark recognition, it was clear he had concussion as well.

Unfortunate. It would have been easier in a lot of ways if MacKenzie had just killed him.

The name burned; a white-hot poker in Boyle's mind. The memory of MacKenzie, gun in hand, having the audacity to tell him what to do. The fucker would already be dead if they hadn't been interrupted. Still, at least Murphy had got that right. He had blown MacKenzie's friend away without hesitation or regret. It was almost enough to make Boyle reassess his opinion of the man.

Almost.

Yes, he should leave. Again, the thought of how much easier the situation would be to manage if Murphy was dead crowded into his mind. He pushed it back. Yes, he could kill him, but what message would that send? That he was a mad dog, an indiscriminate killer who took the easy way out when the shit hit the fan? No. There were rules.

Murphy had brought him into this. That made him the boss. And rule one was never break the chain of command; never betray the boss unless absolutely necessary. He had learned that the hard way, in the blinding heat of Afghanistan. Follow orders. Respect the chain. It kept you alive. So get Murphy to a hospital, then out of this God-forsaken rat-hole and back home. The police were already on high alert with everything that had happened at the Alloa House. When the body at the haulage yard was inevitably found – complete with gunshot wound to the head – it would be like sharks scenting blood in the water. Every police officer in the Central Belt – not that there were many these days – would be on high alert. And while Boyle had been astute enough to clean the gun, break it down and scatter the parts from the car as he drove, he still didn't like the thought of being pulled over by the police. The car was clean, but the injured Murphy was still a detail he would rather not have to explain.

So, yes. Leave. Start the engine, head for home. Deal with any fallout from his confrontation with MacKenzie another day. It was containable, after all: the man was hardly likely to go to the police with what he knew. So let it slide. For now.

But yet . . .

The insolence of the man. Glaring at him, gun aimed straight at his chest, manoeuvring himself away and to his car. And then there was the way he had spoken to him. No fear, no hesitation. Just that same cold anger.

Come on then, you fuck.

Boyle bore down on the steering wheel, clung to it like an anchor. MacKenzie had managed to escape. No one ever did that, no one. Not the doddering old fuck in his shed or the snivelling reporter he had found in the forest. He was a predator, a hunter. And leaving prey alive was alien to him.

He twisted, looked into the back seat, Murphy crumpled there like a discarded coat. What would he want? It was obvious. Their business with Charlston was complete, and Boyle knew from the naked terror in the man's eyes that he would stay silent. To talk would be suicide, and not just because Boyle would find him. But MacKenzie – he was something else. A loose end that needed to be tied off. A loose end who knew too much about their operation to remain alive. And he was motivated now: Boyle had seen it in the man's eyes when he had mentioned his daughter, Jen. There were no lengths he would stop at to keep her safe. And that would mean he would be coming for them.

Boyle turned back to the steering wheel, started the engine, a strange feeling of peace settling over his thoughts like a cool silk sheet. The decision was made. He would finish their business here, deal with MacKenzie, make sure he would never be a threat. A tingle of excitement traced its way from the pit of his gut to his groin.

'Come on then, you fuck,' he said.

CHAPTER 69

MacKenzie's car, a high-end Range Rover worth about the same as a small flat on the outskirts of town, was already in the driveway outside Connor's flat when he arrived, parked tight against the thick stone perimeter wall that separated the block from the house opposite. It obscured any sight of the car from the main road and, as Connor kept the location of his flat as quiet as possible, it was about as anonymous a hiding place as MacKenzie could have hoped for.

Connor approached warily, eyes strobing the forecourt, taking in the staircase that led down to his front door. Skirted the car, felt his pulse quicken when he saw the ugly crack in the windscreen, like a spider's web that had been etched in blood. He looked down, saw a large dent in the offside wing, some light scratches to the paintwork.

Blood and dented paintwork. Not a pleasant combination, but familiar enough to Connor from his time in uniform on the streets of Belfast. He'd seen his fair share of RTAs, hit-and-runs, and pedestrians being struck after wandering into the road. Somehow, he didn't think there was anything accidental about this one.

He retreated from the car, cast his gaze around again. No sign of anyone else, not much chance they could sneak up on him thanks to the thick layer of gravel he had put down in the driveway when he had moved in. Glanced at the staircase again, saw a small, brownish-red splotch on the lip of the top step, knew what had happened.

Connor moved carefully to the stairs, made his way down as

quietly as he could, following the trail of blood, ears straining for noise. Felt no surprise when he saw the door to his flat was open slightly, the wood around the lock and door jamb splintered and raw, like a dog's favourite stick.

He pushed the door open gently, stepped into the flat. Pressed himself against the wall and slid along it to the living room, listening to feet thud dully off the polished-wood floors as he approached. They weren't making much of an effort to stay quiet, he thought. But, then, why would they?

The hallway opened into the living room, Paulie's massive bulk framed in the floor-to-ceiling patio doors that gave out onto the garden. Connor swallowed a momentary flash of rage as he saw the thug standing there, in his home. This was his space, his sanctuary, and to have Paulie here was a violation.

He stepped from the shadows, cleared his throat. 'Nice to see you're making yourself at home,' he said. 'Though you could have—'

The words died in Connor's throat as Paulie whirled on him, raising a gun in one fluid motion as he did so. Again, Connor was reminded of how dangerous this man was, moving with a speed and precision that his bulk should have made physically impossible. And now, just to add to the problem, he was holding a gun, the blank, empty maw of it glaring straight into Connor's chest, stabbing at him with an invisible finger.

'Jesus, Paulie, it's me!' he said, arms raised in an 'I surrender' gesture. 'Put the fucking gun away, will you?'

Momentary confusion flashed across Paulie's face, the killer draining away as recognition set in. He shrugged his shoulders, lowering the gun and tucking it behind his back.

'Fuck, Fraser, almost took your head off,' he said matter-of-factly. 'You move too fucking quietly – anyone ever tell you that?' He dropped his eyes from Connor, stooped towards the couch, the back of which was to Connor. When he spoke, his voice was gentle, almost soft. The only other time Connor had heard Paulie use that tone was when he spoke to Jen.

'Boss? Boss, it's Fraser. He's here.'

Connor approached, looking over the back of the couch. Duncan

MacKenzie lay there, face down. His shirt had been removed, revealing a lightning-bolt-shaped wound that twisted its way up his back, from his hip to his shoulder blades. It was a clean, neat cut, marred only by the ugly stitches that had been used to sew it together, telling Connor that whatever had inflicted it was razor sharp. And deadly.

A sudden memory of Mark Sneddon's mutilated body flashed before his eyes, all glistening intestines and lolling head, and his stomach churned as he realised that the marble-like pallor of MacKenzie's skin mirrored the colour Mark had been when they'd found him.

'What happened?' Connor asked, MacKenzie twisting on the couch and hissing in pain as he spoke.

'Boss got jumped at the yard.' Paulie spat the words as if they were hard pellets. 'Fuckers used a knife. But the boss got away. Winged one of the cunts as well.'

'Yeah, I saw the state of the car,' Connor said, moving around the couch and crouching in front of MacKenzie. 'You've brought a world of shit to my door, Duncan. Want to tell me what the fuck is going on and how this all ties in to Blair Charlston and what happened this weekend?'

MacKenzie stared up at him, brow glistening with sweat, skin sallow and slack around his cheeks. It was, Connor realised, the first time he had looked truly old, the man he was rather than the persona he projected for the world.

'Aye,' he said, after a moment. 'But, first, get me a drink, will you? Paulie can help me up.'

'Boss, I dinnae think you should . . .'

MacKenzie waved a dismissive hand. 'You've done a good job patching me up, Paulie. I'll be fine. Get me up. I can't do this lying down.'

Connor reflected on MacKenzie's words as he crossed to the drinks cabinet and poured two large whiskies. So Paulie had patched up MacKenzie – the stitching job had been his work. Connor wouldn't have thought Paulie possessed either the skill or the knowledge for such a task. And underestimating the man would be a profound mistake.

He took the glasses to the couch, tried to ignore the piles of his gran's papers that were stacked up around the room. It wasn't just his privacy these two were invading. It was hers.

'So what happened?' Connor asked, passing one glass to MacKenzie, the other to Paulie. 'And how does it all connect to your dealings with Charlston, Perigee Distribution Services and a man called Ian Murphy?'

Paulie's head darted up, eyes filled with a simple, stark message. *Don't you fucking dare. Don't you fucking dare betray me.*

'See, I found those names in company records relating to Perigee and your dealings with them,' Connor said, partly to fill the rapidly souring silence, partly to allay Paulie's fears. The last thing he needed was to get into a confrontation with the man. Not now. Not when MacKenzie had answers he needed. A picture was forming in Connor's head, a view of what was going on and why so many people had had to die. But it was jumbled, incomplete, an abstract that took time to decipher. And MacKenzie had the key. Connor could feel it.

MacKenzie took a gulp of the whisky, grimaced. Connor noticed his hand shake as he lifted the glass, wondered how much pain he was in. Wasn't surprised to find he hoped it was a lot.

'Okay,' MacKenzie said, the whisky bringing hectic splotches of colour to his pale cheeks. 'But this goes no further, Fraser. Are we clear? And I'm only telling you as I'm not convinced these bastards won't use Jen to get to me.'

Wouldn't be the first time, Connor thought. 'She's safe,' he said. 'I called one of my people. They'll watch her at the gym, make sure she gets home. Wasn't sure what type of shit you'd stepped in, but after this morning's little chat about "heavy people", I thought it made sense while Paulie was here with you.'

MacKenzie grimaced, twisted his face into an expression that was meant to express thanks but just came out ugly. 'I told you most of it when we met earlier,' MacKenzie said. To Connor, it seemed a lifetime ago. 'There were some heavy people up at the Alloa House this weekend, and I didn't want Jen to get mixed up with them.'

'Why?' Connor asked, frustration itching at his skin. He knew, but he had to get MacKenzie to tell him so Paulie was protected. And besides, MacKenzie might just mention something Paulie had missed out – after all, he had only grudgingly told Connor.

MacKenzie exhaled loudly, his breath strangely liquid, took another heavy slug of the whisky. Looked over Connor's shoulder, focusing on something only he could see.

'It was about five years ago,' he said slowly. 'The business was just starting to get big, really big. Between us and Robinson Haulage, we'd divvied up most of Scotland, from the Central Belt down to the Borders. Not quite as big as Stobart's, but getting there. Things were going well. Did a few press articles – local boy does good, the MacKenzie magic, that sort of thing. Which, I suppose, was part of the problem.'

'Oh? How so?' Connor asked, shoulders tensing as he felt Paulie shift his weight from one foot to the other.

'There was a feature done on us – same magazine that did the spread that kicked Perigee into high gear, now I think of it. You know the type – all happy-family pics, me fucking around with one of my cars, Hannah . . .' He trailed off, voice softening, then he coughed. 'Hannah in all her best jewellery. That sort of shite. Stupid, really. Anyway, couple of weeks after that, I started to get post.'

Connor bit his lip, willing MacKenzie to keep talking, mind filling with thoughts of Kim George. What images of her had been found?

'Go on,' he prompted, snapping MacKenzie from whatever memory he had lost himself in.

'Little things at first,' he said at last, raising the whisky to his lips then dropping it. 'Cut-outs from the magazine spread, stuff like that. But then it got more specific. Blow-ups of Jen, cut-outs of her, or images circled in red ink. No notes, just the scrawls. I made sure she was safe,' a glance at Paulie, 'that she was covered. But then it got worse. Pictures of her on the street, at college, in the pub. All with the same creepy red ink.'

'Okay,' Connor said, trying to keep the impatience from his voice. 'So how does this tie in with Davis, McIntyre and Robinson? Why were you so adamant that you didn't want Jen anywhere near them?'

'They got the same kind of pictures,' MacKenzie said flatly, eyes glittering like the glass he held. His face was paler now, pinched tight by stress. 'Audrey doesn't have children, but McIntyre and Davis do, boy and a girl. They got in touch when Jen was pictured with their kids, told me they'd been getting the same packages.'

Connor folded his arms. So far, MacKenzie hadn't told him anything Paulie hadn't earlier in the day. He needed more. 'So, let me get this straight. You, McIntyre and Davis were each getting pictures of your kids, leading you to believe they were in some kind of danger, being followed at the very least. What I don't see is where Murphy fits into this, and why you didn't just go to the police.'

MacKenzie's face contorted into a sneer. 'Come on, Fraser, you're not a fucking idiot,' he said. 'You know my business hasn't always been carried out in the sun. The last thing I want is the police sticking their nebs in. Besides, it would make me look weak to the others if I cracked or suggested we go to the police.'

'Weak? What do you mean? This isn't the fucking *Sopranos*.'

MacKenzie barked a toneless laugh then stopped, arching his back, pain etching itself into the lines of his face. He closed his eyes, composed himself. 'You ever hear of the Ice Cream Wars, Fraser?'

'Vaguely,' Connor said, the phrase ringing a bell in the back of his head. It had been a turf war in Glasgow during the 1980s. The popular story, as told by headline-hungry tabloids, was that ice-cream vans were used as fronts to move and sell drugs, guns and other items on the streets. He had heard from veteran police officers that the drugs line was spurious, that the truth was it was purely a battle for the lucrative routes the ice-cream vans used. But by then the tabloids had spoken. The legend had become fact, and the fact had become a headline. And that headline featured ice cream.

'You telling me you're a drugs runner?' Connor asked. This was new.

MacKenzie looked at him, as though sizing him up. How far would he go? What could he say? 'You can infer whatever you want, but all I can tell you is haulage and transportation is a tough business, and getting tougher. You want to get something to someone with no questions asked, how would you do that? We go everywhere, from Shetland to Selkirk, and my competitors can be very, ah, protective of their businesses. And showing weakness against them, well, you might as well lube up your arse and bend over.'

A thought hit Connor. 'You think the pictures were an attempt to intimidate you, Davis and McIntyre into pulling out of specific routes? Which ones?'

MacKenzie held up a hand, shook his head. 'Not saying that. Never got that far anyway.'

Connor felt the hairs on the back of his neck stand up. Here it was. The crux of what Paulie had told him. The reason Jen was still being followed whenever Daddy MacKenzie got a little jumpy. The reason he had got pissed and blurted out a warning to Jen in the first place.

'It was a ransom job,' MacKenzie said at last. 'The last pictures were sent with a note, telling us all that one of our kids had been taken, that we were all to throw money in and pay it at the appropriate time.'

Connor stood up straight, felt the sudden need to move. Glanced at Paulie, saw the same urge written all over his posture. 'Where did they take her?' he asked.

MacKenzie swallowed the last of the whisky, tears that were nothing to do with the drink threatening in his eyes. 'That's where it gets clever, Fraser,' he said. 'See, they didn't. Not really. The images they sent were mock-ups – you know, like that fake-porn crap? Jen's head pasted onto another body, some child stripped and tied up. But we couldn't reach her on her mobile and no one had seen her at college or her job. She disappeared off the face of the earth, just like the other kids had. And we were given a clock. A very specific one. The money had to be ready in two hours, delivered to a handler of the kidnapper's choosing.'

Connor stared blankly, letting this all sink in. 'Let me guess,' he said. 'Ian Murphy.'

'Aye,' MacKenzie said, anger sparking in his eyes, drying the tears, turning them hard again. 'Ian Murphy. Came up in Wester Hailes in Edinburgh. Nasty wee shite, got a reputation as a fixer and a go-between for shite like this. So we contacted him and his pet psycho, Boyle. They collected the cash, ferried it to the location specified, then dropped it off.'

'Why him?' Connor asked. 'Why bring another face into this?'

'Like I said, Murphy has a reputation. He'll sort things out, act as a middle man. He's amassed a contact book you wouldn't believe over the years, fuck knows how. From judges to coppers, civil servants to a few serving politicians, word is Murphy has a name for every occasion. And he's silent as a monk, too. Give him his ten-per-cent fee and he's the equivalent of fucking Switzerland. Totally neutral. Totally discreet.'

'And I take it this "pet psycho" you mentioned, Boyle, he's there to enforce that neutrality if needed.'

'Aye,' MacKenzie said. 'He's a nasty wee bastard. But he keeps Murphy safe. Well, he did, until today.'

The smile on MacKenzie's face told Connor not to push the point, but he had a sudden idea about whose body had put the dent in the car outside.

'So you paid the cash, Murphy took it to God knows where.' He realised he didn't want to ask the next question. 'Then what happened? To Jen? Was she . . .?'

'No!' MacKenzie spat the word. 'No. She was fine. That's the thing. It was all a confidence game. We found out later that she and the kids had all had their mobile phones targeted earlier that day, and then they were mysteriously waylaid as they went about their days. Davis's daughter got stuck in a lift at a multi-storey car park in Glasgow for two hours. McIntyre's boy spent the day trying to get his car to start after it died the night before. And Jen . . .'

Connor leaned forward.

'She was fine,' MacKenzie said, answering the question Connor hadn't asked. 'Friend got clipped by a taxi when they were crossing the road outside her college. She took the girl to hospital, made sure she was okay. But you know what hospitals are like, Fraser . . .'

Connor nodded. All too well. 'Long waits to see a doctor unless you're dying, cramped waiting rooms, overpriced coffee and a lack of public payphones. And with her not having a phone . . .'

'Exactly,' MacKenzie agreed. 'She disappeared off the face of the earth just long enough for her mother and me to go out of our minds.'

'Like you said, clever,' Connor said, thinking about the level of organisation it would take to delay three kids for a specific length of time. To target their phones, then take them out of the picture for just long enough to . . . 'So you paid the ransom, the kids came back home, then what? Surely you didn't just let it go.'

MacKenzie exchanged a glance with Paulie, then turned his gaze back to Connor. Hard now. Defiant. 'Course not,' he said. 'We tracked down the taxi driver who clipped Jen's pal, had an, ah, in-depth conversation with him. Tough wee bastard, but eventually he admitted he'd been paid to target the wee girl, make sure Jen wasn't hurt.'

'And did you find who paid him?' Connor asked, knowing the answer.

'No. Cash payment. Guy just got into the cab and started talking. Knew all the right buttons to press. The guy, Sloane I think his name was, was a little too fond of the cards. Pissed away all his money at a big casino in west Edinburgh, got into debt to some very bad people.'

Smart again, Connor was forced to admit. A malleable blackmail target, cash payment, no chance of being traced. But, still, the level of organisation troubled him. 'So what about Jen? Why keep her away from the Alloa House? Did you know Murphy would be there?'

'Christ, no.' MacKenzie coughed. He raised his glass and shook it, Paulie getting the message and lumbering over to the drinks cabinet.

Connor let it go. Another one to chalk up for another day.

'No, we didn't tell Jen anything about it. She'd seen some of the earlier pictures that came in, the ones from the magazine, so she knew to be careful. That's why she lets Paulie tail her from time to time. She doesn't like it, but she's been the target of a sicko before, knows I'm just looking out for her.'

'So you kept her away in case Davis or McIntyre let something slip?' Connor asked, not totally convinced, but willing to play along. For now. 'But that still leaves Murphy. How did you end up in bed with him over Perigee? And why did you pull out so quickly?'

MacKenzie took the whisky Paulie offered, a considerably bigger measure than Connor had poured. Inhaled half of it. 'Like I said, he was a fixer, a middle man. When Charlston got involved with Perigee, it was Murphy who sorted out the contracts and transportation deals. He knew Davis, McIntyre and myself, so he approached us. I signed on to work with his company as Charlston told me they had some clever way of making sure we got as much cash as possible.'

'So why quit so quickly?' Connor asked, knowing the answer. It was in what MacKenzie had said earlier about the ice-cream wars.

'Let's just say I didn't like some of the items they were shipping. Wasn't my cup of tea,' MacKenzie said, his eyes flat and dead.

Connor considered. How far could he push it? Fuck it. His patience was spent, and the way Paulie was making himself at home was needling him.

'Drugs,' he said, a statement, not a question. 'Like you said, the ice-cream wars. But instead of ice-cream vans and shitty music, it was lorries delivering designer kitchens around the country. Designer kitchens to normally wealthy clients who might want a little dessert and some party favours to go with their new Aga?'

MacKenzie raised his glass in salute. 'And they all lived happily ever after,' he said. 'But not me. No drugs. I promised Hannah.'

'So that's why Murphy came for you today? He was worried about how much you'd told me? Or how much Jen had told me?'

MacKenzie shrugged, a shiver of pain racking his shoulders. 'I think he might have been there to scare me, make sure I kept quiet. But then Boyle mentioned Jen and I just lost it. Things . . .' he coughed, eyes going distant again for a moment '. . . things got a little out of hand after that.'

An idea flashed across Connor's mind then faded, like an object briefly illuminated by a swinging lightbulb. 'So, what now?' he asked. 'You think they'll come for you, right? I mean, that's why you're here? To keep out of sight?'

Paulie laughed, a deep, grating chuckle. 'Aye, right,' he said. 'We just needed a place off the grid to get the boss patched up. And make sure you're on board.'

'On board?' Connor asked warily.

'Aye,' Paulie said. 'We'll deal with Murphy. No way that wee shite Boyle is going to let this one go. But we need you to do your job while we sort this.'

'And what job is that?'

'Protection,' MacKenzie said. 'We'll get out of your hair. Now. But I need to make sure none of this blows back on Jen. Murphy is a nasty wee fuck. If he thinks he can use her, he will. So I need you to look after her until this shite is settled. Okay?'

Connor's eyes fell on one of his gran's boxes. Felt a twist of shame.

What the fuck was he doing, discussing a woman he cared for as though she was a possession, something to keep safe while the big brave men went out and made the world right? Ida Fraser would stand for none of that shit. Should he?

He opened his mouth to answer when his phone began to buzz. He reached for it, turned away from the room and walked back up the hallway. 'Donna?'

'Yeah, sorry, Connor. How's your gran?'

He winced. He had used his gran as the excuse to leave Donna when Paulie had called, made a vague implication that she was having a bad day and the care-home staff wanted him to see her.

'Yeah, ah. Yeah, she's fine. What's up? You find anything?'

'I did,' she replied quickly. 'There was another file. Didn't find it at first as we did that name search and it wasn't there. But I got it. Donald really did his research, Connor. This goes a lot deeper than we thought.'

'Go on,' Connor said, excitement prickling the nape of his neck.

'Not over the phone, too much. Easier to show you. Can you come back, if your gran is okay?'

He glanced over his shoulder, calculated. Shouldn't be too much of a problem getting Paulie and MacKenzie to leave. He would worry about securing the flat properly later.

'Be there in forty minutes,' he said.

'Might want to make it quicker,' Donna replied. 'DCI Ford called just before I rang you. He's on his way here now. I'm guessing you're not going to want to share this with him yet.'

Connor cursed. Calculated. He'd get someone from Sentinel to watch Jen. He could argue the ethics with his conscience later. 'I'm on my way,' he said.

CHAPTER 70

Connor sat in his car, looking up at the window of Donna's flat. He knew Ford was already inside, had seen his car parked further up the road. Interesting, he noted, that Ford was driving his own car – a three-year-old BMW – rather than a Police Scotland pool car. Potentially that meant Ford had come on his own, without a driver, and he knew that his usual sidekick, DS Troughton, was still at the Alloa House Hotel. Connor felt a small spark of hope. If Ford was alone, it meant he wasn't being officially monitored. Meant he could bend a few rules to get the answers he needed.

And Connor knew that Ford was more interested in getting to the bottom of a case then spending endless hours quibbling about how he'd got there.

He was, he realised, procrastinating. Either Ford was alone with Donna or he wasn't. He'd find out soon enough. No. The reason he was still sitting in his car was lying in his lap, a small, heavy chunk of cold death. A Glock 17, glistening like a dark jewel in the fading afternoon light. He had grabbed it from the safe hidden in the floorboards under his bed before he'd left the flat, using all the perfectly valid, reasonable justifications he could come up with. He didn't want to leave MacKenzie and Paulie in a flat with a firearm. Couldn't leave it there anyway, now that the lock had been busted, and he didn't have enough time to adequately secure the premises with anything more substantial than a piece of wood wedged into the door jamb to keep the front door from swinging open.

Perfectly valid. Perfectly reasonable. And all bullshit. He wanted the gun because, after talking to MacKenzie and Paulie, Connor knew trouble was coming. It was like walking into a bar and just knowing there was going to be a fight, some less evolved part of the brain sticking its nose in the air and getting the whiff of percolating violence. Connor had the same scent now.

He sighed, stuffed the Glock into the glovebox, locked it. The last thing he needed was to be talking to the DCI with a gun sticking out of his pocket. It was a quiet residential street and the car's security system was state of the art. If anyone was going to come near it, Connor would know.

The door was ajar when he emerged from the lift and made his way along the short corridor to Donna's flat. He knocked once, gently, sticking his head into the hall. 'Hello?'

'Come on in, Connor,' Donna called, her voice drifting from the living room. He could hear tension in that voice.

He stepped into the flat, ears straining for sounds of other people – Donna's parents, Andrew, Sam the babysitter. Couldn't immediately pinpoint them.

He walked into the living room, saw Ford standing in the middle of the room, arms clamped behind his back. Donna was sitting on the couch in front of him, back straight, her gaze as dark and bitter as the mug of coffee she held.

'Ah, Fraser,' Ford said, turning his gaze towards Connor. 'Nice of you to join us. You've been almost as elusive to track down this afternoon as Ms Blake here.'

'Sorry about that, sir, busy time,' Connor said.

'Hmm, not surprising, given your fortune-telling earlier,' Ford said, eyes growing hard. 'We'll talk about that in a moment. I assume you have no objections to Mr Fraser being here while we talk, Ms Blake? If so, I could arrange for a more private setting, perhaps in an interview suite at Randolphfield.'

Donna twisted her face into a sneer, turned to Connor. 'It's fine. My parents are out with Andrew, so we've got about an hour. I'd like this finished before they get back, if at all possible.'

'We'll see,' Ford said, his tone telling her that if anyone was going to

275

set timetables here, it was him. 'Now, before Fraser arrived, you were telling me about Donald Peters. Specifically, his work on the *Westie* and Blair Charlston. And how that all ties in with Mark Sneddon.'

Donna flashed a hate-filled glance at Ford. Connor could understand it. To Ford this was a case, but to Donna, this was her life. And old friend and her ex, lost to violence within twenty-four hours. Which was, of course, why Ford was so keen to talk to her. She wasn't a suspect, but she was a common thread connecting the two men. It was only now that Connor was starting to understand why.

Donna's eyes twitched to Connor, looking for affirmation of what she was about to do. He nodded. Too late in the day for anything else. He had a vague, unformed picture developing in his mind, like an old photograph emerging from a chemical bath, but there were still too many gaps to see the whole. And to fill those gaps, they were going to have to pool their knowledge.

Donna's shoulders drooped, as though she was trying to draw warmth from the coffee mug she held. Then, in a low, soft tone, she started telling Ford everything they had learned about Donald's work on Perigee, the stories he had uncovered, the pay-off to Graham Bell, the offshore trust being used as a tax dodge. She finished with the legal agreement between the *Westie* and Charlston, and who had really paid that bill. By then she was pale, drawn, as though talking had been a physical effort. Given the subject matter, maybe it had been.

Ford was silent for a moment, considering what he had just been told. Then he spoke, distracted, almost more to himself than to Connor or Donna. 'So how does Mark Sneddon fit into this?' he asked. 'And if Peters was sitting pretty on a massive pay-out, why call you, then try to top himself before you arrived?'

Donna started as though the couch had been electrified. 'Wha'? What did you just say? Top himself? Donald was murdered! You've seen the pictures, what was done to him. No way he did that to himself! Christ, someone pulped his head in!'

'Yes,' Ford said, stance finally easing as he spoke. 'But that was after. Toxicology tests and pictures from the crime scene indicate that, after calling you, Peters went to his garden shed and started in on some antifreeze cocktails. No signs that the liquid was forced down his throat. He might even have been unconscious when the killer found him, Donna. Either way, he was dead the moment he went into that shed, no matter what happened.'

Donna looked from Connor to Ford. Connor could see the calculations running in her eyes as she tried to assimilate what Ford had just told them. Peters had tried to kill himself after calling Donna. Why?

Connor felt suddenly lightheaded as a kaleidoscope of thoughts and images collided in his brain, exploding into a coalesced whole for the first time.

Donald Peters. The note sent to Blair Charlston that had started all this. And that Companies House record he had read, the listing of other companies that connected Charlston and Murphy. He fumbled for his pocket, grabbed his phone with numb fingers. Ignored the grunt of objection Ford made, found what he was looking for. Felt the world surge and brighten around him as he looked at the image he had called up.

'Fraser, what the . . .?' Ford asked, clearly seeing something in Connor's face. Or maybe, Connor thought, he could hear the pennies dropping. Christ, they were loud enough.

'Donna,' Connor said, the word feeling alien and misformed in his mouth. 'Donald's house. You said that the gardens were impeccable. Well manicured, yes? This the place?'

He turned his phone to Donna, showing her the street-view picture he had called up on it. Slow, Connor, he thought. Should have seen it so much sooner.

'Well, yeah, that's the place,' Donna said, confusion and irritation clashing in her eyes and face as she spoke. 'But what the hell?'

'Fraser, what have you got?' Ford asked. No confusion in his voice, just impatience edged with anger. 'What's this all about?'

Connor smiled. 'Shit,' he said simply. 'Shit and ice cream. Sir, I think I know what's going on here. Charlston is starting to get flighty, has started to ask about getting out of here and back to London. I think we agree that's a bad idea. We need to talk to him. Now.'

Ford's back straightened again, face darkening. '*We* don't need to do anything, Fraser. *You* need to tell me what the fuck it is you think you know. And while you're at it, you can tell me how you knew we'd find those pictures in Jonathan George's room.'

Connor hissed out a curse. Fuck. The pictures. He had forgotten about them. Stupid again, Connor. Stupid. A flash of George standing in the fire, body aflame, eyes holding Connor's even as he burned. That pleading, accusing defiance. He had seen the same look in Paulie's eyes when he had told Connor about the pictures of Jen that had been sent to Duncan MacKenzie.

'I'm going to go one better,' Connor said, forcing his mind to slow. 'The envelope the pictures came in. Plain envelope, probably A5 size, right? Central Stirling postmark?'

Ford's mouth fell open. It would have been comical if the look had not been offset by the cold fury in the policeman's eyes. 'How the hell did you know?' he asked.

'Like I said, shit and ice cream,' Connor said, the idea solidifying in his mind. Jesus. He could see it now. Almost. He should have seen it so much sooner. What was it Charlston had said? Shape your own destiny? He would have, if his mind hadn't been so preoccupied with his gran and Jen.

Stupid, Connor. Stupid.

'Look, sir, I can explain all this, but we need to get to Charlston. If you want to have him taken to a police station instead, no problem, but I have to be there, and you know the bureaucratic shit storm that's likely to create.'

Ford glared at Connor. He was right. As an ex-police officer, he knew exactly what would happen if Charlston was formally interviewed. And in no version of that scenario would Connor Fraser's presence in the room be an option. Ford considered calling Fraser's bluff. But then he thought of those pictures of Kim George, heard the creak of a branch as Mark Sneddon twisted in the breeze.

Tennant's words now. *Whoever did this is a savage. You have to find them.*

'Okay,' Ford said. 'Let's go. But no fucking around on this one, Fraser. I mean it.'

CHAPTER 71

Dull shocks ran up Boyle's arms as he hammered his fists off the steering wheel, the car rocking gently as he did so. From the back seat, Murphy groaned, the rocking of the car sparking fresh pain within him.

Fuck it. It was all he deserved.

The message had been simple and direct, catastrophe delivered as banality. *Charlston still at Alloa. Fraser has questions. You clear?*

It was bad enough that MacKenzie and his pet gorilla, Paulie, had fallen off the edge of the world. Boyle had tried all the places he could think of – MacKenzie's home, Paulie's hovel, the bars they were known to frequent. Nothing. He had considered just snatching the girl and using her as leverage, but when he had spotted the man at the gym who was trying oh-so-hard to fit in and not telegraph the fact that he was hired muscle there to look out for her, he knew that wasn't going to be possible. The last thing he needed was more attention. No. This had to be quick. Clinical. Tie off the loose ends, then get the fuck out of town.

But then there had been the message. And the game changed again.

He remembered his last meeting with Charlston. The little shit snivelling and crying at his feet as he begged and mewled for no more. Boyle had been very careful, placing his blows where the bruises would not show, but still the little shit had managed to cough up a wad of phlegmy blood and spit it all over the laptop and USB stick on the desk he was sitting at. It had almost been too much for Boyle, who had only backed down when Murphy had restrained him.

Looking back now, Murphy whining like an abused dog behind him and the message fresh in his mind, he wished he had listened to his baser instincts.

He sighed, forced the tension from his body. Considered. What could Fraser know? Really? That Charlston had made some calls to clients after Sneddon had been found. That his financial handling of Perigee wasn't as above board as it might have been. That he had worked with Kinross Construction and Robinson Haulage previously. So what? He was a businessman, an entrepreneur, only natural that he would call on local talent.

And yet.

If Fraser started tugging at the loose ends, he might come across Murphy. And his links to MacKenzie. And if, after their little chat at the yard, MacKenzie had decided to burn his bridges and tell Fraser everything, it could mean the end of all of them.

Again, the message flashed before his mind. *Fraser has questions. You clear?*

He knew the meaning of the message. Are you safe? The answer, he realised, was no. Not until he was sure Charlston would keep his mouth shut, and Fraser would stop digging into something he didn't understand.

But there was, Boyle realised with a cold thrill, only one way to make that happen. He felt a weary frustration seep into his bones. Simple. It was all so simple. If only Murphy had listened to him in the first place, let him deal with this situation as he had with Sneddon and Peters, none of this would be necessary. Murphy would be house-hunting with his wife and brain-dead daughter on the islands, and Boyle would be . . .

Well, he would be doing this for another client. But it would be on his terms. Instead, Murphy was crumpled into the back of the car and Boyle was being forced to react rather than act.

He turned the ignition, put the car in gear. Fine. So be it. He would dump Murphy at a hospital or a doctor's surgery – fuck it, a vet's if that was the first possibility he came upon – then head for the Alloa House.

And by the end of the day Charlston would look into the void again. But this time he wouldn't be coming back with some half-baked life-coaching bullshit.

Boyle laughed at the thought. Maybe this wasn't so bad after all. No more Blair Charlston, no more ITOI, no more bullshit. And as for Connor Fraser?

Plenty of other meatheads out there. What was one less in the world?

CHAPTER 72

The hotel was mostly empty now, guests cleared out as the Health and Safety Executive moved in to begin their in-depth investigations of what had happened the night Jonathan George had leaped into the fire. But Charlston had booked out the hotel for the entire weekend and not cancelled, so he was still able to use the facilities. When Connor arrived with Ford, he found Charlston's PA, Anne, had arranged for them to meet in one of the conference suites on the third floor. Just a day ago, it had been a green room for VIPs attending the ITOI event, all pop-up bars, soft furnishings and refreshments on demand. Now it had been stripped back to a more functional guise – a big room with a conference table in the middle, a sofa pressed up against the back wall, a large-screen TV in one corner and a whiteboard stand in another. It was not unlike some police interview rooms, Connor thought, just bigger and without the graffiti-scarred furniture and underlying stench of tobacco, sweat and desperation.

He looked at Ford, who was pacing around the perimeter of the room. Connor pushed down the irritation he felt towards the policeman, who had stopped him learning whatever it was Donna had found. Thought instead about the number of rules he was breaking to do this. A potential suspect being brought in and interviewed in an unsecured location, with no legal representation and no formal record of the interview. It was, at best, questionable. The only fig leaf they had was that this was a post-event briefing between Connor, as a representative of Sentinel, and his client. The fact that a police officer was present was merely evidence of Sentinel's professionalism, and the close working relationship they had formed with law-enforcement professionals in the area.

Connor coughed back a laugh. Yeah. Fucking right, he thought. And if you believe that one, there's a bridge over the Forth that I can offer to you at a really great price.

He turned as the door opened, Anne entering the room followed by Charlston, Kyle bringing up the rear. Connor caught his eye, nodded his thanks and Kyle retreated, leaving them to it.

'Blair, thanks for waiting for me while I tied a few things up,' Connor said. He watched as Charlston sat at the conference table, noticed how the man winced when he moved. Overdoing it on the punch bag, or something else?

'No problem.' Charlston smiled, perfectly at ease. 'Always happy to help, Connor, you know that. And if it means we can get the contract wrapped up and a final fee for your work this weekend tidied up now, with a discount, then so much the better. Though I am little surprised to see you here, DCI Ford.'

Ford smiled, tilted his head in acknowledgement, then gave the line he and Connor had agreed on the way there. 'I was meeting Mr Fraser to go over some of the logistics of what happened this weekend. He suggested I stick around for this meeting, but I'm happy to step out if . . .'

Charlston raised a hand, oversized watch glinting on his wrist. 'Oh, no, no. Not at all. I'm sure this won't take long, will it, Connor?'

Connor smiled, settled into the chair across the table from Charlston. Christ, it really was like being in an interview room again. He shrugged off the thought. Time to focus. 'Just a couple of things, Blair, a few loose ends to tie off. I appreciate you being here in person, would have been harder to do this with you back in London. And that is where you're heading back to after this, isn't it?'

A flicker of confusion on Charlston's face. 'Of course. You know I'm based down there, Connor. My main office is in the City.'

'Of course,' Connor agreed, pulling a sheet of paper from the folder in front of him. 'Old Broad Street, London. Right? The same office you used to use in your financier days with Charlston Capital Investments. The same office that this was sent to?'

He turned the folder around, showing Charlston the copy of the note he had been sent, the note that had drawn Connor into all this. A single sheet of paper, stained black brown with something vile. Two sentences slashed into the paper in angry red letters, like a kid being let loose with lipstick instead of a colouring pen.

Graham died because of you. And for that, you'll pay SCUM.

'Why – why, yes,' Blair said, tongue flicking over his lips briefly. 'But you looked into that. It was just a crank, right? Nothing more? And with what happened to poor Jonathan after, I hardly think . . .'

Connor held up a hand, conscious of Ford, who was now sitting at the far end of the table. Had he figured it out? Seen what Connor had? It was all there. Shit and ice cream.

Well, not quite shit. Manure.

Connor turned the note around, read it. So obvious now. 'See, I never understood this,' he said. 'Who writes a note like that, smears it in shit, then uses a word like "scum"? With all the anger in the writing, I would have expected "fucking cunt" or something else. But "scum"? Not much of a threat, is it, Blair? Unless it's not a threat. At least, not the type of threat Anne thought it was, the type that made her contact Sentinel in the first place.'

Anne fidgeted in her seat, Charlston paling. His eyes darted across Connor's face. Then his expression hardened. And, again, Connor found himself wondering what type of poker player Charlston would be. Knew the answer: a poor one.

'I'm not sure what you . . .'

'Oh, I'll admit, it had me confused for a while too, Blair. Too long. And with everyone focused on poor Jonathan George and what happened to Mark Sneddon, this kind of got forgotten, didn't it? Which is a pity, because if we'd focused on it sooner, we might have avoided some of the bloodshed.'

'Fraser, what are you saying?' Ford asked, a warning tone in his voice.

'Sorry, sir, I'll get to it. See, this note isn't what we all thought it was.' He turned his gaze to Charlston now. 'It is a threat, but not of physical violence. It's a blackmail note, isn't it, Blair?'

Charlston sucked in a breath, paling beneath his false tan. 'I, ah, I don't know what you mean, Connor. I thought I was coming back here to agree a final fee, not be subjected to your insane conspiracy theories. I missed a flight for this. I'll make sure I bill your employers and—'

'South Caymans Utility Management,' Connor said.

The words hit Charlston like a punch in the guts. He rocked back in his chair, gaze flitting around the room, head jerking to keep up with his eyes. 'What?'

'You heard me,' Connor said. 'South Caymans Utility Management. SCUM if you prefer. Took me long enough to see it, wouldn't have without the stories and background checks on you and your pals that Donald Peters carried out. See, he found out about the tax dodge and the directorships, and I think he found out about the drugs you were shipping around the country with your kitchens as well. That's why you paid him off, not because of your fucking around with Kim George or Graham Bell. But, see, a friend of mine, she tells me that a journalist never stops digging. You might have paid him off, agreed he would retire and put down his pen, but he just couldn't. So he kept digging. And he found South Caymans Utility Management. Nice little company. Does a hell of a lot of business, money flying in and out all over the place from multiple sources. And, being offshore, not overly audited or scrutinised. Unless you know what you're looking for. Like Donald did.'

'I, ah, I . . .' Charlston flailed for words, like a landed fish gasping for air.

Finally, Anne spoke up for him. 'I'm not sure what you're implying, Mr Fraser, but I think that, before this goes any further, Mr Charlston should seek legal representation.'

'No problem.' Connor smiled. 'Though quite what defence a lawyer is going to mount against money-laundering and conspiracy to commit murder is beyond me.'

Charlston bucked in his chair, as though Connor had reached over and struck him. 'How dare you? I—'

285

'Enough,' Connor said, feeling hot anger sear his throat. 'I know it all, Blair. Or most of it. That note is the key. The Stirling postmark. The shit it was smeared in. Or, rather, high-quality manure. Just like the kind used in well-maintained gardens. Peters sent it to you, didn't he? As a warning. How much was he asking for this time? Another half-million? More? Just how much was his silence worth this time?'

'Hold on,' Ford said. 'If Peters was blackmailing him,' he jutted his jaw towards Charlston, 'why did he decide to—'

'Shame,' Connor said quickly, not wanting Charlston to hear that Peters had been planning to take his own life. It was too easy, absolved him of some of the blame for all this. And that was the last thing Connor wanted.

'I'm pretty sure that if you dig deeper into Peters's home and files, you'll find that he sent those pictures to Kim George's dad. See, he didn't stop digging, he kept looking. What was it the note to Jonathan said? *I know what happened to your daughter*? I think that's why he called Donna. Maybe a moment of conscience, or Blair here decided to play hardball. I don't know, but I think—'

A sudden clatter as the door to the conference room bustled open, a waiter pushing a tray of coffee and sandwiches in front of him. He surveyed the room, offering the polite, empty smile mastered by catering staff around the world. 'Refreshments?'

The world slowed. Stilled. Connor saw Charlston turn towards the waiter, a ripple of shock twisting his face into a mask of terror. He flailed back from the table, chair clattering to the floor. Got tangled in it, fell back with a shrill cry even as Anne scrabbled out of the way and bolted for the door.

Connor exploded up, vaulted over the table, eyes fixed on the waiter. Plain, boring, forgettable face, framing eyes that were barely human. The knife appeared in his hand in a heartbeat and he rammed the tray aside, backing round to face Connor, who put himself between the waiter and Charlston.

'Let me guess? Murphy? No, Boyle,' Connor said, taking in the man in front of him. Slender build, exuding the type of sinewy strength martial artists seemed to radiate. Eyes flicking over Connor expectantly, steady breathing, the wicked knife he held like an extension

286

of his arm. What was it MacKenzie had called him? Murphy's pet psycho? Looking into those dead, alien eyes, Connor could believe it.

'Fraser, been looking forward to meeting you,' Boyle said, a smile as empty as his eyes pulling his face taut. 'Though I'm not sure I've been introduced to . . .'

'DCI Malcolm Ford,' Ford said, circling the table slowly. 'Put the knife down, now.'

Boyle glanced at it as though he had forgotten it was there. 'Nah, don't think so,' he said, eyes fixing on Charlston over Connor's shoulder. 'You see I . . .'

'Boss? Boss, I just saw that secretary and—'

Boyle snapped around, a viper striking at its prey, and drove the knife forward as Kyle stepped into the room. His eyes bugged wildly, all surprise and shock and terror as the blade sank into the soft flesh of his throat, blood boiling from the wound and soaking his chest and Boyle's hand. Graceful as a ballet dancer, Boyle whirled around his victim, got Kyle between himself and Connor, eyes glittering over Kyle's shoulder as he gasped and clawed for his neck. Then, with a horrible liquid sucking sound, Boyle hauled the knife free and shoved Kyle forward. Connor caught him, fell with him even as he registered Boyle sprinting for the door to the conference suite. He clamped his hand to the wound in Kyle's neck.

'Hold on, Kyle, hold on!' Connor shouted, Kyle's blood scalding his hands, thick and viscous.

Connor sensed Ford drop to his knees beside him as he called it in. Felt the policeman's hand on his shoulder, whirled, saw the answer to the question he didn't want to ask written all over Ford's face.

A slight shake of the head told Connor everything. Kyle wasn't going to make it. His windpipe was punctured. The dark arterial blood gouting from the wound told him that his jugular had been cut. He was dead.

Connor held him, not wanting to lay the man down in the widening pool of his own blood. Forced himself to release Kyle. Took a second to freeze the image in his memory, digest it. Make it part of him.

He rose to his feet, felt Ford's hand on his shoulder again. 'Fraser.

Connor. Whatever you're thinking, don't. Officers are on their way. Let my men handle it.'

Connor turned to Ford, looked at him as if it was the first time he had seen him.

Felt something feral claw at the back of his eyes even as the world seemed to collapse around him to a single focal point. 'He was one of my men,' Connor rasped, gesturing down to Kyle. He stared at Ford, making sure he got the message. Then he headed for the door, his only thought of wrapping his hands around Boyle's neck and squeezing, leaving nothing but smudges of Kyle's blood in his wake.

CHAPTER 73

'Stupid.'

Boyle hissed the word repeatedly, a mantra as he ran. When he had arrived at the hotel, he had told the girl at Reception that he was joining the meeting Charlston was holding. All too eager to please, she had told him exactly where the party was. It had been painfully easy to find the drinks trolley and a jacket that made him look like one of the waiting staff – as he'd expected, there had been a small room before the conference suites where refreshments would be prepared for whatever business was being held there that day.

And that day, it would be a very bloody business indeed. Boyle had spotted Fraser's car on his circuitous approach to the hotel, knew he was already there. Which made his priorities clear, his objective simple. Get into the room. Deal with Charlston and Fraser. Get out.

But the plan had gone to shit when he had entered the room. Charlston had reacted like the coward he was, giving Fraser too much time to make a move. Despite himself, Boyle was impressed by what he had seen. No hesitation. No fear. Fraser had vaulted the table with admirable speed and grace, put himself between Charlston and the knife. It was only thanks to the other security guard entering the room when he did that Boyle had managed to get away. But there was another problem. He had allowed instinct to take over, murdered a man with witnesses present – one of them a senior police officer.

He could worry about that later. Right now he had to get away.

He ran to the end of the corridor, hit the button to call the lift, then bolted for the door to the emergency stairwell instead. Got into it, rammed his back against the door and braced. Closed his eyes, drew strength from the weight of the knife in his hand. Think. Where could he go? The main entrance to the hotel was out: the police would be swarming over the place at any second, Ford no doubt pulling whatever officers he had left guarding the crime scene in the woods or at the bonfire to sweep the hotel for him. Which, Boyle realised, gave him a possible solution. If, as he suspected, any officers in the vicinity came running for the hotel after the report that a man had been stabbed and the armed assailant was still on the premises, that would leave the grounds clear. At least, that was, until back-up arrived. And he planned to be gone by then. He could slip out of the hotel, get into the grounds, use the same trail Sneddon had been on when he had found him, get onto the back road and walk the half-mile to the layby where he had dumped the car. Perfect. But, still, how to get out of the hotel without being seen? There wasn't a—

He stopped, the thought hitting him. Of course. A sudden image of Charlston, breathing heavily, panic pulling his face into a tight, pale mask as he was pushed roughly against a wall. Yes. Of course. It was simple. So, so simple. He felt the laughter bubble in his chest.

Maybe Charlston was a lifestyle guru after all. Hadn't he just shown Boyle the path to his own future?

CHAPTER 74

The gym was deserted. Boyle crept into the large room just off the main gym where the punch bag so favoured by Charlston hung, waiting. He smiled at the bag as he wiped his hands with the towel he had grabbed from the reception area, blood quickly staining it a dark, angry red. He tossed it aside, approached the bag. Pathetic, really, and all Charlston was fit for. A fake opponent who would never strike back. He suddenly thought of Sneddon, the guttural grunts and muffled screams hot against the back of Boyle's hand as he took the knife and sawed it across the man's midriff, exposing guts and viscera in a glistening black morass.

He stabbed forward, inflicting the same wound on the punch bag, listening as the sand inside poured out with a soft static hiss and pooled on the floor. So much messier than blood, all those granules that you would never quite finish picking up.

He pushed the bag away, letting it haemorrhage as it swung. Headed for the mirrors on the far wall. Found the one Charlston had shown him, pressed and heard it click. Remembered the last time he had been here, with Charlston and Murphy, handing over the key that would unlock millions. Enough to set up Murphy and himself for life. Of course, that was before Murphy had been injured and he had dumped him outside a vet's surgery. True, Murphy would have to talk fast, pay highly to get treatment and buy silence but, still, Boyle had all the details he needed to enjoy the fruits of their labours.

And he would.

He pulled the mirror back, swinging the door open on its hinge. Stepped into the gloom of the service corridor, already planning how he would get to the woods that bordered the hotel and—

Something exploded in his chest as he felt a fist hammer into him and he flew backwards, losing his footing and landing roughly on the hard wooden flooring of the gym. Kicked backwards as a figure loomed out of the shadows at him, as if the darkness had coalesced into the shape of a man.

'Boyle, 'bout ye?' Connor said as he stepped into the gym, face dead and empty. 'Funny meeting you here, though pretty fucking obvious. See, I pointed this place out to one of my guys the other day, told him it was a nice way for the hotel to move equipment and people around without being noticed. Nice way to get out too, or arrange quiet meetings with people you don't want to be seen with, right?'

Boyle sprang to his feet, raising the knife as he backed off. Felt the gritty crunch of sand under his feet, winced. 'Fuck you, Fraser,' he hissed. 'I'm leaving now. You saw what I did to your pal. I'll do the same to you if you don't get the fuck out of my way.'

Connor smiled – little more than a baring of teeth – as his gaze blackened. He stared at the knife, seemed transfixed by it.

'Kyle,' he said, after a moment. 'The name of the man you killed. It was Kyle. Kyle Munroe. Good man.' He shook his head, breaking the spell the knife had cast on him, looked up at Boyle. 'Tell me, that the same knife you used on Sneddon?'

'So what if it is?' Boyle said, something in the detached calm of Fraser's voice unsettling him.

'Thought so,' Connor replied. 'Let me guess. He called Charlston, probably used the number on that same shitty mobile he called you on, told him he had the story about the pay-off to Peters? Charlston told him to come in the back way, through the woods, then sent you out as a welcoming committee?'

Boyle sneered. 'Who fucking cares? Fucking useless cunt deserved to die. Threatening to blackmail folk or he'd spill his guts. Well, I just spilled them for him.'

Connor smiled in agreement. 'Course,' he said. 'That's why you caved Peters's head in as well, wasn't it? Something about using his head and staying out of things? Kind of literal, isn't it?'

'Poetic justice,' Boyle whispered, raising the knife. 'Now get the fuck out of my way, Fraser. *Now*.'

'I've got a gun,' Connor said, making no move to draw it. 'Glock 17. Standard issue for police in Northern Ireland. Started carrying it with me a bit more after I got stabbed last year. Want to know a secret?'

Boyle blinked, confusion washing over him, needling his unease. *What the fuck?*

'Go on.'

'I left it locked in my car,' Connor said, amusement in his voice. 'Didn't want to bring it into a room with DCI Ford. Know what, though?' He paused, the humour melting from his voice as his face became a set, hard thing carved out of stone. 'I'm glad I didn't because I'm going to fuck you up with my own two hands.'

Boyle lunged forward, slashing the knife in a wide, sweeping arc aimed for Connor's head. Instead of backing off, Connor surged forward, into the path of the blade, bringing his forearm up to meet Boyle's arm. Boyle yelped as his arm smashed into Connor's forearm, pain exploding like napalm through the bone. Drove his head forward blindly, felt his skull glance off bone as Connor whipped his head to the side, his cheek taking the worst of the butt.

Boyle grunted as something exploded in his belly, Connor driving his knee into it. He slashed blindly with the knife as he doubled over and forced himself to breathe, backing off, trying to get some space.

Connor stepped back, assessed. Boyle had handled the forearm block well, kept hold of the knife. Reacted quickly with the headbutt. And now, instead of crumpling to the floor, he was backing off, catching his breath, getting ready for the next round. Connor felt the smile play across his face, made no effort to stifle it. So he knew what he was doing. Therefore no reason for kid gloves. Good. He would make this bastard suffer. For Kyle.

He surged in, Boyle stepping forward and slashing the blade up to meet him. Connor stepped to the side, snapped his leg out, aiming for Boyle's knee. The cracking of bone was like a gunshot in the confines of the gym, drowning out the animal howl Boyle made as his leg collapsed beneath him. He flailed again, Connor dodging back as he felt the knife cut through the air around his stomach.

'Fucking cunt!' Boyle screamed, falling to his knees. 'I'll fucking gut you for this!'

'Not today,' Connor whispered, closing in, eyes on the knife. Decision made. He was going to break Boyle's wrist to get it, even if he didn't have to.

Boyle whipped his free hand up, throwing the sand filling of the punch bag into Connor's face. He staggered back, blinded, coughing, trying desperately to blink it away. Heard Boyle's cry, felt the air grow dense in front of him. Brought his hands up in a defensive block, cold fire lancing across his forearm as the blade seared across his flesh. He flailed out with a wild punch, felt it connect weakly with something, then backed off, wiping at his face. Cleared his vision just in time to see Boyle lurching towards him, dragging his ruined leg, knife held backwards and tight to his arm, the blade running up his forearm, ready for a slashing strike.

Fuck that.

Connor stepped forward, dropping into a lunge as he did so. Then he exploded up and forward, putting everything into the strike as he pivoted his hip and used inertia to pull him forward. His fist crashed into the bottom of Boyle's jaw and Connor felt the bone shatter against his knuckles even as he heard teeth squeal and grind together. He sprang forward as the knife clattered to the floor, getting his other hand around Boyle's throat, catching him as he arced backwards, twisting to smash him into the wall. Boyle screamed as the mirror cracked and splintered beneath the force of the impact, shards pushing into his back.

Connor leaned in close, felt fury prickle across his brain as he saw the undimmed hatred in Boyle's eyes. He thought of Kyle, his eyes wide and pleading as he tried to breathe. Of Jonathan George holding his gaze as the blaze consumed him. Squeezed down on Boyle's neck, as though he could force all the rage and pain he felt into the man's body with his grip, brand him with it. Swatted away hands as they batted against his forearms, Boyle's eyes bulging from his sockets as he fought for breath. Thought again of Kyle, of the dead weight of him.

Squeezed harder . . . harder . . .

'Fraser! Fraser, stop!'

Connor whirled, as if woken from a dream. Ford stood in the door of the gym, flanked by two uniforms. 'Connor, he's not worth it. Let him go. It's done. Come on, you know it's right. This won't help anyone.'

Connor considered the words. Turned slowly and studied Boyle, whose head was now lolling to the side, his face a dusty pink. Turned back to Ford, paused, then to Boyle. Forced himself to ease his grip until the hitman started to choke and gag on the air Connor had let in.

A sudden clatter of heavy steps on the wooden floor of the gym as the two uniforms rushed in. Connor turned, watched them come. Glanced up at Ford, then back to Boyle. Released his grip when Boyle began to slump down the wall, then smashed a jab into the man's ribs, felt something snap under his fist.

'That's for Kyle, you fuck,' he whispered.

The uniforms paused for a second, stared at him. Connor tensed, unsure whether they were going to try to arrest him as well. They looked back at Ford who shook his head, then crowded in on Boyle.

Connor backed away, picked up the knife lying discarded on the floor and held it out to Ford. 'Here,' he said, exhaustion suddenly rolling over him in great, crashing waves. 'Think you'll find this matches the wounds found on Mark Sneddon.' It was a large, wicked-looking weapon with a serrated edge and an oversized wood-and-brass handle. Heavy, too. Like a small hammer. Perfect for metal work. Or caving a head in. 'Probably the primary weapon used in bludgeoning Donald Peters to death as well.'

Ford took the weapon, bounced it in his hand, disgust on his face. Possible. Very possible. 'Fuck,' he whispered.

'Yeah,' Connor said, casting a glance at Boyle. He took the blade back from Ford, calculated. He could do it. He was fast enough. The officers holding Boyle wouldn't be a serious impediment. So easy. So, so easy. And no more than he would deserve. And yet.

Connor whirled around suddenly, buried the knife to the hilt in

295

what was left of the punch bag. Ford nodded, something like relief in his eyes.

'You ready to give me that statement now?' Ford asked.

'Oh, yes,' Connor said. 'On one condition.'

Irritation flashed across Ford's face. 'What's that?'

Connor turned, spat on the floor, in the direction of Boyle. 'I need a drink. Get the taste of that fucking punch bag and that arsehole out of my mouth.'

Ford smiled, hard and humourless. 'Whisky work for you?'

CHAPTER 75

The interview dragged on, Connor laying out everything he had learned and everything he suspected. Even as he spoke, he knew it was all supposition and hearsay, backed up by financial records that could be twisted any way a good lawyer decided to do it, and a third-party source, whom Connor couldn't reveal in case he somehow compromised Duncan MacKenzie. He felt no great guilt over the prospect of putting MacKenzie or Paulie in the shit, kept silent only because of Jen. She might not know exactly what she had been part of five years ago, might only suspect some of the lengths her father went to in order to protect her, but Connor thought she had suffered enough.

And, besides, he had his own feelings for her to work out.

It was, he told Ford, a fairly basic shell game. With his background as a financier in the City, Charlston was at home stepping in and taking over companies from bankruptcy. From football clubs to bars and restaurants to bowling alleys, Charlston Capital Investments had dipped its toes into them all at some point. And invariably, when it did, South Caymans Utilities Management got involved. Whether providing loans, taking payments for services rendered or offering tax-relief services, there it was.

So when Perigee ran into trouble, it was only natural that Charlston would show an interest. What wasn't to like? A business going to the wall with a celebrity clientele and a national distribution network already established. It must have been like Christmas for Charlston and his associates when they opened the books on Perigee. And, as MacKenzie had said, some of the loads that were being shipped around the country contained more than dishwashers and designer kitchen units: some came with additional bags of pills or white powder that you definitely couldn't use as detergent. But how to clean the money that was being made from the drug sales? How to make the cash seem above board, and take a fat pay cheque home without overly bothering the tax man?

Again, step forward, Blair Charlston and South Caymans Utilities Management.

It was, Connor was forced to admit, almost perfect. Charlston gets into Perigee, uses the firm as a front to move drugs around the country, then washes the proceeds of drugs offshore. But it had got messy when Donald Peters had involved himself and Kim George had caught Charlston's attention. That was when the shit had hit the fan and Peters, being an old-fashioned journalist, had decided to dig a little deeper. Connor wondered, what had changed? What had made Peters approach Charlston and blackmail him rather than just publish the story and do the job he had spent the last twenty years doing?

A background check Connor carried out on Peters offered a possible answer. His wife had died suddenly years ago, and his daughter had emigrated to Australia as a result. Putting aside the cost of travelling halfway around the world to visit her, which Peters had done on a fairly regular basis, a life move like that took money, and Connor wondered how much Peters had funnelled to his daughter over the years to make sure she was comfortable. Of course, Ford would have his officers check, but to what avail? The money was Peters's – he had earned it, even if it was by means that were less than ethical. What were the police going to do? Bankrupt his daughter to reclaim it? Hardly.

The other piece of the puzzle surrounding Peters was more clear-cut. It was something that had been bothering Connor since he had found out Peters was a dead man even before Boyle fell on him. Why go to all the trouble of calling Donna, arranging for her to visit him, then hitting the antifreeze before she arrived? The answer was in a note found pinned to a loose-leaf folder stuffed into the boot of Boyle's car under the spare tyre. The contents of the folder were similar to the files Donna had managed to dredge up – Peters's unedited stories, research notes on South Caymans Utilities Management, records from Companies House putting Charlston at the heart of the money-laundering web. But there was more, stories and research on Charlston and, in particular, Kimberley George.

The note, which Ford had shared with Connor – off the record, of course – was written in the same jagged, angry lettering that had been present on the blackmail note sent to Charlston in London.

Donna,

This folder represents everything I managed to dig up on Blair Charlston. It made me a rich man, but a haunted one. I thought I could live with the weight of what I had found in return for the money I took from him, the money that made sure Janet could have the fresh start she wanted. But the truth is, that's blood money. Read the files. You'll see what I mean. I'm sorry, Donna, I thought I could tell you this myself, help with one last story, but the truth is I'm tired. Janet is happy in Australia, and that's enough for me. When this story breaks, and I know you'll break it big, my name is going to come up. After what Murdoch did for journalism with phone hacking, it's a shit show I really don't want to be around for. No, I just want peace now, if I'm lucky, with Carrie. So take this file, use it. Leave as soon as you've read this and call the police. They'll find me soon enough.

I'm sorry I let you down, Donna. Be brave. I know you are.

Donald

A suicide note. Connor remembered Donna's haunted glance after they had found Mark's body, her whispered questions, *Is it me? Am I cursed?* Wished Boyle hadn't arrived before her, that she'd found the note before he had taken the whole folder, probably from the table she had described in the back garden. It would have made everything a lot simpler, maybe even have saved Mark and Kyle. And it would, Connor thought, have given Donna a measure of peace.

He finished the interviews about three hours after he had stepped into Randolphfield, leaving with the promise that, no, he wouldn't go anywhere and, yes, he would be available for follow-ups if needed.

He wondered what type of story Charlston would spin. Yes, the allegations against him were serious, but it was either historical or circumstantial. Neither Murphy, who had been found in an alleyway off Craigleith Street, not far from the veterinary hospital, nor Boyle had implicated him in their statements, and he was, understandably, keeping quiet. Connor had no doubt that, when the number-crunchers prised the lid off In Thine Own Image, they'd find South Caymans somewhere along the way. It made sense to Connor. With his self-development weekends going international and attracting ever-bigger names, the amounts of money Charlston was generating were phenomenal. And if a few million of dirty cash somehow ended up in the mix and came out clean, where was the harm? After all, everyone involved was just creating their own destiny, right?

Yeah, right.

Connor made his way home, thoughts and half-formed ideas clawing for his attention. Got into the flat, pausing again to inspect the damage to the door Paulie had done when he'd broken in. Amateurish. Sloppy. Ugly.

He made a circuit of the living room, clearing away any trace of Paulie or MacKenzie's presence. Dumped the glasses they had drunk from and the towels MacKenzie had used to mop up his blood in a bin bag and deposited it outside. It wasn't that he was worried about forensic evidence, but he wanted to purge the place of their presence.

This was his home. His sanctuary. And he would be discussing the finer points of personal privacy with Paulie in the not-so-distant future.

He was just picking up the whisky he had served MacKenzie and Paulie, considering whether to empty the rest of the bottle down the sink, when the doorbell rang. He paused, glanced at the coffee-table, made his way towards it, grabbing the Glock, which he had laid there when he came in. Edged his way up the hall, gun tucked behind his back.

'Hello?' he called, back pressed against the wall.

The door swung open a little and adrenalin clawed its way up Connor's throat like ice.

'Hello? Connor? You there?'

He sighed, let his grip on the gun ease. 'Donna? Jesus, you almost gave me a heart attack.'

Donna's head appeared around the door. 'You okay?' she asked.

'What? That?' He gestured to the mangled door jamb. 'Yeah, just a – a minor misunderstanding. Nothing to worry about.'

'No, not that,' Donna said, impatience in her voice. 'What happened at the Alloa House? When you and Ford dumped me, I checked in with the newsdesk, just heard what happened. How are you holding up?'

He shrugged, made his way back down the hall. 'I'm all right,' he said. 'Sorry about leaving you high and dry earlier. What brings you here anyway? Everything okay at home?'

'Yeah, all fine,' Donna replied.

Connor busied himself at the drinks cabinet. 'You want a drink?' he asked.

'Yeah, please. Vodka and soda, if you've got it.'

Connor raised an eyebrow, made the drink. Poured himself a whisky, careful to avoid the bottle he had used with MacKenzie and Paulie. 'So, what brings you here?' he asked again as he handed her the drink. 'You wanting the scoop on what happened up at the Alloa House?'

'Not quite,' she said, sipping her drink. 'But I thought you'd want to see this.' She hefted the bag from her shoulder onto the kitchen counter, pulled out a laptop. 'It's what you were coming to see me about when Ford interrupted earlier on.'

Connor started. Of course. She had called, telling him she had found something else in the files. 'What you got?' he said, stepping closer, leaning over her shoulder.

Her fingers flew across the laptop, unlocking it. Then she turned it to him, a triumphant smile on her face. 'The final piece of the puzzle,' she said.

CHAPTER 76

It didn't take long to track Charlston down, thanks to his taste for upmarket hotels and his arrogant insistence on checking in under his own name. Connor made a few phone calls and found him at the Colessio, a conference hotel that sat on the steep incline of Spittal Street as it twisted its cobbled path through the granite and sandstone canyons around it to the castle at the top of the hill. One last night of luxury in Scotland before an early flight back to London in the morning.

Driving into the hotel car park, Connor confronted memories of the last time he had been up near the castle and the Holy Rude. Another night, another lunatic determined to end his life with a blade. A friend had been with him – Simon McCartney, his old partner from his days in the PSNI in Belfast. Thinking about it now, Connor wished Simon was with him now. Not to help him – he needed no help with the likes of Charlston. No, he wished Simon was there to stop him if it came to that. And it could. It so easily could.

After reviewing the files Donna had brought to him, they had made a plan. Donna wanted no part of seeing Charlston, perhaps having the same doubts about how far she would go if she did. And there was another reason, a simpler one. One that Charlston had understood all those years ago.

There was no story to report. Anything that hit the press would just tarnish the memories of a family that had already suffered too much.

He got out of the car, leaning in for the printouts that Donna had made for him. Paused for a minute, gazing up at the imposing stone façade of the hotel. Reached into his pocket and made a phone call. Smiled at the irritation in the voice at the end of the line. Explained what he needed. Waited for a reply.

'Great. Ten minutes, then,' he said, killing the call before he could hear an objection.

If it was easy to track Charlston down to the hotel, it was even easier to find his room. The Colessio had a suite on the top floor, and Connor knew that Charlston liked his little comforts.

Knew now that he liked other things, too.

He knocked on the door, forced himself to keep it gentle. 'Housekeeping,' he called, speaking as he exhaled, trying to keep his voice meek as he stood away from the peephole.

A moment's pause, then the sound of the lock being disengaged as the door was swung open. Connor didn't wait, put his hand to the door and shoved it wide, Anne stumbling backwards as he followed her into the room.

'Sorry about that, Anne,' he said, grabbing her by the elbow and steadying her. 'Got a little carried away. Blair here? Got a few things to chat to him about.'

She looked up at him, confusion, panic and dull anger flashing in her eyes. 'What are you—'

'Connor!' Charlston yelped. 'What the hell are you doing here? After your little performance earlier, we have nothing to discuss. And I'll be contacting my solicitors about possible defamation and slander proceedings against you.'

Connor stepped around Anne into the suite. It was a large, spacious room, modern and airy in the same way that the suite at the Alloa House was antique and cocoon-like. Nice enough, Connor thought. Just ruined by the current occupant.

'Go ahead,' Connor said, heading for a table under one of the eaves of the roof. He threw the file onto it, pointed. 'When you do, you might want to mention that to them while you're at it.'

Charlston's eyes flicked from the file back to Connor. He brought himself up to his full height, struck his usual pose of relaxed confidence. Even that was a lie now, Connor knew. Just more bullshit this con man had layered onto his façade.

'And what rubbish is that?' Charlston asked. 'More crap you've made up about me?'

Connor smiled. 'Not me, no. Everything in there was written by Kim George. Remember her, Blair?' Anger rose, cold and scalding, and he grabbed for it. Not yet.

'Wh—' Charlston took a half-step back, paling. Connor noticed a small tremor in his left hand, the oversized watch twinkling in the light as it jerked on his wrist. Good, he thought. Let the bastard suffer.

Charlston composed himself. 'What the hell is this?'

'Kim's diary,' Connor said, looking down at the folder. 'You knew she was keeping one, didn't you, Blair? After all, it's a common enough therapeutic technique for those who are suffering from depression or going through a rough patch. You know, the kind of thing you might run into after you lost a baby and your ex-boyfriend took his own life.'

'Well, I – I—'

Connor held up a hand, Charlston's mewling grating in his ears. 'Kind of lucky for you that she did, isn't it? Looking through it, she was a studious type, was Kim. Borne out by her academic record, too. When she started to go to therapy, she really researched it, dived into neurolinguistic programming, cognitive behavioural therapy, all of that stuff. The diaries show how fascinated she became, how she was going to try to use it to help other people with problems like hers.'

Charlston lowered his head, shook it slowly. When he spoke, his voice was soft, grave, just this side of tears. Connor wanted to step across the room and punch him.

'Yes, that was Kim,' he said. 'Always trying to take the worst of what happened and make something good from it. It's one of the many reasons I loved her, Connor, one of the reasons I do what I do now, to try to honour her memory.'

Connor laughed, the sound ugly to his ears. He could hear his anger in that laugh, snarling to be free. Wondered if he should let it. '"Honour her memory"? That's a good one, Blair. Especially as it was her memory you were so worried about the night you murdered her.'

Charlston darted a glance to Anne, who was now backing away

304

from the living area of the suite. 'What did you say?' Charlston whispered. 'How dare you? How . . .'

Connor opened the folder, the page he was looking for at the front. It had been in the files salvaged from the *Westie* – Peters's research notes and background, anything to do with the Perigee story. Connor didn't dwell on how Peters had managed to get hold of Kim's private papers, knew from the phone-hacking scandal of a few years ago that it wouldn't have been that hard.

'"I'm dead inside",' Connor read. '"No matter what I do, no matter how much I try to look to the future with Blair, it's like there's an empty hole in me now, a piece of me that died when I lost little Alison. The therapists tell me it's all perfectly understandable, that it's a symptom of post-traumatic stress. But what they don't understand, what no one but Blair understands, is that I don't want it to get better. From losing Alison to what's happened tonight, I deserve to die. I'm a horrible person. But at least, after tonight, I know I'm not alone any more, that I won't be taking this journey myself".'

Connor looked up. Charlston stood rooted to the spot, face haggard, eyes wild. 'Want me to go on?' Connor asked. 'I really should – the next bit is good. And you have a starring role.'

He didn't wait for an answer, started reading again.

'"Blair came to me earlier, told me they'd found Graham at the plant, that he'd killed himself. He was crying, ranting, inconsolable. Told me that he'd made a mess of it all, that by trying to pay Graham off he had risked exposing everything he had built. I couldn't believe him when he told me he was being blackmailed to use Perigee to smuggle drugs and launder the money. Said he was the only one with the key to the main account. When everything happened with Graham, he panicked, tried to buy him off with some of the money, which he transferred from the Caymans. And now, with Graham dead, the men he was working for were worried about exposure. He broke down and cried then, begged for my forgiveness. Said I was the only thing he had to live for. And for the first time since I lost Alison, I felt something, something I shouldn't.

'"Hope.

'"We're going to the hotel now. Blair has written a note, which he'll leave for the police, explaining everything. We're going to be together one last time, one last night. Then we're going to rest. And maybe, just maybe, if I'm lucky, I'll see Alison in the dark.'"

Connor paused, looked down at the page he held. Felt the weight of it pushing down on the back of his neck, prickling at his eyes.

'So, how did it go?' he asked when he trusted his voice again. 'You went to the hotel after making some kind of suicide pact with Kim, then made sure she couldn't tell anyone about what you were doing at Perigee? And just to make it convincing, you made sure you were hurt just badly enough to make it look like you had tried to take your own life too. Tell me, Blair, the towels that were delivered to the room you and Kim were using that night. How long after you slashed your own wrists did you call for them? And how long had Kim been bleeding out by then?'

Charlston's mouth opened, closed, his throat clicking softly as he did so. 'I . . . I . . .'

Connor threw the file at him, pages fluttering to the floor like confettti. 'You stole her fucking life!' he shouted, the anger rearing in him now, licking hungrily at his raised voice. Feeding on it. 'You manipulated a girl with mental-health issues, killed her to keep her quiet, then stole all her fucking work on behavioural studies to build this fucking life for yourself. And all for what? So you could keep laundering cash, keep the money flowing? You sick fuck, you sick, sick bastard!'

Charlston held up his hand. 'Now – now just wait a minute,' he said, voice quickening, all traces of the cool, aloof communicator gone. 'Yes, Kim was troubled, but there's no evidence that I—'

Charlston's words died in his throat as Connor produced a USB stick from his pocket and held it up. It wasn't the original, but it was good enough.

'Look familiar?' he asked. 'See, it's all in there. Seems once you started talking to Kim, you couldn't shut up about how clever you were. About how only you had the details and security for the master account in the Caymans, about how it could only be accessed from a secure site and a specific laptop and one USB drive. That's why Murphy and Boyle were here, isn't it? To collect what you owed them.'

Charlston buckled, staggered forward. 'I, ah, I . . .' He coughed. Cleared his throat. Blinked. 'Look, Fraser. Connor. I have money, I can . . .'

'Forget it,' Connor said, disgust souring the back of his throat. 'People who take money from you don't seem to do very well, Blair, so I'll skip it. And much as I want to exact a price from you right now, I'm not going to. Because I think the one thing a man like you fears more than a physical beating is a public one. Jonathan George certainly thought so. See, Donald was a good reporter, kept notes on all his meetings with contacts. It's all in there . . .' He gestured to the papers strewn across the floor. 'Says that, in one meeting with Jonathan, the man told you he wanted to take everything away from you, see you suffer the living death he had since Kim died. See, you were never the target when he jumped into the fire, Blair. Your reputation was.

'So enjoy the ride. A friend of mine, Donna, you met her at the Alloa House, is going to do a nice package about all this. She'll keep Kim out of it as much as she can, of course, but you'll be front and centre. And,' Connor leaned forward, bunched Charlston's shirt into his hand, fighting back the urge to lash out at him, 'I'll make sure every one of my police contacts knows to look into every company, every deal you've ever made. You're fucked, Blair. See what destiny you can make out of that.'

He pushed Charlston back, watched as he crashed into a chair and toppled to the floor. He turned then, heading for the door, Anne skittering out of his way as though he was toxic. Maybe I am, Connor thought. Maybe I am.

He stopped. Turned. 'Oh, one last thing, Blair. I might be leaving, but I'd stay put if I was you. See, I called DCI Ford before I came up here, asked him to look through Murphy and Boyle's belongings. Guess what? They found a USB stick just like this one, paired it with the laptop they found in Boyle's car. So don't bother running anywhere. See ya.'

He stepped out of the suite, breathed. Wasn't surprised when he heard the door open behind him, Anne joining him.

'Mr Fraser,' she said breathlessly, looking up at him. 'I'm sure you understand that I didn't know anything about . . .'

'Boyle,' Connor said bluntly, cutting her off. 'It's been bothering me, Anne. How did Boyle know we were bringing you and Charlston back to the Alloa House? Then it occurred to me. You've organised everything this weekend, all the logistics and rooms. Only makes sense that you organised the meetings for Murphy and Boyle too. And I'm just betting that when the police look – and they will – they'll find it was you who messaged Boyle about our movements.'

Anne paled. Connor leaned in. 'See, thing about that, Anne, is that what you did meant a friend of mine got killed. So, yeah. Think on that.'

He turned to walk away, Anne retreating into the room. Got about halfway down the corridor when a scream froze him in his tracks. He whirled, sprinted back to the suite, barely slowing as he crashed into the door and burst through.

Anne was curled against one wall, trying to make herself as small as possible, hiding her head from what was in the centre of the room. Lying there, surrounded by the printouts of Kim's diary, a diary of pain and darkness, lay Charlston. His eyes were open, naked chest rising and falling rapidly as he took small, birdlike sips of air. His hands were out at his sides, cross-like, twin gouges running like bloody rivers from his wrists to the brachial artery in the crook of his arm. Blood was pooling out, soaking into the carpet and printouts, turning them black. In the middle of the pool of blood, glinting like a glacier in the harsh Arctic sun, was a knife. A knife Connor recognised from the Kim George scene-of-crime pictures he had culled from a contact as part of his background research when he was first approached to handle security for Charlston.

Connor moved to him, dropped to his knees. Saw from the grey of his skin and the bluish hue of his lips that he might be too late.

'No,' he said, trying to staunch the flow of blood. 'No, you bastard, come on. Stay with me and we'll . . .'

Charlston's head turned to him, eyes sharpening briefly. His lips pulled into a dead leer of a smile, teeth horribly white against the ashy blue of his gums. He licked his lips, tried to say a word.

Connor leaned in close, straining to hear.

'Now,' Charlston whispered. 'Now.'

CHAPTER 77

Three weeks later

The world darkened, became a thing of blunt edges, muted sounds and pain. It felt like a thousand cigarette butts were being crushed out on his skin at once, or his arms were being licked by fire.

The thought – and the memory of another fire, of the smell of burning flesh and eyes boring into his own – galvanised Connor. He closed his eyes, concentrated, completed the curl, then let the weights clatter to the floor. He leaned forward, arms shaking as he placed them on his knees and took greedy gulps of air, forced the nausea back into his gut.

'Hey, you know you're not meant to just drop weights around here, right?'

He blinked the sweat out of his eyes. Smiled. 'Jen,' he said. 'Sorry, guess I got a little carried away.'

She smiled back, waved away his apology. 'Don't worry about it. Everyone does it. How you doing anyway?'

He considered that. Since the end of the Charlston case, Connor hadn't had a moment to stop. The Sentinel board was insistent on playing up his role in uncovering a multi-national money-laundering and drug-smuggling operation, underlining the firm's reputation for 'security and investigation services'. Thanks to some selective reporting from Donna, the story stuck and the clients started flowing. Connor kept himself out of it as much as he could, his eagerness to take any credit for what he had done tempered by four people having died, thanks to Blair Charlston, and Connor being too slow to see what was going on.

'Ack, not bad, just busy as ever, you know,' he said, hauling himself back to Jen, admiring her smile. 'How *you* doing? How's your dad? I heard he got a bit hurt up at the yard.'

Jen's smile faltered, became serious. 'Yeah, he took a spill, cut his back open. I keep telling him to watch what he's doing, let the other guys do the heavy work, but he never listens.' She paused, eyebrows furrowing into a frown. 'Anyway, how did you know about that?'

'Ah, Paulie,' Connor said, expression neutral. 'I ran into him outside and he told me what had happened.' In truth, MacKenzie had phoned Connor after word had got out about what had happened to Charlston and they had agreed an explanation for his injuries.

'Jen doesn't need to know about that side of things, Fraser,' Duncan MacKenzie had warned. 'I've kept it from her this long, no reason to get her involved now.'

Again, Connor had felt a bristle of discomfort at making choices on Jen's behalf but, in the end, he had agreed. After all, some things you were better off not knowing.

Jen's eyes moved away from Connor's. He twisted on the bench, spotted the fat kid from the ITOI weekend – what was his name again? Michael? – walk into the gym. Instinctively, he looked around for the young men who had tormented him before, felt something like disappointment when he couldn't see them.

'How's he doing?' Connor asked.

'Who? Michael?' Jen replied, turning her gaze back to him. 'Not bad, actually. Getting regular, form is improving. He's still got a hell of a lot of weight to lose, but at least he's putting the work in. Who knows? Maybe that self-development thing he went to did him some good after all.'

Connor grunted. It was all bullshit, just a front for Charlston's money-laundering and a chance to get rich clients together and sell them his 'tax solutions'. Connor had kept in touch with Ford, who told him that financial-crimes teams on both sides of the border and beyond were looking very closely into just who the ITOI weekends had been doing some good for. By the time they had finished, Ford promised him, Charlston was going to wish he had been successful in taking his own life. Connor doubted that. From what he had learned, Charlston was a survivor, a taker and a user, nothing more.

'. . . tonight?'

He blinked, startled from his thoughts. 'Sorry, Jen, what?'

She smiled, swatted at his shoulder in mock irritation, the feeling of her fingers on him lingering. 'I asked what you were doing tonight,' she repeated.

'Oh! Oh, not a lot. Going through more of my gran's things. Found a report card the other night, think it's one of my dad's, and I wanted to see if there was anything else related to it.'

'You going to ask your dad about it?'

'As if.' Connor snorted. No, that door had well and truly closed. But he was forced to admit that he wanted to. There were things on that report card, what Connor could read of it, that intrigued him, hinted at a version of his father he could scarcely believe was the man he knew. And then there was the mark on the card itself, old, rust-coloured, like an angry splash of sauce.

Connor had seen enough blood spatters to know it for what it was. And it raised questions he wanted answers to.

Later. The card had waited in that box for him for years. It could wait a little longer.

'You want to get something to eat after your shift?' he asked, not knowing he was going to speak until the words were out.

Colour brightened her cheeks. Then she flashed that perfect smile. 'Promise we're not going to be interrupted by your work or that reporter if you cook for me?' she said.

Connor raised his right hand, like the Boy Scout he had never been. 'Scout's honour.' It was a promise he could make with confidence: his new assignment for Sentinel, babysitting a backbench MSP who had been receiving hate mail for his support of decriminalising class-A drugs, wasn't due to start until next week and Donna had finally decided to take a holiday. Just her and Andrew, some time together.

'Okay,' Jen said cheerily. 'I finish at six. Want me to come round to yours for half sevenish?'

'Perfect,' Connor said. 'But let me pick you up. That way you can have a drink if you want.'

A silence fell between them for a moment, the implications of what he had proposed going unsaid.

'Okay,' she said eventually, eyes not meeting his. 'See you at mine at half seven.' She turned to leave. 'And rack those weights before you finish!'

'Yes, ma'am,' Connor said, turning to the mirror in front of him and watching as Jen wandered away. He fumbled into his pocket, fished out his mobile and plugged in his earphones. Selected a Mozart concerto and turned the sound up. Was just getting ready to start his next set when the phone pinged with a text message.

He sat up, read it.

See you're talking to Jen. Boss is grateful but, remember, you treat her right, okay?

Connor turned, looked through the glass partition that separated the gym from the main reception area. Saw Paulie there, all width and attitude, skull glistening under his bristle cut. Connor raised his phone and waggled it, smiled as anger surged through his temples like a headache. Caught himself. Forced himself to breathe. Relax. Remembered the words he had read in Kim's diary: *It's like there's an empty hole in me.*

The words had haunted Connor, needled him. He hadn't realised that the anger he felt, the anger his father had counselled him against as a child, had burrowed that deeply. But it had. It was, as Kim had written, an empty part of him. A vacuum. A dead zone. And, for reasons Connor didn't fully understand, now he wanted to fill it.

He turned away from Paulie, gazed at himself in the mirror. Saw his grandfather stare back at him, the broad shoulders, the heavy brow that was almost thuggish, the high cheekbones and thin nose framing those jade-green eyes. That was the man he wanted to be. The man who had taught his grandson how to lift weights, how to take a lifetime of seeing violence wrought in the name of religion in Northern Ireland and harness it, use it to build something positive. A family, a home. A life.

Connor grabbed for the weights, saw from the corner of his eye that the fat kid from the ITOI weekend was watching him closely, mirroring him. Learning. Connor smiled, went through the weights slowly, one eye on the kid, making sure he was okay.

He recognised the laughter about ten minutes later, looked into the mirror, saw the kid's three tormentors – what had Jen called the biggest one? Darren? – form a loose knot at the back of the gym, pointing and sniggering.

Took his time racking the weights, just as Jen had asked. Then he turned, looked across at Darren and his hyena-like pals, who were now pointing at Michael, slapping each other's backs. He glanced across at the kid, saw his shoulders going down, the reddening of his face nothing to do with his workout.

And still there was the laughter. The bullying. He surveyed the three again, studied them until they fell quiet, feeling his gaze on them. Got moving then, slow and steady, a direct line to Darren, hoped Michael was watching.

Some lessons, after all, could only be taught by example.

Acknowledgements

Thanks, as ever, to the usual suspects at the scene of the crime who are always on hand with bad jokes and good advice.

Special thanks to fellow writer and all-round nice guy Derek Farrell for his technical advice, which gave me the answer to a question I had been circling for far too long. Thanks also to book reviewer and crime fan extraordinaire Louise Fairbairn (@scarletrix) for the early feedback, and to all the bloggers who have supported and championed my books along the way. And, of course, thanks to Alasdair Sim for again delivering the all-important red folder verdict.

I wouldn't be the writer I am without the help, advice and support of Craig Russell, my agent Bob McDevitt and my publisher, Krystyna Green. Thanks also to Douglas Skelton without whom, quite simply, this book wouldn't have been finished.

And lastly, to all those who have ever bought one of my books or taken one out on loan from a library, thank you. As writers, we tell ourselves stories – having people to share them with makes all the difference in the world.